Players, Pimps & Tricks

A Novel
Marcella Andre & Joseph Bergmann

Copyright © 2012 Marcella Andre & Joseph Bergmann

(Andre-Bergmann) All rights reserved.

ISBN: 978-0-9852127-2-8

Cover Design and Graphics by Andy Cialone

Adult Reading Material

For Anju & Hera

1

October 1990
(Day One)

"MOTHAFUCKIN' RADIO PROGRAM GUY tells me he didn't get his mothafuckin' money. I say, 'You mothafuckin' callin' Vishnu a mothafuckin' liar?'"

I flatten my back against the wall.

"So where's the Play Money?" A Deep Voice.

"How th' fuck I know? Handed it to Beany. He done got arrested again." The Vishnu Voice.

"So the cops copped it?" The Deeper Voice.

"Naw, Beany be too smart for that shit." The Vishnu Voice. "It be someplace."

"Then shouldn't that be where to look—someplace?"

"Done that. Ain't there."

"So then, it's not a matter of where, but of who?"

"Who? Why?"

"WHY? I DON'T GIVE A FUCK ABOUT 'WHY.' Find out WHO has the fucking Play Money and make them see the terror of their ways."

Why is he so upset about play money?

The Deep Voice continues. "A LESSON MUST BE TAUGHT. YOU FUCKING UNDERSTAND ME? I WANT BLOOD AND SCREAMING. WHOEVER IS OR WHOEVER ARE PLAYING WITH OUR PLAY MONEY

SHOULD NEVER BREATHE OR WALK AGAIN. You getting my subtext here?"

Maybe this isn't the right time for my job interview.

So I pick up my ice cooler and tiptoe down the hallway.

"Who da fuck are you?" An African-American gentleman glares at me. He's wearing a navy blue Polo shirt and gray sweatpants. Down the side of his pants, in large letters, is the word "Mecca."

"I'm, uh, Lily White."

"I can see that. What you doin' here?"

The Deep Voice inside. "Who's that?"

To the office—"Findin' out now, boss." To me—"Come in."

"I had an appointment with Mr. Bigar Kahn and..."

His thumb jabs at the office. "In there."

Despite my gut feeling, I walk in.

Sitting on a plush leather chair with his feet on a glass coffee table is a man with very short silver hair, a black shirt and yellow eyes. He's chewing on an unlit cigar—it's enormous. Standing in front of him is a muscular black man, wearing an over-sized Def Kahn-5 T-shirt. "What the fuck is that?" Sounds like Vishnu.

Relax, these are just some co-workers chewing the fat at the end of the day—it's happy hour in the record business.

The Yellow Eyes guy takes the unlit stovepipe out of his mouth. "You from the agency?"

"Yes, sir."

"Yes, sir?" Vishnu, wide-eyed, looks at his co-workers.

Yellow Eyes is suspicious. "Where's the other girl?"

Other girl? Roberta said this assignment was a sure thing.

"What's with the ice cooler? You servin' bev'rages?"

"Uh, no. Well, in a way, yes...it's for milk...for my baby."

"Spare us the mothafuckin' life story," Vishnu says. "You'll get your money." He clears the objects off the desk with one sweep of his hand. "You want to go first, boss?"

"Why not." Yellow Eyes stands and undoes his pants.

Vishnu lifts me and my Igloo onto the desk.

"Uh, I was told to meet Mr. Kahn in his office at six today. Anyone know where he is?" This stops the Yellow Eyed gentleman's pants mid-thigh. "I know you're all busy. A lot on your plates. I should go find Mr. Kahn. We had an appointment to discuss my responsibilities and…"

Vishnu interrupts, "Thought you said you was from the mothafuckin' agency."

"I am—TempNation."

"What the fuck kind of mothafuckin' ho service is that?"

"We specialize in typing, filing, reception, you know, administrative assistance."

The three guys look at each other.

"I knew that," says Yellow Eyes, fastening his pants like he was just tucking in his shirttail. "It's these guys who don't."

Vishnu says, "So why'd you mothafuckin' come in here?"

"This gentleman invited me." I point to Mr. Mecca Pants. He shrugs his shoulders in a don't-look-at-me way. "Been in the waiting area for over an hour. I'm a bit surprised by Mr. Kahn's lack of punctuality. Me, I tend to run early. It's simply a matter of professional courtesy."

"How'd you get in here anyway?" asks Mr. Mecca Pants.

"I walked in."

Vishnu says, "What tha fuck?"

Yellow Eyes says, "Fucking security in this place is for shit. Am I right? Anyone walks in."

Mr. Mecca shakes his head. "Just fucked up s'what it is."

Interesting place, this Def Kahn-5. Of course, it was too dark to see much in the hallway, but it kind of gives you the feeling of being outside, even when you're inside.

Yellow Eyes walks to the door, "You, Milk Maiden, grab the beer keg and come with me."

Sliding off the desk, I straighten my skirt and lift the ice cooler. "By the way, this isn't a beer keg. It's an Igloo."

"Yeah, well, who fucking cares?" He walks down the hallway without looking back. "If you want to talk about a job, there's no now like the present."

I rush after him. "I would, but it's after seven o'clock, my babysitter is waiting and…"

"Up to you." He walks. "It's now or nevertheless."

Guess the babysitter's gonna have to wait.

With my mini-dairy farm in tow, I try to catch up. "Are we going to see Mr. Kahn?"

He stops, turns. "Is this what it's like to work with you?"

Not sure how to answer that.

A woman's heels click quickly toward us in the darkened hallway. She's wearing a long fur coat, which she unbuttons to reveal a short red lace slip and an eagle killing a snake tattoo on the inside of her left thigh. Up top, she is amply endowed and proud. She stops, stares, smiles. "Thought we was taking care of business in Vishnu's office."

Clearing his throat, he adopts a professional demeanor, while salivating at her chest. "Uh, yes, Miss, uh, Missy meet Miss, uh, her." He points at me.

The woman shakes my hand. "Nice ta meet ya. Nobody say nothin' 'bout a three-way. What's with the ice chest?"

"It's breast milk. I'm…"

"What tha fuck? Kahnie, you be one twisted dude."

What did she call him? "Are you Mr. Bigar Kahn?"

"In a minute." He turns to the lady in the fur coat. "Why don't you go into Vishu's office and start consultationing. Miss, uh, Missy and I need to interface."

She looks me over. "In-her-face?" Closing her coat, she walks away. Her perfume remains as her heels click down the dark hallway. Suddenly, "Breast milk! Lordie, Lordie! Lordie!"

Mr. Kahn stares after her. "This way."

He walks. I follow.

We stop in front of an office door, where this gigantic guy is sitting, reading "Prevention Magazine." He looks up. "Hey, boss, you be needin' some priv'cy? I can turn down m' hearin' aid."

He puts his face up to the guy and shakes his head. "NO NEED TO, ALONZO. IT'S LEGIT!"

Alonzo stares, nods and goes back to his reading.

"Hi, I'm Lily White." I put out my hand.

He shakes it and then looks at the cooler. "Got any ginger ale? Stomach's been acting up." He stares at my mouth.

"No, it's milk for my baby."

"Sprite's fine."

I enunciate. "Milk-for-my-baby."

"Sorry, can't read lips. You gots to talk louder."

"MILK FOR MY BABY! IT'S MILK FOR MY BABY!"

From down the hall. "YO, SHUT THE FUCK UP! HOW'S SOMEONE SUPPOSED TA FUCKING FUCK AROUND HERE WITH ALL DA FUCKING NOISE OUT THERE?" Sounds like Vishnu.

Kahn yells from his office. "GET IN HERE AND LEAVE MY BODYGUARD ALONE."

Inside his office, is this black and gray weave L-shaped couch that's covered in pistachio nutshells. In front of it is a crystal coffee table etched with fish. The table is covered with bowls of candy and cigars. Balanced on an arm of the couch is a large glass swan ashtray.

I rest my Igloo and tote bag and then brush enough pistachio shells off the couch to sit. Slowly sinking into the cushions, I look around for something to compliment—a very powerful job interview technique that my husband, Hank, taught me.

The walls are yellowish tan burled-wood. Ebony cabinets run across the length of the room. Inside them there are silver knick-knacks and trophies. Above the cabinets are gold and platinum records in square frames. Around the room are four bronze ashtrays with carved holders for cigars and Def Kahn-5 matchbooks. The floor is covered in yellowy-brown leather that matches the walls. There's a worn path from Mr. Kahn's desk to the large windows. On the window ledge is a collection of wind-up Victrolas and antique radios.

His desk is a single sheet of three-inch thick glass, etched with fish, matching the coffee table. The fish seem to float inside the glass. But what dominates the room is a large black and white photograph of a naked black woman trying to break through the picture frame—her mouth open—about to scream. It's breathtaking.

This is the office of a tasteful, thoughtful person. Maybe I shouldn't jump to conclusions about his professionalism.

Mr. Kahn paces back and forth.

With so many things to compliment, where do I start?

"That's some picture you've got there."

"What?" He stops and looks at it. "That piece of shit? The fag

decorator said it was art. I've seen better, so I never look at it."
He starts pacing again.

I wait a few seconds. "Mr. Kahn, what kind of person are you looking for in this position?"

He stops, looks at the picture again. "What? Oh, that piece of shit? The fag decorator said it was art. I've…"

"No, I mean, the job."

He blinks a couple of times. "What job?"

"The one you called me here to discuss."

"To discuss? A job? Here?" His eyes go blurry for a moment. "I need a star." He looks me over. "You a star?"

Careful, this might be a trick question. "How would you define a 'star'?"

"Someone who needs more than a job. Resumes we get by the shitload. What I look for is someone who's willing to burn their britches, someone who'll do whatever it takes to get a job done— no bullshit, just results." He starts pacing. "Everyone here started at the bottom and worked their way to the middle, except for me. I started everything. From no record label, I built a power in the industry. So I only want people, who got what it takes, whatever it takes. That's what gets me hot for a person."

I sit straighter. "Well, I don't like to brag, but I'm very organized, detail-oriented, reliable, and a real self-starter."

"Yeah, yeah, so what's your name?"

"Lily White."

He stops and stares. "That's your name?"

I nod.

"No shit?" He walks back and forth again. "So, Lisa, tell me something about your goals. What do you want when the Grim Rapper finally comes for you?"

"Do you mean personally or professionally?"

"Yes." He stops and squints like a tailor sizing me up. "You want to be rich. Am I correct?"

"I am looking for a place where I can grow."

"Won't money help you grow?"

"Can't argue with you there." I try for a genuine smile.

"To get these growing riches, I need you to understand your relationship to the label—and so must you. You need to be dedicated to make us all successful. You must dig inside yourself and be willing to make personal sacrileges for the company. You must be willing to handle any situation even before shit happens—and shit does happen. But most important, you must be willing to walk through a wall of such shit, to get shit done. You understand the jism of what I'm saying here?"

"You bet!" I chirp. *Don't really, but I need the job.*

He walks to the window and speaks to me with his back turned. "You must..." He stops. He's filled with emotion. "You must, must..."

"Be punctual?" *I'm trying to fill in the blank.*

"No..."

"Be reliable?"

"N, no..."

"Loyal?"

He starts to breathe heavily.

What's he doing?

"No, that's not what I want to hear." Mr. Kahn gasps, " I want you to say, 'whatever it takes.'"

"Whatever it takes—to be punctual?" *What should I say?*

He can hardly get his words out. "Forget that punc-TU-al SHIT. Just...say...'Whatever it takes.'"

"Okay. Whatever it takes." He hunches forward.

Is he going to up-chuck?

"Again...SAY IT!" His right arm starts moving quickly.

"Whatever it takes." *What does that mean?*

"Louder!"

"Whatever it takes!"

"Whatever it takes—like you want it bad!"

As loudly as I can. "WHATEVER IT TAKES!"

He convulses once, then again and again. "Oh, yeah, yeah, oh that's good, yeah, more, there it is, baby, YES!"

"Mr. Kahn, do you need some Tums, or something?"

"Oh, yeah, yeah, oh that's good, that's so good. Mmmm, Mmmm. Mmmm."

I must have done something right.

Kahn spins around to me. His—you know what—is in his hand. Behind him, on the floor-to-ceiling windowpane is a glop of goop.

Did he just do what I think he did?

"The Rap business is about taking it to the edge. Making your mark. You, Lisa, you want money?"

I nod.

"Lots of it?"

I force another nod.

"You'll get it, but only if you're willing to do what?" He points at my face.

"Wha…wha…wha."

"Whatever."

"What…ever."

"It. SAY IT!"

"It."

He tilts forward, his face in my face, and spits, "Takes."

"Tttt…akes."

"Get stuck with me and you'll learn when to whip it out and when to hold back." He zips his pants.

I feel like the woman in the photograph above his desk, desperate to escape, but trapped in this position.

He extends his right hand—the one he used to—yuck.

"Welcome to Def Kahn-5."

2

The Next Morning

IN THE PAST MONTH my life's become a big wait. Waiting in the free clinic to find out why Ivy, my baby, is sniffling. Waiting to hear when Hank is going to move back in with us. Waiting to see if the Legal Services lawyer can prevent us from being evicted from our apartment. Waiting for the babysitter, hoping she'll show up, so I can sit here, waiting at TempNation to say that I will not work at that place, Def Kahn 5.

There are three of us in TempNation—Roberta, her overstuffed Rolodex and me. And guess what's getting all her attention?

Not me.

The exact pronunciation of her name is Ro-boy-tah. After four marriages, she has this theory about men. They're all aliens, spies that come here from another planet to probe our women and return to base. I used to think she was kidding, but after my interview with Mr. Kahn, I feel she may be onto something.

The phone receiver is velcroed to her ear. She's lost in her wheels and deals. In one hand she uses a felt-tip marker, which stains every exposed part of her skin. The other hand holds a cigarette.

Roberta's got a black belt in nicotine. But without her, I wouldn't have had any work these past few months. My typing is barely adequate. The one thing I've always had is good organizational and problem-solving skills. Maybe not in my personal life, but in business, I was forced into action.

Dad used to say that we lived from foot to mouth. One day, when I was twelve, I came home from school, opened the refrigerator and found nothing. NOTHING! Since my father hadn't been paid for his last two jobs, and my mother only worked for the Lord—for free—we couldn't afford to buy groceries. That's when I realized I had to do something, especially if we were going to eat. So I became his booker and bill collector.

Dad is a piano-player for special events like weddings, school dances and farm foreclosures. Made it my job to make sure he got to the gig, got set up and then made real sure he got paid. Left up to him, he'd just sit on his favorite chair, feet up, and stare out the living-room window for hours, humming melodies, accompanying himself on air piano. He's an artist. What he isn't is a businessman. So he hummed. I dunned.

Early on, I learned many ways to collect overdue bills. Pretending to be an agent, a lawyer or a collection agency, I became a pretty good arm twister. If Daddy ever found out what I was doing, he'd, he'd…well…he'd probably just sit there and make mind music. But we never had an empty refrigerator again.

As for Mom, she spent most of her life trying to be more intimate with God than with Dad. The church took away her fear of death and marriage.

Seeing how my parents were (or weren't) with each other, I always wondered how my brother and I were born.

After Hank and I got married, it was just natural that I do the same for him—I mean, collecting money owed and being supportive. He thought he would make a fortune selling Herbalux. "America, Get Ready For Some Colon Cleansing!" is what the brochure read. But now, all we have to show for it are the bruises on my legs from tripping over the cardboard boxes of unsold Herbalux that cleaned out our savings.

So to get by, I do temp work.

At least, that's what I thought I was doing. It's eleven a.m., and Roberta seems to be ignoring me. I walk over to her desk (using the term desk loosely here, because it resembles a paper recycling plant). Behind her are Christmas decorations piled on top of a computer, still in the box. Roberta never got around to setting it up. Her excuse: "Done twenty years without one. I'll get to it."

She looks up at me. "Be wid yas in a moment, doll." Then into the receiver, "Send ya some resumes today, hon…of course…of course…" Roberta winks and lights up another cig. "Yeah, natch…" She exhales a cumulus cloud. "…Right, that's all I got is perfect candidates…bye, babe." She hangs up the phone, two-handed, like a dynamite plunger. The result is an explosion of hacking and spitting into extra-strength tissues.

Following each coughing fit, she reapplies her lipstick. Roberta takes a great deal of pride in her appearance. Today, she's wearing a floral print blouse and too-tight designer jeans. It's not that she's overweight. She's just right, for being a Ro-boy-tah. And a compliment like "love the daisies on your fingernails" or "those red streaks in your hair suit you" goes a long way.

She's been very good to me, but lately it's been slow, according to Roberta. "What can I do ya for, doll?"

"Just wondering if there was any work."

"Ain't cha supposed to be at that record company? It was a sure thing."

"Is there anything else?"

Roberta torches up, and uses the long thin cig to point at the chair next to her desk. "Move that stuff somewhere. Let's chat."

I pick up some papers and look around for a place to put them. She points to pile of old pizza boxes.

"Ova der."

I stack the papers neatly and sit on the rediscovered folding chair.

"So."

"So." Then a silence which is broken by the exhale of her chimney. "Honey, I got some bad news. Straight talk—no one wants to work wid ya."

"No one…?"

"Reports I'm getting is that ya got a mouth on yas."

"What does that mean?"

She leans forward, lacing her fingers around her cigarette, which makes her knuckles look like they're smoking. "The law office I sent ya to a couple weeks ago?"

"Yes."

"Well they almost wouldn't pay. A simple two day assignment and you fricked it up, pardon my French."

"What did I do?"

"Doll, ya can't stick your nose in a lawyer's briefs."

"His briefs?"

"No, no, no, not his briefs," she says pointing to her private area. "Rewriting his legal briefs." She does a writing motion. "Whatever you did, dat lawya got his ass chewed out by a judge. Not good. Not good."

"All I did was make it sound like plain English. I was just trying to improve it."

"Right." Roberta lights a new cig with the old one, and exhales a lung-full. "And wad about that insurance salesguy? What happened widdat? He calls me yelling he lost half his sales. What's widdat?"

My face flushes.

Roberta stares over her reading glasses and coaches me. "Sum'pin about his suit."

"All I said was that if he dressed better, you know, two, not three patterns at a time, he'd attract better customers."

"But dats how he makes his livin'! The guy is a slob. He dresses for success with his clientele—other slobs. Who else is gonna buy his crapola? Pardon my French. It's supply and demand, doll, basic economy. Sheesh!" She drags deep and continues, "Honey, ya can't mess wid an insurance salesman's mind. It's a delicate balance up there. And ya know what happened widdat? Now he's almost outta business. He runs back to the Salvation Army and tries to buy back his attire wardrobe— that he gave away on your advice. Not good. Not good."

Roberta waits for the long cigarette ash to drop.

Wonder if Hank felt the same way. Did I open my mouth too much? I only meant well. I wanted Hank to succeed. Heck, I even told him that his success was our success. Of course, that meant his failure was mine too.

The ash just hangs there. "Sorry t' tell yas these things."

"But, Roberta, it was good advice."

"The advice may be good, but wasn't asked for. Hates ta tell yas, but youse have a new name round here."

"A new name?"

"Finish this. John Lennon was married to Yoko…"

"Ono?"

"Bingo! I mention your first name, 'Lilac,' to a client and they all say the same. 'Oh no! Not her'...Ya gettin' to be famous, doll, for all the wrong reasons."

"Famous?"

The ash drops. "Sorry to have to spill it on ya like dis." Roberta lights up the tenth cigarette of the morning.

Is this where my life is going—from one lousy job to another? Now not even that—nothing. My baby? My bills? Why did Hank have to leave? Things would have worked out. Don't cry. But if I could crawl into a hole somewhere, I would. All I can manage to get out is "Gotta go."

Roberta hands me a lipstick-blotted tissue.

I stand and blow my nose.

"Doll, I hates t' be the tiding of bad news. But maybe there's some good news too."

"Th, There is?" My voice is trembling now.

"Sure. Ya got a baby to pay for. Just cause I'm being honest, don't mean I'm gonna let yas down."

"You're, you're not?"

"Wadda take me for, the angel of debt? Look, this job I sent you on yesterday could be temp to perm."

"You mean that record company?"

"They need a replacement for someone who's in the hospital for awhile."

I should have recognized the look on Roberta's face, the shaky cigarette, the perspiration on her upper lip, the way her perfume went from sweet to sweat, and the way she pushed her glasses back onto the bridge of her nose—like she was hiding behind her ashtray-thick lenses.

Wait a minute—I don't want to work there. That place is a nightmare. Maybe I should tell her about what Mr. Kahn did on his window and my hand.

"I'm booking you tomorrah." (Rhymes with Gomorrah)

"Where?"

"Where!" She shoots back. "There!"

"I can't."

Roberta stares at me. "Can't or won't? Cause if it's either, I'm done. Ya costing me too many sleepless phone calls."

I realize that it's this job or an empty refrigerator.

"Okay."

"But yas have to promise me sumpin'."

"What?"

"Don't go der wid that nosiness. Jus be D&D."

"D&D?"

"Yeah, blind, dumb and deaf."

"Isn't that B, D&D?"

"Right, be D&D. It's an attitude adjustment kind of thing. Ya understand?"

"Yes."

"Ya better. Look, honey, please don't frick this up. Pardon my French. Your operating words from now on are Blind, Dumb and…"

…Def Kahn-5.

3

Long Gone Daddy

ALL RAP SONGS start with a beat. In this case it's the beat of a baby crying. My baby. Two months after giving birth to Ivy, my life has taken on her rhythm. Every time I'm in a deep sleep, she wails her hungry tune, and I do my groggy dance—body shoots upright, legs drop alongside the bed, pink robe tied around my poochie belly, grab the nursing towel, swollen feet slipped into fuzzy pink slippers, and flap, flap, flap, zigzagging through cartons of unsold Herbalux. Learned the routine in my sleep. After two months, the path to Ivy's room is almost as worn out as I am.

> Three a.m.—Ivy bawling, me flapping.
> Six a.m.—No milk run, just a burp-in-waiting.
> Nine a.m.—Wake up in the rocker next to her crib.

It's too quiet. I lean forward, praying that she's still breathing. She's fine. Snoring like a baby.

Wish I was.

But for some reason, I'm as close to awake as I've been in a long time. I look around. So many improvements I'd like to make in her little room. Actually, it's a large closet painted pink. I believe that things can always be done better.

In this case, much better.

Wow, I feel almost human this morning. Might as well get ready for the day. Let Hank have some extra sleep. Into the kitchen for my usual decaf coffee with cream, Wonder Bread toast with butter—fast and foolproof.

Holding the plate and coffee mug, I push my elbow across the kitchen table to clear an eating space. The stack of bills falls to the floor. I groan past my stomach to pick them up.

Since Hank's not selling too much Herbalux these days, we live on what little savings we have. Just enough to eat, buy diapers, be two months behind in our rent and one month on the utilities.

It's a perfect arrangement—I stack the bills and he avoids them. Poor Hank. Sometimes I'll wake up after midnight and find him soaking in the tub. He takes baths in the dark. That's because the tub is in the kitchen, and the kitchen is where we keep the bills. Asked Hank if he'd like me to store them in another room.

"No, Lil'. That's what they want. You see, in the dark they can't collectively peer on my nakedness."

What's really troubling is how he sits in the tub, chanting:

> *God only knows*
> *Only God knows*
> *Knows God only*
> *God knows only*

Over and over.

It's good that he's getting some extra sleep. Sometimes being unconscious is the best medicine.

But I believe in him. He's got the gift of gab. That's what everyone back home used to say. Hank's a good, strong man, who feels responsible for Ivy and me. He's our rock—the foundation upon which we built this family—even when he's acting a little loopy.

Only problem is, every time I think about our situation, I get this knot in my stomach. My insides have always reacted to what's happening outside. Back in Puce, Missouri after each of my grumpy tummy incidents, Mom would testify, "Thank the Lord for outdoor plumbing."

I do have an addiction—Tums. My Dad does too. He's the one who suggested I start popping 'em. They work. So every time my tummy acts up, I reach for those little white chalky dots. But they can't spell relief from past-due bills.

Relax, everyone's still asleep, and nothing's going to ruin my first free morning in months. What to do? Clean up that mess of dishes? Scrub the sink? Sweep?

A rotten-egg smell makes the decision for me. Those diapers have to go. Phew! Holding my breath, I place the mustard-stained disposables in a plastic shopping bag. Tie the handles together and head outside.

This isn't how I imagined my life would turn out. My goal was to have a family and a career on the side. Used to think that being a nurse, or a teacher was in my future. Somehow I never got around to learning those things. Thought about being an office manager—you don't seem to need much education for that—but people seem to want you to have some experience managing an office. So I settled for working as a receptionist or typist. I've temped in many types of businesses, but can't seem to get the permanent hang of taking orders. The folks that hire you act like they want you to take charge—until you do. Then you're a troublemaker or have a mouth on you. Work gets kind of confusing. But soon, I know that the right job will come along.

Problem is, if the phone were to ring, I'd have to say, "Not today. Waiting for my baby to do her business."

Having a child is something we hadn't planned. Just sort of surprised us one day. Hank said I did it on purpose. What purpose, he can't say.

He's just feeling bad, cause he's a failure.

I didn't mean to make it sound like that. What I meant is he's "feeling" like a failure. Things'll turn 'round for him soon. I just know it.

Enough reflection for one morning. After three straight hours of sleep, I'm raring to go. What a luxury.

First thing is to get rid of this garbage bag before the fumes overwhelm me.

Walking downstairs to the street, I see the baby throw-up and breast-milk stains on my robe. In daylight they look awful. Maybe if I cross one arm over my chest and hold the bag, like this, in front of me, no one will notice.

The cold morning air numbs my bare legs. I rush to the garbage area in front of the apartment building. Our neighborhood is the upper part of Manhattan, almost Washington Heights. It borders Highbridge Park to the east and the George Washington Bridge to the north. You can tell our block once had lots of trees by all the square dirt holes in the sidewalk. Each one contains a stump. One stump is upholstered with red vinyl and brass tacks. Who would want to sit on a tiny stool surrounded by stinky garbage?

I throw the used diaper bag into a dented can and rush back up the steps before any of the neighborhood crazies can make any comments about the way I look.

Something catches my eye. Jackpot! There, on a pile of old newspapers, last week's TV Guide.

Hank hates when I bring stuff in from the trash. I explain to him that many of the programs are the same from week to week and that it's one less expense. He just can't see the diamond in the refuse. Sometimes we'll use the same TV Guide for a couple of months. But now, ta-da, we're only a week behind in our entertainment debt.

I find a spot where I can pick up my treasure without getting too much grease on my fingers. Holding it out in front of me like a stinky fish. I walk up the hallway, hoping none of the neighbors can see me. Probably doesn't matter though. We haven't made too many friends in the building, or should I say, we haven't kept too many. Hank's tried to sell Herbalux to each of them.

Inside our apartment, I put on my yellow rubber gloves to check the listings. Surgically, I peel away each page until I uncover Wednesday, nine o' clock:

> Channel Two—Martha Stewart
> Channel Seven—Regis in the Morning
> Channel Five—I Love Lucy

Lucy? I love Lucy.

Just going to be a lump on this mushy thing we call our couch. I stretch out, and feel like I'm twelve again, except how did my legs get so veiny? I whip my robe around to hide the roadmaps on my thighs.

Hey, they're showing the one where Lucy, Ricky and the Mertz's are in California.

I hug my knees and bury my mouth in them to muffle my laughter. Don't want to wake Hank or Ivy. Nope, this morning

I'm a kid without a care, just enjoying what's here and now and fun. My response is to wiggle my toes.

This is great!

Lucy is upset, because even the bellhop has a part in a movie.

The phone rings.
Oh, no!
Choking the receiver quickly, I whisper, "Hello?"
"God be with thee, child."
"Who's this?"
"We have met once. At one of our Realizations."
I'm half-listening, because I'm trying to see if Lucy's going to do what I already know she's going to do.
"Thy husband brought you. But, alas, you decided to travel the unfortunate path."
"What? We're not interested."
"Harken to my call, woman…"
I hang up—telemarketers!
Back to Lucy.

Ricky tells Lucy he's gotten her a part in a movie.

The phone rings again.
What now? I lift the receiver mid-ring and hang up.
The phone rings—again.
I answer. "What?"
"How well dost thy know the Book of Job?" The deep baritone on the other end asks.
"Please, stop calling."
"I warn thee, child, don't hang up. People who have done so have experienced years of torment."
"Who's this?"
"The Right-Reverend Sky Fogg."
"Who?"
"Thine husband's spiritual advisor."
"Spiritual advi…? Oh yeah, from Hank's church thing."
"Astronomous asked me to call you."

The director shows Lucy how to walk down the stairs.

"I'm sorry, Hank's asleep."

There's a muffled voice in the background. Then I hear Fogg speak to that other person. I think he's trying to cover the phone's mouthpiece.

Lucy puts on her big headdress, which makes her nearly fall over.

I giggle.

"What?" The voice says.

"I'm sorry. What's your name again?"

"The Right-Reverend Sky Fogg, PC."

Lucy stumbles down a staircase, trying to balance her headdress.

I bust out laughing.

"What's so funny about that?"

"What?" Trying to catch my breath. "What?"

"Thine husband, Astronomous, formerly Hank White, is leaving thee and obliging his soul to the Fogg Ministries."

My brain isn't functioning. Is this guy saying that Hank is leaving me?

"Worry not, God shall protect those who come to him."

Lucy, without her headdress, acts like she's been shot.

That makes me double over and snort.

"Only then can thou redeemeth thy soul and thy mate."

What's this guy trying to do, ruin my morning?

"Thine husband reacheth for an Epiphany to become a fine-tuned instrument of Our Savior."

Praise be—a commercial. "You just hold on right there. I'm getting my husband." I drop the receiver and march to the bedroom.

I just told Hank to find a church to help work out his problems and enjoy some fellowship. Now this guy is ruining my first free morning in months.

"Hank, wake up, honey. Your Reverend Flogg, is yammering on the phone and..."

I'm staring at the bed, where Hank has left an impression—of where he used to be. The covers are on the floor. I lift them.

No Hank.

I look in the bathroom. Where is he?

In the kitchen? Nothing.

Searching the apartment, I can't see anything different. Except for Hank's closet and dresser being empty, everything is...

EMPTY?

What's going on around here?

Sitting on the edge of the bed, I tell myself this is a nightmare and it's time to wake up. But I am awake. How could he be gone? His smell is still in the air.

The phone in the living room...

Rushing in, I turn the TV sound down and put the receiver up to my ear. Before I can say anything, I hear a muffled conversation on the other end of the line.

"She'll find you've gone," says Fogg.

"Think so?" It's Hank.

"Hello, Hello! Put Hank on the phone."

They keep talking.

"Hellllooo! Excuse me, Reverend, uh..."

"Child, thou hast uncovereth the truth. Deny it not."

My knees buckle. I fall to the couch.

"Astronomous asks you to realize all this is for the best."

For the best? I rub my eyes. "Tell Hank to please come back home—RIGHT THIS MINUTE. He can't just leave us. What about our daughter?"

"Testify to her that the Lord is eternal. Life temporal."

"She's only two months old."

In the background—Hank's voice, "Tell her not to worry. I'll be back soon."

Sky Fogg says, "Doth thou understand commitment?"

"But what if I want to visit?"

"You don't know what you want, do you?"

"No, but I don't want her to worry."

"HELLO! NEED AN EXPLANATION HERE!"

The Reverend hears me and ends his conversation with Hank, "Look, we shall talk about this later. Let me deal with one sinner at a time. Thine own turn will come after I enlighten your woman." To me. "What's thy name, child?"

"Lily."

"Yes, Lily, you will have to go on as best you can. We have our work to do here. Thy have thine there."

"Work? What work? The place is full of unpaid bills. They're piled up all over the house. What about our baby?"

"Lily, if thee had 'the understanding,' thy would know it's Astronomous's time to find meaning in his life."

My hands are twisting the telephone cord into a ball like the one inside my stomach. My insides are about to drop.

Breathe. Breathe. Please, be a dream.

"Let me talk to Hank, or Astronomy, or whatever the heck he's calling himself."

"Not now." Fogg says. "His journey is begun. By the way, we'll send some parishioners over for the boxes of herbal potions."

"Oh, no you…"

The Reverend hangs up.

"…won't."

I collapse on the couch.

Got to do something. What? I can't move. Oh God, I've got to do something. Think.

Luckily, Ivy starts to cry.

I trip on a box of Herbalux, kick it, and then limp to pick up my beautiful baby. We sit in the rocker that Hank's mother gave us. I pull out my breast and invite her to partake. Good ol' reliable Ivy. My body relaxes. I need this more than she does.

The three of us rock together—Ivy, me, and the large lump in my stomach.

A tear lands on her face. It's mine. She pulls away and squints. Ivy's making the same face as me—all scrunched up, so sad. How could Hank leave us?

Another tear lands on her. I wipe it away.

Stop crying, you fool, you'll drown her.

My dad once said, "A baby should be the most important thing in your wife."

Obviously, that's not the way Hank feels.

What am I going to do? How long has he been planning this? Who'll take care of us? What did I do that made him run away? He'll come back—soon as he realizes we have so much more to offer him than that silly church—just a matter of him getting his head on straight—that's right—Hank'll be back.

This is my first free morning. Come on, Ivy, let's go see the rest of the show. Can't afford to be worried.

Heck, can't afford nothing.

I carry Ivy into the living room and see...

> *Lucy, totally covered by a sheet, is on a stretcher.*
> *She wrote her name on the bottom of her shoes.*
> *Ricky has one of those wide-eyed "I can't believe it" looks*
> *—Oh, Lucy!*

Oh, Hank, why didn't I see the handwriting on the wall?

4

Def Khan-5
(Day Two)

THOSE LAST TEN PREGNANT pounds make me huff and puff up the Canal Street subway stairs. With each step, my crisp blue business suit strains to stay in its original shape. I'd use the railing, but my right hand holds a large totebag, stuffed with bottles, a breast pump and extra AA batteries. My left hand grips my Igloo cooler, the heavier one, filled with ice to keep my milk fresh.

I've become a working dairy farm, expressing milk three or four times a day. But it'll be the babysitter who gets to feed Ivy. My turn will be once—during the night.

"Come on already," A man behind me whines.

Can't turn to say what I'd like to, so I just keep groaning upwards—step-by-step-by-step. Finally, I'm at street-level and catch my breath. A crowd of people rushes past, taking the Lord's name in vain—at me.

Made it. Mott Street. It's chilly, but I'm sweating. Set my stuff down to rub the red and white creases out of my hands. Unbutton my jacket. Whew! That's better.

Take a deep breath.

WOO-WEE! A breeze fills my nose with ginger, garlic, grease, all roasting together. One whiff of Chinatown is all it takes to move my stomach up into my throat.

My first business decision of the day is to exhale only.

Everyone moves in double-time as I waddle.

It was different in Missouri. I was the speedy one, the one who'd get frustrated when anyone talked or walked in Puce-time. Don't get me wrong, some folks there are very nice. They just live life a little slower and saw my pace as strange. That's why they didn't want anything to do with me, my family or even Hank (after we got married). In their eyes I was that "crazy girl," rushing around like a woodchuck caught in daylight. Some people thought I was pushy. Others thought I was just plain rude. But to make sure we ate, I had to hustle.

Now, here, I'm the slow poke.

Crossing Mott Street, where Def Kahn-5 has its offices, a large four-wheel-drive screeches up to the curb. I jump out of the way. The windows are pitch black. The whole truck seems to expand and contract like it's breathing. Three of the truck's doors open and music explodes. Stepping out are three foreign-looking gentlemen. One wears a long leather jacket, silver goggles and carries an aluminum briefcase. The second is in a deep blue warm-up suit with loose laces on his sneakers. The gold rope around his neck looks like a shiny python. This gold Belgian waffly ring thing (the size of a small paperback book) covers his left hand, the one firmly attached to his private parts. His other hand gestures wildly with a painfully bent wrist. *You could get a cramp in that position.* The third guy, who has solid gold teeth and very loose pants, joins the other two. *Oh my, you can see the tops of his Polo underwear.* His snap-brim hat reminds me of what Mr. Echols used to wear when he drove his MG around Puce. He smoked a pipe, had this fake English accent and wore the same hat as this fella. Only this guy, whose pants are barely hanging on, wears his sideways.

Honk! Honk! The guy with the silver goggles locks their SUV with a press of his car key.

They talk loudly. Their arms punctuate the foreign language they speak. So I enunciate carefully. "You in No Parking Zone. No Parrr-king."

They turn to me.

"Policeman come." I mime someone writing a ticket. They just stare. Then I act out steering a car, pretending to hit the horn. "Beep! Beep!" I point to the car "You move car. Move car."

In unison, they spit on the sidewalk.

"Get ticket. You-no-want." Hopefully our language-barrier

isn't too great. I point at their SUV and the No Parking sign above. I cross-uncross my hands and shake my head. "No Parking. No Par-king." That's as clear as I can make it.

The guy in the warm-up suit sniffs the air. "Yo, you be smellin' somethin'?"

It's English, but I look at the others to get a translation. They try to stifle a laugh, but fail.

"Prob'ly," says the nearly-pants-off one. "There be lots o' foul things cookin' chere in Chinytown."

The guy with the silver goggles giggles. "Looks like we gots chickenhead on the men-yoo."

They slap hands and chuckle. Wobbling back and forth, the happy trio tries to regain their collective balance.

Great—they do speak English.

"Maybe that's why I feel so pukey." They freeze, but I continue. "Do Chinese people really eat chickenheads? Just the thought of that makes me gag."

In unison, they roll their eyes, and walk away.

"Okay, don't say I didn't warn you."

The fellow in the warm-up suit turns quickly to engage me in conversation, but his goggled friend wraps his arms around him. "Don't bother with that one, bro. You da big dog. She be da flea. Scratch da bitch off. KnowhatImean?"

All three gentlemen give me a nasty once-over (or thrice-over), then amble into the black marble building—where I'm going. So I decide to wait for a few minutes to let them get where they're going—just to be safe.

The street has come alive with hundreds of people. It's world-famous Chinatown. Relax. Enjoy the sights and sounds. Traffic roars. People yell. Smells smell. My breakfast is starting to come up. Hang on, tummy, won't be long now.

I hop from one leg to the other—like when you need to tinkle, puke and your milk's about to geyser.

Those guys have to be gone by now. Even if they haven't, that's about all of Chinatown I can inhale at the moment.

I enter the lobby. It's empty. Great, and great timing, because the elevator's here. Rushing to get inside, I bump into three very large people, already wedged inside.

The three guys turn to see what just hit them.

I'd let them have the elevator all to themselves, but my fluids need a quick outlet—and all are doomed if I explode.

Squeezing the cooler, totebag, and then myself into the three square inches left, I snake carefully between them—to respect their personal space. "Excuse me. Excuse me. Sorry." The tip of my finger just makes it to the eighth floor button, which is already lit up. *Uh-oh.* But nothing can happen here in this sardine can, can it?

Each fella takes out a cigar and lights up. The elevator door closes.

Five Years Ago

Puce, Missouri is a one-elevator town. And that elevator lifts wheelchair-bound members of the Veterans of Foreign Wars from the ground level into the Lodge Hall. That's where most parties, weddings and other events happen. The Hall is where I met Hank. His dad, Reverend White, was conducting a wedding. My father was playing the piano with his dance band.

After the third rendition of "We've Only Just Begun," the wedding reception ends. Time to get payment for services rendered. The bride's father, who's in a wheelchair, wearing a VFW hat covered with pins, says he'll mail us the check.

I know better. "The agreement is that we'd get paid in full the day of the wedding,"

He sneers up at me. "You know, they weren't that good. Thought they're supposed to be professional."

"Professional? Obviously you haven't ever heard of Willy Lamb and His Swinging Flock."

"Sounded like they ought to be swinging shovels."

Not sure why I did this. Just snapped. "Fine, don't pay, and you're not getting out of here."

"What're you talking about?"

"You're in a wheelchair and I have the key to the lift, so…"

He laughs nervously, "You're kidding me, right?"

"Not kidding. No pay. No way…out."

Hank, hearing the to-do, walks up, dragging two nearly full plastic bags of wedding garbage.

The bride's father calls out. "Hank, this little ass-wipe won't let me ride the elevator down."

"Unless he pays the band what he owes them."

"I said I'd send you the check!"

"That wasn't the agreement." Making my case to the cute trash-toting guy.

"You know what?" Wheelchair Daddy folds his arms across his chest. "I ain't gonna pay you nothing. Fact is, I don't believe you got the key."

Caught me. I don't.

Hank extends his hand. "I'm Hank. I clean up after Reverend Thaddeus White's weddings. He's my dad."

"Lily Lamb. Kind of do the same thing for my dad."

He squeezes my hand and smiles. "Nice to meet you, Lily Lamb." There's something in my palm—the key.

I can hardly talk. "Nice to meet me, too, Hank White." He's so cute! Those gray overalls fit him real fine. Thick black hair, neatly cut. Nice open smile. His tan makes his blue eyes pop. I could stare at him all day.

Got to concentrate on the business at hand.

Turning to the non-paying VFW Daddy-of-the-Bride, I show him the key. "Now, about what we agreed to...?"

He looks at me and then at Hank, as we try hard to not eye each other. He slumps. "Okay, what I owe ya?"

While writing the check, he mutters about getting Jewed-out of his hard-earned money, that he's a chair-bound veteran, and that young folk got no respect for what he's gone through for defending our country. But I got the payment, and eventually a husband.

Hank says that he admired how I stood up to that man in the wheelchair. "Spunk's important in a woman nowadays."

But, nowadays, I'm supposed to keep a lid on it. Maybe a little less spunk will help me keep this job—make me a better person—maybe even get Hank back.

Oh well, maybe some day someone will walk up and hand me the key again.

Back to Def Kahn-5 (Day Two)

The elevator door opens. A wall of smoke bursts into the hallway before I do. Coughing and gagging, I set down my equipment, fanning my hands back and forth to clear out a breathing space. "Against...law...to smoke...elevator."

The three guys walk out, lit cigars clenched in their fists.

Surrounded, I lift the Igloo to defend myself.

"You da law?"

"Somebody oughta teach you the law lesson."

Their hands slap in appreciation of their wit. A small opening appears between them. I run to the glass doors marked with the Def Kahn-5 logo—a radar screen with five green blips.

Locked. I slam the cooler against the glass.

The receptionist, a young African-American woman, sits inside a glass booth and gives me a dirty look.

I mouth, "HELP ME!"

My elevator-mates are approaching. *OH MY GOD!* The receptionist takes her own sweet time to buzz me in. Not actually buzz—more like loud clicks.

They're almost here. I bang louder. The clicks speed up, but I can't push the doors open. I push harder.

"Hey, lawya, leave them doors be."

"Yo, you break them doors, it be a mis-de-meanor."

"You don't want no police writing you no ticket."

"That be hard time."

I'm surrounded. *Think.* I turn to them and plant my feet. "I work here and that receptionist has a direct line to the Police Department, and they'll be here in five, no two minutes."

That seems to stop them.

The one with the gold teeth grins. "Then we'd best get our business done quick."

OH NO!

The door clicks again and again.

The guy with the silver goggles points. "'Scuse me, but you gotta step away from the door."

"Look, I'm sorry about what I said. That wasn't nice. Smoke in the elevator all you want. No sweat off my..."

"That's right. That's right." The warm-up suit guy says. "Now, move away from the door so we can pull it open."

Pull it open? Pull? You have to pull the darned thing?

At the same time, the receptionist pushes from her side and pins me against the wall. Her face is close to mine, the glass door between us. "What the fuck you doin'? You don't be breakin' my door!"

Why is she talking to me like that? Is my nose bleeding?

To the guys she's all hugs and kisses. "Yo, boo, how ya doin'? Come on in. Don't let this skank ho keep ya here."

Skank ho? Is she referring to me?

My voice is muffled through the door. "Excuse me, but I'm from TempNation to see Mr. Longo."

"Girl, you ain't here till I takes care o' these gentlemen. They's artists. Don't know what th' hell you are. Now, you go sit ovah there and wait'll someone gives a shit."

That breaks everyone up, but me. She gives the "artists" a sweet wink. They ogle back appreciatively.

She lets go of the door. I check my nose. No blood.

The receptionist, having finished her reception, steps into her plexiglas fortress and slams the door with a thud.

The inner doors click open. My elevator buddies disappear. For a moment, I hear a thundering BOOM BOOM BOOM from inside. Then the doors close and it's silent. Just the smell of their cigar smoke choking the air.

I sit on what looks like two manhole covers welded together. It's good to get off my feet. *I hope this is a chair.*

Rubbing my hands together, I try to straighten my stiff fingers from the Igloo cooler I've been clutching. Also, my breasts need expression and I've got to tinkle badly. This is a big mistake. But my promise to Roberta still stands—keep your mouth shut and just do what they ask—nothing else. Be D&D. Nice start. Great impression I just made.

The receptionist opens a small window in her glass cube. "Mr Longo's in a meeting. Says you should sit here and wait." She slides the window shut.

"Uh, okay," I say in my professionally cheerful way. She isn't buying into it, or me.

What can I do or say to make her like me? I know. Hank says that people like to hear positive things from positive people.

Look around. Find something to compliment.

I don't know, looks like this place just kind of fell into place. The black leather couch across from me is nothing special, other than the few gouges and some funny yellow writing on it.

But sitting on the couch, opposite me, there's this incredibly handsome African-American man. Where'd he come from? I pretend to read what's written on the gold and silver records hanging on the wall above his head. They look like the one's in Mr. Kahn's office. The only thing is, I don't recognize any of the names—XYZee, Axx¿, Ma'am-Ree.

Must mean something special since they're framed.

There's a closet door, half-torn off the hinges. Inside are some coats, bent hangers and a box of rolled-up posters. The floor is covered with flat, gray and dirty carpeting. That's ugly. What else?

Above me, bolted to the wall, is a TV. It's on, but no sound comes out. The logo on the bottom of the screen displays the words "The Box," but the picture is very fuzzy, like it's been on for years and needs a rest.

Better forget saying something positive for now.

I need relief from my breasts, bloated bladder and gnawing tummy. I'd take some Tums, but I'd like a glass of water before chewing the chalk. So I walk to the glass booth where the receptionist is eating what looks like her breakfast in a styrofoam container. "Excuse me" She must not hear me. I tap on the glass. "Excuse me."

With an angry look, she stops chewing and slides the window panel open a bit. "What?"

"Have you got a restroom here?"

"Yeah." She slides the window panel shut.

"Could I use it?"

She slides the window open. "What?"

"Could I use it?"

"Use what?"

"The little girl's room."

"Mr. Longo'll call you in when he's done." She slides the panel shut with a thump.

Guess it's time to say something positive.

Behind the glass partition, she looks like a doll in a case. She has this very tight miniskirt and a very low-cut dark purple top. You can see every dimple and curve on her ample frame. She's cute, has a nice smile, and was very pleasant to those three guys.

Maybe if I ask her about herself, she'll warm up and let me in.

Hank says that people love to talk about themselves—and all you have to do is ask.

"Where did you get that beautiful top?" Her eyes go dead. "Wish I could wear clothes like that. Some people just look good in anything." Her stare becomes deadlier. "How rude of me, my name's Lily White. What's yours?"

She thuds the glass panel open. "I told ya whatcha need to know." The panel thuds shut.

So much for making friends.

"Don't take it personally. Once you get to know her she's worse." It's the guy on the couch. He's wearing big, baggy bluejeans and a dark grey hooded sweatshirt with Fubu written on the chest. He has these small braids, not exactly braids, more like little volcanoes of hair. Very cute. Warm smile. His eyes are large and sad. He looks at me like, well, I don't know if I've ever been looked at like that.

Without thinking, I start rubbing my aching breasts.

Why is he smiling? Then I realize what I'm doing. I blush.

"Anything I can do for you?"

I won't even allow my mind to go there. "No. No, thanks. Well, yes, maybe. Do you know where the little girl's room might be?"

"Tamyka's got the key." He points to the receptionist.

"Oh, uh, okay, thanks." Then I say, "Tamyka, do you have the key to the little girl's room?"

The sliding panel thumps open. "Now what?"

"Tamyka, do you have the key to the little girl's room?"

"Don't you be calling me my name, girl! You don't know me like that!"

I guess she sees the pain on my face, because she reaches under the counter and slides me a vinyl LP record, attached to a chain with a key.

"Be sure to flush." She adds as the glass panel slide-thuds.

"Is it out in the hall?"

Slide-thump. "What you need now—instructions?"

"Kind of. Is it out in the hall?"

"No, in there." She points to the inner doors.

"Could you buzz me in? I really need to go."

By now I feel like a mess of liquids are about to come out of every opening.

"When Longo's outta his meeting." Slide-thud.

"Then why did you hand me the key?"

No slide, no thud—just her back.

"Tamyka, let her in. Won't do no good her relieving herself out here." *My hero.*

Slide-thud. "You just shut yo mouth, Jiggity Man, or I'll be gettin' Security t' kick yo ugly ass outta here." Slide-thud.

Jiggity Man? That wasn't a nice thing to say. And he's far from ugly. "Sorry," he says. "I'm not the most popular person 'round here, right now."

"Right now? You ain't even here. You be the ghost of Christmas passed."

So she can hear us inside her doll case.

They trade insults for a while. I learn that this guy was an artist on this record label, but something happened. The receptionist says that he's "so over." He says that she doesn't have to be a "hater." She says that he needs to get a life—a new one. He says that as soon as he gets his masters back, he'll "bounce."

WHO CARES! My insides are screaming for help.

I look at the bathroom key, and start praying that Mr. Longo will keep his meeting short. Then it hits me—*why do I need a key for a bathroom that's inside their offices?*

Can't wait. "Look, Tampopo, Takaka, Kayaka, or whatever, I'm about to explode! If I don't get to a bathroom, I'm going to redecorate your waiting room!"

That stops their argument. She looks at me and slide-thuds her doll cage window closed. The inner doors start clicking. I rush in with my heavy equipment.

Inside, I'm almost knocked over by the sounds—the BOOM BOOM BOOM of Rap music, Rhythm and Blues, and screaming disk-jockeys. People rush around, shouting—music blasting from every office.

The walls are covered with gold and silver records in picture frames just like in the waiting area. Each hallway has a name—like Axx¿ Avenue, RamBone Boulevard, Ma'am-Ree Lane.

The floor is cracked concrete, filled potholes and curbs that run along both sides of the hallway. It's a city street with even a slight hump in the middle. Except for the ceiling, you'd think you were outside—during rush hour.

Tightening the grip on my cooler, my tote bag and the vinyl record key, I keep walking. Posters display artists, who look like they need to find a bathroom too. And the smells—I can make out bacon, eggs, cigar smoke, colognes and floor cleaner.

Then I turn the corner.

Def Kahn Avenue, the Main Street of this place, is full of people running, walking, and gesturing wildly. Trash flies across the avenue with the movement of bodies. Boxes of vinyl record albums are stacked everywhere. In one corner, used computers lie stripped and abandoned.

"Where's the little gir…? Where's the lady's…? Whe…?"

No one slows down.

Behind me, three voices.

> *We be blowin' up!*
> *We be Godzilla!*
> *We be Orca!*

"Excuse me, I'm trying to find…" But the trio has vanished into the indoor urban nightmare of Def Kahn-5.

Then, there, staring at me is a little boy with a pit-bull with one eye missing (the dog, not the boy).

"Wanna pet Thuzy?"

The dog growls. I step back.

"Can't." He tugs her leash. "Thuzy, she hon-gree."

The dog looks at me and strains its leash to take a bite.

Step back. Relax. "Do you know where the bathroom is?"

He points. "Boys ovah der."

"And where is the girls…?"

Suddenly, six SWAT team members in full body armor rush by me. One of them has a bullhorn. **"POLICE!!! EVERYONE**

IN YOUR OFFICES! EVERYONE IN YOUR OFFICES! NOW!!!"

The hall empties. I look around. Even the little boy and his hungry Suzy have disappeared. Papers, settling to the floor, are the only indication of people having been here. It's a ghost town. You can almost hear the wind blow. What next, a lonely coyote?

"WHAT ARE YOU DOING OUT HERE?" a SWAT guy bull-horns at me.

"I'm from Temp…"

"GET IN YOUR OFFICE. NOW!!!" He and another Swat team member scan the hallway with their rifles.

It's now or never. I'll either go in my panties, or…

I rush to a door with the figure of a baseball cap on it, try the key. IT FITS. I leave the key in the lock, run in, close the stall door and tinkle my brains out. Still sitting on the toilet, I whip out the breast pump and start milking. Ahhh—double relief. My handy little battery-powered expressing machine brings me back to reality.

The bathroom door opens. Heavy footsteps. A SWAT team guy, rifle-ready, peers under my stall. Another appears from above. Caught in the crossfire, I raise my hands above my head. Luckily, the breast pump is hanging on for dear life.

The policeman underneath the door bullhorns, **"WHAT ARE YOU DOING HERE?"**

"I'm a temp."

This seems to satisfy their curiosity. They stomp away.

GET ME OUT OF HERE!

Before I can flush, the bathroom door opens again. This time it's lighter footsteps and heavy breathing. Covering my ears, I wait for the next amplified command.

Instead, a thick white envelope slides under my stall. I peek out the door. It's a short, skinny guy in enormous tan pants, a green Def-Kahn-5 T-shirt and a sideways baseball cap. "Hide it." He lies on the floor, spread-eagle. "Close the fuckin' door. You want 'em to see it?"

I slam the stall door shut, latch it and hide the envelope in my bag. Then, I pull my knees to my chest and turn off the breast pump and hold my breath. I'm sliding slowly into the toilet.

This is so gross.

The little guy on the floor whispers, "Get it back soon as I'm back. KnowwhatImean?"

"Okay. What is this?"

"Play Money."

Play Money?

Some SWAT team guys crash through the door and surround the little fella. All I can see are the little guy's face and the legs of the police.

"Okay, Beany Baby, you know the routine."

"No problem, officer ."

Handcuffs rattle shut. With his hands behind him, the little guy's face turns. He gives me a gold-toothed smile, and is lifted away.

Wait. Make sure everyone's gone. After a few moments of silence, I try to put my legs down, but my rear end is wedged into the toilet. I pump my legs down and up and down to unwedge my behind.

Can't budge.

I reach back to flush. Got it. I push the handle down and kick down hard with my legs. Flush again and kick. Finally, with a third flush, a kick and a pop, I'm unstuck.

Disgusting.

I check the envelope. A bunch of hundred dollar bills. Play Money? Looks real to me.

What on earth is going on around here?

I tuck myself into the nursing bra, the milk into the cooler and the money back into the envelope. Wait, didn't Mr. Kahn talk about breaking the legs of the person who had Play Money? Or something like that? Better get this envelope back to that little guy.

Peeking out the bathroom door, I can see the police turn the corner, carrying the little fella horizontally—one officer holding his collar, one his belt and the other his legs.

I wait for a moment, take the bathroom key out of the lock and then tiptoe into the hallway.

The place slowly comes back to life, like nothing ever happened. I walk up to people and ask for Mr. Longo. But it's like being one of those homeless folks that everybody walks by, trying not to notice. Except for the boy and his one-eyed Thuzy, who run directly at me. I turn to get away, but trip on a box. It breaks open, spilling vinyl LPs across my path. I slide on them like a cartoon character about to run. All that's missing is the fast bongo drum beat. Instead of getting traction, I trip and fall. My cooler opens, spilling ice and bottles.

The man-eating pit-bull just about reaches me, when I hear, "YOU TELL HIM THAT IF WE DON'T WIN THE RAP RUMBLE, I'LL KICK HIS FUCKING TESTICLES UP HIS THROAT! YOU GET MY SUBTEXT HERE?"

The dog stops, looks back, growls and then yelps away.

I scream, "WHAT KIND OF PLACE IS THIS? WILD DOGS ROAMING FREE, POLICE WITH GUNS, GARBAGE EVERYWHERE, AND MONEY IN THE TOILETS...THIS IS NO WAY TO RUN A BUSINESS! IT'S, IT'S SO...UNPROFESSIONAL!"

Dead silence. Finally, I'm noticed.

Someone exhales a painful "Dayamn."

Uh, oh. Be D&D has just become Y-O-Y-B-M-A—You Opened Your Big Mouth Again.

Standing over me is Mr. Kahn. He now looks like one of those devil spirits that made my mother hide behind the dresser to escape. His silver hair is so short that I can see his scalp redden. He looks at the man on his right. That fella next to him is very hairy. His shaved head and face are covered in a five o'clock shadow. Beside them are my three elevator pals, who are speechless, and a busty girl, whose eyes say "You're about to die. Can I watch?" The looks on their faces make me long for the man-eating Thuzy. One of the big guys makes a fist that creaks and groans.

Yikes!

Mr. Kahn looks at the others. "Ex-actly. It's what I've been saying for years, money down the toilets. Am I right in this?"

The hairy guy says, "When you're right, you're right."

The busty girl nods in agreement.

Mr. Kahn leans forward and sniffs me like I'm dinner. He unsnaps his gold watch and puts it in my hand. It's heavy. "For you." He turns to his hairy associate. "Rich, this is the kind of person I want working for me. You hear? This is IT!" He stares at me. "That's why I hired you, isn't it?"

"Yes?"

He turns to Rich. "So where were we?"

"You were going to kick his fuckin' testicles…"

They start walking. "RIGHT, TELL HIM, TELL HIM I'M WATCHING HIS USELESS ASSHOLE UP AND DOWN THE BLOCK…"

I start to clean up my mess.

The busty girl leans over and rasps, "Don't get too comfortable, y' hunnerstan'?" I nod. "Better, meat." She smirks and then runs to join them.

They disappear around the corner. The sounds of Def Kahn-5 roars back.

Oh, I forgot to ask where my desk is.

So I'm standing here with a gold Rolex, encrusted with diamonds and an envelope filled with real-looking hundred dollar bills. Not bad for less than half-an-hour's work. Ro-Boy-Tah would be proud, except for the fact I got it by forgetting to be D&D.

The vinyl record bathroom key reads, "Rappers Bizarre" by Jiggity Man. Why is his name on this? Jiggity MAN? This is for the men's room. That nasty receptionist gave me the wrong key.

Or did it turn out to be the right key?

End of Day Two

Just spent the day getting paid for sitting in a cubicle outside an empty office and reading old copies of "Billboard" and "Vibe."

Mr. Longo said to answer the phone and take messages.

The phone never rang.

Lifted the receiver to check on Ivy—the line was dead.

5

My First A&R Meeting

Smash
Blazin'
Smokin'
Da Bomb
Off the hook
Has a groove
Whack juice on it

"IT'S REALLY COOL."

Why is everyone looking at me and rolling their eyes?

Between songs, each person must voice his or her opinion of the individual tracks from the soon-to-be-released album by Filthy Lukre. It's entitled "Look at me MF." They're all using genuine Hip Hop responses—all, but me. I don't know if cool is hot, or blazin' is cool.

I need a new vocabulary to talk shop here.

So I sit, dreading every time it's my turn to respond. But after each song plays, after everyone else has put in their two-cents, eventually all eyes turn in my direction.

In the past couple of weeks I've gone from barely employable to barely understanding what to do.

To add to life's confusion, I've gone through three babysitters. The first one, Muki, a depressed older Filipino woman, was rummaging through my things. The second, Anna, a Colombian student, had a nervous stomach—worse than mine. She actually walked around with a Milk-of-Magnesia mustache. Had to let her go. Didn't want my baby's first word to be "Burp!" And now, there's Monique, the joyous Jamaican, who has taken my place in

Ivy's life.

One good thing, because of this job, the Legal Services lawyer managed to prevent us from getting evicted. I had to sign a promise to pay off our bills, as well as Hank's Herbalux debt.

So here I am, sitting at my first A&R meeting for Def Kahn-5. A&R stands for Artists and Repertoire. That means finding, signing, and guiding artists. Sounds like a cool thing to do. Or is "cool" the right way to put it?

All of us in the A&R Department, plus Mr. Kahn's bodyguard, are in an elegant hotel meeting room in Short Hills, New Jersey. Behind us are two long buffet tables on which are chicken wings, iced shrimp cocktail, slices of barbecued beef and an assortment of salads, fruit, vegetables, cheeses, breads and desserts.

Should have skipped my Wonder Bread toast this morning.

And even though it's just eleven-thirty a.m., there's enough alcohol on hand to drown an army.

The floral arrangements are beautiful.

Even my dad never played a gig this fancy.

Look at all these fashionable people. The men display loose-fitting Hilfiger, Mecca and Fubu, the women tight-fitting XOXO, DKNY and Miu Miu. You can actually read the labels right there on their clothes.

My no-name white blouse and tailored navy blue skirt look odd here. At least I took off the matching jacket. "Dress for Success" takes on a new meaning in this Hip-Hop business.

We're in what Mr. Kahn calls a "trust circle," surrounded by his cigar smoke, trying to read between the puffs. Our group consists of:

> **Mr. Bigar Kahn**, The Founder and CEO of Def Kahn-5. His eyes seem to penetrate your thoughts like x-rays. I avoid direct eye contact with him, because of what he did in his office that first day. Truth is, part of me secretly wants to be that crazy, but the other part wants to wash his mouth out with soap and his windows with glass cleaner. Mr. Kahn's not what anyone would call handsome. He is

seductive, intimidating and encouraging (sometimes). The most attractive thing about him is the assuredness with which he operates. He can correct album copy, conduct a newspaper interview, approve ads, all while negotiating face-to-face with an artist's manager. Mr. Kahn said that he likes the level of professionalism that I bring to Def Kahn-5. Professionalism? Me? He said, "We're becoming too big to walk around like an up-start company. The nincompetents here give me acrid reflux. You represent where I want Def Kahn-5 to go." He even offered to become my "mental" (I think he meant, "mentor"). Then there's the way he talks. It's sometimes difficult to understand exactly what he's saying. You get the meaning, but sometimes it sounds like English isn't his first or second language.

#2Girl. Next to him, always next to him, is #2Girl. She's white and too tanned to be true. Mr. Kahn calls her his VP of go-fer. I guess she's called #2Girl, because that's how he treats her. He once told her to assume the fecal position, and kiss her you-know-what good-bye. Her voice is wet and raspy, and she uses her whisper like a belt sander. You do what she says, because you don't want that voice to grind your brains into pulp. Beany Baby warned me to "Keep that baddass bitch way away from you, because she'll stab you in the back, front and sideways." But I'm determined to win her over.

Beany Baby is the little guy who introduced me to "play money" in the men's room. He's the one who the police seek out whenever they raid the label. Since he's low-man on the totem pole, he takes the blame for other people's mistakes. Poor guy's been hauled away so many times that the police joke about putting a handle on him so he'd be easier to carry.

Mr. Top Dogg or T Dogg, aka Ron Smith, just out of jail for beating up his girlfriend and threatening to kill her family. He's the head of A&R, but Mr. Dogg doesn't act the least bit interested in listening to new songs. He just takes up most of a couch. Tall, slim and smooth, he only seems to wake up when a female walks by. "Mmm-mmm-mmm, lookin' good, baby!" Then he returns back to his own thoughts. His second job, VP of Special Projects, seems to entail helping artists when they're having personal problems. That seems to keep him very busy.

Sik, aka Philip Orr, an ex-drug dealer, is head of his own sub-label called "Sik Joint Records." Many of his Rappers seem to be just in or just out of jail. Sik goes from giggly teeheeing to sullen chewing grunts. Story is that Mr. Kahn had owed him money for drugs. So rather than suffer the consequences, he gave Sik his own label. Sik is what they call the Master of Dope. That means expensive clothes, cars and marijuana. He blows a great deal of money on all three. It was his son, Malik, and the one-eyed pit-bull, Thuzy, who greeted me on my first morning. Sik likes that I always have candy and dog treats. What he doesn't know is that these are for self-protection.

Mae Pellor (Her real name). She's tall, black and beautiful. Her smile is irresistible. Mae can make you feel like the most important or the least important person in the room. She always wears Gucci and a touch of Prada, which accentuates her perfect breasts and behind. She's executive material, but whenever someone talks about her, they always refer to a part of her body, never her accomplishments. Mae's job is to make sure artists actually sign and live up to their contracts. She's expected to do "whatever it takes" to make that happen. The company even paid for the surgery to make sure she puts up a good front.

Clete is Mr. Kahn's security aka bodyguard. The previous bodyguard, Alonzo, quit. Rumor was that a Rapper's wife sneaked up and stabbed him in the abdomen. But he's doing better and is studying to become a nutritionist. Mr. Kahn even bought him a more sensitive hearing aid. The new bodyguard is a former professional wrestler, Clete Clydesdale. This sweet, smart, mountain-sized man is always in the landscape just behind Mr. Kahn. Clete's long, dark coat conceals a pump-action shotgun and a Magnum. He's always reading a book. Today it's Kafka's "Metamorphosis." Did I mention that he carries a purse? A small European one. It's heavy, because that's where he keeps his extra bullets and the pictures of his family. Clete is very dark-skinned. He has a shaved head and his eyes can go from "I understand" to "You're dead."

Rich Longo, lurks in the corner, unable to light his cigar. He's the company lawyer and Mr. Kahn's "left nut." Wonder if that's on his business card? He's white, but with a dark hairline that starts at the top of his head and ends on the knuckles on his bony toes. I know this, because Rich sometimes walks around the office in shorts, flip-flops and no shirt. He's not exactly a real lawyer—have to pass a bar exam for that. Ask him if he's licensed to practice and you'll never get a direct answer—but he does conduct a thorough cross-examination of your chest.

And finally there's me, Lily White. I've got my papers neatly spread on the coffee table and plenty of sharpened pencils. I'm alert. I care. I'm on the job.

Exactly what that job is, no one's said. In the meantime, I've learned things—like the difference between Rap and Hip Hop. (Rap is the music and Hip Hop is the lifestyle)

The only person who explains things is Beany Baby. He has never asked about the money he threw at me on my first day. I've tried to mention it, but he says he doesn't know what I'm talking about. Then he adds that if I'm smart, I shouldn't know what I'm talking about either. So the envelope is hidden in a shoebox at home.

Getting paid twenty-five thousand dollars a year. So much for getting rich. But Mr. Kahn says that this is only the beginning. "Soon you will take on more responsibilities, and increase your 'worthlessness' to the label." For now, I make just enough for rent, food and the babysitter—and to give Hank a little money to live on.

Beany told me that many of the people here make ten or twenty times as much as me. He added that it wasn't all salary. Some was borrowed income. So I should be making more money soon. Mr. Kahn says it's possible. Beany does too. Guess I have to rely on their word.

"So, Lily, what do you think?"

What's Mr. Kahn asking me about? Oh, the song.

"It was interesting, but…" *Fake it.* "…does it meet the label's professional standards?"

He smiles. "Didn't I say this one's a star? Exactly what we need in this shithole—processional standards."

No one responds.

All I want to do is get a handle on what's actually happening here, while being D&D (Ro-boy-tah would be very proud of me, so far). It's always been my way to get the lay of the land before venturing forth with an opinion (remember, I'm from the Show Me State). Except here it's different. Here, you're expected to show them by being loud, decisive and opinionated.

The music reviews come to an end, except for Mr. Kahn's. It doesn't seem to matter what anyone's opinion is. His response is the final verdict.

Everyone waits for him to speak. The cigar smoke obliterates his head. All you can see of him are his white fingers snapping.

Mr. Kahn exhales a cloud. "I thought it was da' bop."

No one is going to correct him.

He leans forward to show us that he's thinking. "But the title of the album is whack. 'Look at Me MF?' What's that, a whiny titty baby wanting attention? That's double-whack. What we want isn't to just want attention. It's to GRAB it. So how's about

'Look at Me MF!'" He flicks his fingers. "See the difference?"

No, but I don't want to say anything uncool or whacky.

He makes the finger gesture again. "You put an exclamatory point at the end of it and 'Look at Me MF!' becomes a demand. It's much more commandatory. 'Look at Me MF!'"

#2Girl rasps, "That's why you're the boss!"

Mr. Kahn smiles, satisfied. "Creativity is our most important product, people. It's obvious to anyone with any kind of intellegenitals."

He makes the "!" finger gesture again.

I try to make a mental image of that gesture.

"Look at Me MF!"

Still don't get it.

"Now that we met our professional standards," Mr. Kahn points to the food tables. "How about another round of drinks? Dope? We're cooking on all cylinders here. Don't know about the rest of you, but creative juices make me have to piss."

He exits. Clete follows.

Everyone else retreats to the food and drink.

This table reminds me of my wedding reception. Well, sort of. This one's a mite fancier.

Wedding Belle

Dad referred to me as the Gushing Bride, because of the big grin on my face—like someone who'd just won a full scholarship to Life U. Looked it too. Mom made this dress that was part graduation gown and part choir robe. But she didn't come because "marriage is the Devil's deception." Even so, this bride looked like she was about to sing a hymn or a get a diploma.

But I was too happy to be embarrassed.

At the reception Willy Lamb and His Swinging Flock played. We all danced to their version of Duke, Satchmo and Bacharach. Hank looked uncomfortable. He told me that he wasn't much for dancing. His parents had only stayed long enough for his dad to conduct the ceremony. My new mother-in-law got a bad headache that got better a few minutes later, when she met her friends at the Big Mo Cafeteria.

"Where's everyone going?" I whispered to Hank.

"The parking lot," he said, squeezing my hand. "Lily, I want you to look me in the eye."

"Which one?"

He stays serious. "Now that we're married, we have to make our own way. We can't rely on no one—not Pastor White or Mom—not no one. But don't worry your pretty little head about it. I have a plan to make us rich and respected in this community."

"Plan?"

He pins a big white button with red letters on the lapel of his suit that reads "Ask Me About Herbalux Before It's Too Late."

"Yep. I've found a sure path to big money."

"Hank, is this the right time to wear that?"

"The future starts now, hon. That takes planning, strategy, and focus. Been reading about what I need to be a great salesman. Even took the test in the back of the Herbalux Handbook, and know what, this boy's got what it t-a-k-e-s."

"You sure do, hon." I'm winking and hoping he'd start thinking about s-e-x.

"So don't go worrying 'bout those folks that didn't show, or those that didn't stay."

Hadn't thought about them—until now.

"They'll be eatin' out of my hand in six months."

"Can we talk about something else? It being our wedding day and all."

"What?" Hank is in a daydream. "Okay. You wait here. I'll get some brochures."

That night at the Holiday Inn we got down to business. Hank got turned on when we went through the Herbalux Handbook. I tried to get turned on too. Even took off all my clothes and stood there—buck-out-o-luck naked.

He gawks at me.

"Hank, hon, what could you be possibly thinking about?"

He grins like a billygoat. "Don't worry, if you catch a chill. I got something here that'll fix you up just fine."

Rubbing up against him. "And what would that be?"

"Snicklewort. One of our top sellers."

Dad once said that only an asshole thinks turds are treasure.

Back to My First A&R Meeting

"Okay, everyone. I'm done." Mr. Kahn's voice pulls me back to now. "Time to shit or get off the spot! What's next? Let's keep the energy moving, people."

#2Girl reads from her notes. "Willy B. His next single is back on schedule, but we need him to do a remix and..."

"Postpone it," Mr. Kahn interrupts.

"Why postpone it?" #2Girl hands him his mimosa.

"You never hear of postpone? It's a word. It means 'not now.' Get it? NOT NOW!" He throws his drink against the wall.

Whew! Better find out what angers him—and avoid it.

Mr. Kahn motions to Rich, but Rich doesn't notice, because he's still trying to light his cigar.

"Rich, tell them."

"Wha'?" Rich grunts with the cigar between his teeth.

"Tell them about, you know, Willy B...last night."

Rich takes the cigar out of his mouth to remember.

"Oh yeah. Last night his uncle's brother killed his girlfriend's sister, then shot at Willy B, but missed, then killed himself."

Good to see that the others are also trying to figure out the sequence of events.

Mr. Kahn breaks the spell. "So I don't think Willy B will be able to focus on his single until next week." A light comes into his eyes. "Hey, I just made a joke."

We all look at each other.

"It's metapharsical." Kahn is disgusted that we don't get it. "What Willy B will be. Am I the only one here who's getting this wittiness?"

#2Girl tries to help. "Sure, it's like in the song, 'Que Sera Sera,' people. 'What will be will be.' Duuuh!"

"Shut your hole," Kahn screams. "Anyway, what does that have to do with one of our artist's personal tragedies? You have to explain a joke, it's not funny anymore. That's why it's called a sense of humor, not an explanation of humor. Fucking idiot."

She looks down, waiting for the next blow. Her eyes roll sideways to look at me for help.

No thank you, not going to stick my neck out today.

Mr. Kahn shoves her shoulder. She spins. He turns to us. "Okay, enough pity, what's next? Anybody need anything? The catering cost plenty. And the dope, it's for all of you to enjoy. We want you to know how much you're depreciated. Lily, eat. Sik, have another blunt. All of you, whatever you want." He turns to #2Girl, whose vicious tan is now deathly gray. "Next topic…Pleeez."

#2Girl whispers, "Jiggity Man."

Kahn raises his hands. "I, I, I'm just not feeling him."

"He's really getting pissed." #2Girl tries to keep her voice down. "We keep promising him his masters…"

Want to ask what "masters" are, but it seems Mr. Kahn is trying to teach us a different lesson today.

"I'm not feeling him! You got ears? Then use them. I'm—not—feeling—him. Am I alone with this feeling?"

Silence.

"Then get rid of him," Rich spits out. All eyes turn. He's shaking his head side-to-side, which makes him look like a pit-bull, trying to kill a cigar. "Fuck him. He's over."

Kahn sits back and grins. "That's right. And over is not good for what?"

He looks around the room and then answers his own question. "Not good for what the lego stands for."

This is the final word—Lego. No one dares breathe after that. The only response allowed is a silent nod. Exactly what the lego (logo) stands for, no one is sure. To this day, there's no complete answer. Maybe it's because anybody that has anything to do with Def Kahn-5 is in it for his or her own reasons. The label, lego, stands for something different for each person involved—employees, artists, producers, managers, hangers-on and the public.

Vishnu O' Brien, our marketing head, calls it "branding."
I asked him to explain.

Vishnu: "You know that white-hot feeling that
makes you desire a hot car or a certain champagne?"
Me: I shake my head "No."
Vishnu: "What about the cool factor, the badge-
value of the latest line of sneakers?"
Me: I shake my head again.
Vishnu: "Okay, does anything turn you on?"
Me: Shoulder shrug.
Vishnu: "Then let's pretend something does excite
you. Why? Why would that something excite you?
Because it makes you feel special or that you're part
of something bigger 'n yourself."
Me: "Like a religious group?"
Vishnu: "Yeah, something like that. Only we sell
that feeling with music not salvation."
Me: "My husband sells Herbalux and he's very
religious, but he hasn't had much luck lately. Maybe
he's seeking his own branding—his own lego."
Vishnu: "Fuck, girl, are we havin' the same
conversation?"

Kahn stands, stretches and then tilts his head until two
vertebrae crack. "Who brought a writing pad?"

Seizing the moment, I raise my hand.

"Good. Take minutes. Make sure everyone gets a copy."

Isn't it a little late to start minutes? But what comes out is "Yes,
sir!" *Steno-girl is on the job!*

Topp Dogg opens one eye at me. "What th' fuck?"

"At least someone here comes prepared." Kahn gives #2Girl
a look of disgust.

She looks at Kahn—hurt, then at me—hate.

Trying to recoup, she says, "But Jiggity Man's contract says if
he's released, he's entitled to his masters."

Rich says, "You a lawyer?"

"No."

"So that's settled." Rich puts the unlit cigar in his mouth like
the period at the end of a sentence.

She whispers in Mr. Kahn's ear. He turns quickly and puts his fist in her eye. "That's not a word I ever want to hear from anyone. Do you all understand me?"

We all nod. *What word is he referring to?*

Mr. Kahn mumbles through his cigar, "Bootlegs." He turns to #2Girl. "You going to keep giving me more shit?" She holds her bruised eye, shakes her head. "Because others here want to be in your position."

Why is he looking at me?

She slips away to ice the swelling. Maybe that's why she wears so much make-up.

He's all smiles now. "What's the next agenda? Lily, have a real drink or some dope. Refresh yourself."

"Doing fine. Thanks."

He snaps his fingers to emphasize that he means it.

Having just witnessed what he did to #2Girl, I pour a glass of white wine. He's watching, so I take a pretend sip.

"So, Lily, are you still breast-feeding your child."

"Uh...yes. I'm trying to..."

"Then drink up, have another. It's good for the tits."

So much for nursing my drink.

He smiles and nods in approval. "We're here to let our hairs down," Mr. Kahn turns to Rich. "Can we get out of Mr. J Man's contract with ownership of the masters?"

"No sweat."

"By the way, Rich, you have to cut the end of the cigar. It's like circumcising a penis." He does a scissors motion. "Like this. Snip snip. Snip snip."

Sik and Topp Dogg respond by covering their crotches.

"Okay, peoples, it's seventeen-thirty Europe time and that makes it twelve-thirty our time. Time for our problem-solving time. Any problems? We have an hour left."

Silence.

"Come on, peoples, it can't be perfect. There has to be some fucks-ups. This is a safe, trusting environment we're building here. See, we're even sitting in a trust circle. Time for tight assholes to loosen up, if you get my subtext."

Silence.

Mae raises her hand.

Kahn smiles. "Yes, Mae, how may we help you?"

She stands in the center of the circle, her smile lighting up the room. "Well, I'm finding that too many of our potential signings aren't, well, signing. I'm not sure why. Does anyone have any ideas on…?"

"Ideas? Ideas?" Kahn stands and starts waving his arms. "What the fuck you asking for? Do your motherfucking job! We're trying to be open here and you come in with this shit! Fucking won't sign! If you can't get it done, there's plenty of bitches out there that can!"

I'm glad for that drink. Mostly glad that isn't me.

"Ideas?" He spits out. "We're trying to branstorm here and you want motherfucking IDEAS?"

Kahn twists his neck and calms down. "Honey, Mae, you're a beautiful, strong woman." he coos. "I expect so much of you. You're the best. You've spoiled me for mediocre. Don't you see, I yell, because I'm careful. Just business—nothing personal."

Mae, that beautiful smile extinguished, silently slips back into her chair.

Never seen anyone as ferocious as Mr. Kahn.

He cracks his neck again. "I'm getting pain in my cervical, people. Any more problems?"

#2Girl returns and starts to massage his neck. With each squeeze, he groans like a hibernating bear. His cigar hangs loosely on his lower lip. "No problems," he moans. "Oh, oh, that's great."

Sik awakens. "We done?"

#2Girl, kneading Kahn's shoulders, leans her large breasts against his cheek and whispers so everyone can hear, "You wanted me to remind you about the pillow."

Smothering in her chest, his response is, "Vee whaff?"

"The fluff your pillow." She whispers louder, "That lyric in Marquee Da Sade's song."

He remembers and pushes her chest away. "Right! T Dogg, this guy's your artist. What's he doing with lyrics about fluffing your pillows? What are we doing here, FAG RAP? It's not good for the…"

Top Dogg bolts out of his boredom. "Words are, 'Open yo

legs and lemme fluff yo' pillow!'"

"I'm not going to have a fluff your pillow on this label!" Mr. Kahn breathes fire with his smoke.

Top Dogg screams at me, "If I asked you t' open up yo' legs and lemme fluff yo' pillow, would y' think I's a fag?"

Mr. Kahn yells, "You can't ask her that, she's a mother!"

Topp Dogg says, "Jus' tryin' t' get her opinion."

"She just started. Before I listen to her, she needs to earn some mighty big balls."

I look around the room for clarification.

"She's still be a woman, bro," counters Topp Dogg.

"Not yet! Not here! What I mean is, you can't ask her, because she can't have a real opinion here and be a woman. You understand? You have to be a man, even if you are a woman, because it takes balls—big ones—to make decisions. Except, of course..." To Mae. "...you. You need to go out. Get those artists. Then, it wouldn't hurt you to be more of a woman, and let them sling a little dick."

Mr. Kahn turns to me. He gives his cigar two loud sucks. "You see, Lily, I'm basically a feminist, you understand? Someone freshen up the lady's drink. I believe in equal rights. So until you earn your balls, I'm gonna treat you like any other bitch around here—I'm talking metapharsically, but you get my subtext here."

No, but this is not the time to admit it. So I nod.

Rich says, "That means no dick-slinging for you."

"Ex-actly," Mr. Kahn adds.

Clete is staring at me. Our eyes meet. My eyes are saying, "Help!" But he just dives back into Kafka.

We all sit, waiting for Kahn to rip the flesh off the next item on the agenda.

And I'm wondering, "Who would even want to get big you-know-whats or to sling a thingy?"

6

A Short Seminar

DICK SLINGING (DS) and BIG BALLS (BB) are the nuts and bolts for success in the Rap music business. Don't even think about sticking your toe in the Rap world without these tools—in tandem.

For dick slinging without big balls is meaningless, and big balls without dick slinging is useless. Whereas, dick slinging with small balls won't get you noticed. Conversely, with big balls you might just get away with a little dick slinging.

To understand this aspect of the music business, you'll need some definitions.

Dick slinging is what a player does to make his mark. It's how he struts into a room, into a deal and into a fight. It's pure high-grade, high-test testosterone. It's crotch-grabbing, Bentley-driving, Rolex-watching and model-dating. It's baggy clothes in studied-disorder and money in man-sized wads.

In short, it's style points.

Big balls is a major component of having juice.

> Juice: The ability to make something happen—to influence events. (It is too big a topic to be graphed or grappled, and outside our purview at this time.)

It's defness and dopeness. When an artist's name is on the tip of everyone's lips, that's big balls. When people sleep overnight at a record store just to be one of the first to buy their new album, that's bigger balls. And when you wear anything and next week thousands of fans are wearing it, too, that's the biggest balls of all—merchandising, TV guestspotting, hootchie-satisfying, kung foo fightin', intercontinental ball-istics.

Okay, now, you get the meaning. But do you get the relationship? That is, dick slinging in ratio to big balls.

To see how they work together, here is a graph.

BB Axis

DS Axis
(∞ = meaningless)

Dick slinging (the DS Axis) is relatively meaningless. You can sling dick to DS infinity (∞) and no one will notice, except for some frightened tourists on the subway.

But slightly modify that dick slinging with an increase of big balls and look what happens.

Minimal BB Increase
BB Axis

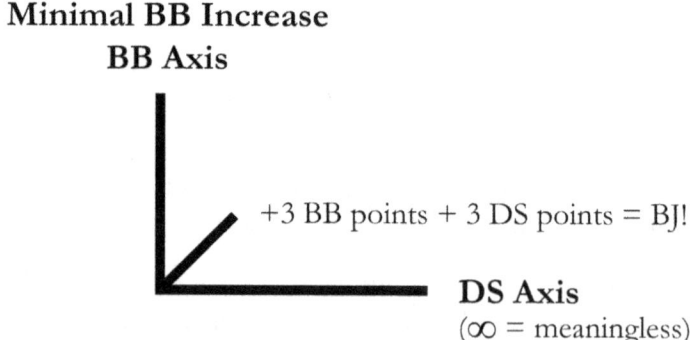

+3 BB points + 3 DS points = BJ!

DS Axis
(∞ = meaningless)

Further increase those BBs and enjoy the results.

Juicing Up Your BBs
BB Axis

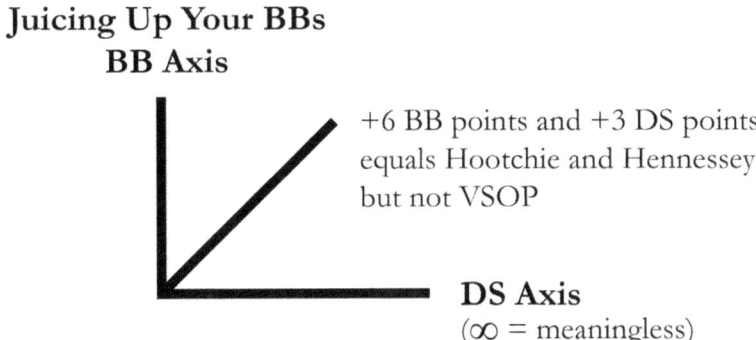

+6 BB points and +3 DS points equals Hootchie and Hennessey but not VSOP

DS Axis
(∞ = meaningless)

You see? The bigger the balls, the higher the level at which you sling dick (+3DS points as an average). For example, let's say your record just charted on "Billboard," say #99 (+2BB points). And you've just been asked to read for a small role in a Spike Lee film—but end up as an extra (+1BB point). That's a total of +3BB points. Your total is 6 points. Not high enough to get you on the cover of "Vibe," but may earn a few minutes with a chickenhead.

> Chickenhead: a woman, whose head movements resemble a hen pecking. These movements can be observed in conversation, but preferably in sexual practices, as most Rappers don't care about what a chickenhead has to say.

Everyday life and events can affect your rating. For instance, your crew laughs at your jokes (+1 BB point), even though your girlfriend doesn't (-1 BB point) or a recent run-in with the law (+1 BB point, +3 BB points if it makes the papers—publicity). Get the idea?

If you want to Rap with the big boys, then you must develop some big ball-oonies.

Here are some career moves and how they affect one's big balls rating:

Guest on a sitcom	+2 BB points
Be a sitcom regular	-1 BB point (Overexposure)
Do a talk show: Howard Stern or Oprah Jay Leno or Letterman Rosie O'Donnell	 +1 BB point 0 BB points (Wrong audience) (You're kidding, right?)
Cause a concert riot	+3 BB points (Publicity!)
Believe in God	+1 BB point (Can't say motherfucker without faith)
Get out of a management contract with an uncle, who still calls himself SuperFly	+2 BB points -1 BB point (If you sign with another relative)
Date models	0 BB points (Who doesn't?)
Write your book	0 BB points (Who reads?)
Sell movie rights to your book no one reads	+4 BB points (That's book pimpin'!)

Conversely, a recent study of Rappers, who have gone mainstream, not aged well or are incarcerated have found that even as their big balls increased, they actually scored lower on the BB/DS grid!

"They is ovah!" is the insider's term for a Rapper's big balls having deflated over time. This can cause their dick slinging capabilities to shrink.

Theory has it that this is due to the negative effect of Senile Sluggishness Syndrome (SSS) or State Penile Stagnation (SPS).

Both the SSS and SPS phenomena lessen the effect of big ballism. But no one really knows why. We suspect it's because a Rapper is either:

A) Over-the-hill, but don't realize it yet—SSS
OR
B) In jail and their crew spent all their cash (cache)—SPS

More studies are under way to help understand the how and the why big balls and dick slinging are affected by a loss of juice.

That's it for today's seminar.

7

Girls' Night Out

"THAT IS THE FINEST butt I've seen tonight."

"Shh, he can hear you."

"Yeah, so? Look, Lilac, ya gotta show some appreciation for God's handywork."

"Roberta, he's looking at us. Maybe he doesn't like to be referred to in that way."

"Sue me for harassment. Guilty! He can collect my fine—any time."

"Criminy, Roberta."

"What're you so uptight about, doll?"

"Just don't want him to get embarrassed."

"Hon, you don't come to a place like this unless you intend to end up some kind of bare-assed."

I'm out with Ro-Boy-Tah. We're at Finnegan's Wake. Wanted some insight about Def Kahn-5. So far—nothing. That's because Roberta is on a manhunt.

In this place you can smell the beer, the brogues and the brawls of every person who's ever bellied up to the mahogany bar—since 1938. On weekends, Finnegan's Wake is a singles' hangout, complete with sports TV screens, lots of beer on tap, loud music and sawdust on the floor. On a weeknight, like tonight, patrons crawl in to get progressively morose.

"You know what I hate? Those baggy pants guys wear nowadays. Hell, if you got a nice butt, it don't do no one no good to hide it. Call me old-fashioned."

"Roberta, could I ask you a question?"

"No, I ain't a virgin."

"Not that."

She shakes her head. "It's a joke. Jeez, lighten up, girl. Look, I'm here. I came to this dump, cause it's less than ten blocks from your apartment like you wanted, right?"

"Need to be close, just in case."

"Yeah, but you promised to loosen up, have some fun. You gonna start soon? Cause I'm worried that the one-half decent guy in here will go back to his New Jersey convent."

She scans the bar and orders another Mai Tai.

"Sorry. If you want to flirt, I won't interfere."

"Flirt? Who's flirting? I'm looking to get laid—plain and simple. I only flirt if that's the last choice. Jeez, if I'm not mistaken, I'm the older one of us here."

Can't argue with her there. She's somewhere north of forty, but who can tell? Her hot pink stretch Capri pants and the feathers on her spiked sandals match, but not with her body. Up-top, she's got this tight, bright yellow sleeveless turtleneck with a pink and yellow scarf around her neck tied to one side. Her toe and fingernails are a fluorescent pink and match her lipstick. The only thing not yellow or pink is her eyeshadow—baby blue. Roberta's outfit makes it clear that she's ageless and available.

I have to keep reminding myself that this woman runs a very successful business.

Her Mai Tai arrives. She puts the little umbrella in her hair. That's three she's got sprouting out of her head.

"'Y' know, Lilac, I think this joint's played out. How about we go to Honkers?"

"That place where the waitresses wear skimpy, uh, tight, uh, very tiny uniforms?"

"Can you think of a better place to meet men?"

"Aren't most of them there to ogle those girls?"

"Exactly. Soon as they discover that they ain't gonna take any waitress home, guess where they'll be looking next? Roberta plumps up her orangy-red hair and umbrellas.

"Roberta, I'm still married."

"That husband of yours, he feel the same way?"

"The important thing is that I still feel it."

"Well, my philosophy is better laid than never."

"Sorry."

"Okay, okay, another drink?"

"Sure, Diet Coke with lime."

"Regular wild woman." We order. "What time you gotta be back home"?"

"Ten."

"Okay, one more hour. One—whole—hour. So if you're not going to scope out men, whadda you wanna do?"

"Talk."

"Talk? Talk I can do in the office. The night was made for action. You know, rubbin' around, screamin', bitin', scratchin'" She counts off on her fingers. "And there's one more. What is it? Don't tell me—rub, scream, bite, scratch, what's the fifth one? Oh, I remember—cuddlin'. One of my faves."

We order another Mai Tai and Diet Coke with lime. It's a treat for me to be out, even at Finnegan's Wake.

"Roberta, I have a work-related question."

"So, doll, you obviously discovered that Def Kahn-5 is a little different than you thunk."

"Kind of. The thing is, well, I'm not sure how to put it, without sounding silly."

"Ya want me to apologize and find you another job."

"No, that's not it."

"You been working at that place for nearly a month, a world's record I might add, and you don't want out?"

"It's a great opportunity."

"Op-por...? We talkin' about the same place?"

"Yes."

"Def Kahn-5, the Rap record company?"

"Why are you so surprised?"

Roberta lights up a cigarette. A beefy waiter in black pants and a stained white shirt rushes over and, in an Irish accent, says that this is the "no smoking section."

"Bring me ovah an ashtray, doll, and I'll give your tip a little extra tip later." She winks, and runs her tongue over her lipstick-stained teeth.

The waiter stands there, not smiling.

Roberta bats her lashes. "What time you get off tonight?"

"Way past yer bedtime, granny."

He wipes the table with a rag, yanks the cigarette out of her mouth and walks away. Roberta sits there in shock.

I run up to the waiter, who's about a head-and-half taller than me. "YOU APOLOGIZE TO HER!"

He smirks.

"I WANT AN APOLOGY NOW OR I'M GONNA TELL THE MANAGER!"

"I am the manager, darlin'. And I want youse both out of me place, as of now."

"How do you keep any customers, with that attitude?"

He reaches over the bar and heads my way with an iron pipe. "I'll be givin' ya one chance to leave me premises or there's gonna be…"

Roberta pulls me out the door. "Let's get outta here before you get us busted up and arrested."

We walk.

Wow! Haven't gotten that mad in a long time.

"Damn-on-rye, doll, you got some temper. Roberta hooks her arm in mine. "Thanks for defendin' my honor back there."

"We're buddies, aren't we?"

"No, but thanks anyway. Guess we'll have to find a place eleven blocks from home. Can you handle the distance?"

"Maybe. Let's see."

A half-block farther—The Smurf Bar. Roberta freaks out. Most of the people's hair color is wilder than hers. They're also pierced from head to toe. In here, Roberta is tame. That dampens her manhunt for a few minutes.

Maybe now is the time to talk about DK-5.

She orders this strange drink—a Smurf Breeze. It's blue booze of some kind with pink hair (cotton candy, I think) on top. But, Roberta likes it, even without the umbrellas.

Bottled water for me. Two Diet Cokes are my limit. Need to think clearly. "Def Kahn-5 is kind of weird, but I've got a great feeling about the place."

"Yeah, doll, I got a feeling, too. The kind you get when you need Kaopectate. Look, I've placed two other people there. The first left after an hour, and the other, the girl you replaced, was there for a week. Now she's out of the hospital and moving back to Chicago for physical therapy."

"What happened?"

"Bad performance review, if you catch my dlift."

DLIFT? *Time for Roberta to slow down on those Smurf Breezes.*

"But I think I could have a future there." I'm trying to get her to talk seriously, but...

"Poor girl got the pissbeatout o' her. Somepin' 'bout sayin' one of the singers wasn't no good. His girlfriend brought some of his buddies to...aw hell, what the frick, pard-on my France, we're here to enjoy ourselves. She'll be all right ina foo monts."

Interesting story, but Roberta looks like she'll be passing out soon, so..."I think I can build a career there—with some advice."

"What dadvice can I give? Eve'y time I call to colleck m' fee, dey threaten t' send ove' some biguy t' beat m' fuckin' brains out. Not good. Need my fuckin' brains, y' know."

"It is a tough place, but the rewards are amazing. Just need to get a foothold there."

Roberta uses her fingernail to stir her drink. She stifles a burp. "'kay, but I can't be reespinsible held for the results."

"I understand."

She lights up, misses her mouth the first time, but on the second she takes a deep drag. Words flow with the smoke. "Get a rep. You know, like someone who gets sings done—no BS, no BS, jus' results. To get ahead, you got to give a head."

She said the last sentence a little too loudly. The Smurf crowd is staring at us.

Leaning forward, I whisper "Are you suggesting I...?"

"No, no, no, not like dat, doll. Like Marie Antonio-ette"

"The French Marie Antoinette?"

She nods as if her head weighs a ton, "Stick out your neck out. Jus' do. No asking why. Like you did widdat cute waiter in Finnegon's Wok. Well, maybe not s' cute, but he'd o' done for t'night. It's hot in 'ere. But you get the idea, doll? How's 'bout we drink somewhere elf? Too many fricking Smurfs in here."

"Maybe we should order some coffee."

"No cof-f-fee. Make me stay up allll night. Allll A-lone."

"Sorry if I ruined your evening."

"No prob, doll. Night's still young, even if I'm not."

"Excuse me, ladies, this is a no smoking establishment."

The waiter stands at our table, holding an ashtray. Roberta puts out her cigarette and then lights another. He puts the ashtray on the table. She stubs out her cigarette. "Strike twooo!"

"If you like, we've got tables outside." The waiter is about Roberta's age and not bad looking, except he's pierced through the center of his nostrils.

Her eyes focus on him. "How'd you sneeze widdat ting?"

"Let's go out sometime and I'll show you." He winks.

Wide-eyed, she turns to me. "How many Smurfs I had?"

"One."

"Gimme two more and I'll consider it."

He walks away, disappointed.

"Roberta, wasn't he cute?"

"Yeah, like my three, third husband—da geezer."

Touching Roberta's wrist, I see her watch.

"Oh, no! It's ten-fifteen."

"Yeah?"

"My babysitter!"

Hank

BEEP! *Peace on you two. This is Astronomous. I'm calling to say The Lord is my shepherd, I shall not want, and to say, 'Hello.' The best part of where I am right now, is that I'm growing inside—in my soul. The Right Reverend Fogg said the other day, "Astronomous, let me shade my eyes. Why you are positively beaming with inner light. Yes, the Lord is shining through you. Be sure to tell that lovely wife of yours that her kind generosity is bearing fruit." Ain't that something, Lil? 'Cause of you, I'll be back sooner rather than later. Blessings on you and Ivory. Praise the...***BEEP!**

Hank calls Ivy—Ivory. He decided that her Christian name should also be a strong brand—like the soap. I wanted to name her after something beautiful that grows upward—Ivy.

It's been a battle between soap and hope ever since.

Hank leaves a message at the end of each month. That's when he gets the Reverend's invoice from the Fogg Ministries.

I mail him money now and then—can't afford much. The Hank that I married is still inside him, somewhere. He may have lost himself, but he hasn't lost us. Just wish I could do something to snap him out of it. What that "it" is, I'm not sure. I'd do anything to get him back.

Back in Puce, when we were first married, I'd take on jobs like serving croquettes at Big Mo's Cafeteria, typing death certificates and invoices for the Jonquille Funeral Home, or ticket taking at Puce High football games—anything to help him reach for his herbal dreams.

Hank devoted himself heart and soul to Herbalux Designer Colon Supplements. He'd go door-to-door, spreading the gospel about how this special mix of herbs and enzymes could change your life. It was his calling.

I had to take on a second job to pay for the inventory he couldn't move. That and collect money from some poor farmer who just spent most of the day on the toilet.

"Hank, maybe Herbalux isn't so healthy."

He'd smile and touch my cheek. "Li'l, it's just a matter of time and we'll be living in luxury."

"But why do they keep sending us all this stuff, when we haven't sold out the first box?"

"Headquarters seems to have more faith in my salesmanship than anyone in this household."

"I believe in you. It's just that people around here are getting tired of having to take their loved ones to the emergency room."

That's when Hank realized that it wasn't <u>what</u> he was selling. It was <u>where</u>. Puce wasn't a big enough market for herbal laxatives. Maybe some place like New York City.

Fine with me. Daddy retired to his recliner, Mom was in heaven, my brother lived in his own place, and Puce had lost its luster. Actually, the reason I agreed to the move was that I had dunned just about every family in this rural community—first for Daddy, then for Hank. It got to the point where people would walk across the Interstate to avoid me.

So New York it was.

Funny about New Yorkers, sometimes they treat you like family. Other times they're just, well, like Midwestern farmers that owe you money.

The upside about the Big Apple is that since there's more opportunity floating around, your debts can disappear in months instead of years. The downside was, we kept losing whole new sets of friends. Hank saw every couple, every person we met as a potential sale. People tend to avoid you when your conversation works its way into their colons.

So, we had to live on Hank's optimism and my temp work.

But now, at DK-5, for the first time, I have an opportunity to accomplish something of my own—take some control and make some real money. It flows around here like a stream during spring thaw. Just have to find the right bucket and dip in.

At least, that's what Mr. Kahn said. "The people who stick it out the farttest" are remembered at bonus time. So I asked for some special assignments "to help the lego."

Memo

To: Mr. Bigar Kahn,
        Chief Executive Officer, Founder,
        Def Kahn-5 Labels

From: Mrs. Lily White,
        Coordinator of A&R,
        Def Kahn-5 Labels

Re: Extra Assignments

I've noticed in the past few months that there are many assignments, which have yet to be completed. For example, last week you asked if someone would show Filthy Lukre around the city. Since no one volunteered, he was forced to travel around Manhattan alone. As you know, he was severely beaten. I wonder if someone, who knew the city, could have prevented this incident. Had Mr. Lukre been taken to museums, a Broadway show or the Circle Line, maybe he would not have traveled into Spanish Harlem and angered the people who didn't appreciate his pet name for them. Plus, I am sure he would have had a better time. So what I am suggesting is that I be allowed to oversee certain projects. I make myself available to help Def Kahn-5 succeed, and our artists survive.

Thank you for your consideration.

Roberta would be proud. This girl is about to stick her neck out—like Marie Antoinette.

8

An Overnight Success

MY FIRST SPECIAL ASSIGNMENT was at HorseHoof Recording Studios with the group XYZee, one of our marquee artists.

Ten hours later, about one a.m., everyone's exhausted, especially the three guys who are XYZee.

They're puffing blunts, and me, wanting to make a good first impression, asked if I could try to make one too.

Figured a lot of the older men in Puce rolled their own cigarettes and Mom loved Crafting.

Here's what they showed me:

> **Step One:** With a razor, slice the cigar wrapper lengthwise. Then insert your finger and gently slide the tobacco out.
> **Step Two:** Lick the inside of the entire wrapper and spread this other type of tobacco, chronic, evenly inside it.
> **Step Three:** Roll tightly around the contents. To seal it, lick the last inch or two of the wrapper and then stick one half of the blunt in your mouth and moisten it. Flip it over and moisten the other half. Run a match or lighter quickly up and down the length of the blunt.
> **Step Four:** Light up and enjoy, responsibly.

Almost got it. Problem is how to keep one's blunt from unrolling or drooping. These guys are experts. They laughed at my attempts. But we bonded. Glad I don't smoke though. Why go to all the trouble of replacing perfectly good tobacco with chronic? Seems pointless.

Later, I learned that chronic is NOT another form of tobacco.

The recording studio is now filled with a strange burning smell. It's everywhere. The engineer, producer and I are moving in slow motion. Exhaustion makes us giggle a lot—it's not funny.

After listening to the track they've just recorded, the producer, Doodles, presses the talkback button on the console and says to the Rappers in the recording room, "That was dope. Let's take a short break and lay it down one more time."

XYZee starts to complain in unison.

> *We done be working too long.*
> *Needs me an inspiration break.*
> *Could use some pussy, too.*
> *Got your head on straight with tha shit.*

Their hands clasp each other in brotherly appreciation.

"Any strip joints around here?"

Doodles pushes the talkback button. "Few blocks down."

They start to leave.

"What are you doing?" Pressing the talkback button, I try to bring order. "Guys, guys, excuse me, we're running very late. The release date is only EIGHT weeks away. The music was due at the plant TWO weeks ago."

"'The fuck you doin', slave-drivin' us?" Master X stares at me through the recording room window.

"Don't be treatin' us like that." Gargantu-Y joins in.

"Need to get my willy wonka-ed," pleads Zee-Diki Boy.

Got to take control. "Do you realize how much money we're spending on overtime? How..." Doodles reminds me to push the talkback button. "Do you realize how much money we're spending on overtime? How about a little cooperation?" This time they hear me.

"Fuck that shit!" yells Master X.

As one, each guy displays his immediate need by grabbing his own privates. They're in full rebellion, screaming, cursing and gesturing at me.

Should I call Mr. Kahn?

Can't. Took me two months to get this chance. Need to show him that I can handle a tough situation. Show my strength. Flex my big you-know-whats. Kahn warned me that missing the release date would be a "disastrophy." But they're already halfway out the door to find a strip joint.

Stop them. The album must be done tonight. These guys are twice as wide and twice as tall as me. *Think fast.* I jump in front of them with my legs and arms spread. "Gentlemen, gentlemen, let me take care of it!"

They look at me, then at each other.

"I need me a girl with some meat on her," Gargantu-Y says, "You too scrawny."

But the other two tilt their heads and size me up.

"No, not me! I'll go out and find you, you know, what you...want. Just keep working. We're almost finished. Leave the rest to me. At Def Kahn-5 we take care of our artists."

They look at each other and then nod in agreement.

"You guys are the best. There's nothing too good for XYZee. The label is lucky to have such professional and talented people—and we'd like to prove it."

Once, I saw Mr. Kahn pour praise on an artist. It worked.

"Well, fellas?"

They look at each other, waiting for someone to make a decision. It's got to be me. "Bet I'm back before you can roll another blunt, plus travel time."

"We ain't gonna work until you come back with the hos."

Great! I leap down the stairs to find and transport three companions back to HorseHoof Studios. Figure there's about an hour before they'll start their own search—and how would I explain that to Mr. Kahn?

The night is fresh, smokeless. The air stings my goosebumps.

I hail a cab and ask the driver if he knows where to find prostitutes in the neighborhood.

"Ah, marmnavacharrner."

Houston, we have a problem.

Nine Hours Earlier

Traveling the Midtown Manhattan streets in search of artists' companions, my thoughts go back to earlier that night. This is the first time I've ever been in a recording studio. The smell is what hit me first, a brew of musty carpets, burnt leather upholstery and the ozone of electrical wires.

What's impressive is how XYZee creates a Rap song.

These multi-platinum artists arrived two hours late, laughing like they don't care. Their first concern is getting several pints of Hennessy, ordering ribs with biscuits, collard greens, macaroni and cheese, and Captain Crunch Cereal. Master X wants a specific brand of cranberry-apple-peach drink.

While waiting for food delivery, we wake up the engineer, Steve, whose long reddish curls and pizza-stained beard are stuck to the console. He snores and drools on the million-dollar equipment, having just finished a two-day session with a pop boy group.

XYZee's manager, Meaty, has brought in some beats he'd recorded in the basement of his New Jersey mansion. Now, in the studio, they play them over-and-over for about three hours.

This drives me crazy.

Meaty, Steve, Doodles and I sit there, waiting.

It would be nice if someone, other than me, recognizes we need to record—something.

After the fortieth playback of a single beat and a stomachache full of ribs, Master X starts to clap his hands in counterpoint.

More time passes. When should I say that time is money?

Zee-Diki Boy begins to experiment with what he calls R&B vocal samples. Meaty said that sampling is like a baker making a cake mix and adding an egg that someone else layed. So, Zee starts creating his own mix by speeding the R&B samples up and then slowing them down until they blend with the beats.

I thought that the best recipes were made from scratch.

The big one, Gargantu-Y, sits there eating Captain Crunch. Suddenly, he throws the box of cereal away and takes out a red marker and starts to write on a yellow legal pad, then on his hand. He refers back and forth to the paper as "the verse" and his palm as "the hook."

Then, Gargantua matches a rhyme to the different beats. He replaces and chops up words. Some vowels and consonants expand and contract.

It's like watching my dad in his chair, humming tunes, never getting to the point—and it's making me crazy. "Exactly when do we start recording something?"

Zee-Diki Boy says, "Got to write th' thing first."

"You came into the studio without any songs written?"

They look at each other, then Gargantu-X says, "That's the way it's done, 'xcept if y' keep yappin'."

Are they're trying to pull one over on the label?

Doodles gets an idea. "What if we be addin' that Clyde Stubblefield 'Funky Drummer' sample to the track…about there?"

They listen to the beat and Doodles points when the drum should come in. There's total silence. Doodles slides a DAT into the console and cues the track. Just as the beat starts, he flicks a button, turns a switch and the two separate sounds are welded into something new.

Master-X says, "That be 'bout right, but how 'bout we speed it up a mite."

The result is, got to admit, thrilling. Eyes meet. They agree, without saying a word.

Then Gargantu-Y gets inspiration. "Need a girl singing high shit, about here." He falsettos a riff. In six notes his voice soars to show what he means. "What 'bout endin' on the low shit two times, then endin' high on th' fourth?"

Gargantu-Y demonstrates the new, improved riff.

A moment of silence and Zee-Diki Boy is stunned. "That be stupid sexy, bro."

It's interesting, but "stupid sexy?"

"No doubt," says Master-X, as they high-five.

Did they or didn't they like it?

Master-X practices a beat, then suddenly stops. "Yo, Gar, what this muthafuckin' rhyme be about?"

Gargantu-Y says, "It be 'bout ill hootchies wantin' yo monies. How I'm gonna fade me them bitches. Yo, check this rhyme…"

> *Some fucked-up bitch I'm gonna be toastin'*
> *Gonna git in that muff, I ain't flamboastin'*
> *Gonna blindside yo' snatch,*
> *With m' gas and m' match*
> *Then I be furry biz-kit roastin'*

"Whatcha think?" Gargantu-Y asks in all seriousness.

Master-X is reviewing the words in his head. He makes a sour face. "That be whack."

"Why for you be dissing my rhyme like that, bro?"

"Gar, I ain't dissin' you, I just be thinkin' whatcha really need to be doin' ta git back at those ho cakes. Nobody gonna believe yo gonna burn them pubes. Furry biz-kit—that be whack, bro, knowwhatImean? Y' needs mo pimpin' sense. Mo propa mackin' in yo words."

Have no clue what they're talking about.

Gargantu-Y thinks for a minute. "Whicha, bro. I'm whicha." They do a choreographed handshake, thump their chests twice and point two fingers at each other. Gargantu-Y continues, "I be bearin' to yo ad-vice, bro."

Zee-Diki Boy gets serious. "Yo, 'member when that pimp, Deegan or sumpin' like that, up in da Bronx, find out his ho be stealin' his benjies, and shit, and wantin' t' be leavin' town, knowwhatImean? He do her up how?"

Gar concentrates. "You mean Slice Deegan?"

"Yeah, that be him."

"Da guy takes him a blade t' her."

"Yeah, that be the one."

Gargantu-Y thinks. "Blade, huh? Thinks that be betta 'n burnin' bush?"

"Sound bad, Gar, knowwhatImean?"

They nod in agreement.

Does bad mean good?

"Dime, bro." They high-five.

So Gargantu-Y writes lyrics which, when translated, say that XYZee is going to find all the ladies who've done him wrong and cut their faces up.

"Excuse me, but are you planning to write a song about

cutting up a woman?" Their eyes freeze on me. "Because if you are, I have to protest. Being cruel to women is not what this label is about." They look at me like I'm from another planet. "Look, I know you need creative license, but there is a line you shouldn't cross. There is such a thing as bad taste."

That's when their manager, Meaty, takes my arm and escorts me to the back of the studio.

"Could I talk to you, Miss White?"

"It's Mrs. White. But you can call me Lily."

Zee-Diki Boy squints. "Who da fuck she think she be?"

Gargantu-Y explains. "She jus' one o' them Kahn hos."

Master-X watches as Meaty and I leave. "No shi'? She look like one o' them stewardesses. Thought she be 'bout t' show us seatbelt shit." He starts mimicking a stewardess giving her take-off speech.

"Look like Meaty be showin' dat bitch the e-mergency exit." The group laughs so loud that I can hear them in the hallway behind the control room.

Outside, Meaty scratches his head. He's trying to figure out what to say, and how to say it. "Miss White, I don't know what you think you're doing, but it's not helpful."

"Well, I'm here to make sure that Def Kahn-5's interests are represented."

"Interests? Excuse me, but do you know how many albums XYZee sold last year?"

"Quite a few."

"Quite a few? Try eighteen million. Let me repeat that. Eight-teen mil-li-on albums. So, as you can see, whatever this group does, and however they decide to do that, determines what the best interests of the label are. And if I'm not mistaken, it's still about making money."

"Yes, but there's money and then there's money."

"What the hell's that mean?"

"Well, there's making money by entertaining people and then there's making money by hurting people."

He shakes his head. "I can't let you be in there if you're going to interfere with their work."

"Interfere? Interfere? I'm here to make sure they arrived on time—which they didn't—and also to make sure the company's money is used effectively—which so far has been a mixture of Captain Crunch and slicing up women. If you think I'm going to be bullied out of that room, you are so wrong, Mr. Meaty!"

"Okay, okay, don't get your panties knotted up. Just try not to do anything that stops their flow. Any time you got something to say, we'll come out here, you can say it to me and I'll communicate the message." He extends his hand. It's his left one—the one with the hammered-gold and diamond Rolex. He smiles. "Dealy-yo?"

Reluctantly I say, "Dealy-yo-kay."

We shake hands. Only I can't actually see mine, because of Meaty's mighty mitt.

Walking back into the studio, he yells to everyone, "Lily White in da house!"

Back to My Quest

Dootie Fallopian, my Armenian cab driver, cruises down Eleventh Avenue as we hunt for what XYZee desires.

Past the Javits Convention Center to the bridge over the train yard, we find what looks like Hooker Headquarters. To the right, against a concrete wall, there's human activity.

"Slow down!" We creep down the long, wide avenue. "Stop!"

Dootie hits the brakes.

There, on the curb, is the silhouette of a very tall hooker. Between the platforms and pouffed-up hair, this one is about seven feet tall—just the right size for Gargantu-Y.

I roll down the window. "Excuse me."

The lady passes into the light, into view and into my window and says, "You looking for something different, honey?" That's when, through her make-up, I see the shave bumps on HIS face.

"Excuse me, but are there any women around here?"

REMINDER: NEVER SAY THAT TO A TRANSVESTITE.

The counterfeit daughter explodes with rage. Platform shoes bang the side of the car and a stream of curses machine gun at us. She/He is denting and venting.

I roll up the window quickly. "DOOTIE! DRIVE!"

The taxi tires squeal, and so does our tall friend.

A few blocks down—paydirt. The women talk money. All I have is twenty-three dollars. But I have the next best thing—DK-5 business cards.

One woman, a bit on the fleshy side, wearing the miniest of mini-skirts and a black lace bra under a short rabbit fur jacket, looks at my card. "How'm I gonna spend this?"

Another, younger, woman with bruises on her face looks at the DK-5 card. "Damn, girl, I hand this to Flash and he'd wire-hanger my ass."

There is general agreement on that point.

Guess they need assurance. "Look, ladies, do you realize how much money you're about to make? In one shot you'll make more than you would in a whole night." *Do I know what they make?* "And these Rappers wear lots of expensive jewelry. Need I say more?" They look at each other. "You'll get the money up front—soon as we walk in the door. I promise you." They're still wary of me. "All I'm asking is for you to come with me to the studio. You'll meet some famous artists. Soon as you see them, you'll know who they are. Then it's up to you. Look, I can't force you to do anything."

I'm telling hookers that No Means No.

One of them, wearing red vinyl hotpants with a large front-to-back zipper looks at me like she intends to do damage. "You tryin' t' save souls or some shit like that?"

Just my own. What comes out of my mouth is "No."

The hooker, wearing nothing but a very stretched out maroon leotard moves in "Smell like cop t' me."

The others quietly circle.

Throwing my hands high. "Okay! Fine! Reject the offer. Someone around here is looking to make a lot of money. Quit wasting my time. I'm on a deadline." Starting to sound like the way Mr. Kahn treats women at the label. And, gosh darn, if it doesn't work.

Crammed into Dootie's's cab, we hightail it back to HorseHoof.

Once inside, well, push comes to shove, and shove comes to grope. Doodles, the producer, and Steve, the engineer, edit what they've recorded so far. My eyes fix on the mixing console. The wagging needle on the sound meter is hypnotic. I'm afraid to look up, because XYZee and the ladies are going at it like it's their last day on earth—hooting and howling.

How will I explain this to anyone?

The phone rings. "For you." Steve hands me the receiver.

At 3:30 a.m.?

"Lily White."

"Not done yet?" It's Mr. Kahn.

"Oh hi, what are you doing up this late?"

"The question is what are you doing up at this time of night?"

"Well you know how artists are. And these guys are perfectionists. So, I'm letting them do some fine tuning."

Their banging shakes the console. I look up and Gargantu-Y has the smaller girl pinned against the glass wall of the recording booth—like a smashed bug on a windshield. They're screaming, cursing at each other and doing it so hard that the partition rattles.

Thought this was supposed to be soundproof. Then I realize the recording room door is open. I reach my hand out to close it, but the phone cord is too short. I try to kick my leg out, but…

Mr. Kahn barks. "Are you feeling it?"

I try to retain my composure. "Uh, yes."

"You sure? Cause I want this album real raw."

"That it will be." I'm sweating through my jacket.

The couple-under-glass arrive at their destination simultaneously. The noise is nuclear.

"What was that?"

As non-nonchalant as I can. "The rough mix."

"Oh, baby, oh baby, it's so good…"

"Remember, we need a clean version."

"Working on it." *Got to get him off the phone.* Mr. Kahn must sense this, because I answer a little too quickly. Luckily, another couple is still going at it full tilt.

"Oh, yes, baby! Oh, baby! That's it! That's it! Oh fuck me, baby, fuck me! I got it! I got it! I…Yeoooow!!!"

Did he hear that?

"Sounds good. Keep it real."

"Promise."

I hang up.

The artists zip up.

The hookers settle up.

The tracks are buttoned up.

XYZee is on their way to their hotel to pack up for the flight back to their girlfriends and wives.

Silence.

Tossed rib bones, torn scraps of lyrics, smoked blunts, used condoms, smashed microphones and music stands—no longer standing, Captain Crunch crumbs and almost-empty Hennessy bottles litter the studio.

And me. I'm wasted—but this girl got it done.

Whatever it takes.

9

Tricked Out

MR. KAHN HAS GENEROUSLY given me a ticket to the Grammys for bringing in the XYZee album on time. Well actually, only two weeks behind schedule. But that's a record for them.

Imagine—the Grammys, Radio City Music Hall, TV beaming us worldwide, red carpet interviews, famous people inside and screaming crowds outside. Def Kahn-5 has four artists up for six Grammys. That's why Mr. Kahn ordered us to dress for impact. He even paid for my outfit.

Vishnu worked out all the artist's thank-you speeches.

The talking points are:

        1) Thank your personal savior
        2) Recognize your wife and children, if you can
        3) Mention Bigar Kahn—in a nice way

Beany is babysitting Ivy tonight. Honest. Only took a call to his grandma for permission. She's very strict because she doesn't want him to grow up to be a criminal. If she only knew that he's the label's Play Money courier and the police take-out guy.

He refused to be paid for babysitting, and said, "Ain't business. It's fun."

Tonight, Beany and Ivy will watch the Grammys. If they see me on TV, he'll point and tell Ivy, "There's Mommy!"

That would be so cool.

My first awards show. A limo to pick me up. All right, it isn't the power limo, that would be a stretch, but I've never been in a car with a real chauffer before.

Mae, me, and a very upset #2Girl share the ride. She feels that she should be in a #1 limo with Kahn—not with the field hands.

Even so, this is exciting. Haven't experienced exciting in a long time. Went overboard with the dress and shoes. Shopping for clothes is another thing I haven't done in awhile. Gave me a lift. Heels, strapless, silver-sequined dress. Hair in a French Twist. Nails match my ravishing red lipstick—glamorous. Need a better coat, but one has only so much time and money to get gorgeous. So my long tan Missouri winter wool will have to do.

Inside the limo, it's a lady's powder room. All three of us are checking everything from hair to panty lines.

#2Girl's even checking up on a couple of coke lines. She offers some to me. "No thanks, but that dress is gorgeous. Some people just know how to wear clothes."

I still haven't given up trying to win her over.

"Yeah, well, you look like shit. That coat is whack. You look like a Republican Tranny." Her beeper goes off. "Fuck!" She checks the message, takes a snort of coke, flips her cellphone open and makes a call. "It's me…Yeah? No shi…Great, just fucking great…Any idea where she is?…" #2Girl looks at me, then smiles. "I got the perfect person for it…Lemme go." She hangs up.

"Something wrong?" I ask.

"Big time." #2Girl yells to the driver. "Stop the car."

"What's up?" asks Mae.

"Kahn's upset. Phatigue's fourten-year-old cousin is missing. She's supposed to meet her aunt at the bus station, but the little bitch didn't show."

Phatigue is one of our artists. He's nominated for best Rap album and single.

#2Girl says, "Sounds like she disappeared."

Mae says, "Or she could've gotten off somewhere on the way and didn't get back on the bus."

"Not likely. She's from New Orleans and never been to New York before. A girl like that wouldn't get off the bus in fucking Kentucky."

I'm shocked. "Why would someone put a fourteen-year-old girl on a bus by herself?"

#2Girl and Mae make eye contact. Some secret message passes between them.

"That's just awful."

"Isn't it?" #2Girl mocks me. "But Kahn's relying on Mae to find her."

"Me?"

"But the Grammys…" I say.

"Okay," #2Girl flips open her cell and hands it to Mae. "Go on, tell Kahn that you prefer to take your fake ass to the show."

"Bitch, you been snortin' too much of that pixie powder. Kahn would never ask me that. He called your beeper. You're just trying to fuck me over, ain't ya? Well, it ain't gonna work, 'cause this is shit work. That's your job."

#2Girl pulls out a knife and pops the blade. "How'd you like me to cut out one them silicone tits o' yours?"

"You pullin' a knife on me? You pullin' a motherfuckin' knife on me, cunt?"

They start swinging at each other.

What should I do? Conflict resolution. Conflict resolution.

"Warning you—Get outta my face, and outta the car, fucking skank ho!"

"How you'd like me to take that knife and open up a new hole for Kahn to fuck?"

I raise my hands. "Ladies, ladies, this is no way to act. Put that knife away! I'll go find her." They look at each other. "I'll go look for Phatigue's cousin. Just stop fighting. This is supposed to be a happy night."

A long silence. Even the driver turns to see what's up.

#2Girl puts her knife away. "Okay. You got to meet with Topp Dogg at the P-A-B-T."

"The P-A-B-T?"

Mae and #2Girl speak simultaneously.

"Port Authority Bus Terminal."

"Which way is that from here?"

Mae points. "Two blocks that way and seven blocks down."

"And where will Topp Dogg be?"

"In the front."

"In the front?"

"In the fucking front!" says #2Girl. "What the fuck you need, a mutherfuckin' map?"

I step out of the car. "One thing, what's the girl's name?"

"Tahini Johnson."

"Tahini Johnson?"

"We're late." #2Girl closes the limo door. I hear Mae. "You are one fucking crazy bitch." Sounds like they're laughing—or are they still fighting? Whichever, they're only a block away from Radio City Music Hall, so there won't be too much damage, I hope. The limo speeds away. Me, towards the P-A-B-T.

Oh no! I forgot to ask what Tahini Johnson looks like. Maybe Topp Dogg knows.

Crossing Times Square, the streets are crowded with people headed for a fun time. Hope I can get back, to enjoy some of the evening.

It's cold, but clear. It feels good being away from those two. They fight so much. I'm afraid one of them's going to end up hurt, or worse.

There it is—the P-A-B-T.

Where do I start looking?

Outside the bus terminal most of the people seem to be going nowhere, just hanging out. Some yell at their crying kids in strollers. Others take quick sips from bottles in brown paper bags. One couple seems to be there just to argue in public.

The Port Authority Bus Terminal is a big place. Looking for Topp Dogg is going to be difficult. Not even sure which entrance is considered the front. I walk inside, up to the most normal-looking man and woman I can find. "Excuse me, where is the front of the bus station?"

The woman and man, leaning against a bank of phones, stare at me. She passes a small green bottle of deep red liquid to her companion, and then lifts her pointy chin. "Wha de fuck you are, a Princess Pussy? Hey, is Princess Pussy, no?" This sets off her male friend with black and green teeth. He doubles over, laughing, choking for breath.

I walk deeper into the bus station.

She screams after me, "Princess Pussy, coming to here and give my man what he is needing."

Where is Topp Dogg? I wander around, scanning every entrance. Stopping at this large glass-enclosed sculpture, I watch a ball slowly roll down some wiry mechanism then ding and clang its way to the bottom. It's one of those things that does a lot of activity and ends up doing nothing but repeating itself. What's it called? Rude or ruse something. The movement hypnotizes you, ball after ball being lifted, and curling a long path to the bottom. You have to force yourself to look away.

There, looking through the glass box, is Topp Dogg on the other side, watching the movement too. He just stares at the balls rolling downward.

"Topp Dogg, where have you been?"

He looks around to see who's talking.

After knocking on the glass box and waving, he sees me. His eyes are two watery slits. I walk around to his side of the sculpture. "T Dogg, what does Tahini look like?"

The guy next to him says, "Tahini? Ain't that that shitty brown stuff that smells like shitty brown stuff?"

Stoned humor overtakes them.

What is this, comedy night at the Port Authority?

"Come on, we've got to find her."

Getting his bearings, T Dogg finally points in a general direction. He and his friend gently bump fists.

"Stay poppin', bro."

"That 'n more, blood." T Dogg walks away.

I run to catch up. He's got his green camoflauge jacket and matching pants, and a black doo rag. His unlaced Timberlands make me want to scream "Tie your shoes. You could trip over those things."

He looks me over. "What the fuck you dressed for?"

"The Grammys."

"That tonight?"

"Yes, but we're here to find Tahini Johnson."

"Oh, yeah, right" He stops walking and uses his nose to point. "Up there."

"Up where?"

"We stays here. They be comin' down from up there."

"Who?"

"Prime."

"Prime?"

"Yeah, girls be getting' off'n da bus. Prime meat. Pimps know the schedules."

"They do?"

"Sure, 'spot a runaway hick right off."

"How do you know about this?"

"Ain't always been in tha music business. See th' two dudes there—yellow suit, other's wearin' 'didas warm-ups?"

Their eyes are fixed on the top of the escalators.

"They be waitin'. One sign of awk'ardness—lost eyes, slow walk—and they start workin' the confusion. Watch."

A tall, blonde girl with a large backpack and purse rides the escalator down. She looks around, appears lost.

"Should we warn her?" I whisper.

"Don't have to. She be foreign. A pimp be givin' up when she opens her mouth an' they ain't understandin' what the fuck she sayin'."

That's exactly what happens.

When she reaches the bottom of the escalator, they fight for her attention. She opens a map and asks them for directions. The guy in the yellow suit walks away. But the one in the Adidas warm-ups looks around, grabs her purse and runs. She pursues.

Topp Dogg has a big grin on his face. "That bro ain't no pimp. He be a thief—in it for the short haul."

"Shouldn't we call the police?"

"What for? That girl just learned her a New York lesson. Now, Phatigue's cousin, Tahidi…"

"Tahini."

"Th' fuck don't matter. Dat prime wadn't smart 'nough to have her purse stolen, knowhatImean? You got money?"

Checking my purse—"Ten dollars."

"What you go outta da house with only ten dollars for?"

"How much do you have?"

"Gots what I need."

He walks to the man in the yellow suit. I follow.

"Yo, Donald, wassup?"

The guy almost jumps out of his skin, but then sees Topp

Dogg. "Ron? Ron Smith? Thought you was in jail."

"Was. In th' music biz now."

They do a hand and hug ritual.

"Donald, you lookin' tight 'n propa."

"Yeah, well, so it goes." Donald, in the yellow suit, wags his head back and forth. "Only changed m' name. I ain't Donald no more. I's Teserac."

"No shi'? I be Topp Dogg now too."

"No shi'."

Have to get this project moving. "Excuse me, but we have to find someone."

Teserac looks at me. "Who da bitch?"

"She work with me at the label."

"I beg your pardon. Who you calling names, mister?"

Teserac glances at me, then Topp Dogg. "Dat ho needs her a good whoopin'."

"Nah, she just be the jumpy type. She all right."

Teserac grins, looks me over and rubs his chin. "Maybe get me a taste o' that. Waddaya say, bro?"

"Okay, enough. We're looking for a Tahini Johnson. She's fourteen, from New Orleans, and was supposed to arrive here at the P-A-B-T this afternoon."

"She a cop?".

"Nah, a suit."

"T Dog, are you going to help me find her, or not?" In my sequined dress and tan wool coat, I feel like a Republican-in-waiting, waiting for someone to say something that makes sense.

"Yo, Teserac, we be looking for this prime come in this afternoon from N' Orleans. Big girl, fourteen, real hick."

"There's a reward if she's returned unharmed," I say.

Teserac becomes sly. "Like t' help, but they's so many prime come down that esc'later, a man jus' can't 'member."

"I'm sure Mr. Bigar Kahn will show his appreciation. I'm guessing at least a hundred dollars." I give him a sly, knowing grin.

The yellow-suited guy starts laughing. "Hunnerd bucks? Damn! A whole hunnerd? Hear that, bro?"

Topp Dogg looks at me with pity. "Fuck, Lily, that ain't even a han-job, 'c ept fo' crack hos."

"Word." Teserac agrees. "Muthafucka can't even get his wick wet for punk change like that."

"Fine, but I got a feeling you know the girl we're talking about. Only you don't know who she is—she's Phatigue's cousin. She ain't no prime, chickenhead, hootchie or hick. This girl's family is getting real angry that someone grabbed her outta the P-A-B-T. Y'unnerstan' what I'm sayin? She isn't returned, there's gonna be cons'quences, bro, bad cons'quences." I've gone ghetto right before their eyes. My gestures are big and aggressive.

But this guy is slipperier than a Puce pig. "You know how it is, baby. I got me a repute' to maintain. Y' gots ta respec' m' position here. I's Teserac. Everybody on th' street knows I'm straight up, sugar."

"That be fact, proppa," says T Dogg.

They do some pimp-inspired handshake.

I glare as T Dogg, but change my tone. "Mr. Teserac, that's a beautiful suit. Some people just know how to wear clothes. What color is that? Canary?" He preens. "A canary is a bird that sings beautiful music to attract females, am I right?" *Okay, so I'm laying it on a little thick.* It works.

Teserac improves his posture. "Could tell you was a lady from the start."

"So would you help a lady find someone that's lost?"

Sweat, cologne and BS radiate from him. "Here I am, baby. Jus' waitin' t' be of service."

"Please, have you seen Tahini Johnson?" I smile. "She's very special to some people, who'd be very grateful if she was returned to her family." *Keep smiling.*

He grins back—lips together, twisted—like he's got a secret. His eyes look up and to the left, but not at me. "Lots of prime come through. Some stick in yo mind, othas don't. All depends on how much they be stimulatin' yo mem'ry. Y' unnerstan'?"

I'd like to stimulate that smirk off his face with a shovel.

"Def Kahn-5 Recordings will want to reward anyone who had a hand in her recovery."

Topp Dogg is staring at me like I just sprouted horns.

I reach inside my purse. "In fact, I have this ticket to the

Grammys tonight. It starts in fifteen minutes. It belongs to the person who helps us find Tahini Johnson."

"Lemme see." Teserac reaches for the ticket.

"Don't touch. Just look."

He reads and BITES. "Folla me...Stay 'bout half a block back. I'll takes off ma' hat, rubs da inside, where she be. Then, I'll walk back t' ya." His eyes never leave the ticket.

"You'll get this when your hat comes off, but if she isn't there, you're gonna get the ticket from hell, y'unnerstan'?"

"Baby, I ain't foolin' wich choo? I gots famb'ly too."

"Yeah, right—innocent as pie."

Canary struts out of the bus terminal. We follow, uptown, at a distance. Eighth Avenue is a pee-utrified frozen hellhole. Peepshow hustlers snap flyers to *check it out!* Pushers chant *smoke, smoke*. Tourists gawk as hookers hawk:

> *Hey, baby, going out?*
> *Looking for a date?*
> *Got some free time?*
> *New in town?*

The only time Topp Dogg says anything is to instruct me in street etiquette. "T'ain't ladylike to sass a pimp."

What do you say to that?

Teserac crosses Forty-Second Street. Each porno house has a guy standing out front, and each one knows our point man. Can't hear them, but when they talk, frosty air puffs from their mouths. Hands slap and clasp as he slides and glides up Eighth Avenue. The Broadway theatre crowd flows around us, but that yellow suit is our beacon. At West Forty-Fifth Street he takes a sharp left, and then a quick glance back at us.

I wave.

He keeps walking.

We follow, turning the corner. The street is dark. T Dogg and I walk past an empty Broadway theater, which has boxes and blankets of the homeless under it's marquee.

A few doors down, Teserac stops in front of a brownstone. His hat comes off. He rubs the inside band, looks at the building, then puts his hat on and walks back towards us.

As he passes, I whisper, "If this is a wild goose chase, you're going to be one dead cockatoo, you understand?"

He nods and grabs my ticket to the Grammys.

A flash of yellow, and our canary has flown.

"Now what?" Silence. "Top Dogg, now what?"

"Go in."

We reach the brownstone. I have a plan. "Now remember our goal is to see the girl, make sure she's alright, then get her out. The most important thing is to stay calm." *If he was any calmer, I'd have to drag him up the stairs.* "I'll say that the police are outside in unmarked cars. If we don't get her in three minutes, they'll be coming in. Can you remember that?"

He rubs the back of his neck. "Lily, do me a favor."

"What?"

"Shut th' fuck up." Topp Dogg moseys up the stairs. "An' don't diss anyone."

"Diss? Why would I…"

"Lemme take care of it."

"Do you know what you're doing?"

Turning to me, frustrated. "See? Y' jus' dissed me and we ain't even rung th' bell. Can you jus' not open that mouth of yours?"

"Maybe."

He shakes his head and rings the doorbell.

The front of the building is covered in ancient Egyptian carvings. The stair railings end in two stone Sphinxes. All the windows are painted over. A few stabs of light shoot through where the paint has peeled.

"Can I help you?" a scratchy voice says from an intercom by the black door.

T Dogg leans forward. "Teserac sent us."

I grab his arm. "Why are you using his name?"

"Can't just walk in. Teserac be the key."

"What is this place?"

"Where you from?" He makes it sound like an accusation rather than a question.

"Puce, Missouri."

"An' I s'pose they don't have no ho-houses there?"

Before I can ask "ho-houses?" the door opens.

In the foyer, through a very dim red light, stands a squat figure. "Who can I say is calling?"

"I's Topp Dogg." He enters boldly. Then me, less boldly.

"Need t' talk t' the lady of the house."

Lady of the house? What is this, Avon calling?

The figure steps into the light. Is that a woman?

"We be looking for a lost sister."

"Cousin," I correct him.

The squat thing gurgles and giggles. "My, my, my so many lost children. Whatever are we to do with them all?"

That voice—sounds like we just entered a brothel in the seventh circle of hell.

My eyes are getting used to the dark. Too bad, because I'm looking at one of the most grotesque things I've ever seen. Every part of her visible flesh is covered by tattoos. Two jutting, off-center teeth are all that's left between her melon-like cheeks. And her overripe body odor—you could drown in that smell.

"Tell the lady we got 'portant business t' discuss."

Inside, the air suffocates with stale perfume, snuffed cigars and pine disinfectant. My nostrils already need a break.

The stinkheap beams at T Dogg and then motions us to a waiting area, encircled by floor-to-ceiling green velvet drapes and decorated in tag sale Egyptian furniture.

She disappears through an opening in one of the drapes.

"T Dogg, is Tahini here?"

"Could be."

What would happen to Ivy if something happened to me? She wouldn't even have Hank, because even Hank doesn't have Hank. She'd be all alone. Maybe it's time to cut my losses. My quiet life—the impoverished routine and feeble hope that things will get better—seem very attractive now. My stomach and bladder are telling me it's time to go—one way or another.

Why does this always happen at the wrong times?

T Dogg sees me squirming. "Be cool. They be watchin'."

I decide to keep my coat on—in case we have to scoot.

There's a rustling behind the green velvet curtain. It opens and a tiny, white-powdered and overly-rouged woman enters. On her feet are miniature versions of shoes. So small—they can't be real.

She tiptoes across the room like a ballerina. Her white feather boa floats behind her. The caftan she's wearing looks like it's made from the same material as the drapes. Following her is our friend from the foyer, cradling a baseball bat in her tattooed jelly arms.

My spine just froze into a fearsicle.

Through pouty red lips, the tiny woman squeaks, "My dears, please, could I offer you any refreshments?"

She sounds like Minnie Mouse on helium.

Topp Dogg scratches his crotch. "Yeah, thanks. We here on business though. M' name is…"

"I know who you are. Who is this lovely lady?"

"This be Lily. We from Def Kahn-5. Cousin a' one of our artists 'rived here today by bus from N' Orleans. May a' got primed. Hoping we'd come to some kind of 'greement."

The Minnie Madame thinks. "I'm not sure I can help you, as much as I'd like to."

T Dogg asks me. "What's her name?"

"Tahini. Tahini Johnson."

The assistant chub sniffles. "Adorable name, isn't it?"

"Adorable." Her smile never changes.

I hand my business card to Minnie. "Bigar Kahn, the CEO of Def Kahn-5 would take it as a personal favor, if she was returned unharmed. A reward is being offered."

"As it should be. In the right hands, investments made in young ladies are quite profitable. Vida, make us some tea."

Vida, the bat-wielding scratch and snuffler, rushes out.

"We don't often recieve women from the corporate world here."

"Well, we don't have this kind of situation—very often." My stomach is about to run away and leave me behind. "May I use the powder room, Ma'am

"Of course, dear. Behind that curtain is a door. It's quite tricky after that. Keep to your right. Wherever you have a choice, go right. Please, don't open any door except for the one with a lady's silhouette."

"Thank you, ma'am." I take off my coat, revealing my sparkly Grammys gown.

"Lovely dress." Minnie smiles.

T Dogg smiles. I smile. *Why are we smiling?*

"Thank you." Before leaving, I turn to Topp Dogg. "Be right back."

TRANSLATION: YOU BETTER BE HERE WHEN I RETURN.

He looks at me, leans his head to one side and…why does he have to touch his privates every five seconds?

Leaving, I hear Minnie say to T Dogg, "I do hope you received the fruit basket I sent while you were upstate."

Fruit basket?

Behind the heavy curtains everything is in dark blue light. The sequins on my dress glitter. The hallway looks endless. Take a deep breath and try to see. One step at a time.

Keep right. Turn right. All right.

As my eyes and ears get used to the environment, I hear quiet voices and thumping sounds. Laughter. Muffled lust? Next to each numbered door is a woman's picture. Like an address. This must be where they deliver her male.

Footsteps? Stop. Listen…must be mine echoing.

Going to take a long shower after this. Not sure if it's going to be hot or cold.

This would be a scary place for a fourteen-year-old girl—if she's here.

Stop. Look back. No beginning or end to the hallway now. Just a bunch of doors as landmarks.

There, the last door on the right is the silhouette of a lady in a bonnet, hoop skirt and pantaloons.

What happened to the Egyptian motif?

Guess the bathroom doesn't go back that far.

Above the door is an open transom. Inside, it's pitch black. I can't find the light switch. Where's the toilet? Found it.

Lift my long dress. Ahhh!

Something in here smells funny. Maybe it's just as well that it's dark. Where's the toilet paper?

There's a squeak. Mice?

Up there, in the small window above the door, is the outline of a head, moving. Heavy breathing. That odor.

Vida! She's peeping at me. *Where's the darn toilet paper?* Smellosaurus snorts and snuffles, trying to get a better view.

FLUSH. I quickly open the bathroom door, knocking Vida off a stepladder. She lands with an oof, gasping for air. The door is between us. I rush down the hallway.

Hurry. Keep left.

She's trying to roll off her back. Her fingernails scrape like a dog on slippery linoleum.

Is Tahini in one of these rooms? I flatten my ear to each door—first on the right, then on the left—nothing, just sexual rock and roll. *Please, don't let it be her.*

At room number nine, the picture frame next to the door is empty. Covering one ear, I press the other one against it.

A TV's on.

I hear Vida breathing hard. Her feet thud, thud, thud, thud in my direction. *Try the knob.* It opens. I enter and quietly shut the door.

Thuds rumble past the room and fade into the distance.

The only light in the room is from a television. Sitting on the bed, motionless, watching the TV, is a young girl in blue jeans and a, "I ♥ New York" T-shirt. She's chubby with long legs. Hands folded on her lap. Her attention on the screen.

"Tahini?"

"Yeah?" She doesn't look up.

"Tahini Johnson?"

She turns her head and drawls, "Who're you?"

"Lily White—from Phatigue's record label, Def Kahn-5. Are you Tahini Johnson?"

"Yeah."

"We've come to get you out of here."

"Why? It's nice."

"Nice?"

"Sure, The Grandma and Aunt Vida say I can stay here as long as I want, and I can stay up as late as I want, and…"

"Do you realize what kind of place this is?"

There's laughter and applause from the TV.

"A hotel."

"A HOTEL?"

"Not a 'hotel' hotel, but one o' them hotels for models. Tol' me I's gonna be a model."

"You have to come with me. Now!"

I grab at her. She pulls away. "I don't know you."

"Do you have any idea what they have in mind?"

"Sure, they gonna go picture shootin'. Goin' to the State of Liberdee, Times Squared, Empire Statue Building…"

"How would you like to go to the Grammys?"

"Doin' that already." She points to the TV.

"Tahini, there's a difference between seeing it on TV and being there live."

"Hey, there be Duane."

And darn, if the camera isn't showing the entire DK-5 crew, sitting in their seats. AND, THERE'S TESERAC IN HIS YELLOW SUIT, APPLAUDING!

Don't scream. Keep your cool. "Wouldn't you like to be there when Phatigue wins?"

"Phatigue? Real name's Duane. And Duane ain't gonna win nothin', 'cause Biddly Diddly gonna. He da bomb!"

"Tahini, it's against the law to hire fourteen-year-olds as models without their parent's consent. If you don't leave with me, the Grandma and Aunt Vida could go to jail."

She looks at me. "That so?"

"Tahini, do you have your parent's written consent?"

"Didn't knowed I had to."

"If we can get your parents to sign a form, then we'll see about getting you on the cover of 'Vogue.'"

"Gots my eye on 'Jet.'"

"Okay then, 'Jet.'" But you have to get permission first. Then you'll need an agent. Can't be a model without an agent. Tahini, we should go. The police could be here in a few minutes."

"Should I leave m' clothes? They ain't for real fashion."

"Up to you. Me? I'd take them, until you can buy a new wardrobe, of course. That's what most models do, right?"

Tahini thinks, then forces the drawers open on the cheap dresser. She stuffs a few outfits into a small plaid suitcase. "Yeah, iffin I don't bring my clothes back, my mama's gonna whoop me."

"Good decision."

Both of us take one last glance at the TV.

Could have been there tonight.

"I'm gonna be a model." She's confident.

But not today.

We leave the "model's" room and head down the hallway. At the green curtain, I stop. "Now, whatever happens, say nothing, get out the front door, and wait for us in the street." She stares. "You understand what I just said?"

"I ain't stupid. Just tryin' to figger out the order."

Take a deep breath, exhale slowly, and enter.

Tea is served. Topp Dogg and Minnie are laughing.

"Oh, there you are, dear. Thought you might have gotten lost. Red Zinger? It's herbal, you know."

Tahini enters after me.

What will Minnie's and Vida's next move be?

Nothing. Vida, still breathing hard, just stands there with a baseball bat. Minnie pours me a cup.

"Look who I found in the hallway." I put on my coat.

Topp Dogg looks Tahini up and down. He tweaks his nose and grabs his favorite body part. "Who?"

Did he forget why we're here? "Tahini Johnson."

She gives a dimpled smile and raises her hand. "Hi."

Minnie sips her tea. "I know how Mr. Kahn repays his favors. Shall we say thirty?"

"Yeah, okay." T Dogg takes one more sip and stands.

Thirty thousand dollars? This cartoon character will get more from a kidnapping than I make in a year?!

Minnie leans forward. "All I need is your word."

"Word." T Dogg arranges the front of his pants like he's swearing on the Bible.

Minnie relaxes back into her chair. "More tea?"

"Actually, we're supposed to be at the Grammys." I push Tahini towards the door.

Vida steps forward. "The lady just offered you more tea."

"Thank you. We'd love to stay, but the sooner Mr. Kahn sees Tahini safe, the sooner everyone will get satisfaction."

"She's always been safe." Minnie smiles. "I realize this must be your first time."

"First time?"

"No worries, dear. We have a deal. Word is bond."

T Dogg kisses two fingers, then shoots out a peace sign.

"Thank you, Topp Dogg. You always been proper."

Vida steps forward. "But I don't want her to go."

"Nevertheless, we've struck a deal." Minnie says. "And, after all, we are honorable people here."

Vida says, "But you promised her to me first!"

"Vida, behave yourself."

Almost have Tahini at the door, when Vida rhinos towards us, swinging her bat at everything. Tahini and I duck. She raises her arms high over her head. Just before she strikes, Topp Dogg swings his beefy hand into her face. She stops and drops cold. The bat flies forward, knocking over a lamp. The bulb shatters. Vida is now an unconscious pile of blubber.

Tahini stares at her. "Dayamn, you colcocked her."

Topp Dogg smiles shyly.

I grab the bat.

But Minnie just sits there with a smile on her face.

Topp Dogg rubs his hand. "Sorry 'bout yo' prop'tee. T'ain't po-lite, I know, but she be one crazy bitch."

Vida starts to move and grunt.

"Please leave now." Minnie is upset. "This is not a place of violence."

"You've got to be kidding." *Be D & D, remember?*

Topp Dogg pushes Tahini and me to the front door.

Minnie Madame says to Vida, "Get up you old fat pig."

Vida's breathing sounds like a clogged street sweeper.

I open the door. Vida gurgles out a threat, "I glyo crjtslivg (Huff) vbrdingtump (Puff)."

Topp Dogg turns to Minnie. "Thanks for the hospitality."

"Yes, dear, you're welcome. Nighty-night."

Nighty-night?

The door slams shut. On the way down the stairs, Tahini starts crying. I put my arm around her. "You'll be alright."

"No I won't. Ain't never gonna be no model now."

10

A Month Later

Dear Lily,
This is your chance to share in God's good fortune.
Imagine, receiving a hundred thousand dollars, or
getting that Mercedes you've always wanted. That's
what happened when others like you sent this
message forward. Simply by mailing this letter to ten
other people, you can make your dreams come true.
But hurry! You only have forty-eight hours to
achieve your goals, or bad luck will befall you.
Isn't God great?
Your husband,
Astronomous

SINCE OUR NEW PHONE is unlisted, Hank communicates
by chain letter, faithfully.

Finally realized that there wasn't going to be a miracle. The
only things waiting at home for him are the six boxes of
Herbalux. And to lighten the load—no more payments to the
Fogg Ministries.

The weight just isn't worth the wait.

It gets lonely sometimes, but there's not too much time to
think about myself—Ivy and DK-5 make sure of that. Don't
mean to sound bitter. Just kind of worn out.

Back to work.

"Those names aren't spelled right, are they?" I'm on the
phone, trying to straighten out some inconsistencies.

"That's how they spelled them." Blochead doesn't want to lift a finger to help me.

"You're telling me that PhuzzBusterPhlash is all one word with PH instead of F for Phuzz and Phlash?"

"He should know."

"That's not how it was spelled on his last album."

Got a new title—Manager of Special A&R Operations—totally meaningless, completely undefined and certainly no extra pay.

Kahn volunteered me to identify samples. Sampling is reusing another artist's music. But that means you need to get permission and pay to use someone else's work. Even so, illegal samples can be found in many Rap songs. Like gun possession, selling drugs and prostitution, there's no problem—until you get caught. But once caught, a label can be sued for hundreds of thousands of dollars per sample. And with up to seven or eight samples in a song, that can be a major problem.

Often, artists or producers don't admit they have borrowed another artist's work. So constant oversight and careful listening has to be done.

Sik is our sampling ears. Amazingly, he can find a single note from the background of a song and identify it. Then suddenly last week, he decided he didn't want to do that anymore. So now, along with my job of making sure the liner notes and credits are correct, I was assigned the sample chores.

Lucky me.

Since I don't have Sik ears or any background about this music, I rely on the artists or the producers to tell me what samples they used.

One positive thing, this is the longest job I've had—six months. *Could we be talking career?*

My office is a long narrow rectangle filled with file cabinets, a Danish breakfront and two aluminum outdoor chairs for guests. The desk is a slab of blacktop. It looks like tar and smells like it too. Down the middle, runs a double yellow line that looks like a No Passing Zone. I have permanent bruises on both knees thanks to the ugly grey blobs of concrete that hold up the whole mess. My leather chair can swivel quickly to face my computer or tape player or files or the phone or bang into the concrete columns. Speed is necessary, since I have to solve every sampling problem before it's on-record or on-the-record.

After a hasty lunch, I made a hastier call to PhuzBusterPhlash's producer, Blochead, for the tenth time, to give me the correct information for his artist's upcoming album, that is, song titles, credits, liner notes, acknowledgements and samples.

"I wasn't his producer on the last album."

"And that affects how he spells his name?"

My other line rings. "Hold on, I'll be right back. Don't hang up, we have to get through this and that means samples too."

I hold line one and hit line two. "Def Kahn-5, Lily White here."

"This is long distance. I have a collect call for Lily White from Willy Lamb."

Dad?

"Will you accept the charges?"

"Yes, yes I will."

"Go ahead."

Silence. "Dad?" Silence. "Dad? You there?" Sniffling? "Dad, hold on, I'm on the other line."

Hold line two and hit line one. "Okay, Blochead, since when did Jon Womack start playing the conga drums?"

"Didn't he?"

"Thought he was a pianist."

"What difference does it make? He's credited."

"It'll make a difference when you have to pay for the album art to be re-printed."

"Okay, okay, I hear you. That all?"

"No. Stay there. Be right back."

Hold line one and hit line two. "Dad, what's wrong?" More sniffling. "Dad, got a call on the other line. Can I call you back?"

"I just miss you so much, Lily."

"What's wrong?"

"Can't a father miss his only daughter?"

"Of course. Just a little surprised. Hang on."

Hold line two and hit line one. "What about the samples?"

"Don't know of any."

"You were in the studio with him. Look, why do we have to do this dance every time? Also, I heard two samples in one song. And if I heard them, you can bet there are more. Need ALL this information before five o'clock today."

"You got it."

"Wait, don't hang up."

Hold line one and hit line two. "Dad, sorry, it's very busy here today. What's wrong?"

"Well, you know how I'm still playing 'round here now and then? Last week, I done this gig and they haven't paid me yet. The ice box's 'bout empty. Don't know what to do-hoo..." Is he crying?

"Be right back." Put Dad on hold again. Feel guilty, but I need the information from Blochead or we'll miss the album's scheduled in-store date.

Kahn enters, sits down and puts his feet up on my desk.

"Be with you in a moment." *Why is Kahn here?*

Hit a button. "Okay, Blochead, I need correct name spellings, instruments they played and sampling credits. It's your responsibility. I don't appreciate you making me do all the legwork to find out this information. Maybe we should talk about how much money Phuz and you will lose if the label gets sued."

"Lily, what're you talking about?" It's Dad.

"Sorry, be right back."

Hit line one. "Okay, Blochead, correct name spellings, instruments they played and sampling credits. no fooling around this time. If I don't get the information, the album release date is bumped, and you're taking the blame."

Kahn smiles.

"You wouldn't do that, Lily, would ya?"

"Don't push me." I hit the phone. "Need some cooperation from you or...."

"Lily, that you practicin' collectin' my fee?" It's Dad.

"What are you doing on line one?"

"Lily, gotta go." It's Blochead.

"Blochead, don't hang up, I mean it."

"Lil, why are you calling me a blockhead?" Dad.

Great, somehow I've got them conferenced. Kahn pumps his

fist at me. He's mouthing, "Go, go, go!"

"Blochead, don't make me call you again or there will be some major problems. You get my meaning?"

Kahn chants. "GO, Lily, GO, Lily…!"

"Hold on."

"GO, Lily, GO, Lily…!"

"Lily, I don't understand this attitude." Dad.

"GO, Lily, GO, Lily…!"

"Hold, please."

Hit the hold button and turn to Kahn. "Yes?"

"Don't mind me. Kick butt." Kahn smiles. "I'll wait."

Hit the flashing button. "I'm not kidding, Blochead. Get the information I asked for by five TODAY, or the PhuzzBusterPhlash release gets bumped."

"Lil, hon, you act like that, and you're sure to get my money." Dad again? "I wasn't talking to you. Got to go. I'll call you back later. Promise."

Hit the other button. "Who's this?"

"Jesus Christ, I'll get the information! Just don't bump the album!" At the same time, it's Dad. "You sound busy. So could you call th' guy that owes me? His number is 417…"

I just hit a button—disconnect. *Didn't mean to do that. Calm down. Take a deep breath.*

To Kahn: "So, how can I…"

The phone rings again. *What now?* "Hey, it's me, Jiggity. S'up? Was in reception, wonderin' if you'd like to go have some lunch?"

"Can't. Swamped now. Call you later."

"Oh, just thought…"

"CALL YOU LATER. Right now, I'm juggling my left and right ones."

"Sure, I…"

"Thanks."

Hang up. Swivel my chair to write something down about PhuzBusterPhlash and a Parental Advisory sticker.

I close my eyes, take a deep breath, open them. *Why is Kahn here? He never comes into my office.* I swivel to him. He's looking around.

After a few moments of watching him scan the room, I say. "And?"

Kahn smiles. "What's different about this place?"

Here it comes. "You tell me."

"Sure, there's something different. I can feel it." He stands up and walks around. Not far, because my office could double for a linen closet. "Isn't this where we keep the big swinging dicks?"

"Beg your pardon?"

"Definitely. This is the office of a big swinging…

"I get it. I get it."

"So, Lily, are you ready to take the next step up your career ladder?"

What's he got up his pant leg this time?

Kahn looks me in the eye. "Lily, you've become a presence here at the label." *Does that mean I take up space?* "So I have a favor to ask, but it needs the big swinging dick that's populating this oroffice." *Why is he acting like this?* "I want you to be my big balls…at a very important event. Lily, you are to speak on my behalf about the Rap music industry to a very important audience. You need to help them understand how we do business and how we've influenced the world. The press may be there, so be sure to look your best." He leans forward. "Think of yourself as a speakeswoman for the label. This special task, I only offer to someone special, someone who's ready. And you know what I'm thinking? I'm thinking you're ready."

Wow, a high profile speaking engagement. He's starting to recognize my value to the company.

Class Act

"How come you're white?" is the first question from the back of the room.

"People of all races are involved in the music business." Trying to be politically correct. "Although the initial Rap beats and rhymes may have started in the ghetto, there are themes that have crossed over to all cultures. Any other questions?" I point. "Yes?"

"How come Afrodeesha got such a big butt?"

I'm doing "Parents' Day" for Lauren, Kahn's ten-year-old

daughter, who is cringing in the corner.

Technically, you could call it a speaking engagement. High profile? Technically, not at all.

The teacher warned me that fourth graders have an attention span of less than ten seconds. So I've brought some hands-on activity to get the students involved—a copy of "Billboard Magazine," color proofs of album packaging and finished CD artwork. My agenda is to explain the record-making process, and get the kids to design their own CD covers.

As for Afrodeesha's behind: "Whatever she has, it's working for her. She's always on the 'Billboard' charts."

"My mom had a song on the 'Billboard,'" lisps a boy whose permanent teeth are almost in and sticking out.

"He's lying," shouts another child. "He doesn't even live with his mom."

"Really? What's the song?"

"Something about love and kisses."

In unison, the kids go "Eyuuuh! Yuck!"

"That's great. Now here's how artists and record companies work together. The record company signs an artist to a contract after listening to a demo. A demo is a cassette or CD that has a few original songs on it. Sometimes we even give a group or solo artist enough money to make a demo. If it's good, the record company gives the artist more money to record a whole album."

"An' then, mo' money and mo' money, and then, you be big pimpin'!" a boy shouts from the back of the room. The class breaks into giggles.

"Sometimes." Got to get the room back. "Most artists don't make a lot of money. Eventually, the label let's them go. That's very sad for everyone." Just lost them.

Kahn's daughter hides her face in her hands.

"Who wants to help me design art for a CD cover?" No hands shoot up. "Each of you take a piece of paper." I hand them out quickly. "Okay, now, let's pick an artist."

> *DMX!*
> *LL!*
> *NWA!*

> *Phatigue!*
> *Yo' big butt!*

"Never heard of that last one." They all giggle. "Okay, okay, settle down. Here's the "Billboard" Top Two Hundred Albums. "Let's close our eyes and pick one."

One girl with a hundred little pigtails and ashtray-thick glasses closes her eyes and points.

I read. "Let's see...Ol' Dirty Bastard..."

Before I can recover, the kids are "ohing," "umming," pointing and giggling. Red-faced, I sneak a look at the teacher, who's just staring at me.

Uh-oh. Here I'm trying to explain that Rap music is a business and instead I'm corrupting ten-year-olds.

"Uh, well, maybe we should pick a different artist."

"How 'bout my mom?" The toothy guy pipes up again. "She was on the charts."

"Shut up, you prob'ly don't even have a mom," replies a large girl in the back.

Another girl says, "Yeah, you be the young dirty bastard."

And I thought Rap was cruel.

"You wash yo mouth, girl. Don't be dissin' my mom. She better than yo fatass ho mama anyday!"

A riot of responses fills the classroom. The teacher just sits there—staring at me—expressionless.

Maybe that's the way she smiles.

Someone should exert some control. "Yo-yo-yo! Give me the room." I cross my arms high in that familiar Rapper stance, and lower my voice. "Yo-yo-yo."

It works.

Kahn's daughter, Lauren, is now hiding under her desk. She's embarrassed by me and probably very hurt that her dad didn't show up.

But to the rest of the class, I'm dope, I'm da' bomb.

We design an album cover for Salaam Whichaz. As an added treat, some of the boys get together and do some Freestyle (improvised Rap) about how boring school is.

My talk lasts thirty minutes, a class record.

Packing up, the kids surround me—happy faces and asking lots of questions.

"You ever win a Grammy?"

Should I tell them of my Grammy night adventure? "No, that's mainly for the artists. I did work on some albums that won. It's a team effort."

"You know XYZee?"

"Yes, been in the studio with them. They're nice guys."

This seems to disappoint the boy who asked.

"You ever meet Ol' Dirty Bastard?"

"No, he's with another label." I try to change the subject. "Anyone here interested in the history of Rap?"

Just lost them again.

The kids start yelling Rap lyrics. The Parental Advisory stickers fly out of their mouths.

> *Bang! Bang! Motherfucka!*
> *My dog gonna eat ya*
> *And the pain gonna teach ya*

The child, whose mother may or may not have been on the charts, asks for my autograph. I write, "Even when you're not on the charts, you're special."

The children continue rapping.

> *Cops be snoopin' all over tha place*
> *Tryin' t' find me my homies*
> *To blow up their race*

The teacher walks this way. Her broad face and pink apple cheeks are aimed at me. She approaches, gently pushing aside each child. Her pale blue eyes are fixed on mine. She's about four inches taller than me, and wide-hipped. Please don't let this get out of hand. But if it does, stand your ground. Don't let her get the jump on you."

> *Don't be playa hatin' an' all that shit*
> *Cause one day—the truth will be told*
> *With all my bitches an' ballers an' bros*
> *They all gonna love me til there' ain't no mo*

Why do these kids have to be singing that song?

My ears get hot. The hair on my neck stands up. Attack first, before she gets a good shot at you.

Always go for the juggling vein. That's what Kahn says.

"That vas voonderful."

What?

"You really got zem eenvolved. Look how eggzited they are."

She's smiling.

"I did?" So much for the juggling vein. Wonder where her accent's from.

"Thank you zo much for taking ze time to talk to ze class." She shakes my hand. "It vas most eempressive. You explain-ed everyting zo vell."

Was waiting for her to say something about bad role models, violence, sexism or whatever. Had a speech about racism, abuse, and artistic expression loaded up—ready to respond with facts. None needed. Relief.

"You know my husband iz a musician."

"Uh, really?"

"Vould you be zo kind az to listen to hiz demo tape?"

"Uh, well..."

"He's written and updated zome Serbian songs. Zey are qvuite unyoozual. Yu vill see."

"Sounds interesting. Have him send something to me." I hand her one of my business cards. Not going to put Kahn's daughter's future into the hands of a disappointed Serbian musician's wife? So... "Love to hear it. But you know, my label only does Rap."

"Eet eez Rap." She hands me a cassette.

"Eet eez? I mean, it is? But I thought you said..."

"Eet's Serbian Rap."

What the heck is Serbian Rap?

11

Two Weeks Later

BEEP!
I rape and kill for my cause is just
I rape and kill, with no love lust

AS AN ADDED TREAT, every Wednesday morning, the teacher's husband, Miroslav, Rap name—MC Novi Sad (His hometown in Serbia—without the MC), screams his latest rhyme—on my voicemail.

> *For ethnic cleansing is purer And the Albanians are fewer*
> *In my Serbian Mother—land. (Everybody sing!)*

Kahn was so grateful he didn't have to do "Parents Day" at Lauren's school that he gave me a thousand dollars in cash to go out and buy some new clothes.

Outside of my Grammys gown, I haven't bought anything new to wear for almost a year. Plus my petite figure is making a comeback and I'd like to show it off. So I call, always-fashionable, Mae and ask her where could I get some really fun clothes—the kind that show off your personality. She tells me about a shop in Soho. It's called Chez-D—very urban, very chic and very expensive—but they're having a sale.

I invite her to join me, for style advice.

There's this mini-skirt on display. It's made out of Astroturf and the belt has a lawn mower blade buckle that spins. You have to be careful because you could lose your chin or your kneecaps in one rotation. The blouse is made of plastic strips that come from those folding lawn chairs. Only problem—they pinch your nipples—not exactly comfortable. The salesman, with a constellation of piercings on his ears, eyebrows, nose and lips says that the outfit makes a statement about America.

I model the green turf skirt and lawnchair top for Mae. She rolls her eyes. "Honey, you look like the suburbs."

"Mae, this is not what people wear in the suburbs."

"Not the people—you look like their lawns. Only thing missing is a plastic flamingo."

"Well, I think it's different."

"Right about that."

I didn't buy the lawn outfit, but I did try on some tops, skirts and pants. Even on sale, these Hip Hop fashions are too expensive. A thousand dollars doesn't go too far at Chez-D. Just can't bring myself to spend that kind of money on clothes. Ivy's growing and needs things too.

While waiting in line with Mae to pay for her purchases, I notice she has her DK-5 corporate credit card out.

"Mae, won't you get in trouble for charging those clothes to the label?"

"Trouble? What for?"

"Doesn't someone audit your expense report?

"This isn't an expense account. It's a perk for keeping my mouth shut."

"About what?

"If I told you, then I'd lose my little perk." She waves the card in my face. "You think anyone can live on what Kahn pays people?"

Are others at DK-5 getting paid next to nothing? Have they found ways to supplement their incomes? "So how would I go about getting a corporate card?"

"Do whatever it takes to make it happen, then forget whatever happened."

"'Make it happen'? I've been doing whatever it takes for months and can hardly pay my rent. So what exactly is the difference between whatever it takes and making it happen? And what is the "it" everyone talks about?"

"If you got to ask, you aren't ever gonna know."

Am I over-thinking it or just spinning my wheels at the label?

Just outside of Chez-D are clothing racks and a large folding table on the sidewalk. The racks display clothing, mostly knock-offs of the styles inside the store—a coat for fifty dollars, shirts for twenty and skirts for ten each—very Hip Hop and very affordable. I buy about two hundred dollars worth.

Imagine—I can dress like Mae for a tenth of the price.

On the folding table are boxes of CDs and cassettes. The sign in front of them reads: "All proceeds go to help the Fogg Ministries in its charitable search for God's truth."

Fogg Ministries? *Great, I haven't thought of Hank for a while—now this.*

Mae puts her hand on my shoulder and pulls me away. "Lily, don't buy any of them bootlegs. Kahn catches you and some girl'll be looking for a new set o' teeth."

"Bootlegs?"

"Yeah, they make illegal copies of music, then sell it for five bucks on the street. Kahn goes crazy over that shit."

"Why is Fogg Ministries selling them?"

"Bootlegs are good business. Low margins. 'Specially when you got a not-for-profit behind it—slave labor."

"Has Hank been turned into a slave?"

"Who's Hank?"

"My husband, I think."

"You aren't sure?"

I'm too ashamed to tell her the details.

There, in front of me, is the XYZee album I worked on. The jewel-case, the artwork, even the liner notes are the same, sort of—they look xeroxed, smudgy. I read. "Wait, this isn't right. The producer was Doodles not Meaty. How did you get these?"

The guy standing at the bootleg table gives me a forced smile. "If you're not going buy anything, please move along. Thank you. Isn't God great?"

In his happy-angry face, I say, "Sounds like someone needs an Epiphany."

His smile becomes a snarl. "What's y' problem, bitch?"

Dress for Excess

The next day, I dress for work in my new sparkly tube-top and tight white spandex pants. Add to that my new tan Timberland knock-off boots. Over it all—my white and gray camouflage coat. I'm the picture of Hip Hop chic.

On the subway to work people can't take their eyes off me. One guy makes a "looking sharp, baby" comment. Even the inhabitants of Chinatown notice. Imagine what everyone will say when I walk into Def Kahn-5. I can hardly wait.

Wish I had waited. Along with the strange looks, smirks and shaking heads of my fellow employees, I have to survive a Kahn critique of my outfit.

"What the hell are you—Halloween? You look like a skunk ho, trying to tricker treat. I got an office full of chickencoups. Don't need another. Look at you. Where's the potent professional person I hired, the businesswoman who makes this shithole legit? Are you trying to make your baby daughter ashamed of her mother? Lena, make me and your baby proud. Get rid of that ghetto garb-age and go back to a more professional lookage. Don't worry, I'll give you another chance to make up for this indexicretion."

So I guess I've found my hook, my niche—my "it." I'm the official suit at Def Kahn-5—dependable, predictable and expected to act as a counterpoint to the rest of the people at the label.

And he still doesn't get my name right.

At first, my feelings were hurt. But now, maybe my suitability will pay off in some way. Maybe Kahn has a bigger plan for me.

Kahn's Masters Plan

"Ah, Luna, come in." He stands politely, points to his couch and sits next to me.

He's smiling. *I hate that.* It means he wants something done, so he doesn't have to dirty his hands.

Since I've stopped volunteering for assignments, I get home earlier, have time to play with Ivy, and don't have to worry about dying young—as much.

"Do you remember when I found you out there, in the hallway—lying?"

"Lying?"

"Well, screaming."

"I remember."

"You've come a long way since then. Am I right?"

"Right."

"You've proved yourself to be the consummating professional I knew you'd be. You've proved that DK-5 can rely on you."

This is the guy who made me put my new clothes through the shredder last week.

"So, in appreciation of your contributulating, I'm giving you another title: 'Mistress of the Masters.'"

"Mr. Kahn…"

"Please, here in this office, when we're alone, you can call me Bigar. Just here, I mean, when we're alone, not in front of those other assholes."

"Thank you, Bigar, but I've never heard of that title before. What are the responsibilities?"

"Simple. In addition to what you do now, you'll catalog and keep watch over the DK-5 masters."

"Hasn't that been done?"

"Well, we've been busy for the last twelve years, just haven't got around to doing an inventory. So now that you're here with those big balls of yours, it's time to sling some dick."

"Excuse me, but I find this whole reference to private parts offensive. Why can't you just say that this is a performance promotion?"

"Sure I could say that, but it doesn't have the same impact as a swinging dick. Of course, I'm speaking metapharsically here."

"So does this metapharse come with a pay increase?"

He thinks for a moment and stands. "Follow me." We go into the hallway. People rush past. He stops and extends his arms. **"TELL ME WHO TO FIRE SO YOU CAN GET YOUR FUCKING RAISE!"**

"Uh, Mr. Kahn, I never…"

Topp Dogg, Mae and Clete are just a few of the people that

have stopped to stare at us.

"WHAT? I CAN'T HEAR YOU. DID YOU SAY MR. TOPP DOGG, OR WAS THAT MISS MAE? YOU'LL HAVE TO SPEAK UP. I NEED TO KNOW WHO YOU'RE ASKING ME TO FIRE!"

So much for more money. "Mr. Kahn, could we go back into your office?"

"SURE, WE CAN TALK BEHIND CLOSED DOORS, AND MAKE THESE HARD-WORKING PEOPLE HERE WAIT TO SEE WHO YOU WANT TO FIRE!"

"BIGAR, I DON'T WANT ANYONE FIRED— JUST A RAISE FOR GETTING A PROMOTION!"

The crowd walks away. They already know this routine. But I don't.

Kahn's face is very red.

I try to calm down. "Can we go back in your office?"

Inside, he quickly turns. I jump back.

"I told you to only call me Bigar when we're alone."

"But…"

"Tell you what, Lisa, how about we bury the hatchling? Forget about calling me Bigar. Forget about the money argument. Forget about firing someone. Look, I'll even get you a ticket for the Dough-Boyz concert. Hell, TWO tickets. And I'm going to sweeten the deal. You do this job well, and I'll buy you a Navigator—the big one. Because, nothing's too good for my new 'Mistress of the Masters.'"

Great. More work, no extra pay, plus two tickets that cost the label nothing, for a group whose music I find boring—and who in Manhattan needs a truck the size of a tank? I don't get it. For the same amount, he could have given me a raise.

At Least Someone Got Paid

Finally collected Dad's money. Had Clete make the call—no sweat.

12

Mastering Life

BEEP! *Blessings! Astronomous here. Just calling to tell you I've discovered why I've been such a failure. I was eighty-seven percent spiritually disabled. Can you believe that? But I'm getting better. Reverend Fogg is helping me purge my soul. As of today, I'm only forty-five percent spiritually disabled. Who knows, maybe soon I'll be able to come home. Isn't God Great? By the way, remember those boxes of Herbalux? Think I could drop by some time and relieve you of them? Miss you both.* **BEEP!**

HOW DO YOU MEASURE a spiritual disability? Can you graph it like the Big Balls/Dick Slinging Grid?

Oh, and sure he can relieve me of the Herbalux boxes. All he has to do is purge his wallet of the twenty-five hundred dollars I paid for them. Took me over a year to wipe out that debt.

Hank's spiritual situation is just another part of the last few months of abnormals—personal and professional. That's what my life has become—two abs for each normal.

Days begin with making breakfast for Ivy. She's on solid food. I stopped breast-feeding her two months ago.

Now it's DK-5 that's sucking me dry.

Tada! I've managed to keep a babysitter—Ola—for six months. Monique got her green card, and was out of the nannying business the next day. So the search began. After hundreds of people called in response to my ad in the "Irish Echo" newspaper, Ola was the only one I could afford. She's great, but there is one problem. Ola accuses me of being a child abuser—in both English and Polish. It could be a hundred degrees outside and she'll say what a bad mother I am because Ivy's not wearing a jacket, gloves and a hat. But I trust her.

My other babysitter, Beany Baby. starts the day with a description of his latest date—in too much detail. Beany has a very vivid imagination. He tries hard to be a player, but despite his boasting, he's just a Beanie-pie. Ivy loves him. He loves her. When they're together, he's Ivy's pony, play pal and story-teller-feller. After work, when he's not in jail, Beany takes over for Ola. He gets to have all the fun with Ivy, because, lately, I've had to work nights. Kahn expects us to attend artists' showcases and launch parties.

And then there's my job as "Mistress of the Masters."

Kahn has me spend every Tuesday and Thursday at this storage warehouse on thirty-sixth and eleventh. I've completely cataloged every master recording of every DK-5 artist in the past twelve years. Since then, I've gone from being the Mistress to more like the Librarian of the Masters.

It goes something like this: These scraggly guys show up Tuesday, say a codeword like "boombox" and then leave a thousand-dollar deposit. I go in the back and find the Masters they want. The following Thursday they return with the tapes and get their money back.

Tried to ask Kahn what they did with the Masters. His reply was that they borrowed them, and that was all I needed to know. He said that no one had ever been fired from this job—hospitalized, yes—but never fired. How could anyone have been hospitalized or not fired, when this job didn't exist until now?

It got curiouser and curiouser.

One day, I was asked to help Sik make a secret pick-up and delivery from a warehouse in Long Island City to Manhattan. I rent a white truck with cash. Sik has no license, so I drive. We head from Manhattan through the Queens Midtown Tunnel. Just past the tollbooth. "Didn't we just miss that first exit? Sik, are you sure you know how to get there?"

"I looks for landmarks, then follows m' nose."

"Need to have something more than that to go on. This truck is too big to follow your nose."

"Stay in the right lane. It's over there."

"Over where?"

He points. "There, on the right."

"I see, but there's no way to get off this highway."

"Keep drivin'. We'll get off next exit."

After about twelve right turns and one lucky left, we find the warehouse in Long Island City. Some guys are waiting outside an unmarked door. We stay in the truck. They load us up. Ten minutes later we head back to Manhattan.

"Sik, what are we doing?"

"Drivin' through a tunnel."

"No, I mean, what's in the boxes?"

"Fuck if I know. Kahn wants 'em delivered to this place."

Earlier, Kahn had written an address on the corner of a "Daily News" page, handed it to me, then got very serious. "Keep this a secretion." Took me a half hour to realize he had written our destination backwards—like some code we're supposed to crack.

All I want to do is get out of this smelly truck and away from Kahn's secretion.

We find the place, a large brownstone, and double park in front. Sik runs out and rings the doorbell. A chubby black man in shiny brown pants and a priest's collar opens the door. They do a ritualistic handshake, then a half-hug.

The heavy guy calls into the building, and out come five guys. They start to unload. I see them in the passenger side mirror. *Hey, I think I know one of them.* As he tries to lift a box, I notice how much he looks like...HANK!

Must be my imagination. Try to look out the window, but the view is blocked. So I slowly open the door. The key in the ignition sound dings. I grab the key, slip out of the driver's seat and ease my way to the side of the truck. A quick peek, followed by a longer gaze and there he is.

His head is turned...*Is it?*...I recognize the thin neck and thick hair. His clothes just hang on him. He looks more like the ghost of Hank—not the real live guy I married. His skin is so gray. *Should I say something?* He quickly turns. I pull back, keeping the truck between us.

I used to love it when he came home after a day of selling

door to door. How he'd be so full of hope. Hank would hug me, put his fingers yay apart and say, "We're just this far from our goal."

And it was always our goal. For the first time in my life, I felt part of something. My left-out feeling came later, when he couldn't see the difference between rejection of Herbalux and himself. Back then, I loved it when he would practice his sales pitch on me. We laughed so hard when I found a loophole. He'd touch my cheek and say, "I'm nothing without you."

Looks like his prediction came true.

I peek around the truck again. He's too weak to lift a box.

A big guy helps. "Isn't God Great!" It's not a question. It's a statement. He means that he better hold up his end.

Poor Hank can hardly keep his balance as they lug the box up the steps.

The Fogg Ministries? *So this is where it is.*

Used to think I could talk Hank back to his senses. Now, it seems senseless to try, because he's no longer Hank.

He's almost inside. I should get his attention.

But I don't.

I don't, because I realize I don't want him to see me.

Take a deep breath.

I'm waiting for my tummy to start up. It doesn't. No need to run for the bathroom or pop a Tums.

My Dad once said that things tend to work out, whether you want them to or not. *Guess this is one of those times.*

Who Are You?

"Mr. Kahn, I've taken on many new responsibilities, and I think it should be reflected in my compensation."

He stares at me.

I'm scrounging for a place in an industry that rewards both hard work and no work equally. "When I was first hired, you said that my salary would increase if I did 'whatever it takes.' I've done that. Now I'd like that reflected in my paycheck."

He laces his fingers on his desk and leans forward.

"There are other people here who do much less than I do, and make much more. I'm only asking for what's fair."

Why doesn't he say something?

"Guess the bottom line is, could I have a raise in pay?"

Kahn leans back, twists his mouth and clicks his lips. "Lala, you're very organicized—a real businesswoman. So I'd like us to get to know each other better before I make a decision." *Here we go again.* "It's time we share our innermost feelings and neuroticals."

If he undoes his pants, I'm out of here.

"What I'm suggesting is that before we talk money, we first go to therapy together"

"Ther...therapy?"

"Yes, cuddles counseling."

Cuddles counseling?

Nonsensual Pleasure

And then there's sex. I knew I'd have to get around to it.

The doctor said that as a woman's milk production declines, her libido increases. In other words, I should be going from moo to woof, but I don't seem to have the time or the desire. Wonder if I'll ever have a sex drive again.

A confession: Until I met Hank, I'd only kissed two boys—the first one on the cheek, the next one on a bet. But the second guy was at least honest enough to tell me that his friends bet him that he couldn't kiss me. I asked him how much he bet? He said two dollars. I told him if he could get it up to ten, to come back and we'd split it.

He did.

We did.

You'd have to pay me the big bucks to get near one of those Puce boys. They smelled Future Farmers funky. Except for Hank, a preacher's son, whose cleanliness was next to a godsend. I fell in love with a guy who bathed daily and wouldn't kiss me on a bet.

Then he discovered herbal laxatives.

Can't begin to tell you what that was like. Hank would take the stuff—to prove it worked. It was bathroom hell. I think I only took two deep breaths that first year. Hank would mope around when we hadn't had sex in a while.

I couldn't, because I couldn't breathe.

A few times I suggested we go fool around out by the pond or someone's barn—anywhere other than the bedroom, which abutted the bathroom.

Once I tried to boil apples and cinnamon on a hotplate. Hank walked in and asked me what I was doing.

I wrapped my arms around his neck, looked him in the eyes and purred, "Getting sensual."

He accused me of not having a normal sex drive. "But you could fix that if your colon was clean."

"Hank, the atmosphere is bad enough without my input."

Or would that be output?

I used to thank God that we moved to New York. We were reborn. And soon as we exited the Lincoln Tunnel—I got pregnant.

Now, well, it's not easy to have your only sexual partner living in a cult. That's what it is. There's nothing religious about that church. It's phony as Hank's herba-babble.

Heck, it's been nearly a year, two, if you count my pregnancy, since...you know...

At work the fellas are sexually aggressive. Some have even hit on me, but no one seems to follow through. I think they're just being polite. It's like they don't want to disrespect me by leaving me out of the come-ons. You know, for all the booty booty around here, there's something very un-sexy about DK-5.

Anyway, what would I do if someone did more than talk?

The Concert

Jiggity Man and I are at a concert at the Rajah Theater in Times Square. We're going to hear Dough-Boyz, the hottest Hip Hop group of the moment. The opening act is a gospel Rapper—JC Props.

Never been to a big concert. No one's ever asked me. The same is true for this evening, because I asked Jiggity.

Is this the new assertive Lily White?

Maybe.

Beany Baby and Ivy are doing their usual routine—watching cartoons and then reading "Charlotte's Web." I told him that maybe he should be reading something more age-appropriate. You know what he says to me? "Gettin' smart means challenging yourself. Sure, Ivy ain't readin' now, being twelve-months-old, but 'ventually she'll be seein' how much fun I have readin' to her and then she'll want to read too."

I love Beany.

Anywho, Jiggity and I are at this concert. Security's heavy. Everybody's in line to be body-searched and metal-detected. Ahead of us, Sik passes his gun to a girl, who immediately hides it in her purse. She passes it back to him after he's cleared.

Behind us, stands Topp Dogg, his crew and his son, who's dressed just like daddy—baggy pants, a Yankee's cap turned sideways with the cutest pair of Nikes—untied.

"Yeow!" There's a cold hand up my skirt. It's a female security guard, who's mining for metal. She pats down my body and waves the weapons wand over me.

I'm in.

The guard glares at Jiggity. "Yo, J Man, 'member me?"

"Should, lovely lady like you."

She looks angrier. "Er-Mine, 'member?"

"Must be someone else you're thinking of."

"Jiggity Man, I's yo' top girl. That's what you said."

J Man laughs nervously. "Why, Er-Mine, sure I 'member. My, my, my, looks like security done you right well."

"Spread 'em, muthafucka!"

J Man strains to keep smiling.

The guard frisks him—hard. Er-Mine shoves him around like a raggedy man. *What is going on here?* She slams her wand near his groin. His grin goes limp. She jabs her metal detector into his back—and he just stands there.

This has got to stop. "Jiggity, are you alright?"

The guard glances at me, then goes back to her task. "See you've got a taste for white meat, these days." Her back is to me, but I know who she's talking about.

She turns my way and says, "You better be bringin' in those Benjamins, or he gonna be smackin' yo' cracker ass."

"Now, wait a minute..."

"Lily, keep out of this."

The guard starts laughing. "Lily? What's her last name—White? She snickers at her put-down. J Man and I stare at each other. Our eye-contact must look strange, because she sharpens her gaze. "Get yo pimp ass out of here, Jiggity, before I handcuff you and that ho."

"OK, THAT'S IT..."

Before I get into a mess, he pulls me away. "Nice t' see you 'gain, Er-Mine."

She takes a threatening step towards us.

Luckily, Topp Dogg's son is screaming. "Yo, we gonna get in? I got to go pee-pee."

Thank you.

We enter the theatre.

"Jiggity, what was that about?"

"That's one crazy woman."

"How do you know her?"

He shrugs. "Someone from back-in-the-day. We all make mistakes. Some just got a way of coming back t' frisk you."

"Why did she call you a pimp?"

"Lily, let's enjoy tonight."

"Okay" is what I say. "Not okay" is what I think.

The atmosphere inside the theater is electric. Being here with this legend of Old School, an artist revered in other Rappers' rhymes, makes the night even more exciting. J Man is teaching me about Rap history, the way it's changed and where it's going. There's a generosity of spirit in this guy. There's also a great deal of pride. That's why he wants what belongs to him—his masters. Those tracks represent ownership and identity.

J Man says that he used to experiment in the early days. There are beats and rhymes no one's ever heard. As he talks, I can see that he wants a big piece of himself back.

I can appreciate that. "Jiggity, I'm going to find a way to get your masters back."

"I'm touched, Lily, really touched. You're the first person with enough sensitivity to understand."

It won't be easy to get his masters out. Kahn watches what goes in and what goes out. How can I tell Jiggity that they're sitting in a warehouse, under my protection? Maybe I shouldn't have opened my over-promising mouth.

"You're a wonderful person." He puts his arm around my shoulders. "And I want to help you with what's important to you."

We make real intense eye contact.

No one's ever said that to me. I could rattle off a few hundred things I need, but not now. Well there is one—all I want is to be alone with him. That's what he could do for me. My tongue is tied, so I just smile. He puts his hand on my cheek and smiles. "Let me know, okay?"

I nod. Been a long time since I've been touched in a loving way. He's so attractive. Warm personality. Nice body—lean and muscular—and that smile...

Maybe I'm ready to take a step in that direction. But I see the way sex is used in this business. It's like currency. You trade for what you want. And what you get in return isn't always what you bargained for. Not exactly what I have in mind. I want a loving relationship. The last thing I need right now is to be treated like beef jerky at a truck stop. I'm not an impulse purchase. I want some consideration before a guy buys into me.

Not many men understand that—not in this business.

After close observation of mating rituals in the Rap business, I shall attempt to explain how female desire can slam-bang into male reality.

A Woman's Hip Hop Guide To Relationships
(Eleven Ways To Pick Mr. Wrong)

1) Go For The Money
If a guy has no money, forget it. If he has a little money, forget it. If he's loaded, make sure he doesn't forget you. Many women, especially chickenheads, first take the measure of an alpha bro, a high roller, platinum artist, or a playa before initiating their mating ritual. One yardstick they use are the cascades of cash, which can connect men and women in a bi-fold wallet of lust. And since there is no designated mating season in the Rap world, sexual frenzy can be induced by colors—green (dead presidents), gold

(credit cards, car trim and teeth), and platinum (credit cards, clothes, and huge record sales). Any flash of these hues causes chickenheads to start pecking. In response, Mr. Wrong will strut, representing his desire to mate. All you need to do is keep your eyes and legs open.

2) Trap Him With Sex

Obviously, we're not talking about intimacy—unless, of course, a Rapper is having a bad day in bed. This "Ain't never happened before, honest, baby" can be traced to non-performance anxiety, chronic use of chronic, grabbing one's self too hard and too often in public, or the need to start "esperimentin'." This esperimentin' can simply mean a Rapper prefers male companionship or is seeking to avoid female disappointment. In the rarified air of fame, many Rappers find themselves unable to live up to their pubic personae. The result is looking for gentlemen, with similar issues, for support. But to make sure no one calls it what it is, they refer to it as esperimentin'. This allows a Rapper to have his cock and eat it too. Ladies, this is your opportunity. All you have to do is appeal to his fear of exposure.

3) Grab Your Share Of His Power

Only a fool would think Mr. Wrong is going to share power with you (See #4 "Warm Yourself In Reflected Glory"). You're only as powerful as what you last did for him, or his friends (See #9 "Crew Around"). Power is as elusive as fame, both of which most Rappers use up faster than Cristal. The only power you, as a woman, can exercise is to be silent until he needs you, or be irritating until he gives you what you want. Be careful, though. Mr. Wrong can have you kicked to the curb. That means, streetwalking—not a power move, unless you're working to get your GED, or saving enough to start the nail salon of your dreams.

4) Warm Yourself In Reflected Glory

Hanging with a successful Rapper can have its rewards. Record execs make money on it, homeys get jiggy with it, chickenheads get down with it, and even a Rapper's family will live on it. Each one wants to bask in it—reflected glory. Hey, reflected glory's better than no glory at all. See how the hangers-on roll together on the wheel of his fortune. All you have to do is be a spoke on a Rapper's rims. From the outside, it looks like you're traveling together. Inside, you're just spinning your wheels. But as soon as he stops turning out hits, you better leave that flat MF for this year's ride.

5) Expect Loyalty

Let's not even pretend this concept exists.

6) Dangle Some Props

This is where you can demonstrate your social position to Mr. Wrong's crew, and to the outside world. It's the unspoken, public display of your worth. Flashing diamonds, designer labels, gold jewelry, watches, cars, and, above all, manicures that tell the world that you're tight and right with Mr. Wrong. Keep repeating to yourself that you're his number one until you believe it. It's the props that'll show those playa-haters who's the one living in the lapdance of luxury—you, baby.

7) Become His Baby Mama

It's a big mistake to think a child can chainlink you to a Rapper's heart, and other parts. Monogamy is a word you never hear in his rhymes. One, because it doesn't rhyme with anything (Okay, maybe monotony). Two, because it's a foreign concept. Even though Rappers express the need to spread their seed, they, sure as heck, don't want to get tied down to some skank-assed ho, who's trying to lose those last ten pounds of baby fat. Anyway, birth control "Be da bitch's problem." A Rapper's just doin' the nasty. He's not procreating to promote the species. He's just sharing the love, Mama. Mr. Wrong isn't looking to change diapers, potty train or get baby vomit on his new 'didas.

8) Take On His Mama

Never, never, never, say anything negative about a Rapper's mother—even if it's true. There's no faster way to get Mr. Wrong in a pimp-slapping mood than casting aspersions on the woman who brought him into the world. Even if she is a crackhead hootchie, you mustn't point it out. Remember, you and Mom have a common goal—the need to keep Mr. Wrong sharing the love and the bling.

9) Crew Around

A Rapper's crew gets to share just about everything. That includes you. But rather than becoming some hootchie that's passed around like a moist blunt, you have to be selective. Get involved with only those crewmembers that have been with him since back-in-the-day. That means, they've learned how to pull the wool over Mr. Wrong's eyes, and have done so, for a long time. Props to them. They got nexts in his ball game, and you be the free throw.

10) Answer His Booty Call

Be sure to maintain the body type Mr. Wrong prefers. You can tell what that type is by walking down the street and noticing which women make him tilt his head and say "Mmm-Mmm-Mmm." Make sure you've seen his videos. There are many clues as to which body part he's partial to—learn them. Thank goodness that silicone and other implants can be ordered to suit his taste like a Ben and Jerry's sundae, served up in the right sized cup.

11) Doing The Nasty (Attitude)

If your goal is to be the most important woman in his life, you must commit to the special things you'll have to do that will make you feel like a piece of warm meat with a hole. But even "meating" his needs might not be enough. Some Rappers were once pimps. Most are wannabes. So it goes without saying that you may have to do whatever it takes— even on the street—to prove your worth to him. And what's the best way to cover up the low self-esteem that follows? Why, a nasty attitude. Develop that look that says, "I'm wasting more than two seconds on you for what exactly?" That way, when the truth or Mr. Wrong hits you in the face, you'll be armored, ready to defend your sense of worthlessness.

There is one more motivation for forming a relationship, but it has nothing to do with being with a Rapper. It has to do with just needing someone to love, to touch and to trust. Although this may sound sentimental, remember a successful genre of love songs, Rhythm & Blues, is based on the pain of romantic love in our society.

As with most generalizations, love doesn't stand up to rigorous scrutiny. I was feeling pretty turned-on about being on a date, until I started thinking about this.

Back to the Concert

Jiggity and I find our seats. The crowd noise and pre-recorded music drown out any chance of conversation. So we wait and wait and wait.

Nine-thirty and there are no signs of the show starting.

Finally, at ten, the opening act, JC Props and his crew saunter onstage. They start rhyming slow and cool for Jesus. The audience explodes, arms waving, bodies shaking. It's the same bump and grind, whether it's Gospel or Gangsta. Hank should see this. He'd learn that there's a lot of joy in both the spiritual and in the flesh.

J Man leans against me. "Let's move over near the door."

"Why? These are great seats."

"Don't worry, you'll see what you'll need to see. It's better near the far aisle—just in case."

"Just in case, what?"

He doesn't answer, but pulls me across a row of seats to the right spot. As we walk, people recognize him. Some call his name. Others do ritualized handshakes. Most just point at him and whisper to each other. Jiggity Man may not have a future in Rap, but he does have a following.

We stand in the aisle by the exit. My feet start to hurt.

Forty minutes later, my shoes are off when the next act, Dough-Boyz, bursts onstage. They tornado their bodies from one end of the stage to the other. The crowd goes wild. I tap my toes. Everyone is standing, dancing to the beat. People jump onto their seats, some balancing on armrests, all booty-shaking. I move my arms and hips a bit. The crowd boils. I warm up. Then Dough-Boyz hit a wordless part of their song. All that you can hear are the drum beat and the screaming turntable of DJ-Buxx as he rips vinyl into rhythmic thunder. Something happens to me. My arms fly one way. My hips rotate the other. Jiggity smiles. He's dancing against my thigh. I'm gone. I'm free. *Where did I learn to move like this?* I've never experienced so much joy. I'm laughing, woo-hooing and sweating.

The music I work for is now working for me.

Then the fireworks start. Not the Fourth of July kind, but the concealed weapon type. I hear two popping sounds.

Jiggity pushes me down to the floor and then lies on top. He whips out his cellphone and dials. "Need a car at the Rajah Theater right now."

People start screaming and running.

"What's happening?" That's all I can get out before we roll under the row of seats.

"Tuck your legs in! Lie flat!"

"Why…"

"Pull 'em in, NOW!"

I do what he says. Just in time. A group of screaming people rush down the aisle. They would have crushed my legs if I hadn't tucked them in.

"What's the number?" J Man yells into his cellphone, "Louder! Can't hear you! Right, one-five-seven." He yells at me. "Remember car one-five-seven."

He sees I'm scared. I see he's in control.

"One-seven-five?"

"NO, ONE-FIVE-SEVEN!"

"RIGHT, RIGHT ONE-FIVE-SEVEN. WHY?"

"IN CASE WE GET SEPARATED!"

More gunshots. More screams as the crowd runs in different directions. Thundering feet fade into the background as Jiggity lies on top of me.

One-five-seven, one-five-seven, one-five...

Gee, he smells great.

An Hour Later

The scene has changed, but our positions haven't. Even before the first gunshot, we knew where this was headed.

Back home, I find Beany Baby, snoring on my couch. "Charlotte's Web" is open on his lap. It takes a few tries, but I manage to wake Beany and send him home in a cab.

Jiggity brought a pint of Hennessy (VSOP—by the way). He said it would calm my nerves. It's doing that, and more.

He strokes my hair, my face, my shoulders and then my back. Everywhere he touches, makes me moan.

Better be quiet. Don't want to wake Ivy. "Let me get ready."

He runs his lips up my neck. "Don't take too long."

"I won't. God, I won't. I promise." Running to the bathroom, I turn. "I promise!"

As soon as the door is closed, I rummage for my diaphragm and jelly, condoms, plastic wrap—anything!

It's here somewhere. I tear up the bathroom looking.

Found it—my little rubber bowl and a very squeezed out tube of jelly. It's so old that the label is all crinkled and cracked. I can't even read the expiration date. Who cares? It has to work. I will it to work. Squeezing hard on the ancient spermicide, I manage to get a dribble.

Squeeze harder.

I'm strong. I'm determined.

A tiny bit more plops.

That should do it.

Remember to coat the edges, then make a little jelly circle in the center and squeeze the diaphragm into a closed clam. *Like riding a bicycle, right?* Place my left leg onto the edge of the tub. Insert. It won't go in! I push harder.

Must be making a lot of noise, because J Man knocks on the door. "You okay in there?"

"Just a few technical difficulties!"

I push harder. My chin rising to heaven. *Come on, I need some cooperation here.* Have I closed shut? *Push harder.* The diaphragm shoots out of my fingers. It has taken flight. I slam the lid, just in time to prevent it from landing in the toilet.

Sweating, I take off my dress and throw it over the shower curtain. Determined, I pick up my birth control frizbee and prepare to insert with all my might.

One little problem—you have to take off your underpants, if you want to insert a diaphragm—stupid.

And all I had was a half a glass of brandy.

Panting and pantiless, the birth control device in its proper place, I take this moment of victory to check myself in the mirror.

Awful. What happened to my body? Where's my waist? My breasts used to stand out. Who is this I'm looking at?

"Stop it! Don't start judging. He already wants you."

"Lily, you talking to someone in there?"

Despite a tingling inside me, "Everything's just fine. Be there in a mo…" The tingling becomes burning, which becomes a blazing contraction. It's like I'm in labor again—about to give birth to fire.

I scream.

"Lily, you okay? Lily…?"

What's happening to me? Maybe if I go to the bathroom? I sit and manage to pee on the closed lid. My feet are in a puddle of my own making.

"On, NO!"

I spray bathroom cleaner on the floor. The fumes make me

sick. The burning inside me gets worse. I wash my hands and put some water on my face. Reaching for a towel, I slip on the wet floor and land on my back. "Oh God!"

Jiggity is outside the door. "That sounds brutal."

"Be there in a minute." Panting for air.

Got to remove the diaphragm. It hurts. It hurts so much! Still on my back, I lift my knees and fish for it. One yank and, "OW!" it flies across the bathroom.

Don't see any blood, but the pain is still there. The diaphragm is partially melted. *How?* The only reason I can think of is, the tube of jelly is too old, or maybe I've become acidic.

Jiggity opens the door. "You okay in…"

He sees me on the floor in pain, reading the tube. It's so wrinkly I can hardly make out the words.

"Read this?" I ask weakly.

"For best results sq ze   Contact poison co   Avoid contact w s."

J Man picks me up, gets Ivy, and we cab it to the hospital.

The doctor in the emergency room says I'm lucky that it was Herbalux extra whitening toothpaste and not their silver cleaner.

Either way, my sex life just got polished off.

My In-Box

Tamyka, the former receptionist, is now the assistant to the head of Radio Promotions, Vishnu O'Brien. People can move up quickly in this business. But the job title has gone to her head. She jiggles into my office with her order-of-the-day. "We need you to join the street soldiers tonight."

That means spending all night pasting posters all over the city, and dodging police. Even though we're all expected to help, I remind Tamyka that I have a child at home.

"Who doesn't?" Then she questions my commitment.

I take the breast pump out of my desk drawer, hold it up. "Commitment? What do you call this? I'm expressing milk for my child here so can I do what's good for the lego. So don't talk to me about commitment!"

That shuts her up. What she doesn't know is that the pump is now a prop without batteries. Wonder how long I'll get away with that little scam.

#2Girl is on a vegan crusade. She says that I'll always be a "meat fucker" until I cut out animal products. I once asked her if cocaine is considered plant-sourced. She said that she'd cut my breasts open if I ever talked like that to her again. Her obsession with slicing breasts doesn't have the same impact it used to.

Then there's Rich, our company almost-lawyer. His job has become finding someone to intimidate or sleep with.

I've been lucky. He only tries to intimidate me.

Sik and Topp Dogg are themselves. Making money and hanging with their crews, who help them spend their money as quickly as possible. Once I asked Sik if he took advantage of the company's 401K plan. He just gave me a big grin. "Yeah, I got me a plan, but it's lots more than 401K."

Kahn's been promising me a promotion as soon as I have my performance review. Later I find out that no one at DK-5 ever gets a performance review. Kahn wants to avoid being shot by an employee.

One perk: Got Mae to use her "expense" account to buy me a bunch of MBA how-to books. That way I can learn how a business is supposed to run.

You just never know.

Still wear my blue business suit everyday. Developed new policies and systems to help DK-5 be more efficient and profitable. Have to admit, these ideas have gotten a consistent company-wide response.

> **Me:** These new procedures need to be followed.
> This includes paperwork that has to be completed so
> our work is more accurate and efficient.
> **Everyone Else:** (Silence)

Doesn't stop me, though, because I know with a professional approach, I can move up on the Big Balls/Dick Slinging Grid.

The present system is a mess. There is no system.

Clete calls it Kafkaesque—"There are no rules at DK-5, until you break one."

A company just can't go on like that, can it?

One more thing: Sampling has become an even bigger

nightmare. For example, it's 1991, one of our artists, Clo-Rocks, just sampled two bars of a guitar riff played by another artist in 1989 who had sampled that riff from a 1972 Funkadelic Congress song, which was a rip-off of another song from 1964. The original composer (from 1964) is in litigation, because he says that the credited Funkadelic Congress composer on the 1972 record stole his composition.

Now, both the original 1964 composer and the executor of the Funkadelic Congress catalogue, plus the artist from 1989 are suing DK-5 for over eleven million dollars. That's because Clo-Rocks refuses to admit he used the sample of the sample of the sample of the original stolen music. And he refuses to take it out of his track—"whether he had sampled it or not"—which he did.

To make things worse, the album has been in-store for three weeks. If we have to pull it from the shelves, DK-5 will lose a lot of money, and we'll still have to settle with whoever wins any of the three pending lawsuits.

Even Kahn tried to explain it to Clo-Rocks, who yelled that DK-5 is infringing on his "autistic freedoms."

Then, Clo-Rocks' uncle/manager, Smoove, demonstrated his displeasure about all this by putting a gun to Kahn's head. Negotiations went on for about twenty minutes. Just when everything seemed unresolvable, an order of Pecker's spicy wings arrives. Mae had ordered it for herself, but quickly diverted the Peckers platter to help with the hostage crisis.

Smoove's mind was awhirl with choices. Shoot Kahn or eat wings? Eat wings or shoot Kahn?

Revenge or gluttony?

Clete tried to talk him down, but Mae's simple question "You want sauce with them wings?" broke the stalemate.

Hot barbecue wins over hot lead. It's all good.

Since then, I have the Peckers takeout menu on my bulletin board and their number on my speed dial. Can't be too careful with armed relatives roaming the halls.

And that's just the day-to-day-of it—today.

13

Cuddles Counseling

THE BALD, WHISKERED and professionally sincere therapist leans back in his black leather swivel chair like what he's about to say makes a difference. "So, Bigar, tell me what's happening."

Smart me, I called Kahn's bluff on his therapy offer. This was supposed to be my little ploy to play along and get more money. Now our weekly cuddles counseling sessions have become torture-by-appointment.

Kahn clears his throat. "Well, I've been having these feelings about Lily."

Uh, oh.

"Could you talk about these feelings?"

"Yes, but I don't want her to look at me."

Great, just great, he's sounding like Hank before the Fogg set in.

The therapist's black leather lounger squeaks, as he turns to me. "Lily, how do you feel about that?"

"I'll go to the waiting room, if you want." Thinking, "Oh, please, please, please say yes."

"The purpose of couples counseling is to face each other and work out your issues." Mr. Isador Wild, MFCC-MA, MS, smiles a fatherly smile. "We can't do that if Lily is in the other room, can we?"

Kahn grunts. "Then, at least, she could face the wall."

"That's up to Lily." His lounger squeaks in my direction.

After a few looks back and forth, I move to the arm of the couch that Kahn and I share, and stare at the wall.

Kahn starts in on the most bizarre grouping of anger, violence and pornographic imagery—about me.

And the therapist just keeps repeating, "Go on."

Kahn's monologue includes the twenty-three names Rappers call women—in no particular order—but I alphabetized them.

Baby
Back-seat girl
Bitch
Chick
Dame
First Lady
Girl
Girlfriend
Ho
Honey
Hootchie
Love
Mama
Mutha
Nasty-girl
Punana
Pussy
Skank
Slut
Sugar Pie
Tramp
Trick
Woman

To each, the therapist adds, "I see."
He sees what? All I see is an Audubon print of a dead bird on the wall.
I ask him, if I'm going to get a turn.
His chair groans. "Are you feeling threatened, Lily?"
"Threatened isn't the word I'd use. More like left out."
"Left out of what?"
"This little party we're having here."
"Then why don't you join us?"
"Does that mean I can turn around?"
"You chose to sit like that, Lily."

I feel like walking out. Instead, I slide down the arm of the couch and plop down next to Kahn. My arms and legs have been crossed so tight that the blood flow has stopped.

I unfold my gone-to-sleep extremities.

The therapist's chair squeaks. "Go on."

Haven't got the feeling back in my legs, but this may be my only chance to say something meaningful. "Look, I'm not exactly sure what we're trying to accomplish here. All I asked for is more money for taking on more work."

Kahn shakes his head at me like I'm to be pitied. "You get paid. There's plenty other people who'd like to have your job, for less."

The therapist leans forward. "Sounds like you don't feel appreciated, Lily. Is that it?"

Before I can answer. "I appreciate her. Look at the responsibilities she has. No one else at the label have I ever given such responsibilities. You want to know the truth? The truth is, I don't think she appreciates me."

The therapist sits back. "So there we have it. Neither of you feels appreciated by the other."

"I appreciate what Mr. Kahn's been able to accomplish in this business. I also appreciate that he's given me a chance to grow. But what he has to appreciate is that I need to make more money. There are days at DK-5 when I'm busier than a one-armed paper hanger in a flea circus." I see that they don't understand my analogy. "And I'm raising a child by myself."

"I'm raising a child, too, you know."

He's not raising his daughter. His wife and nannies are. But, I guess, you could argue that Ola and Beany are raising Ivy too. So I say nothing.

"In the time you have left, I'd like each of you to think about how you can appreciate each other. I want you to think of this as a place where you can talk as equals—no employer/employee relationship to get in the way."

Is he kidding?

So, Lily, why don't you start by telling Bigar what you can do to increase your appreciation of him?"

This therapist doesn't understand the situation at all. But I've got to say something. "Okay, I will try to express how much I appreciate that he trusts me with extra responsibilities." *Of course, no one else does these extra jobs because they are dirty, dangerous and don't put cash in your hand.*

"Okay. Now, Bigar, what can you do to increase your appreciation of Lily?"

"I'll remind her that I picked her out of nowhere and that she was hired to turn the label into a real business, and that we haven't become one, because she can't fucking take orders and show initiative without my K-O. So I'm sitting on my balls, waiting for her star to shine. So far, I have a lot of mud on my face from her splashing around without being splashy."

What?

"Now, can both of you commit to what you just said?"

What did Kahn just say?

"I'll do what I can—without limits."

Does he mean "within limits?"

"Yes," I say.

"Good," says the therapist.

The feeling is almost back in my legs. "Do you think we'll ever get to discussing a pay raise?"

The therapist stands. "That'll take some time. First, we have to work on improving your communication, practice being a little more open with each other. Listening to what is being said and hearing what is being meant."

With Kahn? Even with a gun in his ear, he only hears what he wants to hear.

As we leave the session, Kahn goes to the bathroom and talks through the door. "All I'm wanting is a little loyalty in re-run for my caringness—not someone looking to give ahead on my bones. Please, go. I need to evacuate."

I'm going to need therapy after this therapy.

Girls' Night Ouch

Someone needs a break, and she sure looks like me.

Because of my workload, I haven't made many friends outside the business (not that I've made too many inside, either). So when Roberta called, I was excited. She invited me to her

monthly women's meeting—The Too Busy to Be Here Bunch—
mostly recently-single or barely-married women, who
discuss...things.

Must be the only place where anyone will listen.

We're shoeless in a beautiful apartment on West Eighty-First
Street and Central Park West, just across from the Planetarium,
waiting for our Chinese food to be delivered. Outside the large
windows is the street where they blow up the balloons for the
Thanksgiving Day Parade. Inside, I'm deflated by the
perfection—not a scratch on anything, the livingroom is a pearl
matte and the dining room is "color-washed ochre." *Looks golden-
yellow to me.* A lot of work went into making the walls look
weathered. Big ferns and leafy plants in porcelain pots break up
the sharp edges. But the main design element is the coaster—or
coasters—everywhere. There's even coasters for coasters.
Surprised we aren't sitting on them. Everything is in its place, each
doo-dad facing the right direction, pictures perfectly plumb and
carpeting clean as cotton. *The only mess in here is us.*

After debating for thirty minutes about what province of
Chinese food to order and where to order from (each menu has
its own plastic sleeve. All are held together in a taupe leather
binder), we agree upon Sichuan dishes with different flavors of
tofu. *Ugh.*

That done, the regulars start updating the group on their
continuing dramas. How each one of them is coping with a
disappointing marriage, an ex-husband, weight loss, post-divorce
dating, assertiveness, Feng Shui and bikini waxing.

To tell the truth, I kind of lost interest about twenty minutes
ago. Everyone's stuck in her own story, and no one's really
listening—just waiting their turn to out-miserable each other.

I want to say, "Your life—get on with it."

I also want Roberta to show up and bring some energy to this
whine-fest.

She calls to say she has a date, or at least found one "on the
fly." I get on the phone in the ecru—or another tasteful color
name—bedroom to beg her to cancel it and come to the meeting.

"No chance." She giggles. "Gonna make it tonight, just not
there, if you catch my meaning." More giggles.

"But I don't know anyone here."

"Just tell 'em your story—the husband part, the work part. Tell 'em how screwed up things are. They'll love it."

"But I'm not here for their entertainment."

"They sometimes give ya good advice too. Hang in there, babe. Gotta go. A sweaty night awaits."

"Roberta? Rob…?"

Now I'm stuck with these women. They are, Beatrice, the hostess, Blanche, whose husband has a prostate problem, Betty, who's been laid-off twice this year—by her employer and then her husband, and Edith, who's put on a few pounds lately, "but on her it looks good."

I'm having a hard time keeping their names straight, but their "neuroticals" define them.

This evening's hostess, Beatrice, aims her smile at me. "We'd like to welcome Lily White to our meeting. She's a record executive for…which company?"

"Def Kahn-5."

"You're kidding."

"No. That's where I work."

"But they do Rap music!" *Is Betty going to faint?*

"Yes, we're a Rap label."

"How can you, in good conscience, condone that woman-bashing propaganda?" asks the hostess, whose husband left her and this great apartment for a younger, more flexible woman. Since then, Beatrice has dedicated herself to Martha Stewart and Brazilian Waxes.

I try to explain the unexplainable. "It's not, well, not all woman-bashing."

"You can't possibly agree with the lyrics," says Edith, the woman who talks non-stop about her latest diet as she chain-eats celery sticks.

"I don't see it as me agreeing or not agreeing."

This is going nowhere. When is the food going to arrive?

Betty, an older woman, who's coping with abandonment, states, "Well I, for one, will never allow a man to treat me as his property, again."

"Is that what you think I do?" I stare at her.

Betty backs down. "No, I was just emphasizing how important it is for a woman to be respected." She straightens her pearl necklace and matching pearl bracelet.

The dieter jumps in with both celery sticks, "We're not here to be judgmental. All we want to do is be supportive. We're all in this together."

"It's simple, I have a job with a lot of responsibility..."

"And I'm sure you're getting paid as much as the men." She looks for, and gets knowing nods from the others.

"There's plenty of opportunity to grow." *Now, I'm getting a bit defensive.*

"Just keep telling yourself that," says the wife of the prostate problem, like she knows a secret.

"You don't understand," I say.

"No need to." She adds. "I've read about how those Rappers treat their women."

"I'm not one of their women."

"And what about the videos?" the hostess chimes in, bringing out her Martha Stewart-approved plates. "Objectification, if I've ever seen it. And I have."

"Okay," I say, "What do you suggest I do, quit a great job, for your principles?"

After a moment of silence, Mrs. Prostate says, "I just came back from the Galapagos."

The others "ooh" and "ahh."

Beatrice beams. "Nature at it's most pristine."

That's the signal for Mrs. Prostate to continue. "They only allow a certain number of people, you know, on the island at a time, for conservation and ecological reasons."

"Exactly like in the rainforest of Bora Bora," says the hostess, as she lays out the freshly ironed napkins wrapped in rings of "bent elm twigs" and "sisal." I know this, because the hostess tells us the story behind everything she brings in. From first seeing the napkins in a gourmet magazine to how they wash and fold, she goes on to tell us that even at wholesale they were very expensive, but worth it. And what the heck is sisal?

Makes me wonder that if they took this much trouble with her husbands, maybe they'd be happier. But look who's making judgments about relationships.

"Bora Bora, now there's an ecological paradise with one of the world's finest restaurants."

The talk goes on like that for about half-an-hour.

I'm dying for the food to come. Maybe, then, they'll have something to do with their mouths other than yack. The discussion jumps from fine dining to abandonment, from bargaining at bazaars to the latest exhibit at the Whitney that features an artist, who stuffs pantyhose with women's cries of anguish written on feminine pads. The conversation then leaps from country inns to Gurdjieff—I can't talk about any of this stuff, especially with my stomach growling.

Even, when the food arrives, the conversation turns to the cutest little restaurant that each of them has discovered and getting even with their spouses. Since the hostess got the biggest settlement, she trumps all with her story of revenge—her husband's assistant just left him for a much younger rock climber.

"Serves him right!" Followed by angry high-fiving.

Really?! Them?! High-fiving?! What am I doing here?

"So, Lily, I hear your husband left you," the hostess says with a mouthful of brown tofu.

I'm going to kill that Roberta. Setting me up like this, then telling this crew my life story.

The hostess leans forward and bares her Martha-approved capped teeth at me, "Care to share your story?"

She wants to take a bite of me, then spit out the bones.

But I'm not going to let her. "Well, yes, but he didn't leave me. He had a spiritual awakening."

That shut them up for a moment.

"Sounds like he's gay," says Edith the dieter, sucking the end of a spicy green bean.

That causes Mrs. Prostate, Blanche, to choke. After a few backslaps and a feeble Heimlich Hug, she says, "You know, I suspect Arturo doesn't really have a prostate problem. I think he likes boys. He's just using his prostate as a denial mechanism. It hit me in the Galapagos." She sadly nibbles on her tofu.

"Well, that's certainly not Hank's problem—straight as an arrow." I wiggle my hand to demonstrate a straight arrow.

"If that's what you need to think," says the hostess. "No matter what, we'll support you."

"I don't need support. I'm doing fine. I have a job and my daughter…"

"Do you have a good babysitter?" says Blanche.

"Yes."

"Well, then you have everything." She starts weeping. The others surround her with comforting pats on her back.

"What's wrong?" I ask.

Blanche looks at us and then down at the carpet. "I have to admit something. My husband ran away with our babysitter and came back when he needed my support with his problem prostate." She takes a deep breath and exhales. "The babysitter was male."

Just lost my appetite.

The dieter, Edith, says, "I think Gar left me because I never lost the weight after Johnny and Ronnie were born. God knows I tried to burn calories." She sobs.

"There-theres" follow like amens.

"Look, I understand what it's like to feel abandoned, but we're all dealt a hand. It's how you play it that matters. I've got a husband who needed to go live in a church to find happiness. He couldn't find it with his daughter and me. So what do I do, sit around and mope? I did that. It doesn't work. And now, you know what? My life's better. I spend my days and nights with the craziest bunch of people you'd ever meet, but my life is better."

They're staring at me. Did I just reach them in some way?

The hostess turns her head to the others. "Did you hear that Chakra Bagwam is speaking at Alice Tully Hall next week? I have a ticket."

The others say how much they'd like to experience him.

"Not a chance," she says with an evil smile. "It's completely sold out."

A moment of disappointed silence, then Mrs. Prostate says, "You know, I found the cutest pop-over restaurant…"

The "oohs" and "ahs" start up again.

Get me out of here!

Summer Theater

In the summer we usually have half-Fridays. Kahn likes to leave early for The Hamptons. Even so, the rest of us are expected to volunteer to spend the whole day being his "eyes, ears and noses." That's why we're surprised when he tells all of us to take next Friday off—with pay.

I'm suspicious. So I go to the office.

The first thing I notice is that the elevator ride is smooth, like the gears have been oiled. The car is graffiti-free—no more *Yonkrz-189* and *FeverFish* tags—no more urine odor and the floor's been polished. Even the buttons light up. I can actually see myself in the little mirror in the corner of the elevator above me—Toronto Maple Leaf jersey, tight jeans, black Nike's and high ponytail—non-business casual.

Walking in, there's Tamyka at the reception desk. Wait, why is she there? It's been six months since her promotion.

She sees me. Her eyes widen. "Wha, what're you doing here? Everyone's s'posed to be off."

"Then what are you doing here?"

"You can't go in." She unlocks her door.

"Right," I keep walking.

Tamyka jumps out from inside the plexiglass booth. "You can't come in here today."

"Oh, Really?" I slide my cardkey through the slot. Tamyka rushes to block my way. She's sweating. I realize the air conditioner that's usually set to arctic is off.

"Lily, you ain't goin' in there."

"Why are you trying to stop me?" Now I'm sweating.

"This place is off limits today."

"I've got a lot of work to finish."

"Take off 'til Monday. Have a nice weekend." She smiles.

What's gotten into her? Tamyka looks scared. Her eyes dart around. I smile at her. She smiles back. I push her aside and keep walking.

Behind me, I hear, "Oh shit, oh shit, Kahn gonna kill me...Lily, stop! Y' at least got to hit me! Please. I need t' get bloodied so he knows I tried!"

I speed up, turn the corner and then stop in the atrium.

What's different about this place? I know. It's quiet. No music, no screaming DJs, and no yelling employees, just Tamyka's "oh shit, oh shits" in the distance.

The place smells like lemon floor wax. And where are all the boxes of vinyls and the computer skeletons?

Two white guys in khakis and ties walk by, carrying files. The one, wearing penny loafers with real pennies in them, looks at me. He glances at his companion. They shake their heads and keep walking. Other people stroll, carrying magazines and stopping to chat.

Never seen so many Dockers pants outside of Macy's.

A tall blonde guy with a shiny blue shirt and matching tie is pushing a mail cart.

Did I get off on the wrong floor?

There are the silver walls, the rockets that mark each cubicle and office, the space monster chandelier in the main atrium that hangs from the ceiling, and the flashing galactic projections of our artists' images on the walls. Yes, this is the Death Star where I work. Only now, it's populated with aliens—an invasion of preppies. They sit at our desks, sipping lattes and whispering. You can even hear paper rustling.

What in the heck is going on?

I walk to my office. There's a girl sitting in my chair, looking at a glossy photo of herself. In that dark blue suit she could pass for me. She looks up and hides the picture.

She smiles. "Can I help you?"

I smile back. "You're sitting at my desk."

"Actually, I was assigned here by Mr. Longo."

Mr. Longo? Rich?

"If you'd like, I could help you find him. But I don't think he'll like the way you're costumed."

Costumed?

"The call was for conservative business-like attire." She gives my clothes another once-over. "And you were supposed to be here two hours ago. Not very professional, if you ask me."

"Not very professional? Not very professional? Look, babycakes, I've worked in this office for over a year."

She doesn't have a clue about what I'm saying, but that's not going to stop her from being right. So I put my hands on MY desk and lean forward. "Here's the deal, I'll give you a choice. Leave now with all your teeth or leave later with only some of them. Your choice."

She's thinking. Good sign. She packs up and picks up her purse and large totebag, then makes a grand exit. "Well, I'm certainly going to report this to the Union."

Union?

She "well, I nevers" her way down the hall.

What is going on? Have I gone nuts? A few minutes later I find out the answer to one of my questions.

I'm sitting at my desk, coughing, from that girl's lingering perfume. Heavy shoes and heavier breathing—what now? Rich is at my door, WEARING A TIE. His nostrils expand and then contract as soon as he sees me. His jaw opens and closes, then opens and closes again. All that comes out is "Oh, shit. Oh shit"

Seems like the expression of the day.

"Lily, wha, what the fuck are you doing here?"

"Sitting at my desk. Why?"

"Nothing, uh nothing. Do you mind if I close your door? There might be a lot of noise in the hallway. Wouldn't want your work to be disturbed."

Outside of screaming, "bitch" and "fucking cunt," this is the nicest he's ever been to me. And he's clean-shaven—even his knuckles.

"I would, but the girl who was sitting in here wore this perfume, and it would be like sealing me in a gas chamber."

He grabs a magazine from a chair and starts fanning.

"Rich, Rich, hey, Rich…."

"Just trying to help. I know how hard you work…"

There are heavy sweat stains under his arms.

"What is going on around here? Rich, stop that right now and tell me!"

He stops fanning. "That better?"

"Than what? Rich, who are these people?"

He slowly exhales. "Well, we're trying an experiment, uh that is, we may be leasing the office to, uh…" Rich can hardly talk.

Then, the girl who'd been at my desk walks up with an oldish, comb-over blonde man. He wears a camel-colored jacket and houndstooth vest over his middle-aged thorax. His thick horn-rimmed glasses sit atop his spotty forehead.

She points. "There she is. That's the person who threatened me with bodily violence."

The officious-looking man lowers his glasses to inspect. He lightly touches his fist to his lips. "Ahem, young lady, I will need your name for my report."

"You a cop?"

"Well, ahem, in a way..."

"Let me see some ID, then."

Rich starts to leave.

"Hey, Rich, stay here. I might need a good lawyer."

The barrel-vested guy flashes me his card.

"What in the heck is an Actors Equity Deputy?"

The girl covers her mouth like she's just had her private parts described to her. Rich shakes his head.

The guy blinks a couple of times. "Are you Equity?"

"No, I'm Presbyterian. What kind of question is that?"

The Deputy turns to Rich. "It's my duty to warn you, Mr. Longo (soft g), if we find out you have hired non-union talent, there will have to be a full investigation, and if found guilty, the consequences will be dire. This breach of contract will have to be resolved or I'll have to pull my actors immediately?"

Rich, near tears, turns to me, "Lily, please cooperate, for once. Just stay in your office and everything..."

The girl interrupts, "Excuse me, but this is supposed to be my office and my lines are, 'Hello, I am Lily White. It is a pleasure to meet you."

Rich sinks to the floor, holding his head.

The Equity Deputy puts his hand on the girl's shoulder. "Whatever happens, Mitzi, you have my word, this will not affect your pay rate—lines or no lines."

He turns to me—both hands on his wide hips. "Now you, Missy, I need to see some ID."

I'm at a loss for words, so I do something I've never done. I flip him the finger. "ID this."

Never heard someone actually say "Ha-rumph," before, but that's what comes out of the Equity Deputy's mouth. "Ha-rumph! Ha-rumph! Ha-rumph!" Three times—just like that.

We all seem to have crossed some union line here. Gathering what little dignity he has left, the Deputy and the glossy girl try to say something meaningful.

But I beat them to the punch. "Now get out of my office before I call security!"

The Deputy's massive body quivers with outrage. He turns like a mad elephant about to sweep the path before him. But all that comes out is, "This way, my dear."

He extends his arm. Mitzi takes it. She acknowledges the deputy's gentlemanly behavior with a breathy "Thank you." I get the feeling she'd like to kick my behind, but knows she can't. So Mitzi looks at me and enunciates, "Unprofessional." She turns her head away and then turns up that perfect nose that must have cost a fortune. The gallant Deputy and elegant Mitzi exit stage left.

What is this—some English teatime drama?

Rich, on the floor, holds his head and rocks. "Kahn's gonna kill me."

"Rich, who are these people?"

"…Can't…say," is all Rich manages to squeeze out.

I walk to the door.

"Where you going?"

"To find out what this is all about."

Rich grabs one of my legs and puts his sweaty, hairy head against it. "Please don't go out there. I'll make sure you get something out of this, only don't cause any trouble."

That's it. Even if I have to crack preppy heads and be investigated by Actors Equity, I'm finding out…

But Rich is still latched onto my right ankle. "Rich, let go of my leg."

So, with the legal beagle in tow (he must have a nasty floor burn by now), I manage to see around the corner into Kahn's office. Nothing's different, except a bunch of strange people walking around. I turn to ask Rich who these people are, but my feet get tangled on him, and I trip. Rich tries to keep me down. I fight him, but we end up on the floor, rolling around. Never been this close to him. Woo-wee, he smells bad—like battery acid and month-old compost, wrapped in a polyester sock.

"Here, might I help, Miss?"

I look up and there's this thin, pale white guy. He's wearing jeans with knife-sharp creases in them, and penny loafers. The coins in them shine as much as his shoes. His reddish hair is slicked back. He's wearing a dark, slim-cut sportcoat. His eyes are light blue. A few freckles on his nose highlight his peaches and cream complexion. *Was that an English accent?*

Something makes him stand out from the other preppies. I know what it is—he's smiling.

Untangling myself from Rich, I notice the other people with the English guy. #2Girl's spilling out of her business-blue bodice. Kahn is dressed in a conservative dark gray suit. His tie looks like an Armani boa constrictor. It's so tight that his yellow eyes bulge out with red veins. His oily face changes color as he looks at Rich, then at me. Three other men, surrounding the English guy, completely fill out their suits. Bodyguards? They have earpieces that disappear into their collars. I get the feeling they'd like a chance to demonstrate their skills—on me.

So I put my behind back on the floor—it's safer.

The English boy steps forward, his hands clasped behind his back. "I say, are you alright? Might I be of service?"

"I'm okay. Rich and I are just horsing around."

Kahn's and #2Girl's eyes dart back and forth at each other, then at the boy's face for a reaction.

"Very amusing. I fancy camaraderie in the workplace. Much more pleasant that way. What?"

"Yes, much more pleasant. By the way, hello, my name is Lily White. It is so nice to meet you." To Rich: "Did I say my line right?"

He cringes.

The English guy turns his head slightly. "Beg pardon?"

"Oh nothing, just an inside joke."

"Inside joke? Horsing around. Yes. Camaraderie. Quite. You know, Mr. Kahn, I must say, I was a little worried until now. Everything's ever so nicely run here, but I was led to believe that the Rap music business was a little more randy, more nay-teef, if you get my meaning."

Kahn straightens his posture. "Why yes, it can be. But we think that the artists should be the nay-teefs and we should perform like businessmen."

"Yep, just a regular corporate environment around here. Just yesterday..." Kahn's eyes laser at me, so I stop talking.

"What? Yes? Go on, Miss White," says the English guy.

"It's nice to work here."

"Nice to work here," he repeats, as if it's a brilliant concept. "Camaraderie. Quite. Oh pardon, M' name's Bunyan, Bobby Bunyan..."

"Nice to meet you. I'm Lily, Lily White."

"Yes, he knows," Kahn says through his teeth.

Maybe it's time to stand up. Bunyan helps me. We shake hands. He stares at my chest—*what is it with these guys?*—and laughs—*Laughs?*

"I do adore the Maple Leafs. Or would that be Maple Leavvves?" He laughs again. Everyone laughs with him.

What's so funny?

#2Girl fills me in. "Your shirt."

I look at it. "Oh."

"Bigar, how does Ms. White contribute to the company?"

I can hardly wait to hear Kahn explain what I do. But, for once, he's speechless. So I jump in. "If I may, my job is to nurture talent by making sure they get what they need to succeed. Sometimes I'm a friend, sometimes a taskmaster, but most of the time, I try to support the creative process."

"Brilliant. I should think that would be very rewarding. "

"Rewarding? Uh, yes most rewarding in a Mother Teresa sort of way."

Bunyan gets serious. "Tell me, Miss White, do you think that the Rap lyrics are a bit, how shall I say, a bit much?"

"Sometimes. Not all music can be called art. Only a few individuals and groups can claim real artistry. These few have torn poetry from its pedestal and brought it to street-level. These are the Rappers I admire the most. It's their gift that we, in our own way, attempt to nurture."

You should hear the silence. No one at this label has ever heard such BS, even from Kahn.

But guess who just ate it up?

"Ms. White, I look forward to more conversations with you. Such depth and commitment—remarkable. It's been the highlight of my visit meeting you. Bigar, shall we?"

Kahn tilts at the waste like a headwaiter with a fifty-dollar tip. "Yes, Mr. Bunyan."

"Could you arrange for Ms. White and I to talk further?"

"Further?" Kahn mumbles.

"I'd like to consult with her about company morale."

What morale?

"Yes, that would pleasure me to no end," Kahn says through clenched teeth.

"Until then, Miss White," Bunyan says.

"One thing, Mr. Bunyan."

"Yes, Miss White."

"You'll have to call me Lily."

He takes a sweet and deep breath. "Alright…Lily. And you must call me Bobby."

"Okay, Bob-by." I squeeze the be-jebus out of every last letter in his name.

He smiles. "Charming."

They walk. Bobby turns back and waves "Taaaah."

I "Taaaah" back.

Now wasn't that pleasant? I look down and realize Rich has slumped to the floor. His freshly-sheared head of hair is matted down. His black shirt is soaked through. Even his tie is dripping sweat.

"Rich, tell me the truth. What's going on here?"

Rich mumbles something.

"I can't hear you when you talk into the carpet."

He turns his head. "Kahn is going to kill me."

"Then, in your final words, tell me what's going on."

"Actors. We hired actors to impersonate the employees."

"Why?"

"To make a good impression."

"Impression?"

"Kahn didn't want any of those idiots fucking things up."

"What about Tamyka?"

"What kind of Rap label doesn't have at least one black person? So he kept Tamyka in the glass box up front."

"Who's this Bunyan guy?"

"Can't." Rich tries to crawl away, but I kneel on him.

"Whoa there. Tell me now, or I'm going to kick you from here to next Sunday!"

"No."

"HEY YOU, STOP THAT!" It's the overstuffed Equity Deputy. "Thought you could slip that by me, did you? Well, I caught you. Mr. Longo (harsher g). That will cost extra. We weren't told anything about stunts." He exits, writing in a little notepad, and muttering.

Rich scrambles after him. "Look, no one thought she'd show up..."

I head for Kahn's office. My stomach tells me that this isn't going to be good news. He better tell me what it is, or else...or else, what?

The fake DK-5 employees move around the clean version of the label. *But I smell a dirty Dealy-Yo.*

Later, Jiggity Man tells me, "BUG is Bunyan Under Garments. You read th' papers? They're buying up record companies."

"Is Kahn going to sell DK-5?"

"Naw, without DK-5 he's nothin'."

I'm beginning to have the same feeling—about myself.

14

Three Hints

First: One Saturday, while ironing, I realize it's too quiet. Ivy's up to something. So I walk quietly through the apartment. She's not in the kitchen, where she likes to pretend cook. She's not in the bathroom. The child gate is closed—so she's not trying to wash her Barbies in the toilet. There's a tearing sound from my bedroom. I tiptoe in. She's kneeling in what used to be Hank's closet and has opened one of the boxes of Herbalux. "Ivy, don't!" She looks up at me, scared, and starts crying. I pick her up and say, "I'm sorry, honey. Mommy just doesn't want you to get a sick tummy." Closing the box, I notice something's not right. Maybe I'm mistaken, but weren't there six boxes? I only count five. After that, I changed my front door locks and put a childproof bolt on the closet.

Second: Thursday morning: I'm sitting at the warehouse, waiting for this guy to return the PhatPhantom masters. It's almost eleven a.m., nearly time to head back to DK-5. I get a phone call. It's from the guy, who says that he's on a payphone, because the dubbing plant was raided this morning, and that they confiscated the masters. "Why were they raided?" "Why d' y' think?" "If I knew I wouldn't ask you." "Better tell Kahn 'bout th' bootlegs." "What bootlegs?" But he hangs up. Who raided the plant? What plant? Time to talk to Kahn.

Third: Later that day, I tell Kahn about the bootlegs. He closes the door to his office. "Lily, I hate that word. It means someone else is making money off the bones of our artists. If you've had anything to do with this, you could be in some serious trouble." I say, "But I haven't done anything. Even after that guy called, I wasn't even sure what he meant. Who raids a dubbing plant? Other than loaning out the masters to strangers like you told me to do, I realize that I don't know..." Then, a thought crosses my mind: What if Kahn was doing some kind of scam with the masters? Why would he? Bootlegs steal money out of his pocket—unless he's making money on it. But how? "Lily, if you're going to be trustworthy, you have to forget these things." Kahn leans forward. "And forget them as of yesterday." I try to, but the image of Hank unloading those boxes at the Fogg Ministries won't go away. What does one have to do with the other? Doesn't matter. Step back from it. But you know me.

Hampton Races
(Doo-Dah Doo-Dah)

Kahn's suddenly running the label like it's a real business. He's even taking all of my policy suggestions seriously. I mean, really acting on them.

"Lily, I told you from the beginning that we need to become a professional environmental. Now we are. Happy? You made a differential. You made the rules and you play by them. So now, you're a player."

I've learned one lesson here—if you play by the rules, you will never be a player. At DK-5 there's no straight line to advancement—only a crooked one.

Kahn brags about my "potency" and tells everyone, "You got a problem, see the White girl." Now, I'm the go-to person at the label. *Am I?* My reputation has become someone who gets things done on-time, big-time. People even come to me for advice. I handhold, babysit and advise Rappers, their crews, their families and an assortment of chickenheads. Honestly, most of the time, I'm not sure what the problem is, but I try to sound like there's a solution.

Kahn says he always knew I could do it.

Even so, I get the feeling that people here don't like me. It's not jealousy. They must think I have some influence over Kahn. I don't. Maybe they think that I'm turning the label into a nine-to-five business. I've tried to—with no effect—until recently.

Something's up.

Those actors, who stood in for label employees, and now the bootleg incidents, are eating at me. Need to gain some insight from the most seasoned person here—Mae. She's great at assessing a situation, then working it. She knows where the bodies are buried. But getting her alone and talking will take some doing. Mae doesn't do chitchat.

My chance comes at Kahn's house in the Hamptons. We're having an A&R meeting, disguised as a celebration. One of our artists, SmoochEE, has hit the charts big. My name is actually on the album—my first "shout out."

Kahn's mansion is decorated in pickled-white wood and over-stuffed furniture. The spotless beach and gentle waves keep a tasteful distance from the veranda.

Just perfect.

Lainie, Kahn's wife, an ex-model, catered this A&R Beach Party from this very fancy restaurant in East Hampton. The food is so beautiful it makes you gasp. The booze crashes on the shores of the Baccarat crystal.

She opens the glass doors, allowing the gentle breeze to remove the cigar and pot smoke.

Lainie is beautiful and gracious. *What's she doing with Kahn?*

I'm sitting back, enjoying a glass of diet cola, playing with my new mini-Rolex watch. I keep staring at it, twisting it on my wrist, checking the time every few minutes. Kahn gave it to me for "making a profit out of a molehill."

The first watch he gave me stopped. Beany was right—it was a fake. So this Rolex might be another fake-out for a real raise.

Ivy is outside on the beach, playing with the kids of other label employees. Lainie's and Kahn's daughter, Lauren, is also there. She's shy and blushes easily, especially when I remind her of the time I visited her fourth-grade class.

Two nannies watch the kids. There's a pony ride, a clown, a barbecue buffet and wonderful gifts for all of them.

Outside, the weather is calm. Inside, we're "blowin' up." Def Kahn-5 is cooking, operating industrial-strength. The "Billboard" charts have just come out. The responses are:

We be Orca!
We be Godzilla!
We be Dick Tating!

Four albums in the top fifty, three singles in the top ten, heck, we be MegaGodzilla!

Kahn is muscle-bound with success. He's just this side of out-of-control, and his huge cigar is smokin' to the beat.

Sik is sick. He's got a nosebleed, probably from all the coke. Lainie places a box of tissues next to him, so he won't drip red on her white silk sofa.

Top Dogg, totally bonged, enjoys his third helping of brunch. He scratches the plate like a DJ with vinyl in rhythm with the number one single—ours.

But all he's really doing is smearing his food around.

Mae is wearing a metallic blue bathing suit under a Caribbean print, sheer skirt, sea blue sandals and large hoop earrings. She looks cool and distant. I've got to get her away from the crowd without drawing attention.

Sitting next to her, actually humping up against her is Jess-up, an unsigned artist being wooed by the label. He takes his wooing literally, because he keeps trying to stick his tongue into Mae's ear. She's trying to turn him on—to the deal.

Clete is reading Thomas Mann. "The Magic Mountain" lies on the arm of his wingback chair. He's got a plate of Greek salad on his lap. Under his overcoat are a palm tree Hawaiian shirt and a unusual type of shotgun, called a Street Sweeper.

The environment is charged with excitement. Except for Rich. His wife is here. Never met her, but I can see she keeps him on a leash—a short one.

He whispers to her. She hisses back, "You stay right here where I can see you."

Rich is never happy, but today he seems to be beyond miserable. *Could he have flunked his third Bar Exam?*

Anyway, the mood is intoxicating. This is what it's all about— music, food, the beach, a comfortable summer home, and the success that ties it all together.

With all this excitement and achievement, why would Kahn even think of selling the label?

I try to get Mae's attention, but she's busy fighting off Jess-up without looking like she's fighting off Jess-up.

Three DK-5 interns rush into the room. One of them whispers to Kahn. He reddens and whispers back. He pokes one of them twice on the forehead. They leave. Something's happening. I excuse myself, and follow.

Where did they go? Walking down the hall, I look into each beautifully decorated room. Obviously, Lainie was in control of the design. Kahn's taste leans more towards strip joint chic.

I hear frantic sounds coming from a back room. Sounds like an orgy. So, of course, I peek in. It is an orgy. I see five people screaming into their telephones, "SmoochEE." Each one dials a phone and screams, "SmoochEE" again. Dialing and screaming, again and again.

This is how we win the Hip99 RapRumble. The radio station plays the current hit singles of two artists. Listeners call in to vote on the "dopest joint."

Kahn's goal is to win. So, each week, he helps it along a little bit. Anyway, what's the big deal? A little ballot-stuffing never hurt anyone. And our rival, Organ Records, is probably doing the same thing.

Back in the living room, Mae shouts, "Ow, fuck! My ear!"

Jess-up pulls Mae's earring off his tongue. "Sorry, baby, you know how it is."

I try to diffuse the sticky situation. "Would either of you like something? Jess-up, how about another blunt?"

He grins and exposes his gold-teeth. "Always room for a beautiful lady. Get me another Cris-tal and come sit over here next to the man."

Luckily, Kahn clinks his glass with a gold and ebony Mont Blanc pen. The room becomes silent. Everyone seems to know that we're about to play one of Kahn's party games.

"Are we fuckin' number one, or what?" Kahn stretches his arms to form a triumphant "vee" and sticks out two fingers on each hand to complete the pose.

A light dusting of applause.

Isn't that a number two?

Oh yes, #2Girl stands next to Kahn on the L-shaped sofa. She acts more "wifely" to him than Lainie. I'm surprised she isn't wiping his mouth between bites. What she's wearing, actually spilling out of, is a halting halter-top. It's breathtaking. In fact, I hold my breath every time she moves, waiting for those magic mountains to erupt.

Kahn breaks his pose. "We've set a new fucking standard in the business. The word on the street is, we got four more monster joints in the wings. 'Vibe' is doing a profile of me—not too fucking bad."

Not bad? He's incapable of understatement, so I fear what is about to come next.

He turns to Jess-up. "You see, Jess-us, we're the label that's blazin'. Right, Mae?"

"Right. We be da mothafuckin' bomb."

Jess-up is trying to look "not impressed."

"Now, I want us to form a trust circle."

Oh, brother.

"We're going to experience our personal goals."

Each of us is frozen in place, chin-down, eyes moving rapidly back and forth, trying to see if anyone else knows what the rules of this game will be.

Kahn breaks the tension. "After a success it's important to stake stock in ourselves. Focus on our personality goals. We want to show Jess-us how we do business around here. Rich, you're a lawyer..."

He is?

"...Why don't you make an opening statement?"

We wait for this legal beagle to bark his snide remarks at us.

But not today. His wife has spayed and choke-chained him. "My personal goal is to make a lot of money…for Def Kahn-5, and to eventually be a big swinging…" His wife clears her throat. Rich looks at her and changes course. "…player."

Kahn smiles. That's everyone's cue. Now everyone knows what to say. *But wait a minute, that's what I actually want.* Now everybody else will be saying the same thing. And when I say it, it won't mean anything.

"So, Mr. Topp Dogg, what are your personal goals?"

T Dogg, his lips and fingertips stained with food, stands up and lifts one leg. "Piss on the competition, make me a shitload of money." He lowers his leg. "And be a big, fucking movie star like Denzel." He sits, satisfied.

Jess-up and Topp Dogg do an intricate handshake.

"Very ambitious." Kahn smiles. Then, explaining like there's some greater meaning. "You see, the goal of this exercise is to have a goal—and express it."

One of the interns, a young splinter of a guy, rushes in. He whispers to Kahn, who screams, "FUCK! WELL CALL FASTER, GOD-DAMN-IT! WE LOSE THE RAP RUMBLE AND I'LL KICK YOUR FUCKING TESTICLES UP ALL YOUR THROATS. DO YOU UNDERSTAND MY SUBTEXT HERE?!"

The intern nods, then rushes back to the phones.

"Fuckin' Organ Records," he grumbles.

#2Girl becomes a cheerleader. "Everybody knows our joints are hotter than Organ's."

"You," Kahn points to her, "Go in there. Here, take your cellphone and start calling Hip99."

"But what about my personal goals?"

"It just became winning this RapRumble. Anyway, who gives a fuck what you want?"

I almost feel embarrassed for her—almost. She takes a deep breath, then walks bravely forth to clog the phone lines.

What does #2Girl get out of all this? Money? Power? I tell myself that I would never let anyone treat me like that, would I?

A gust of wind from Sik's nose brings everyone back to the topic at hand. His head is tilted back trying to stem the blood-flow with his fingers.

I hand him a couple of paper napkins. "Dab. Don't blow your nose, you'll bleed to death." Kahn turns to us. "That's it for personal goals? Really? THAT'S IT?"

I say, "Sik here looks like he could use some attention."

"Okay, since you're so talkative, what are your personal goals, Misses Lily White?"

"That's easy. My goal is to be you."

Kahn blinks twice as my statement registers. To say there's tension in the room, doesn't do it justice. Even the sea breeze has stopped.

"Yes, I want your job."

"Oh—really?"

"Why not?" I gesture to the room. "I want to have this. I want everything I see here. The house, the view, the cars, heck, I even want a wife like yours."

Kahn stares at me, rolling the cigar in his mouth. His face expands and turns red. What's he feeling? Since he doesn't know embarrassment, all that's left in his range of "red-faced" expressions is rage.

Lainie steps up. "Lily, what a great goal. And what a compliment to you, Bigar." Kahn's head snaps towards her. "That's about as respectful as it gets—not to have someone be just like you, but be you."

Kahn looks around to see how others are responding.

"Lily, what a lovely thing to say."

Kahn steps toward her. "Who the fuck asked you? Go get us more drinks. Make yourself useful."

How can he talk to her like that?

Lainie glides to the glass doors, turns to Kahn. "I'd like to be you too, just so you could know what it's like to be me." She continues out to the beach.

If I were married to Kahn, I'd walk into the ocean and never look back.

He follows Lainie and stops at the door. "You should be on the phones making SmoochEE number one! Earn some of this shit that I pay for." He looks back at us, then puts some caring into his tone, "Uh, you should get some lotion on, honey. Don't get skin cancer out there!"

To Jess-up. "Must always keep your woman in line."

"Hear that. Keeps my bitches on a rope."

Kahn gives him a high-five. Jess-up is very pleased. What he doesn't know is that Kahn's about to rob him blind. Jess-up will sign with Def Kahn-5 and then see just enough money to get a taste of success. Then he'll spend the rest of his life saying, "Know who I used to be?" Poor fool won't know what hit him.

Kahn stares at me. "So, Mrs. White, you've gotten some mighty big balls lately."

"Earned them, just like you wanted me to."

Silence.

He smiles. "Mae, you got any personal goals?"

Mae pushes Jess-up and his tongue away. "A dry ear."

Kahn doesn't get it.

She gets up and walks out the door. This is my chance. The beach is the perfect place. No one can hear us. Somehow, I have to get outside and talk to her.

"Sik, you got a goal?"

I slowly shift toward the door.

"Can't talk," Sik snorts, "Nose shit…blood…"

"You should take care of that." As if Kahn cares. "Call a doctor or a Vitamin C. Anyone else?"

A quick glance outside—I can't see Mae.

"What about Clete?" I ask. "He never has any input, yet he's always here. Am I right?"

Clete doesn't like attention.

Kahn thinks for a minute, then turns to Clete, "Right. Okay, Mister Clete Clydesdale, what could be your personality goal? Tell us. We're here to share."

Clete is thinking.

I'm almost outside.

"You need more time to get that brain going?"

"No, no, I was formulating what I want to say. Clarity is important here, Mr Kahn."

"Can we have a clue when you might be getting this clarity? Hello, I'm talking here."

Did he just knock three times on Clete's forehead? Is he crazy? Clete could break Kahn in two.

I should leave, but want to see what will happen next.

Clete sits motionless, then speaks slowly. "My goal is to finish 'The Magic Mountain' this week."

"A simple and beautiful thing," Kahn says. "I am very proud of you, Clete."

Clete starts shucking and jiving in his chair. "Thank you, Massa Kahn. "I's always be lookin' fer some white folks' approval. Yassah, I does."

This will not end well.

Kahn is getting uncomfortable. Especially when Clete stands up, and up, and up. God, he's tall.

He fixes his eyes on Kahn. "I jes would love t' oblige yo whim, but y'sees, I keeps my pers'nal goals to my pers'nal self. I hope y'unnerstan' a po' boy like me. Das ya?" His voice lowers two octaves. "DO YOU?!"

Kahn's eyes are a mile wide. His cigar dangles from his dried-up lips. He slowly nods.

"Good. Now, next time you want to play your fucked-up games, you leave me out. I'm paid to take a bullet for you, not your bullshit. Do you understand me?"

Time to exit. I slip out and head for the beach.

Mae, I think it's Mae, is a spec in the distance. Run, but my laced-up boots aren't for running or for the beach.

Ivy calls, "Mommy! Mommy! Watch me! Watch me!"

I feel so guilty that I'm ignoring my daughter, but the future is walking away, up there, where the water meets the shore, and I have to catch up. "Mae! Mae!" I feel like I'm running backwards in the sand. "Mae!"

Then from behind me, "What you doin', silly?"

I turn. It's Mae. She's sitting on a beach chair.

Her wraparound skirt is open, revealing her long legs.

"I thought that was you, over there."

She looks. "Where?"

"There." I point to the figure in the distance.

Mae squints. "That's a seagull picking up garbage."

"It is?"

"Why'd you come running after me?"

"I want to talk with you about something."

"This about Jess-up?"

"No."

"The RapRumble?"

"No."

"Our 'personality' goals?"

"No, but… well, sort of."

"Hey, that was five minutes ago. Kahn should be chewin' up a whole new topic by now. Let me guess, how do we get rid of headcount so we can decapitate operating expensivenesses?"

Her perfect imitation of Kahn breaks me up. "It's something else. I mean, I want to talk to you about something…else." *I'm not prepared for this conversation.*

"Mm-hm," she's waiting for the other shoe to drop.

"You're the only person I trust, the only person I truly respect at the label."

"Respect? Truly? Like I'm supposed to buy that shit?"

She raises the trust bar higher. "Mae, I need your advice." She stares, waiting. "I'm not sure how to start this."

"Go ahead."

Go ahead just became going uphill. "Well, there are some strange things going on."

"No shi'?"

"What I mean is, something out of the abnormal."

"Mmm-hmm."

"I wouldn't even bring this up if it wasn't so strange."

"Mmm-hmm."

She's not going to make this easy. Anyway, I'm not sure I can trust her. But the only way to get the information I need is to tell her what I've seen. So I decide to sidle up to the subject. "You know, Mae, we have a lot in common." *That got her attention.* "In many ways we're alike."

Mae bursts out laughing.

"What's so funny?"

Mae tries to talk, but doubles over, gasping for breath.

"I'm serious…Stop laughing."

Mae and her beach chair topple over. She gets up, laughing, brushing the sand off her.

"Mae."

She looks at me and goes into another spasm of laughter.

"We are...we're a lot alike."

That's it. She's on the sand again.

"Mae, what's so funny?"

She collects herself and rights her beach chair. "Oh, my, my, my, can't tell whether you're stupid or ignorant."

There's a difference?

She straightens her skirt. "We're alike, my ass. First of all, I never fucked Kahn"

"Excuse me?"

"I'm not judging. You do what you gotta do, girl."

"Exactly what does that mean?"

"Look, everyone knows you and Kahn got something going Tuesdays and Thursdays."

"Tues...?"

"You think anyone believes that you and him are going to a psychiatrist together. Really? Look, I'm not judging, we all do what we gotta do."

"DO? I AM NOT DOING 'THAT' WITH KAHN!"

"Uh huh..."

"Never...in a million years. I'd rather get my husband back than fool around with that animal. I can't believe anyone would even think that."

"Then what's the dealy-yo?"

"Truth is, I sit in a warehouse with the masters and check them out to people on Tuesdays, who return them Thursdays. Didn't know why, until this guy calls and says that the dubbing studio where he worked was raided and the masters confiscated. Then he said something about bootlegs."

Mae gasps, but recovers her cool quickly. "You better not be jivin' about that shit, 'cause Kahn erases people that even hint this much about bootlegs."

"I know. So why would he make me Mistress of the Masters, and set me up in that warehouse? And another thing—Sik and I went on a delivery run. Everything was very secret. Then, we stop at the Fogg Ministries. Some guys unload the boxes. Worst part was, one of them was my husband, Hank."

Mae seems confused.

"I'm telling you the truth."

"So?"

"So Kahn's doing something fishy with those masters and it has to do with bootlegging. Remember when we went shopping at Chez-D? Outside was this table of bootlegs? On that table was a sign that said something about the money going to the Fogg Ministries."

"And?"

My stomach knots up. "And all this has been bothering me for weeks. Only I didn't know who I could tell. You know this place."

She thinks and then waves her hand, dismissing her thought. "Doesn't matter anyway. Kahn's always into something. He's a money magnet. But, damn, bootlegs? That's somethin' new."

One of the RapRumble phone-callers runs to the beach. He says, "We're losing! Mr. Kahn wants everybody inside!"

Mae looks at me. "Keep quiet about this. Whatever it is, it ain't gonna do you any good to keep on about it."

"Be D&D?"

"How's that?"

We walk to the house. "Mae, did you know that Kahn hired all these actors to pretend they were DK-5 employees? It had something to do with BUG. I mean, Bunyan Under Garments. Ever hear of them?"

"Girl, you just full of shit today."

"Why would he do something like that?"

"He's always mackin' some whack company to give him money. Nothing to worry about. Let a pimp be a pimp."

She sees I'm confused.

"Look, Lily, just do what you said to Kahn. Be him. Be crazy over the small shit and clear-headed about what counts. Find something else to take up your time. Redecorate your office, pad your expense report, look for a new artist, anything to get you away from his business. Hang on and let the other shit slide."

We walk back silently. I'm thinking that Mae's right. Actually, finding a new artist might be fun. And fun would be a nice change of pace.

In the house, Kahn is running around the living room,

screaming. He looks more desperate than when Clete was about to turn him into a squeeze toy. "We have to put the A&R meeting on hold. We need more votes. Everybody got their cells? Take them out."

Everyone flips open their cellphones, like in "Star Trek."

Kahn commands, "Now start calling Hip99."

Everyone starts to dial his or her phasers.

Beam us up!

"Wait a minute!" Kahn interrupts, "My personal goal."

Beam us up!

"I want us to go from the 'Bad News Bearensteins' to 'The Little Engineer That Could.'"

Beam us up already!

"So make as many phone calls as you got fingers. Let's knock that Organ from here to kingdom kong!"

After dialing Hip99 and getting through, I yell, "SmoochEE!"

I redial and get a busy signal.

Mae's right. I'm going to find an artist.

The voice on the other end of the phone says, "Hip99 Rap Rumble. Your vote?"

"What? Oh, uh, SmoochEE!"

Getting the Picture

An envelope came to my apartment today. Inside were photographs of Hank, dressed as some biblical figures.

> Hank as a blinded, bloody Samson (from behind) in a thong and pushing the temple columns apart. His head is turned to the camera. He winks.

> Hank as David in bed with a blow-up Bathsheba.
> Oh my God, Hank as Barabas, smiling, wearing a loincloth made of thorns, crucified next to Jesus, giving him a thumbs-up.

> Hank as Ehud, the king, who was killed on the toilet, with his harem pants pulled down below his knees, saluting.

The note inside read:

> I'm closer to Epiphany than ever. See for yourself. Would like to get the Herbalux boxes from you. Want to share the joy with my fellow disciples here at the church.
> Isn't God Great!
> Eternally,
> Astronomous.

ETERNALLY?

If he wasn't a tax deduction, I'd have written him off by now.

15

A Talent for Talent

WE WON the Rap Rumble—not because we made the most calls. Organ Records had their own counterparts to our crew, who were just as determined to win. Kahn realized we were losing and made a call to some old friends at Hip99.

Cash always gets the best radio reception in this area.

The lesson: This isn't a popularity contest. It's a battle of the bucks. Hardball with underhanded pitching.

Whatever. I just want to sign a new artist.

Listened to a heap of demos we keep in big boxes in an empty office. Wasn't very impressed with what I heard. What's really amazing are the amount of wannabes, the naïve and outright talentless people, who fantasize that they'll be the next LL Cool J or Tupac.

After a hundred cassettes, you stop hearing. After a thousand, you hope the tape deck won't work.

Even gave an ear to the Serbian guy who still leaves his weekly Rap songs on my answering machine, before hitting erase.

That was rock bottom.

At a loss for talent, I referenced the demos of our signed artists. Maybe I'd hear or feel what made them special.

Surprisingly, even they didn't sound so great.

So what made them different? I asked around, but no one at DK-5 gave me a clear answer.

He got the gift
They know how to flow
Dope beats and rhymes

Not much to go on.

Called Jiggity Man. Since that eventful uneventful night at my place, we haven't spoken. He hasn't returned my calls, and he stopped hanging out in the DK-5 reception area.

I know this is sort of a tangent, but it's been bothering me. It's not like I want a relationship. It's, well, maybe I do. I don't know. When I finally do reach him, all he does is ask about what's going on at the label. "Kahn still givin' gifts to the artists, then taking double the cost out their royalties?"

Where did that come from? "I, I don't know."

"That Play Money still flowin' through Beany Baby?"

"That's not my..."

"Heard Vishnu got shot. Anyone know who did it?"

"He got what?"

"My guess it was..."

"He didn't get shot. I was just in his office."

"Did he try to rape you?"

"What? NO! He just tried to pass off some of his work on me."

"But, I heard..."

"J Man, you're not letting me talk."

"Oh, sorry, just tryin' t' show an interest. Work seems so important to you, and all."

"What I need is some advice. Could you tell me what makes a Rapper successful? Is it the music, the words, a vocal quality, or something else?"

He's thinking..."There isn't one single factor. It's the whole package—a standout quality, strong flow, and monster joints. But then, it's money, marketing and muscle aka radio play, word on the street, and wide distribution..."

"I kind of knew that already. What I want to know is there something more that I should look for in a new artist?"

"Most Rappers fit a type—something that's been proven to work. It ain't like the old days, when you just had to be clever. Now you gotta be sort of good, have a look and be able to carry a theme—like money, revenge and big booties. An artist's biggest need is a good producer with a shitload of hot beats. Think too much, and you'll miss the point. It's a gut thing. Why, gonna jack yourself some new blood?"

"No, just trying to understand things."

He clears his throat. "Now about Vishnu..."

"He's on vacation. Jamaica, I think."

"Thought you were just in his office..."

Caught me. "He just left." I get Jiggity off the phone quickly with another fib—something about being late for a meeting.

Got to find a new artist, change my plan of attack. Listen/Look for someone with a good sense of flow and who fits into a character type like a pimp, a gangbanger or a lover. This is what I've been missing. It's like casting a role more than fishing for talent. This new approach should make finding a new artist easier. *And if there's one thing I know, it's how to develop a system.*

First, I go through a bunch of demos, looking at the pictures that come with them. If they don't fit into one of three character types—The Pimp, The Gangbanger or The Lover—out they go.

That leaves me with three piles of pictures and demos. The final jeopardy is an audio daily double. If they don't sound like their picture looks, they're history. I've narrowed it down to the best of each type. Time to do some background checks.

> **The Pimp** is the lead singer of a group called FTGU, From The Ground Up. Three of the guys are in jail. The lead singer is about to go to trial for the same gang rape. Long sentences—scratch them off my short list.

> **The Gangbanger** is Kalik (The sound an empty gun makes). He's about to sign a deal with Organ Records. Too high on the BB/DS Grid for where I am now. And the last person who tried to steal an artist from Organ was almost beaten to death—next.

> **The Lover** is Montrose DeLea. Smooth voice, one raised eyebrow and great teeth. But he's now a preacher for the Reverend JumpMaster-Modee's Methodisk Church—I don't think so.

So I'm out of luck, until I see the picture of this goofy-looking guy at the bottom of the box. The best way to describe him is, think of an annoyed homeboy with thick glasses who wins the national spelling bee.

He doesn't fit into any type. His name is BronxSkee (After Bronx Science High School). Just what I need, another wannabe kid—until his demo starts playing. Never heard anything like it. The bio says his songs are based on a combination of "borrowed" Bach fugues, amplified internal organ sounds and crime statistics.

Over my head, but I like his beats and the royalty-free samples sound even better.

He's a maybe.

So I go to BronxSkee's Riverdale home on a sunny Sunday afternoon. His real name is Henderson James Burgess and his uncle says that his IQ is near one-eighty.

His large family wanders around—an afternoon barbecue in the backyard. Since no babysitter was available, I brought Ivy. She's a big hit. Right now, she's out playing with the other children. Have to admit it, I thought that bringing her would help break the ice.

She's so cute and I'm so shameless.

The Burgess living room is full of friendly people and comfortable furniture. Talk and warmth fill their house.

Seated with a plate of ribs, chicken, collard greens, macaroni and cheese and a tumbler of mint iced tea, I feel like a stranger.

On the phone I told his uncle, who's also his manager, how unique BronxSkee's lyrics and beats were.

He laughs. "Oh, you mean Henderson. Yeah, he's really a brain. Even built all the recording equipment he uses. Ain't that something?"

"Something, indeed. Would he be interested in talking to Def Kahn-5 about his music?"

"Well, can't be sure about that. He's into doing quite a lot o' things. I'll get back to ya."

He did—ten minutes later.

Rap artists being represented by a relative is common. Even more common is that they end up stealing money from their own kin. But I don't think that's the case here. These folks have too much family feeling for that.

I balance my napkin, plate full of food and my tumbler. Time for my pitch. "Mr. Burgess, could we talk about Henderson?"

"I ain't Mr. Burgess."

"You're not?"

"No, I'm Mr. Jackson. The other side o' th' family."

"I'm sorry, Mr. Jackson."

A large lady sitting next to me says, "You call him Mr. Jackson, he liable to get a big head. We calls him 'Smelly.'"

Another woman, a skinny one in a dark blue dress says, "Used to call him 'Stinky.' He wore them diapers 'til he was eight. But, he ain't Stinky no more, just Smelly."

This private family joke breaks up everyone in the room, except Uncle Smelly.

I'm on dangerous ground here. "What would you prefer I call you, Mr. Jackson?"

"My Christian name's Joshua. Most call me Josh."

Before I can say his name, the large woman starts fanning the air in front of her. "Josh, Josh, Josh. Oh, honey, don't let that boy be joshin' you. He still be Smelleee!"

Everyone laughs.

Josh is embarrassed. He turns to me. "Maybe we should discuss business away from these 'interrupters.'"

"Who you callin' 'interrupters?' You go fill up Grandma's tumbler before my foot interrupts yo fat be-hind!"

Josh stands and takes an empty glass from a woman on the couch. She's old, but alert. Everyone in the room is sitting in a kind of circle that begins and ends with her.

Josh, through it all, tries to be a gentleman. "Anything I can get any of you?"

Grandma says, "You're a good boy. Ladies, ain't that so?"

His tormenters nod in agreement, then...

> *Yes, Ma'am.*
> *That Josh is a kind boy.*
> *I always smelt that.*

They lose it. Some laugh so hard that food falls off their plates. Josh stops, but doesn't look back. He looks down, exhales slowly and walks outside with as much pride as he has left.

Grandma sets her plate on the coffee table. "Would y'all please allow Miz White and me some time alone?"

As one, they stand, hands filled with plastic plates and cups, and quietly file out.

"And could ya'll find Henderson for me. Tell him to join us. I'd appreciate it."

"Yes, Ma'ams" as they exit.

They're gone. The lack of decibels disorients me—only the sounds of children playing and laughing in the backyard.

I haven't eaten anything, so I take a bite of a rib, which is incredibly juicy and delicious.

Grandma pats a spot on the sofa. "Please, sit next to me so we can chat."

Another quick bite, I wipe my chin and move to the couch. Grandma smiles. She seems delicate and frail, but her eyes reveal strength. They're Henderson's eyes. That's where he must get his intense gaze.

I figure she's in her sixties.

"Excuse me, Ma'am, but where are you from?" She laughs at my question. "If you don't mind me asking."

"Born in Mississippi."

"Oh, that must have been hard."

"Hon, didn't know it was a bad situation 'til I got a bit older. Just thought everyone was treated like that."

"I'm sorry."

"No need to be. Soon as I figured out what's what, got motivated to get out, do things and move forward. Some hard work, and look what I got now." She points at the backyard full of people. "You come from a big family?"

"No, Ma'am, just Dad and my brother, back in Missouri, and Ivy and her father here."

"You're still young."

Here I am, trying to convince this close family into releasing their golden child into the clutches of Bigar Kahn.

Grandma smiles. "May I call you Lily?"

"Of course."

"If you like, you can call me Grandma."

"Yes, ma'am."

"Lovely daughter you have—Ivy—does that name have any family significance?"

"Yes, but it's kind of convoluted."

"I'd love to hear why."

Should I tell her the truth or make something up? Her eyes tell me to tell the truth. "It was my husband's idea. He liked the idea of Ivory soap. He said it was a good USP."

"USP?"

"Yes, Unique Selling Proposition. It's what makes something special versus other things, like 'ninety-nine and forty-four one hundredths percent pure.' That's where Ivory came from—a sales pitch. I call her Ivy, for short."

"'Y' husband sounds like a piece of work."

"Well, we're not exactly living together."

Grandma slowly, sadly shakes her head. "That's a pity. You able to get by on what they pay you at that label?"

Where is this coming from? "I get by. Sometimes it's tight."

"Don't worry, the Lord will look out for you. I can feel it." *Sounds like Grandma has some great connections.* "So you want to sign Henderson to some sort of contract?"

"I want to give him the opportunity to shine."

"He can already do that." Her voice becomes tough. "What are you offering him that he can't get himself?"

So much for the calm before the storm.

"I'm offering Henderson a chance to get his music out to people who'd enjoy it. BronxSkee 's very talented and his sound is like nothing I've ever heard before. Excuse me, but shouldn't I discuss this with Mr. Jackson? He's the manager, isn't he?"

"You talked to him and you talked to me. Now who do you think has final say on this?"

The answer is obvious. "Okay, let's talk."

Grandma says, "You ever been on a farm?"

"Yes. Many times"

"You remember the sound of hogs wallerin' in slop?"

"Sure." *Where is this going?*

"That's what Henderson's music sounds like to me—hogs wallerin' in slop."

"Well, I guess there's a market for that."

That makes us both laugh.

"You think he'll be making lots of money?"

"Can't say f' sure." My Missourah accent returns. "Just know I'll try."

"So what you offerin' m' boy—upfront?" That takes me by surprise. "You got the authorization to make a deal?"

That really takes me by surprise.

"I wouldn't be here, if…"

She leans her face into mine, and speaks distinctly. "'Cause if you're jivin' me, you can just finish y' plate and go home with a full belly and an empty hand. Henderson be too precious to us to let him be taken in by another un-credentialled, fast-talking, no-juice yahoo."

Another? There are other un-credentialled, fast-talking, no juice yahoos, I mean, labels after him? Got to think. I take a taste of the macaroni and cheese.

"Gosh, this food is good."

She settles back into the sofa.

"Grandma, can I explain to you how Def Kahn-5 operates?" She nods. "Most of the artists we sign don't make it. Before the public can decide, there are layers of people that have to okay each detail—managers, lawyers, marketing people, and so on. Then, even if every i is dotted and every t is crossed, even then, you're at the mercy of the owner and Chief Executive Officer of the label—that's Bigar Kahn. You've got to be on his right side when he shoots from the hip. Only then will he put the muscle behind the radio play, marketing and distribution…"

"And the payola?" Grandma is measuring my response.

"That's not my department. I just try to help artists do what they need to do."

"You buy them drugs? Girls? Cars?"

"No, ma'am, I don't." Not actually lying. I don't buy those things—the label does. But I'm starting to feel guilty.

"Not that Henderson would be taken in by such nonsense. It's just I don't want any hidden expenses taken out of his monies."

She knows more than I thought.

"Have you talked to other labels?"

"Just four or five."

FOUR OR FIVE? Is that true or is she just negotiating for a better deal? Either way, I start to sweat.

Henderson walks in, holding hands with toddling Ivy. They seem to be buddies. He has short, dreadlocked hair. Those wild shocks are like comets shooting out in all directions. His dark eyes, behind those thick glasses, seem to compute you into ones and zeros, and then store the results in his head drive. "Wow," he says with surprise, "You're still here."

Is he referring to Grandma or me?

"Thought you'd forgot something," He raises Ivy's hand. "Man, I can't believe it. You've been in here for over ten minutes with Grandma, and you're still in one piece?"

As he grins in disbelief, I look at Grandma, who just shakes her head at him. I can read her mind—"That's supposed to be our genius. Lord, help us."

"Dis!" Ivy lifts a small black box, then pushes the red button on it. A farting sound comes out of it, which makes Ivy giggle. Then a recorded voice says "Pardon me, Your Majesty." She plops down and pushes the button again. A burp, this time, is followed by "Thank you, Mr. President." Ivy giggles so hard that I'm thinking I may have to change her diaper. "Dis, dis, dis!"

Henderson (BronxSkee) says, "I made this computer software program that digitizes speech and music. You can play it back on anything that reads a special file type. Makes music easier to listen to and share. Thought Ivy'd like it. I think she does."

Henderson made this? He also built his own recording equipment. He'd finished all the Columbia University math and science courses by the eleventh grade. He got a perfect score on the SATs and has full-scholarship offers from every Ivy League college. What am I doing here? This boy could find the cure for cancer in his spare time, and I'm trying to get him to sign with DK-5? How can I put him into a world that might destroy him?

I can't. "Grandma, it's been a pleasure meeting you. Henderson, BronxSkee, you're smart, sweet and very talented. Ivy and I thank you. But I'm afraid this won't work out. Sorry if I wasted your time, although I did enjoy the great food and your wonderful family."

Grandma sits back, her hand on her heart, hyperventilating. I grab her hand. "You okay, Grandma?"

"Girl, you gonna be the death o' me. Here I try to negotiate in good faith and you don't even make an offer. You don't even finish your ribs. Girl, you ever finish anything?" *Where did this come from?* "Lily, hon, you want somethin' y' gots t' use ya mind. Y' gots a chance at makin' lots o' money for you and your young 'un and you don't even put up a fight for it? So what kind o' fight y' gonna put up for my Henderson, 'spec'ly when those hyenas and yahoos start after him?"

She's negotiating with me about how to negotiate?

"Grandma, I'm just thinking that a mind like Henderson's might be put to better use doing something else."

"I'll be th' judge o' that! Henderson's got the gift, but he also has t' move out of m' basement. Be a man. Get out in the world. I just want t' make sure the stage is set properly for him. You gonna help me do that?"

"All I can promise is my best."

"Hope this last few minutes wasn't it."

"It really wasn't. What I want is to bring in a special artist. Someone who'll get my boss excited about him and me."

"And more money." Grandma coaches me.

"And more money."

"That's my girl. Come and give Grandma a hug."

I lean over and hug her.

She puts her arms around me. Her strength is surprising. I try to get out of Grandma's grasp, but... "They hurt my baby and I'll come lookin' for someone's ass." She lets go and smiles. "Henderson James, get Lily a whole new plate. Hers is gotten cold."

"Yes, Grandma." He walks into the backyard.

The sound of a burp/fart machine breaks the silence, then "Excusez-moi, Your Ladyship."

Ivy giggles. "Dis, dis, dis!"

With that, I just signed my first artist.

Or So I Thought

"YOU'RE FIRED!"

"But he's a great talent."

"YOU'RE FIRED!"

"Just listen to the demo."

"YOU'RE FIRED!"

"He invented a new way to digitize music."

"Rich, take over. I must not be speaking English today."

Rich leans over me. "YOU'RE FIRED."

"Get out of my face!"

Rich tries to put his fingers in my ears. "I think she needs a hearing aid."

"STOP IT Just listen to the demo, then decide."

Silence. Soon as I got back to DK-5 and told Kahn about BronxSkee, he called Rich into his office and started screaming, flailing his arms while standing under his latest office painting—a crucified naked female with a switchblade stuck in her ribs. The canvas is pushed in and wrinkled by the thrust of the knife.

"Who told you, you could go out and sign an artist? Where did you get the big balls to start slinging dick?"

"You said to bring anyone interesting to your attention."

Rich stands behind me. "Bring, not sign, you stupid cunt, do you know all the legal implications of making a verbal agreement with an artist?"

I turn to him. "No—do you?"

This hits a nerve. He turns red. I think he'd slap me if he wasn't sure I'd strike back, or worse, sue.

"So what do you want me to do?"

"Oh I don't know. How about acting like YOU'RE FIRED!" Kahn spits the tip of his cigar in the trash. One problem, not all of his spit wants to let go. It just hangs there while he keeps hacking and trying to keep the phlegm off his leather jacket. He pulls his hand back to hit me.

Rich jumps in. "That wouldn't be prudent."

"Fuck prudent and fuck her!" Kahn puts his face up to mine. The chewed-up stale cigar smell makes me queasy. "When did you get the balls to do something like this? To me? I gave you a chance to make something of yourself." He spits as he talks. "What were you before this place?"

"Nothing," Rich says.

"And where were you going with your puny life?"

"Nowhere," again Rich.

"And what did I give that you can't get anywhere else?"

"A chance." Rich again.

What is this—a responsive reading? I wipe my face and try to remain calm. "All you have to do is listen to his demo. If I'm wrong about BronxSkee, then let me take him to another label that sees his value. Only, stop bullying me about doing something that's 'good for the lego.'" *There, I've invoked the magic phrase.*

Kahn and Rich trade looks.

"You still gonna fire her?"

"I don't know." Kahn turns away. "She has the beginning of itty bitty buds of big balls. But I'm not sure if she'd know what to do with them, if she ever really grew a pair."

Rich says, "I don't see any great executive potential. Not everyone has to be a CEO. We can always use grunts."

I'm listening to them discuss my future like I'm not there, but I stay silent to see where this game is going.

"If I do keep her," Kahn says, "I can't give her that raise I wanted to with a clear conscience."

What raise?

Rich says, "Hell, she's lucky she isn't crawling on the curb with a boot stuck up her ass."

"Okay, okay, message sent. I thought we were in the talent business, so I went out on my own initiative and found a special artist. You can accept or pass on BronxSkee, but don't blame me for trying to help."

Rich smirks. "Help?"

"How do I grow big (I point to my privates) you-know-what's, if I get blamed for trying? You know how loyal I am. I've always done what's good for this label."

Why am I'm begging? It should be obvious how valuable I've become. Yet, here I am, having to defend myself for doing something that could reap a high return.

Kahn raises the palm of his hand at me. "I'm still upset, but I'll take my 'you're fired' back if I get another attitude."

"What attitude is that?"

"Don't get me wrongfully, we can still mint our fences."

There's something else going on here—not sure what.

Kahn leans forward. Now I can smell his lunch. "Lily, Lily, Lily, you have so much to offer, so much potency. Please, feel free to talk to me, but to ME FIRST. My door policy has always been open."

I look. The door is locked and Rich is the doorjamb.

"What do I tell BronxSkee?"

Kahn points. "Give the demo to Rich. He's the lawyer, and lawyers have to clean up legal messes—a mess you made. That's why, this is your last chance. I hope you understand what I mean, because you never have a first impression to make a last chance."

I'm beginning to understand what he means.

With that, Rich unlocks the door. I hand him BronxSkee's materials. He throws it onto a chair like week-old garbage.

#2Girl is standing outside the door, smiling. She knows what it's like to be in a DK-5 sandwich, and she's happy that this time I was the lunchmeat.

That afternoon, Beany delivers an interoffice envelope from Kahn. I open it carefully. Inside is a gift-membership to a health club. There's a yellow sticky attached. It reads: "Get back into shape. I depend on your strength."

So let me get this straight—I'm not going to get a raise, because I went out and brought in an artist. Now I'm given a health club membership to get in shape, because Kahn depends on my strength. After all the money I've saved the label and after all the times I've been put into dangerous situations, I'm still only one step away from the street.

I've got to find another job. But where? People who work at DK-5 can't even get an interview at other labels. You have to be fired and totally healed from your injuries before any of them will even talk to you. Code of honor. They refuse to steal another company's property.

I could start at the bottom in another industry, but that would be horrible, and not what I need now.

All my life I've done what was needed at the moment. And at this moment, I realize my fate is tied to Def Kahn-5. The reason is, I still have a chance to make enough money to take care of Ivy and myself.

Sounds crazy when I talk about it now, but back then, it made sickening sense.

A week later, I find out Kahn heard the demo and took over BronxSkee's career. He's gotten Uncle Smelly all excited with the scent of money. He's told Grandma that I'm still watching over Henderson's interests. I wouldn't have known this if I hadn't called Grandma to see how she was doing.

BronxSkee isn't a top seller, but he has a loyal following. Even without a big marketing push or radio play, the sheer genius of his songs and word of mouth, has people asking record stores for his album. He's made enough money to move out of his Grandma's basement into a loft in Manhattan. Kahn gets credit for discovering him. And when I have time, I get to swim laps and take steam. But no raise this year, due to what Kahn refers to as my "indesecretion."

16

Sweet and Sour

"I NEEDED THAT."

"Sure sounded like you did."

I'm in bed with Jiggity Man. We've just—you know.

He's holding me, and repeating, "My, my, my."

How'd we get to this point?

Simple—I called him to see why he wasn't returning my phone calls. He apologized, asked me not to take it personally and then said something about a new business venture that was taking up all his time. Jiggity said he couldn't discuss it. But we could talk about something else at this Japanese restaurant.

At dinner, he didn't mention his masters once. He kept asking about the label's sales and financials. Trying to change the subject, I said that things were as crazy as ever. He didn't seem to be satisfied with that.

After dinner, Jiggity said that what I needed was some fun, to let go. We went to a club, danced, drank a little, laughed a lot, and headed back to my place.

This time things worked out. I was prepared. Still, I went a bit shy on the pharmacist, mumbling something about birth control thingies. Next to me was this girl, she looked fourteen, just out-loud asking for all sorts of sexual stuff, like she was ordering fries. Don't know why it's such a big deal to me—guess it's just my upbringing. That, and the fact I'm still technically, if not emotionally, married.

But here I lie—with this sexy guy.

"What's going on in that head o' yours?"

"Just thinking."

"What about?"

I lift myself up on one elbow. "Why do you think Kahn keeps me around?"

"Whoa, Lily, you been thinking about that guy when you're here with me?"

"No, I didn't mean it that way. I was just wondering why he hired me in the first place. I'm not exactly street or even a street wannabe. According to Kahn, I'm there, because I'm professional. But when I do act professionally, he treats me like some hootchie."

"That's just him." He starts caressing my leg. "You're the only business-type there. Would you call Kahn or Rich businessmen? No, they're players and pimps."

"What about Mae?"

"She's just the company ho."

"That was offensive."

"Don't mean no disrespect, just meant they need you lot more 'n her."

"Yeah, right."

"It's true. They need your skills to make things happen. You ain't the one conning artists and skimming money. You're the one who keeps DK-5 in business."

"Like the place would fall apart if I left."

J Man strokes his fingers back and forth across my stomach. "Kahn depends on you to get it done."

"Get what done?"

"Everyone else is there for the free tickets or to rub elbows or to rob the place blind. You're there to make the business work."

"I am?"

"You am." He touches my breast and gives me a boyish look. I'm melting. "Hear Kahn's planning to redecorate."

"Construction starts next week. It'll be a nightmare."

He kisses my breasts. "You know the name of the company doing the work?"

"ArKan, or something." I can hardly breathe. "Why?"

Jiggity kisses me, then speaks near my cheek. "Bet you could find out something about them (kiss) who they are. Probably in Kahn's office (kiss). If someone sees ya, (kiss) tell 'em Kahn told you to find something." (kiss).

"Something?"

"He's always tellin' people to do stuff, then forgetting he told them." He pulls me to him. "Just make sure you have an artist's name or song title to cover yourself."

I want more of what he's doing and less of what he's saying. "Jiggity, I could get in real trouble."

He kisses the inside of my thigh. "Again?"

The look in his eye makes me freeze.

"And again?" He's smiling like he knows I can't resist.

I'd like to "and again," but something's changed in the atmosphere. Maybe it's the feeling that he's playing me to get even with Kahn. I pull my blanket up to my chin. He tries to pull it down. I resist. He looks into my eyes. I stare at him. At first he's angry, then he gets up, stretches and heads for the bathroom.

Why is my baloney meter registering in the red zone? Because he's been asking one question too many, that's why. Something's up. Could he be sleeping with me to get information? Why? And what about his masters? He's totally stopped even talking about them.

I'm getting that terrible tummy feeling.

That's it—no more thinking for tonight. If he's using me, well I'll just use him back.

Sprawled out in my bed, relaxed, every muscle loose. Every thought gone. I have never felt this clear or at ease. I use my hand to wiggle my thigh. After all my workouts at the gym, my tight muscles just want to be flubbery. Fine with me. My breathing is light and effortless. No tension spots on this girl. Not tonight. That makes me laugh. Even laughter feels good. I'm hungry. So I head to the fridge and open the door. The cold sparkles across the front of my body. I can't remember the last time I actually walked around my house naked.

A lonely plum on the bottom shelf calls to me. I wash it and enjoy the cool water. I can taste the plum with my eyes. The crunch of deep purple skin, then the tart, squishy squirt of juice makes me giggle.

Looking around my kitchen, I no longer see what needs to be done. I see what's there—the chalky tiles, the cracks in the wall, the Buick-like bends and folds of the not so white stove and the Wonder Bread crumbs welded to the chrome Sunbeam toaster. Even the sink's permanent stain looks like a piece of art.

Extraordinary.

Extra—ordinary.

There's a knock on the front door. *At eleven-thirty at night?*

What the heck is that? Ignore it. But I can't ignore that I'm naked. So I cover myself with my arms. My heart speeds up. I can't answer the door like this.

The bell rings.

Have to answer it before Ivy wakes up.

"Be there in a minute!"

Rush to the bedroom, throw on my robe.

The doorbell rings again.

Tying my robe on the way to the door. "Don't ring the bell? I have a sleeping child."

Silence.

"Who are you?"

Silence.

Looking through the peephole, I can make out a man in a parrot green suit. He uses a handkerchief to rub the inside of his wide-brimmed, green, feathered fedora.

"What do you want?"

"Did I wake you, child?"

"Yes."

"Hee, hee, I didn't really now, did I," he grins, revealing a row of gold-tipped teeth.

He reminds me of the pimp in the Bus Terminal, but with a priest's collar that chokes into is his beefy neck.

A priest's collar?

I'm glad Jiggity is within shouting distance.

"It's late. What do you want?"

"I see you're someone who likes to get to the point—an admiral quality in a person."

Admiral quality? Those familiar words start my stomach up. "Get to the point."

"Well then, I shall. We need to discuss Astronomous."

Astronomous? Astronomous. Who is…That's Hank! Oh, no. What's going on? Is he dead? Why is this person…

I unlock the door and open it.

His cologne stings my eyes.

"He misses you and his bless-ed child. Astronomous is ready to return to your lives."

"Wait a minute. Aren't you…?"

"I am that I am—The Right Reverend Sky Fogg, PC."

PC. This is the guy who stole my husband, my life and my hope. I don't know whether to kill him or thank him. What I do know is that my grumpy old tummy has risen from the dead.

"The reason for my visit is that Astronomous is at a crucial stage in his spiritual journey. Epiphany is imminent. That's a rare accomplishment at our church. His soul is rich. Now cometh the tithing. Your husband needeth to invest more than his precious soul. He now hast to invest in the Realization Trinity."

"Would you get to the point?"

"I can see you're a skeptic. Let-eth me continue. In our faith we believe that to become successful, attain true Realization, you must reach-eth Epiphany. That is, the state of perfect union between Man, God and Wealth. Astronomous is now about to reacheth-ed the last step in his Man-God union. That taketh seed money. The Tree of Wealth springeth from sowing sheckles in holy soil. Without these tithes, there are no saplings—no growth to the heavens, ergo no Epiphany."

"Are you asking me for money? For Hank?"

"Child, thinketh, all the watering, caring and fertilizering will not maketh that tree grow. Without that seed money you're just tending dirt. Only with that seed can the spiritual become tangible. And best of all, that investment will bring a new, better man into your life."

Just then, Jiggity walks in—in his underwear. Waves of hot embarrassment flush up to my face.

Fogg looks at him. "Or maybe not. The results are what you want them to be."

J Man stares at the Reverend. "Duane?"

Sky Fogg starts blinking quickly.

"Duane Duran? You ol' ghost, how y' doin'? Lily, you know this guy? He's Duane Duran, or should I be calling you

Foggmaster-D."

Foggmaster-D? Isn't that one of the old school guys, who practically invented Rap?

Reverend Foggmaster-D grins widely. "Brother Jiggity Man, my friend, how hast thou been? He looks at me, catches himself and turns to Jiggity. "Looks like the Lord hath been treating you well, son?"

"Oh yeah. Heard y' went into religion. How's it go, bro?"

Why is J Man going street all of a sudden?

"Lily, when I was growing up in Bed-Sty. this DJ was THE role model." He starts to Rap, "Tokin' jokin' smokin' them bitches. Snatchin' matchin' scrathin' them itches…" J Man starts to beatbox.

The Rev revs up the rhyme, "Get in the way, you be lyin' face up down in them ditches."

They laugh and clasp hands like it was 1977.

J Man sighs. "Back-in-the-day, you was the greatest."

Fogg, in the fog of his glory days, rhymes, "I'm the greatest ever was. I'll always be the greatest, 'cause…"

J Man jumps in, "…'cause you the man. The man wid de plan. Gots t' han'—dit to da man that can. Gotta hand it to the man that be that Foggmaster, Foggmaster, Foggmaster-D, that Foggmaster-D…Word!"

"Enough already! There's a child sleeping in there."

I was feeling so good just a few minutes ago.

They apologize, but continue whispering their nostalgia.

"Heard you'd gone to God after that time upstate."

"Yeah, well we all gots t' grow up some time. Crime ain'teth the way o' th' Lord."

"I hears ya, bro, I hears ya."

Oh, please. "This friend of yours is trying to shake me down for money. He wants me to pay to get Hank back."

J Man looks at Reverend Foggmaster. "That so?"

"Gots to get her husband," To me. "Astronomous," To Jiggity, "on the path to Epiphany."

J Man looks at me. "Something wrong with that?"

"Something wrong? I'll say there is. I don't want Hank back! You understand that? And, I'm not going to shell out sheckles so

Hank can playact at spiritually. It's time to stick-eth a fork-eth in him, 'cause I'm doneth with him. He's on his own. You get my subtext here? So get dressed and get out. I'm sick of you too."

Jiggity puts his hand gently on my shoulder, but I pull away, walk to the bathroom, slam the door and lock it. My grumpy tummy and I try to relax on the toilet.

I won't cry. I won't cry. I won't cry. Then, I hear them.

Jiggity to Foggmaster-D: "How much you lookin' for?"

I shout from the bathroom: "Doesn't matter. He's not getting anything."

Fogg to Jiggity: "Ten bills."

Jiggity: "Ten? Whoa, lighten up, bro. That be steep."

Fogg: "Yeah, well a churchman's gots ta eat, too."

Jiggity: "I hears ya."

Fogg: "Anyway, m' ministries ain't takin' it all. The cracker an' his bitch in there be gettin' a taste of th' investment. That's why we calls it our Gethsemane Mutual Fund. We jus' aks you to pay and pray, and we be all fo'given our transactions."

Jiggity: "Sounds propa to me."

I yell through the door: "Talk all the hood lingo you want, I'm not paying a penny."

Flush.

Jiggity: "So what's the bottom line dealy-yo?"

I holler over the toilet flushing: "Are you two deaf out there?! No money!"

Fogg: "Could get by with a little less, since you blood and all. But this be an investment in the Lord. Y' sees, in Proverbs 23:4 it sayeth 'Don't be wearin' yo'self out to get rich.' So that's exactly what I be doin'—not wearin' myself out—in Jesus's name."

Jiggity: "You always been a man a God," J Man places his hand on the padded shoulders of the Reverend's shiny green suit. "Sounds tight."

Walking out of the bathroom, I see their tableau. "Okay, enough. You two can stop negotiating, because I can't afford to have him come back. In fact, he owes me twenty-five hundred dollars for his boxed-up herbal dreams."

"Woo-wee! Don' want to even think 'bout them herbs! J Man, this Astronomous brings this weed into the Church with him. But it ain't for smokin'. He be telling us it's gonna clean us up inside and purify our souls, and shit. And we believe him. So everybody be taking some o' that and then, ka-boom. Everybody be on the toilet, or some such, foulin' up the rec'try, the kitchen, th' water fountains, even the serenity pond got polluted. Them poor goldfish. Take us two weeks to wipe all that desecration up. I can smell it—like it was yesterday. Lemme tell you, that shit be dangerous. And that Astro-cracker be a faith-tester."

My turn: "And you want me to pay you to get that back into my life? Would you?"

The Reverend Sky Fogg PC thinks. He straightens his lapels, clears his throat, and speaketh: "My child, I see-eth that thou dost have a point. Therefore, let us reacheth an accommodation. How 'bout I asketh for a little less, so you can get-eth a lot more?"

"More?"

"Much more—be riddeth of him. Won't cost much."

"How do you mean 'riddeth of him?'"

"The ancient Ante-Semites, who it has been proven, were of African origin, used stoning to punish transgressors."

"Stoning? Hank?"

"An allegorical phrase, child. Transgression may not have changed, but the 'stones' has become mo' sophisticated."

He's serious. "Transgression? Are you crazy? He's still a human being. All he's done wrong is abandon his family."

"So who hasn't?" Fogg says with a straight face. "But that ain't the trans he's gressed. That guy, that guy, everything he toucheth turns to shit—in both of its meanings. So I'm just suggesting, mind you, just for the good of us all, maybe he should be given another chance—this time in heaven."

"No, no, no, no, you won't harm him in any way, you hear me? I find out you've done anything to Hank and I'll make sure you get to visit God's wrath in person!"

J Man smiles. I think in some strange way he's proud of me— my toughness. If he only knew how weak I feel at this moment. I'm sinking into my own soft tissue. No bones, no muscle—just attitude and bluster holding me up. *Think...*

I start pacing.

"Okay...Okay, child, I shall honor-eth your wishes. Only,

even without the money he owe-eth the church, he's gonna have-eth to come home spiritually unfulfilled, without that final Epiphany—without heaven's grace."

I stop pacing. "That should be his only worry." *Got it.* "Stay here." I go to my bedroom and search through the closet. In a shoebox is an envelope—the one Beany handed me in the men's room on my first day at DK-5—there's sixteen hundred dollars of Play Money in it. I look at the bills. There are a lot of nice things I could buy Ivy with this money. But there's a bigger picture here—those pornographic biblical photos of Hank, half-naked with a blow-up Bathsheba and his pose as Ehud on the toilet—I need to keep Hank (and the Fogg in my living room) away from us forever.

"Here." I hold the bills to Foggmaster-D's face. "You can have this, but I don't want anything to happen to Hank, and I don't want to see him anywhere near this place. He's yours. Now promise, or be damned to eternal perdition everlasting." When my mother said those words to me, I never thought that I'd use them to save myself.

He gulps.

Is he sweating the eternal damnation or estimating the wad of cash?

"As God is m' shepherd." He proclaims, "I shall see no harm comes upon the head of Astronomous."

He reaches for the wad of bills.

I pull it back. "Hank."

"Pardon?"

"I'm paying. His name is Hank."

"Uh, well then, Hank. I just hopeth I haven't giveneth his soul the curse of Balaam."

I hand him the money. "You should read up on your Bible. Balaam was the guy who rode his ass out of town."

"That so." He's not listening—just stuffing money inside his coat pocket.

"One thing: In case you don't keep up your end of this bargain, remember I know all about the bootlegs."

That knocks the wind out of the Rev.

J Man stares at me. That caught him by surprise too.

The Reverend becomes holier-than-thou. "Lost child, you do

knoweth that stoning is also the punishment for both snitches and adulterers."

He straightens his green silk lapels and piously dips and weaves his way to the door. He opens it, turns with a flourish, puts his hat on and smoothes the brim. "Thus ends the homily of Astro..., uh, Hank. Remember, child, ye who opens thine eyes and mouth too much will have many curses visiteth on thee. Proverbs 28:27—let that be a warning to ye, Jezebel."

He's out the door and down the hall.

"What did you just call me?" I run to the door. "What did you call me?"

He walks out of sight.

One last yell into the empty hallway. "Bootlegger!"

No response, just the distant click and slide of his Gucci's on the tiles.

As I step back into my apartment, J Man tries to hug me.

I pull away. "What is it with you guys? All you do is crotch-grab, do the handshake crap, and treat women like property. Don't you have any sensitivity to what anyone else is feeling?"

"Whoa, hon, you're asking too many questions. Things are the way things are. Anyway, you talk like we didn't just make love. Let me tell you, you're something special."

"Special? Me? Oh, I'm getting all goose-pimply all over! DON'T TRY THAT PIMP JIVE ON ME."

"Lily, I don't think like that..."

"Oh, you don't? What did I just witness with you and the Reverend Moneygrubber? He's been putting the squeeze on me for almost a year, holding onto his big fat Astronomous, waiting for a payday. Well, he got it. Now, I don't owe anyone anything. Not him, not Hank, not you."

He shakes his head. "You just don't get it, do ya?"

"Get it? What's to get, a bunch of pimps feeding off people? It's beyond sick. It's always, 'Hey, jus' business—nothin' personal.' I do the heavy lifting while the pimpmasters get rich. I'm tired of being treated like something you guys own. Well, you and your pimp-crew aren't going to use me anymore. It's my time. It's my turn. I'm going to be a player, earn the big bucks too. KnowwhatImean?"

Jiggity stares at me and smiles.

"What?" I say.

"May be wrong, but I think you're getting 'it.'" *Are we having the same conversation?* "Problem I see is that you still think that if you work hard, act smart and keep-it-real, someone's gonna reward you. Ain't gonna happen, girl, never no-how, no way. You got to grab what you can, 'cause if you don't, there won't be nothin' left. It's like them lions. The women do the hunting and the men gets the eats. If you don't put up a fight, you gonna end up unfed."

I sit down on the frayed couch and put my face in my hands. "Is that all there is to this? Greed, need and feed?"

J Man puts his arm around me. All I can think of is my father waiting for me to collect his money, Hank waiting for me to pay his debts, and Kahn barely paying me to do what's good for the lego. All the lions sitting around, waiting for me to bring in the kill. What does that make me—a hungry lioness with a cub to feed? I'm too exhausted to hunt and too hungry not to. Who am I kidding? I'm not a lioness. I'm a hamster on a treadmill.

"You okay?"

I look at him. His eyes are so kind. This is probably the only real moment we've ever had. I feel so exposed.

"What's your real name?"

He swallows hard. "Duane."

"Duane?"

"Yeah, Duane DuPree."

"Is everyone in this business named Duane?"

He laughs. "Sounds like that sometimes, don't it?"

"I'm so sick of people."

"Lily, things are gonna work out. It may take some time, but I promise all your hard work is going to pay off."

"You just told me it wouldn't. Get your advice straight. Why do I even listen to...Look what happened to you, one of the biggest stars in the business, and you end up sitting in the reception area, hoping to get noticed."

"If you're trying to hurt me, you're doing a great job. But I know of some things out there." He kisses my neck. "Big things." He runs his hands down my back. "Happening right now." He pulls me to him. "That'll make a big difference." He puts his hand in my robe. "I promise you there'll be better times." He squeezes my left breast. "One small thing. What did you mean by the bootlegs?"

I'm burning up with lust. "Tell you later. Let's go back in the bedroom."

"Mommy!"

Oh, no!

"Mom-my, I have bad dream." There, in the doorway, stands my sleepy Ivy. She rubs her eyes. "I'm scared."

I push J Man's hand away. "Ivy, sweetie, you should be in bed."

"That Daddy?"

"No, honey, it's a friend of Mommy's."

She accepts the explanation. "I have bad dream."

"Poor baby, let's go to bed."

But she's in a child-mare—part sleepwalking, part awake. You can talk, but you can't touch, because it might frighten her. She walks in wide circles around J Man and me.

"You have bad dream too, Mommy?"

"Uh, kind of."

"Tell me."

My Bad Dream

In my office sit two very obese Rappers, who are feuding. They're from the same neighborhood. Once they were best friends. Now, with success, they have grown apart.

Their opposing crews have had some deadly encounters.

The older one is Phat Dez, short for Phatalistic Deztroyer. The younger one is E-Norm, short for Elliot-Normous-Ness

I'm mediating their feud in my tiny office. Clete sits outside the door. He won't intervene until there's gunfire.

"Phat Dez, why don't you start? Tell E-Norm what's been bothering you?"

For a moment it's so silent, you can hear their lungs straining to take in breath. I better hurry. In ten seconds all the oxygen in my office will be used up. All they'll find are two heaps of melted ego and an asphyxiated small blond woman with a "what have I gotten myself into?" look on her face.

"Come on Phat Des, we're here to work things out. You won the coin toss, so you get to tell your side of it first."

"Well, E-Norm be saying lotta shit 'bout Phat Dez. He become a real playa-hater."

"What shit you talkin', bro?" E-Norm counters. "I ain't said nothin' 'bout you. T' other way 'round."

For someone over four hundred pounds E-Norm has a surprisingly high-pitched voice.

"Y' know damn well what th' fuck I'm sayin'. I be hearin' y' dissed me in that Hustler Mag profile."

"You even read that? 'Cause, I ain't said shit 'bout you. I been mis-quoted. That a fact."

"I ain't read th' muthafuckin' magazine. That shit be for sinners and whack-offs. Ain't no lita-ture in that pussy mag."

Now we know that Phatalistic Destroyer is into literature.

"See?" says E-Norm like he's dealing with an idiot. "See what dis be 'bout? You are one igor-ant un-read nigga."

"Oh, no I'm not. Fuckin' smart's what I am."

Trying to moderate. "Excuse me, but it's still Phat Dez's turn to talk. E, I promise you will get your turn."

E leans back, folding his huge arms across his stomach. The chair creaks, crying for mercy.

"Phat Dez, tell E-Norm what you'd like him to do."

"Wan' th' muthafucka t' stop dissing me in his rhymes."

I write that down. "Okay, anything else?"

"Wan' him t' stop sayin' things 'bout m' crew."

I write that down. "Okay."

"An' I wan' him t' stop seeing m' mom."

"Excuse me?" I look up.

"Stop seein' m' mom."

I turn to E-Norm. "Are you seeing his mom?"

He grins, embarrassed and bobs his head. "Y' know, can't control y' feelins. Phat's mom, Dereatha, an' I gots this ee-motion for each otha."

"You stay 'ways from my mom, or I'm gonna fuck yo' mom," Phat Dez is nearly in tears.

"Y' prob'ly would." E is sad.

"Fuck her damned good too."

"She passed on, y' know. Y' might needs y' a shovel."
With that, the conversation just died.

I'm stuck here with these overfed babies, trying to resolve a conflict that seems to get deeper and uglier as we go along. "Look, I'm not here to judge anyone. Mr. Kahn asked me to help you two come to some sort of understanding. Make peace. The way things are headed, one of you is going to get killed, and the other will go to jail for murder. Either way, no matter who does what, both of you lose, unless we find a middle ground. So I'd appreciate it if you would just help me help you discover a win-win solution."

"Tell E t' stop foolin' with m' mom, and I'll chill wid dat win-win shit."

"Tell Phat that I ain't forcin' his mom t' do anythin'. She be older than him…"

"Now that be a smart thing t' say. She be older 'n me. Now, that be an educated statement."

I try to diffuse the situation, "Remember, we agreed to no negative comments about each other."

E continues like I'm not here. "Yo' Mama she be choosin' a real man. Y' bests ree-specs me. I might be yo muthafuckin' Dad some day."

With that, Phat works his way to a standing position, catches his breath and then takes a swing at E-Norm. He misses and bangs his thigh against the blacktop that's my desktop. It moves slightly. He rubs his leg. "Ow, that fuckin' desk be hard."

"Serve you right, tryin' t' hit E like that."

"Soon as th' pain stops, I gonna whoop yo' muthafuckin' ass, 'cause that what you are, a muthafuckin' muthafucka'."

This is the first time I've ever heard the MF word used literally.

How do I stop this argument without being crushed? "E, Dez, I think there's a solution here."

I point to their chairs. They look at each other and sit. I perch on the desktop, because there's no place to stand. "I thought you were from the same hood. You grew up together, am I right?"

They nod.

"Then how did it ever get to this? How did you start being so angry at each other?"

No response.

"I think I know. It's not you, two. It's the people around you, who caused this. They need you to be feuding."

Phat and E look at each other.

"And why do they need you to be feuding? Because they want to keep you separate. That way they can keep you from being suspicious of them. Ask yourself, 'Can I really trust any of my crew like I can my homeboy?' If you answer truthfully, you'll realize that they're the ones you should be upset with. They're playing you off against each other—dissin' that and dattin' this. You two aren't enemies. You're brothers."

Am I getting through to these guys?

"I ain't got no quarr'l wichoo, Phat Dez. We growed up t'gether. We done our wilding together. We even love th' same woman. You m' brotha, bro. My peeps f' keeps."

They get up and try to hug, but my office is so small that all they do is manage to move my furniture around—a little at first. Then, they decide to really hug. My office is moved, filled with emotion and sliding furniture, by the force of over a half-ton of weeping Rappers, determined to make up.

Is this how Cuddles Counseling is supposed to work?

I step back toward my little window and then signal, "Go ahead. Make friends."

It will take a forklift to put my desk back onto its concrete pedestal. My breakfront is leaning. Even some of my pictures and gold records will have to be reframed. But they're back together. The feud has ended. They only refer to the other's good qualities, like beating hos and f-ing up playa-haters. There's even talk of them doing a tour. They want to call it "The Phat-E Phat-E Two by Four Across America."

The title needs a little work.

I was hoping this was a bad dream, but no, it has become another thing I do at DK-5.

A Label Warning

"You don't have to rip my head off. All I'm saying is that I suspect someone is bootlegging our catalog."

"Who else have you been sharing this suspicion with?"

"No one."

"You know your problem? You're too honest to be trusted. That's my fault." Kahn is breathing hard.

His office. Door's closed. I'm trying to warn him about the bootlegs. "But if you let it go, someone's making money off our artist's work without paying for it."

"And what are you suggesting?"

"Maybe we should take legal action."

"Just what we need—negative publicity, fucking idiot. People on the street saying we can't keep our shit in line. My opinion? It's time for you to move out of this job."

"Are you firing me again?"

"Not yet. Know why? Without you, where would we be—up the toilet without a puddle."

This is confusing. Anytime someone says, "bootleg," Kahn explodes with rage. He wants the bootleggers found and annihilated. Now he avoids talking about it.

He just sits there for a long time, rolling an unlit cigar in his mouth. I'm getting very uncomfortable, waiting for what's next.

Kahn pats the space next to him, inviting me to sit on the couch. I take my time, because he's going to explode.

Instead, he takes my hand and speaks quietly, "You don't know much about me, do you?"

"Just from what you scream out at our therapy sessions."

"Did you know that I started out arranging club parties? I came from a very influent family, and yet, I was in the street, turning minor acts into major events. Then I'd make sure there was an audience to listen. Not much money in those days, just the joy of making it happen. Later, I found myself working with this guy, who was always worried about things. Not me—I just did whatever it took to move forward. So you know what happened to my worrying partner? Sad story. He was perturbed about the Fire Marshall wanting to close the club because there were over a thousand people inside. The limit was three hundred. Outside, I was negotiating with the Fire Marshall, keeping him busy, while the show went on. My partner, his name was Luther, started screaming inside that it was too crowded. Instead of letting things run their course, he got panicky. Then so did the people. While I'm joking with the fireman outside, the audience inside is seriously trying to get out the locked exits. Poor Luther tried to stop them." A pause, as Kahn remembers. "They crushed him into little pieces of Luther. And what is the lesson of this?— That if you get panicky at the wrong time and yell 'Fire Exit,' you'll only get crushed. Are you getting my messaging here?"

I nod.

"I'm hoping so." He walks to his window (*uh-oh*) and looks to the horizon. "There are many ways to get crushed—even to death."

He's threatening me without threatening me. This is the first time I've ever realized that he's not so crazy. He's very clear about what he's doing. In fact, I think he's up to his neck in this bootlegging operation. Why? Doesn't matter. I have to back away—now.

"I'd like to give up my title as Mistress of the Masters and try something new. It's time, don't you think?"

He turns and smiles. "I knew you'd come up with a good idea. That's why you're so potentate."

"We all want to do what's good for the lego."

He hands me a cigar. "Well, we all know you've got what it takes. We've just got to find a place to take it, right?"

"Right?"

17

Go West

Mommy, you get scared?
Yes, sometimes, honey.
When I scared...
What do you do?
...Pee-pee my pants.
Oh my.
It helps.

THAT'S THE BEST ADVICE I've gotten since I started working at DK-5.

Kahn walks into my office and volunteers my big balls to Los Angeles. A West Coast Rapper is looking for a new label because "His current label is spending shit on marketing and promotion. That's why his record sales you could flush down a toilet. He's desperate, but even so, this could take negotiating skills. You may have to sling some dick."

"Excuse me, but..." is all I can get out before Kahn raises his hand. He lights up a Havana, in my office, despite the "Thank You For Not Smoking" sign on my wall.

He puffs. "Pull this off, and I'll double your salary."

Double? I go from almost fired to fifty thousand in one round trip to LA?

Then he throws four thousand dollars cash on my desk.

"What's this?"

"Money."

"For?"

"Unforeseeable expenses."

"Shouldn't I sign a petty cash voucher?"

"No receipts. The only proof of purchase I need is the artist, right here, I mean, right there in my office."

"What if he doesn't want to come?"

"Then you're fucked. Lily, remember, 'whatever it takes.' And I mean 'whatever.'"

That should have been my first indication that something was off. This is Mae's job, not mine.

Another sign I missed was when #2 Girl and Rich walked into my office and wished me a bon voyage. *Since when do they care? And in French?*

At eleven a.m. I arrive in LA, and get my rental car, a subcompact. Very cute. I haven't traveled in a long time, so this could be fun. Fun, until the woman at the desk gives me a hard time about paying in cash instead of with a credit card.

We argue. She makes a call. I win.

After driving for an hour, I realize the woman gave me the wrong directions. I got a Geo Metro and she got even.

Luckily, I get a call on my cell from the artist's manager, with the right route. The trip there is long and slow. There's no way to miss my exit, because the traffic moves slower than a sleepwalker.

Three hours later, my little car throws up a bunch of dust and pebbles in front of a desert warehouse.

Four guys wearing head bandanas, packing Uzis and suspicious looks, eye me as I approach.

"Hi, I'm Lily White from Def Kahn-5."

They look at each other. One spits on the sand. The warehouse door scrapes open. Out flops a very stoned guy with a pistol tucked into his jeans. "I'm (The Artist's Name) manager, (Manager's Name)."

I extend my hand. He doesn't.

He yells toward the warehouse. "Yo, she be here, man."

Out walks a tall, skinny guy, dressed more for Alaska than the California desert. Even though he's wearing an Oakland Raiders down coat with a fur-trimmed hood and loose-laced yellow Timberlands, he's not sweating.

But I am.

Manager introduces us. The Artist gives me a special Rap handshake and then asks me to step inside. "That way no one be checkin' us from the road." He looks worried. His eyes check every movement out to the horizon. Each gust of dry air makes him jump.

Inside, they sit on two broken crates, while I stand next to a rusty oil drum. I start my sales-pitch to get him to sign with DK-5. *Are they listening?* They haven't looked at me once since we walked inside. "So do we have a deal?"

Neither Artist nor Manager answers. *Are they convinced? Are they backing out?*

Artist stands. "When we leavin'?"

"After I check into my hotel, I'll call Kahn and…"

Manager stands. "Nuh-uh. You want 'im, we fly—now."

"Now?"

"That's the dealyo."

I agree. Manager tells me to drive the Range Rover and they'll follow in my rental car. Like an idiot, I agree.

The six guys cram into the Geo. Artist and Manager crouch in the backseat. Two of the others sit on top of them. The door closes. Two more, with Uzis, sit in the passenger seat. Why, with all the room in the Range Rover, do these guys want to squash into a sub-compact? Its tiny engine strains, fights to move. Poor little car, built to hold four small people without weaponry, rides two inches off the ground.

Manager yells. "Don't stop for nothin', not even cops."

"Is there some sort of problem here?"

He says something to his car-mates that sounds like, "Prob'ly knows…Rover…Shoot her, not…"He yells to me, "Don't use the fuckin' car phone!"

Our little caravan takes a slow route to LAX.

With all those guns they'll set off the airport metal detectors before we get there.

Why are these guys so afraid, and of whom? What has Kahn done to me?

"Double my salary" is what keeps my foot pressed to the gas pedal.

Three hours later, we arrive at the airport and then split up. A couple this way, others that way, and me standing in line to book flights for Artist, Manager and myself. Since we just missed the six-ten p.m., the next available flight is the red-eye, leaving at eleven twenty-five p.m. with a changeover in Chicago. We'll arrive in New York at nine a.m.

Although we're all booked on the same plane, they want to meet at the gate from different directions.

It's too early to check in, so I sit down in the waiting area, and put my feet up on my luggage. Maybe a short nap would help. I try to relax, until I see two of the guys with their hidden Uzis standing by an airport newsstand scanning the waiting area. If I were security, I'd pick them out instantly as non-frequent fliers. How did they get their weapons past the metal-detector? I've been to enough concerts to know that getting guns past security seems to be the norm—but never at an airport.

I can't afford to get caught up in something like this. Why is Kahn going through all this trouble to bring in a minimally-talented guy whose albums barely break even? Then, there are the rumors that the head of his label has been implicated in some murders. *Something's way off here.*

I decide to call J Man for help. All I get is his voicemail, but I leave a message.

> **BEEP!** *Jiggity, this is Lily. Hope you're well. I'm calling because I'm in this situation in LA. Can't go into detail, but something's going on with this Rapper out here moving to DK-5. Not sure about what's up. I'm scared and not sure what to do next. Please, call me back on my cell. I really need to ask your...* **BEEP!**

His machine is set for thirty seconds.

I call home to check on Ivy. Ola answers. "Ya, ya, dat girl eez fine and snorink avay, oh my tired girl. Yoo stayink avay froming her too lonk. Not goot mozer yoo are."

Add feeling guilty to being scared.

Now what? There's still three hours left before we board.

I call Kahn to tell him when we'll land. He wants to make sure that no one knows what we're doing. Then he says that at La Guardia, a driver at the luggage pick-up area will hold up a sign with a false name on it. Kahn will tell me the name when he makes one up.

THE RENTAL CAR! I FORGOT TO RETURN IT! My Uzi-packing partners don't remember where they left it. I look around the drop-off area. The policeman at the curb tells me that if it's been there over twenty minutes, it's probably been towed. And it's rented in my name.

All the clocks seem to have stopped. My stomach starts up. Thank goodness, because it gives me something to do—buy some Tums. I chew them slowly.

My dad once told me *You can't kill time. It kills you.* Now, I know what he means.

Passing a magazine stand, I see "Billboard." The headline reads "Is BUG About to Devour Def Kahn-5?" *What?* Kahn would never sell the label. Just another made up story by "the industry bible." You can choose to believe it or not, right? So why do I feel so uneasy? I saw Bunyan at DK-5 a couple of times, and yet, no one seems to know anything about any sale.

I was hoping to have some time to relax in LA. Oh, well…

Finally, the friendly voice on the loudspeaker tells us to board. I wait and wait…and wait. *Where are those guys?*

Just as they announce the last call, Artist stumbles out of the men's room. He's so stoned he can't stand. One of his headkerchiefed crew and his Manager hold him up. I have their boarding passes. Where are they going? "Hey, your tickets!" I have to chase them, because they're going towards the gate without even looking at me. "Your tickets! Hey!" They stop and grab the envelopes out of my hand and walk to the gate. "Wait! You took my ticket!"

At no time during the flight does anyone talk. That's okay. I'm exhausted. *Got to think. Got to sleep.*

The change in Chicago is a blur.

When the plane lands at La Guardia, a car is waiting, under the name of "D. Slinger." Kahn is being his usual subtle self. He calls me on my cellphone and asks if I recognize his voice.

"Yes."

He asks if I have Caller ID.

"Yes."

Then Kahn asks me to use it. I try, but disconnect him. He calls back and yells at me to never do that again. I ask him why everything's so Secret Service-like?

"Mind your own business." It sounds like he's covering the

mouthpiece of his receiver because I can hear his nose breathing. "The driver will bring you here. You bring them to my office— the private entrance."

What private entrance?

"Then leave like nothing is going down. Stay with your traveling companions until then. Let no one see or talk to them." He hangs up before I can ask the ten questions in my mind.

I've just spent nearly twelve hours flying, ten hours in LA, and now, I have to spend even more time with the Artist who seems to have a contract out on his head rather than on his career. But my salary is supposed to double after this project, right?

We're finally settled in the limousine. I ask the Artist what's going on. He says he can't talk about it, but he could use a blowjob. He's so stoned that it sounds like "lowglob."

"Sorry, not in my job description."

This upsets him. "Pleeeze?"

Manager says, "You want me, I'll make her."

"Naw, I'm soo high to getit-up." To me. "Sorry."

Don't want to look at him, but I do. "No problem."

The Manager puts his arm on the Artist's shoulder. "Jus' lookin' out fo' yo' in'trest. You're m' 'sponsibility." They hug.

Thank God for jet lag and pot.

Another blunt is rolled and lit. Getting carsick from the smoke. Determined not to puke. But if I do, it'll be on them.

I'll never forgive Kahn for this.

The trip to Twenty Mott Street is painfully slow. It consists of me rolling down the window, then them rolling it back up. I roll it down. They roll it back up. Down. Up. I'm beginning to get a contact high. Luckily, when we enter the Queens-Midtown Tunnel, they get scared because "Yo, what happened to the fucking sunlight, man?"

We near Mott Street. The Artist whines, "Whoa, bro, I be losin' m' eyesight. Those letters, 'can't make them out."

"It's Chinese," I say. "Welcome to Chinatown."

Just as we turn the corner, the Manager screams. "Shit, man. Shit, Shit, Shit."

"Wha'?" says the Artist who's still trying to make sense of the signs in Chinatown.

"Look. There."

A stretch Hummer with blacked-out windows is double-parked in front of DK-5. A huge guy in a shiny black suit, black tee and curved teardrop sunglasses leans against the block-long military-style limo.

"It's Big Bic."

The Artist is suddenly wide-awake. "Where?"

"Over there. Th' Hummper."

He looks. "Oh, shit."

The Manager pushes the Artist to the floorboard and leans over him. "Drive around the block."

"Why?" the limo driver asks.

"Do it, muthafucka! You want to die?"

All of us crouch down, even the driver hunkers below steering wheel-level and drives around the block.

I ask, "Who's Big Bic?"

The Manager says, "His muscle."

"Whose muscle?"

He says the name of the Head of the West Coast Label (HWCL).

"Is that a problem?"

By the looks on their faces, I can see it is.

We're about to drive past the label again. A police car is parked nearby. I tell the driver to stop. I get out and walk to the officers with a shy grin. "Excuse me, officers. I hate to bother you with something so trivial, but there's this very long Hummer double-parked over there. It's just blocking the whole street. I tried to ask the gentleman nicely to move his car, but he cursed at me, right in front of my little girl."

All right, so I'm laying it on a little thick. It works. The cop slowly cruises up to the Hummer.

"You got a choice," the officer blasts out of his loudspeaker. "I get out of the car, or you get in yours and drive away."

This takes Big Bic by surprise. He looks around, sees the police car, and does a passive-aggressive saunter into the Hummer. After buckling up, he takes a quick "I'm gonna take my time" look at himself in the side-view mirror, then drives away. The patrol car follows. We pull up to where the stretch had been, and I try to get Artist and Manager to follow me. They refuse. But they promise to stay in the car. Hopefully, they're too stoned to move.

In the elevator, I start to get real angry. *What kind of situation has Kahn put me in this time?*

Inside DK-5, Jiggity is sitting in the reception area. He hasn't done that in a long time. He stands up, smiles and says, "Hi."

"In a minute."

"But I got something important to..."

I walk faster. Suddenly, Tamyka waddles up in front of me and says, "Where the fuck you been? Vishnu been all over me 'bout those "Axx¿" album credits!"

"Get out of my face!" I walk through the Death Star décor to Darth Kahn's office.

"Who you talkin' to like that you ofay bitch?"

I get in her face. "Get out of my way!"

A crowd gathers. I have to dump those guys in the car on Kahn. But Tamyka keeps pushing. "Get me those radio edits or I'ma fuck you up, bitch."

"Then do it!" I stop and turn. "Do it, or shut your big mouth and get out of my way!"

She tries to hit me. I duck, rear back and with my best Puce punch connect with her nose. There's a crack and blood explodes everywhere.

Gasping, gushing, Tamyka falls to the floor.

I keep moving.

An intern exhales, "Dayamn."

At Kahn's office, #2Girl, Clete and Sik stand outside the closed door. What catches my eye is that Clete's not reading. He's holding his shotgun—outside his overcoat.

Never saw that before. I reach out to open the door.

Clete, in his "no-nonsense" voice says, "Where you going?"

"I've got Artist and Manager in a car downstairs. They're too scared to come up."

Sik jumps, waves his arms and whispers, "Shit, what the fuck, get 'em da fuck outta here. Put them someplace—on another fucking planet. You know who's in there?

Clete adds. "It may be best if you get out of this vicinity, as well. Might be some trouble."

"Trouble? You haven't seen trouble yet."

I burst into the office.

The first thing I notice is a small black man, wearing a silver-blue Adidas warm-up suit and lots of gold. He has Kahn bent backwards over the back of his ergonomic chair. The top of his head nearly touches the floor. Kahn's spine is about to snap.

Kahn sees me and gasps out. "Ah, Lily, just mentioning you to Mr. HWCL."

He chokes out to the HWCL, "This person. Her idea. She runs things."

I WHAT?!!!

The man slowly brings Kahn and his office chair upright. A couple of Kahn's vertebrae crack back into place. I look around and see another man, whose muscles show through his tight black turtleneck. He's sitting on the sofa with a large shiny automatic pistol in his lap—and not smiling.

I extend my hand to the HWCL. "I'm Lily White. Nice to finally meet you."

He and the other guy look at each other. HWCL starts to speak, but stops. He stares at my chest. His eyes widen. *Come on, I'm not that well-endowed.* I look at my blouse. Oh my, I have Tamyka's blood all over me.

In three seconds he'll remember why he's here. In two, I speak, "Don't like employees dissin' me. Didn't get where we are by takin' sass from anyone, knowwhatImean? You understand. That's why you are one of the most respected people in this industry." I pause to let that soak in. What I'm thinking is HELP!

Kahn tries to talk, "Lily, why don't..."

"Shut your face!" *This idiot will get us all killed.* "Haven't you messed up enough?" I turn to the HWCL. "Has anyone asked you if you'd like something to eat, drink or to take care of your secular needs?" He shakes his head. "There. You see? That's what I have to work with—a bunch of no-mannered fools."

I open the door. Clete, #2Girl and Sik jump. "Get Mr. HWCL AND ALL OF US SOMETHING TO EAT AND DRINK. RIGHT NOW!" Turning to our visitors, "Ribs, chicken, the works for you gentlemen?" They nod. To the DK-5 people who must think I've gone nuts, "Well, you heard me! A full feast for our honored guests—Peckers Chicken Wings and Ribs Double Deluxe—Lots of sodas and champagne—NOW!"

They jump. I quickly close the door so no one can ask me what I'm doing. *The answer is, I don't know what I'm doing, other than trying to stay one step ahead of these guys.* "Now, gentlemen, while we wait for your Pecker's to arrive, how can I help you?"

The HWCL booms, "Heard DK-5 stole one o' m' artists an' ya' can't have 'im."

Stay calm. "I see. Exactly who are we talking about?"

He says Artist's name.

"Him? How many units did he sell last year?"

The HWCL looks at his larger partner on the couch, who speaks, "'Bout hundred thousand."

"A hundred thousand?" I say as fake-shocked as I can. "A hundred thousand? Do you honestly think we would steal an artist that only sells a hundred thousand albums in one year? We can't even break even with those sales numbers. Can you?" They look at each other, confused. "Plus, gentlemen, we'd never do anything like steal another company's artist. Not only is it disrespectful, but also bad business. An East Coast/West Coast feud is only good in print, not in reality, and certainly not in record stores."

Let that sink in—but not too long.

"If you'd like, I could make some calls and see if we can help you find your Artist. Let's consider this our first joint venture. Who knows where this could..."

"Kahn says you went to LA an' snuck m' artist out." HWCL looks a little confused.

I glare at Kahn. He set me up to be blown away, to save his hide. All this was his idea, and now...*Deep breath. Think clearly.*

"I'm afraid Bigar has been doing a little too much blow. You'll have to forgive him." I shake my head at Kahn. "You made these gentlemen come all the way to New York just because you were hallucinating again? You're pathetic." I start pimp-slapping Kahn. "Apologize to HWCL and his associate right now!"

A few more slaps and Kahn holds his cheeks. One more makes him apologize. The HWCL relaxes a bit.

"Mr. HWCL, I have never been to LA. Spent the last few days on the L.I.E. (Long Island Expressway), moving masters to our new warehouse."

Kahn's head turns to me. He's shocked that I know. Maybe I should have made up another L.I.E.

The food arrives. We have a great meal and a nice chat. I offer him and his business muscle tickets to a Broadway show "Les Miserables." They quickly decide it's time to go. "Les Mis" tickets scares music industry-types every time. Now, to get them back to LA. First, as a surprise, I send HWCL and his crew to La Guardia in a double-decker bus filled with strippers, Cristal and blunts. Then, I arrange for Artist and Manager to fly coach from Newark, booking them on a flight that arrives in LA before HWCL does.

Like Nothing Happened

Next morning, Kahn is in a neck brace. "You salted and battered me in front of HWCL. You humiliated me in the eye of the industry. It's insupportination!"

"If it wasn't for me, you'd be broken in half. You should double my salary, like you said, for doing what's good for both the lego and your neck. "

Kahn doesn't see it that way. He says I should feel lucky I don't end up as a receptionist, or worse.

There's worse?

He is upset and disappointed in me that I told a lie about moving the masters.

A lie?

He says that, now, we have to act like nothing happened.

Like nothing happened.

18

Sneaky Peaky

OPENING THE WAREHOUSE DOOR, I turn and smile. "Follow me."

I have to push Jiggity Man inside and make sure the door doesn't slam. He must think I'm crazy to bring him here at this hour. But his dream is about to come true—he's going to get his masters back—only he doesn't know it, yet.

J Man asks, "Why are we here?"

"It's a surprise. Just leave it at..."

Sounds—hissing of something being dragged across the floor, muffled voices, and the occasional squeak of a sneaker on the concrete floor.

We duck behind a stack of boxes.

"YOU FUCKING TELLING ME IT WAS AN ACCIDENTAL?" It's Khan.

SMACK!

"I's tellin' you the truth."

That other voice is familiar. Is that Foggmaster?

SMACK!

I peek around the corner. Four guys carry boxes of masters on handtrucks and then head to the loading dock.

They ignore Kahn and Foggmaster who are making the big noise here. A bodyguard I've never seen before holds Foggmaster's arms behind him. Kahn is beet red. "HER HUSBAND, JUST BY ACCIDENT, JOINED YOUR FUCKING CHURCH?"

"It's a coincidence."

"YOU EXPECT ME TO BELIEVE THAT SHIT,

MOTHERFUCKER?"

"I'm ain't foolin' wid choo, man."

SMACK! Kahn slaps him so hard I can feel it.

Foggmaster pleads, "Go meet the muthfucka. Tell me what you see. That guy be a fool. He actually believes what I'm sayin', knowhatImean? Even tol' him straight out I was playin' him an' his bitch, an' he still be believin' that Epiphany shit."

"And did you stop to think why? Why would he believe your bullshit? Because he's playin' you. The guy could be a Fed or a Hip Hop Cop. Shit, he could be Jesus fucking Christ and you wouldn't be able to tell the difference."

"No way, bro. No way. I've gots an eagle eye. No pigs gonna be dupin' this brother."

"Shut the fuck up!" SMACK! "Look what you've done." Kahn points to the guys moving boxes. "You're fucking forcing me to move this shit to fucking Jersey City."

Why is he moving the masters again?

"YOU'VE INCOME-VENIENCED ME!"

SMACK!

"Hey, man, you hired her, not me," Fogg cries out. "Why'd you do that?"

"That? That's different. She's my *cuntingency* plan. Just in case someone like you fucks things up."

Had a feeling Kahn was into something. That something, I'm still not sure of—but now I know who'll be blamed.

Jiggity Man puts his hand on my shoulder.

The Reverend says, "You want me to ice 'im, just say so."

"Too late for that, Mister Jesus-Man. Looks like you're going to have to die for his sins."

"Why? I didn't do nothin'!"

Two men head our way. We hide. They load more boxes onto their handtrucks. One whispers, "Fucking Foggmaster gonna eat dirt soon."

The other, "So fucking what."

They turn the corner.

We have to move. They'll be back for the boxes in front of us. I motion "across the aisle" to Jiggity. We move behind some metal shelves, where it's darker. *Smells like something died back here.*

Sik saunters in. "Yo, man, full up. Needs a bigger truck."

Kahn turns. "What? That truck is plenty big."

"Nope, full up. Got more boxes than truck."

Kahn stares at Sik in disbelief. "So rent another one."

"Eleven at night?"

"There's a whole parking lot filled with trucks next door. Crack one and we'll return it when we're done."

Sik shakes his head. "I don't boost. I sells smack and chronic—pure an' simple."

"Just what I need," says Kahn. "A fucking specialist."

Foggmaster says, "I used to hotwire back-in-th'-day."

"Back-in-the-day, you were worth something."

Sik shrugs his shoulders and leaves.

Kahn watches him walk away. "Fucking amazing, I give the guy the world and he still acts like some street nigger." He turns to Foggmaster. "Looks like I'm not going to kill you—yet. Because you're going to make yourself useful. But if I don't get a truck in ten minutes, you're back to dead." Kahn waves his hand. The bodyguard lets Foggmaster go. They walk out.

The place is empty.

I take a step toward the boxes. Jiggity grabs my hand. He motions for me to come back. I pull away.

Looking at the box labels, I see what I'm looking for. Quietly I pull the sealing tape off and look through the plastic cases. Here's the batch I want.

I slide Jiggity's boxes of masters to him. I open one, and hand him a DAT (Digital Audio Tape). He stares at it, then opens the box and looks inside. His eyes look away and then back at the DATs. He holds some of them, turning one over and over. "That was my first gold record." There's a lot of thinking going on. He seems sad and angry. I can't tell.

"What's wrong?"

He snaps out of his thoughts. "They're gonna miss 'em."

"So?"

"So they'll get suspicious. Put 'em back. I mean it. Put 'em back." He throws the DAT back in the box.

"The point of coming here was to get your masters."

"Just thinking of you."

"Me?"

"Don't want you to get in trouble when things go down."

"What things are going down?"

"Shh, someone's coming."

Dumpster Diving

Out front of the DK-5 building, a dumpster appears a day before office renovations are about to begin. A month later, the renovations aren't happening. *So why is that thing still there?*

One evening, I see our clean-up crew emptying trash into the dumpster. Seems like an expensive way to get rid of garbage. Kahn's papers are usually shredded, but Rich bags his garbage and leaves it for the crew to dispose—even though it's supposed to be shredded.

Could there be anything about the BUG/DK-5 sale or non-sale in Rich's trash?

I want to look inside his bag of tricks and see what's up. But each evening his office is the second one to get cleaned. Need more time. The other choice is to look in the dumpster.

So, I tape a piece of paper with the letter R (for Rich) onto his bag. That way when I search in the dumpster, I don't have to go through every bag.

Later that night, I open the dumpster door, turn on my flashlight and start looking for the marked bag. It's like being inside a loaded boxcar. The smell is the DK-5 perfume I'm used to—spoiled food, tangy cologne, burnt tobacco and beads of booze inside bottles—only concentrated and composted.

The garbage in the front of the dumpster should be the most recent. So I check each bag for the R tag. Nothing. After a while, there's a tall stack of bags behind me.

We really produce more garbage than actual paperwork. How much of this stuff could be recycled? *Not here for environmental reasons. Need information—soon.* The stink seeps into my skin. Hold my breath. Exhale. Keep looking for Rich's bag. A few minutes deeper in, I look back at the wall of trash bags behind me.

THE DUMPSTER DOOR CREAKS AND BOOMS SHUT.

Don't panic.

There are voices, but they are outside. I listen. Just muffled street sounds of people and traffic.

Why did I let Jiggity talk me into this?

Rich's garbage is here somewhere. I know that the cleaning crew emptied their bins in this dumpster. Maybe I went too far? I go back and re-examine the bags behind me. This time I open each one. Mostly it's food wrappers, drink containers and some papers, mostly with drawings and a few words.

What do people at DK-5 do all day?

There is a promising bag. It has a piece of tape and a slip of torn paper under it. This could be it.

But no, it's #2 Girl's trash—it has her scent. Let's see—used feminine products (in her office?—Really?—Disgusting), clothes catalogues, lists of Rappers and money figures by their names, phone messages on pink sheets and a wet legal pad with a Fifth Avenue address written on it.

I pick it up by a corner and read the word BUG with an address and phone number. Could be Bunyan's office or home. Thank you #2 Girl for being un-secure—in so many ways.

Now to get out of here.

No handle on the door. I push. Nothing. Harder. Nothing. Guess they never thought someone could be locked inside. I bang on the door and yell for help. The people near the dumpster seem to have quieted. But no one helps. Bang and yell again.

Nothing.

So I get my cellphone and call...who? It can't be Beany or anyone from the label.

Ola.

She has to bring Ivy with her. It takes a few minutes for her to figure out how to open the door.

I exit. There, stands a very angry Ola. "You no goot muzzer, you are."

Ivy's nose twitches. She smells something weird—it's me.

19

Snatch

MY APARTMENT DOOR is open—nearly off it's hinges.

Inside, the living room's a mess. The rug's been pushed up against the wall, the coffee table is broken and "Peter Rabbit" is on the floor—one page torn.

"Beany? Ivy? Hello?"

I run into Ivy's room. She's not there. To the kitchen—no one. The bathroom. Back to Ivy's room. On the floor are some of her clothes and her favorite stuffed animal, a tiny pink bunny, named Funny. She goes everywhere with it.

No note, no sound, no nothing. Only a smell—kind of like men who just got off a hot day of farm work. Who was here?

Call the police.

By the time they arrive, I'm hysterical.

A Detective Wary shows up a few minutes later to "secure the crime scene," which I've already turned upside down twice. He opens a notepad. "How did you discover she was gone?"

"I walked in and no one was here."

"Who was with your child?"

"Beany Baby. He's been my sitter for over a year now. He watches Ivy when I have to work late."

"When was the last time you spoke to him?"

"Right before I left for an in-store at Tower Records."

"In-store?"

"That's when artists make a guest appearance to promote a new album."

"Where do you work?"

"Def Kahn-5. It's a record label."

"I see." He writes in his notepad. "Where's the father?"

"He lives at the Fogg Ministries. Hank, that's his name, well not exactly. His name now is Astronomous."

Detective Wary looks at me. "Astronomous?"

"That's the name they gave him at the church."

"How do you spell that?"

"A-s-t-r-o-n-o-m-o-u-s."

The detective writes as two uniformed officers walk through my apartment. They don't seem to be doing anything but gawking at the mess.

"Does the father know your daughter's missing?"

"We haven't spoken in about a year-and-a-half. Shouldn't someone start looking for her?"

"Just a few more questions. Does the father know about this babysitter, Beany Baby? What kind of name is that?"

"What difference does it make? When are we going to start looking for Ivy?"

"I know this is hard, so let me get the information I need to help you, okay?" I nod. "Good. Now, has this babysitter ever taken your daughter out overnight?"

"No. Never."

"You're sure."

"He'd never do anything like this. Beany's very responsible. He'd fight anyone that would try to harm Ivy."

My body starts to shake. I sit down before I faint.

"Anything unusual happen in the last couple of days?"

"Look, detective, my daughter's gone. Beany's gone. The apartment is trashed. Isn't that unusual enough for you?"

I lose control and can't stop crying.

The detective puts his hand on my shoulder. "Would you like to go to the hospital? They could give you something to calm your nerves."

"Don't want calm nerves. I want my little girl back."

"I understand"

"DO YOU? DO YOU? Then, why aren't you out there looking for her?"

The uniformed cops are watching me.

"A few more questions."

"How long is this going to take?"

"Was there a note left?"

"I don't know. Did they find one?" I point at the cops.

They say they haven't found anything.

"Finally, could you reconstruct what you did today?"

I tell him as best I can—the usual sampling headaches, scheduling studio time, calming managers, listening to radio edits, and finally the in-store event, where some kids broke the plate-glass window, trying to be the first ones in.

He must think my life is crazy, but I don't care.

"Hodge, any recent Family Services complaints?"

"Listen, you're wasting your time there."

"Would anyone have anything against you?"

"No, I, I can't think of anyone."

Then it hits me. Ever since I learned about the DK-5 sale and the bootlegs, Kahn's been acting strangely. One day, he walks into my office, closes the door, stares at me for a moment, and asks about how my life was progressing. "Does your baby have everything she needs? We take care of each other, our little family. Of course, unless someone spills their guts to the press, there could be some very converse consequences, if you get my subtext here."

Could he have been threatening me? At the warehouse, Kahn called me as his "cuntingency plan." What did he mean?

"Any idea what she was wearing?" The detective brings me out of my thoughts.

"I'm sorry."

"Wearing, what was she wearing?"

"When I left the house, she was wearing a 'Power Puff Girls' T-shirt. But those clothes are on her bedroom floor. Ivy's out there somewhere, probably frightened, maybe even…Can't you do something?"

His eyes meet mine. *Is he trying to stare me down?*

"Something else you'd like to add?"

"What else do you need to know?"

"Little unusual for a babysitter to be male."

"And he's black too. Are we talking about babysitter stereotypes or about finding my daughter?"

"You have relations with the sitter? "

"WHAT? NO!"

"Sorry, have to ask."

"Can we get in your car and start looking?"

"That wouldn't be productive, Mrs. White."

"I'm sorry, I thought you were on-duty. Just tell me when you punch in so you can start doing your job."

He puts his hand on my shoulder and squeezes—to what—comfort me? I pull away. Detective Wary just crossed my boundary. He must realize it, because he turns his head to "look" like he's looking around. There's a long, uncomfortable silence. The only sound comes from a uniformed officer in Ivy's bedroom. His radio squawks.

Why didn't I think of this before? "We should call Beany's grandmother. Maybe she's heard from him."

She answers the phone, hysterically, "They done taken my Trevor to jail. He call me and say they callin' him a burglar! God knows my Trevor ain't no burglar. He got a good job and he be sittin' yo' daughter. Them police just bust into yo' house and grab him up like a criminal."

POLICE? Like DK-5, the SWAT team enters. Beany gets carried away. Only, this time, it's in MY APARTMENT!

"Where's Ivy?"

"He done nothin' wrong. He ain't a bad boy, my Trevor."

"DID BEAN, UH TREVOR, SAY ANYTHING ABOUT MY DAUGHTER, IVY?"

She stops. "Trevor ain't said nothing 'bout her. He tell me to call Mr. Kahn to gets him out."

"Well, Ivy's missing. Trevor was watching her. How could he not say anything about Ivy? Why did the police come here?"

"Oh, he did say someone complaint there was a burglar in yo' house. An' the po-lice done thought it was my sweet baby. Now, who woulda call in sump'n like that?"

Yeah, who would have?

I tell the detective to drive me to the police station, where they're holding Beany.

The A&R Meeting (A Week Ago)

A dingy after hours club, eleven a.m., the stench of last night's beer, vomit, and pine cleaner take my appetite away. The catering consists of stale potato chips, warm bottled water and slimy pasta salad. We're cutting expenses, even though it's our best year ever. It's BYOB (Bring Your Own Blunt). Kahn's explanation—singles are doing well, but album sales are below projections.

I know better. This is about playing BUG.

Kahn wants DK-5 to look like we're swimming in profit. There's even a tourniquet on the flow of Play Money—never a good idea.

It's a sham. But why go through all that effort, unless...?

Why do I feel like the bottom is about to drop out of my world? So I take another Tums.

Smoke circles our little group. We've just listened to all of our artists' upcoming releases. The responses are:

> *Hot joints*
> *Off the hook*
> *Da bomb*

Same old, same old. Sik and Top-Dogg are stretched across two torn leather chairs. Wonder how they're going to react if Kahn dumps them. These guys don't take rejection lying down.

Thank God, Kahn doesn't ask us what our personal goals are anymore. Mine would be to get some fresh air.

The next subject on the agenda is what are we going to do about Axxẹ's arrest last night for rape, sodomy, aggravated assault and abduction of a fifteen-year-old girl?

"Was she a hooker?" Kahn asks.

Rich responds, "No, someone's honor student of a daughter—middle class and black."

"So rumor around that she's a suburban hooker. The press eats up that shit."

Rich shakes his head. "They're already playing this as another 'Rapper-Goes-Wild' story. Bail was set at two hundred thousand dollars. He'll be out by tonight. In a couple of weeks it'll blow over. Fucking bitch couldn't just chalk it up to experience."

Kahn sits there, puffing on his dead cigar. He has that look on his face like he's really thinking. No one breathes.

"I need the room. Take a walk everybody, a long one."

The sun is supposed to be shining. It's one of those beautiful New York days in June. What a relief.

"Rich, Lily," Kahn barks. "Stay."

Why do I need to be in on this?

"What about me?" asks #2Girl.

"What about you? You got some need-to-know thing up your butthole today?"

#2Girl shakes her head.

Kahn doesn't even look at her. "Then it should be easy for you to move your fat ass out the door."

As #2Girl walks by, the heat of her hate radiates in my direction. I want to tell her that I'd prefer it if she stayed and not me. She looks at Kahn. "Anything I can get you while I'm out—that yogurt you like?" Kahn dismisses her with a flick of his hand. She walks away like someone has just kicked her in the stomach.

A quick flash of sunlight from outside, then the dark returns with a door slam.

Does this means I've become one of them? I'm here, aren't I? Just Kahn, Rich, me and…I look for Clete…but even he's gone.

No sound, except the screeching of metal chairs, as we form a tighter circle. The exposed lightbulbs directly above spotlight us.

Smoke rises.

"Time to barnstorm about Axx¿'s future with the label. The question is, do we want him out of jail?"

Rich says, "If we don't bail him out, his crew will."

"Those assholes? They want him in jail so that they can mansack his crib. Okay, let's talk pro versus con. Pro: We get 'Lord' Axx¿ out of jail, then what?"

Rich says, "We can pay the girl off. That means she agrees to no trial, no book deals, and no movie-of-the-week for her—zip. But to settle, we're talking big bucks. It would be easier to destroy her rep so that she's not a credible witness."

"Then, if it goes to trial, no one will believe her?"

"Yes and no. If they can prove Axx¿ did all that shit, well, she could be whore central and he'll get serious time."

"And if one of them should disappear?"

This is beyond hiring, firing or flooding the phone-lines for the RapRumble. We're talking life and death here. Yes, I have just graduated from backup to one of the leads. Time for my solo.

"Ice the girl?" says Rich. "That's an option."

"We can't." I interrupt. "We do any damage to her and she becomes talk show material. Picture her mother and father crying, as Oprah hugs them. 'Another Innocent Victim of Rap. Give Mama a makeover!' Applause! And guess who'll be the villain of the story—not Axxʒ. No, all fingers will be pointed at us. Especially in the black community." I let that sink in. "Gentlemen, that's just not good for the lego!"

There, I said it. I'm in control now.

A thoughtful silence.

"She has a point, Bigar. If Axxʒ is found dead, we could make some money on the reissues and box sets. Hell, the studio costs will be next to nothing. Fuck me, but that's a strong option."

"You can't be serious," I say. "Killing an artist is...is...it's bad business is what it is. You have to think ahead. Axxʒ is one of our top-sellers."

"Not if he's dead," Rich says.

"Murdering him will kill Def Kahn-5!"

"Never has before." Kahn smiles. "But, hey, we're only barnstorming ideas here. We're looking for some new conceptions." He turns to Rich. "That's the pro, now the con. What if he cops a plea?"

"No can do," Rich says. "Either we go after the raped girl's rep or ice Axxʒ."

"Or a third choice." My turn. "What if he just takes his lumps and repents?"

"Repents?" Kahn stands and screams, "I'm not gonna have another preacher Rapper on this label! You fuckin' hear me? I got enough with that Reverend Nigger Shit from up to here." he demonstrates how high, "You can suck my dick and shove whackjuice up your assholes, if you think I'm going to waste my fucking time on a no-sales religious Raper-Rapper! If that's the only choice, icy-icicle him!" Kahn throws his soggy cigar into the far darkness and spits out, "Repents."

Can't let this moment go. "Think in the long-term. What I'm saying is let Axxȥ take responsibility for his actions."

A pause, as they try to take in that novel concept.

"Kahn, what's she doing here?" Rich says. "Now she has big balls in this company, or something?"

Uh oh, anatomy. If I let this reference go by, I'm history. "I don't need them. I have something better—an idea." I stand, then pace back and forth "He's going to jail anyway. So let him cop a plea. Let him go to jail. Axxȥ will still be valuable to us there."

Their eyes move with me like four pendulums. It's my time— my beat—the blood is pumping. I stop, turn, and spell it out to them slowly, teasingly. "Twenty-five percent of all black males will be in jail some time in their lives. Read the statistics. How many millions is that—two, three? Now that's what Vishnu would call a 'captured' market. And that's why we should let Axxȥ be convicted and do time. It'll be keeping it real, and profitable."

Rich says, "What does 'real' have to with anything?"

"Think. He's in jail. He starts recording—in jail. Axxȥ becomes—'The Voice of Conviction.'" I pause to let that sink in. "He speaks 'The Word' for convicts, for their families. He becomes the conscience of a nation that incarcerates young boys for just being black. He has no name—just his prison number. Axxȥ is now 100101." I'm on a roll. "He's able to keep it real, because his imprisonment is 'real.' That's the way to turn a problem into an asset. That's the way to open up a whole new market segment—convicts and their immediate families. And imagine the wannabes. Imagine all the white boys at the mall wearing prison outfits. I'm telling you it's a whole new clothing line. Look. See them? They're exchanging handshakes you can only learn from being on the 'inside'—the slammer. We'll be creating a whole new category of music—'Slamma-Rap.' More than that, we'll create a movement. By the time it reaches the suburbs, we'll have five to six years of big profits. We've just turned a bad situation into a moneymaker. And people will thank us, yes, thank us, for giving voice to a whole new population. Bigar Kahn, you'll be celebrated at the White House, in the news, and even appear on Oprah—but for a good reason. You'll be known as the humanitarian who revived the soul of a jailed nation. And Axxё is only the beginning. Now, every time one of our artists gets convicted, or even indicted, we just move him over to 'Slamma-Rap.'"

"So are you, Bigar Kahn, ready to make history and, by the way, a whole lot of money?" I can hardly catch my breath, because I know I've blown him away. This time it's my eyes that zero in.

It's so quiet you can almost hear a thought forming.

Kahn leans back and tilts his head. He chews on his lower lip and stifles a smile. I bet he's trying not to show that he's impressed. "You have some interesting ideas for someone who can't control her mouth or her artists."

What is he saying?

"If you had listened with your ears to Axxё a little more, and not opened your big mouth all the time, none of this would never have happened."

Did I hear him right?

"So before you do anything else that might hurt the label, maybe you should just do your job. Leave the talking to the guys with the big balls and keep your pussy-brained ideas away from my sights!"

"You're, you're blaming me, because he raped that girl?"

"The jury's still out, so to speak," adds Rich.

"Then why did you ask me to stay?"

Silence.

I can't let this go. "You know that Axxё has always been out of control. It's not anyone's fault, but his. What about 'Slamma Rap?' Don't you see how amazing it could be? Rich, Bigar, how many ideas like this pass our way?"

"Exactly," Kahn says. "Bad ideas I get by the dozen. This one is number eleven, just today." He tosses a music trade magazine to me. "Read it."

"BUG to Devour DK-5?" I look up at Kahn. "Thought you wanted this kept quiet."

"I still do. But what I'm finding is that someone I trusted is trust-worthless."

"Do you think that I..."

Rich gets in my face. "You fucking cunt, no one was supposed to say anything!"

He raises his hand to hit me, but I push his arm away. "Don't you threaten me."

"Rich, control yourself. This is a corporal business meeting." Kahn smiles. "Lily, why did you tell the reporter about our private business?"

"Tell what reporter? I didn't talk to anyone. I don't even know what this BUG business is about. Why would I want to ruin what I've worked so hard for?"

"Exactly what I've been pondering to figure out."

"I would never do something so stupid. A fool like Rich would, but I've never done anything to harm this label. You should know that by now."

I can see he's having second thoughts. Rich stands by, waiting to see if he can go for one of my major arteries.

Kahn rolls a fresh cigar in his mouth. His eyes narrow. "I want to believe you, Lily, but this BUG business is too important to let anyone, ANYONE, fuck it up. So I want you to understand— any more leaks or open mouthings or loose tongueings and I'll have to stop them any ways I know how. You understand?"

I nod.

"Good, cause I'd hate for anything to happen of a negative nature to anyone. Especially, if they have a child to think of."

So Where Is Ivy?

The leaks continue. Not from me. But if Kahn still suspected that I...

Can hardly catch my breath. My stomach is erupting. My eyes tear up. My hands shake.

Stop it! Stop it! Don't cry. Don't feel. Just find Ivy.

Who would do this? If it was Kahn or Rich, the police would never have been called. They'd hire someone to take care of the details. No, whoever did this had something else in mind. This isn't about keeping quiet. This is about making a statement. Someone's trying to show me how powerful they are. I could be wrong. My thinking's become just one what if, after what if, after what if.

A few minutes later, we're in front of the jail where Beany Baby is locked up. The detective tries to talk me out of going in. "Did you know this Beany Baby, whose real name is Trevor Lee, has an arrest record you wouldn't believe."

"Any convictions?"

"That the kind of person you want babysitting for you?"

"Look, I happen to know that all of these arrests are work-related. He's a good person. Anyway, don't you want to talk with the last person to see my daughter?"

Inside the jail a bruised, bloodied and swollen Beany tells us that the police knocked on my door. He wouldn't open it until they showed him some ID. They battered it in and threw him to the ground. He fought back—to protect Ivy. But there were so many of them. They took turns kicking and punching him.

"With all those cops, how could Ivy just disappear?"

"There was this white dude, claiming to be Ivy's father. Was rappin' weird things like 'God only knows. Only God knows. God knows only.'"

HANK!

Hank kidnapped Ivy? Why? After all this time, why would he do something like that? It's him. Who else would chant something so stupid like "God knows only, Only God knows?"

God only knows where they are now.

I call the Fogg Ministries and ask for Hank, I mean, Astronomous. The person, who answers, says he's not in. I ask if Ivy is there. He says that he doesn't know anyone by that name.

What do I do now?

First, I cry. On the way home, I make the cabdriver stop twice so I can open the door and throw up in the street.

Maybe I should call some people from DK-5, but would anyone really help me? Kahn will get Beany Baby released, but will he bail me out of this situation? I have to do something, so I pick up the phone to call Kahn's home. That's when I notice the light flashing on my answering machine. I push the button.

BEEP! *I AM ASTRONOMOUS. I possess Ivory. Did you think I shall allow her to be raised in a hell, where strange men come in and out at all hours of the night? Thou, my wife, hast become a fornicatrix to the devil sons of Ishmael. I shall not summon you until after a prolonged period of purification. You must purge your putrefaction. I shall, then, determine what is best for Ivory's soul FOR I AM ASTRONO...***BEEP!**

A couple of days? For purification? Ivory's soul? And, how did he know about forni...uh, Jiggity Man?

How did Hank get this number? It's unlisted.

I go to the closet to check on the boxes of Herbalux.

They're all gone.

Did he kidnap Ivy to cover up stealing the boxes of herbal laxative? Has he lost his soul and his conscience? Hank hasn't seen Ivy or helped with her needs in eighteen months, and now he's become the caring father? I'm the one who works like a dog and takes responsibility for everything, and now that creep takes her from me, for what—that godforsaken church and crappy colon cleaner?

THAT DOES IT! I'm going to the Fogg Ministries. I put on some dark clothing, then slide a kitchen knife into the pocket of my tan coat.

Whatever it takes, I will get her back.

I practice pulling the knife out of my pocket a couple of times, just to make sure the handle is where I can reach it.

Whatever it takes.

The door to my apartment won't shut. The police broke the whole frame. Doesn't matter. Every second I waste on stupid details takes time away from finding Ivy. Running, I slip on the stairs in front of my apartment house. My ankle makes a cracking sound. I gasp, then hop around, trying to keep moving and at the same time run away from the pain. My ankle swells immediately. But even that won't stop me. Perspiration runs down my face. It's summer, fool. No one wears a wool coat. I take it off. My sweat-soaked blouse is stuck to my back.

WALK! I force myself to move a little bit and then bend over to rub the sore spot. I repeat the walking and rubbing a few times until I can handle the pain. *What now?*

In the shadows across the street, I see a large figure. It's a man, sitting in a black Hummer.

Is that Clete? I limp across the street. "Clete?"

He jumps up in surprise, banging his head on the roof.

"Clete, what are you doing here?"

"Lily? That you?"

"I said, what are you doing here?"

"Reading"

"In an SUV, in front of my apartment house, at one-thirty in the morning?"

"It's a nice night."

"I know why you're here—someone thinks I'm interfering with that Bunyan business—right? Well, I'm not."

He doesn't look at me.

"Did you see the Police or Beany or my daughter enter or leave my place?"

"Was just tending to my own business." He shows me his copy of "Heart of Darkness."

"Did you know that my husband, soon-to-be ex-husband, kidnapped my daughter tonight?"

"Do now."

"Clete, please help me. I have to get Ivy back."

"Would like to help, but I'm on company time."

"Look, I won't mention to Kahn that you're doing a lousy job of spying on me."

He looks at me—not his "friendly" look.

"Clete, I'm talking about the safety of my daughter and you're playing the 'just following orders' game?"

He places a bookmark into "Heart of Darkness" and steps out of the Hummer, and warns, "This isn't a game."

Don't know why, but I start hitting him. "Why don't you have the decency to help me? How can you be so cold-hearted?" It's like slamming your hands against a brick wall. The harder I hit, the less he reacts.

He scans the street and grabs my wrists. "Stop it. I sent my little brother to follow them."

"Them? Who's 'them?' Oh, you mean Hank and Ivy?"

"Couldn't tell for sure. There was a whole crew of them. Should be getting a call soon about where they are."

I hug him and start crying. Now, he's embarrassed and pulls away. The knife falls out of my coat pocket.

Both of us stare at it.

I pick up my weapon and put it back in my coat.

He smiles. "Now, if you were to go traveling somewhere, I'd have to follow. That's part of the assignment."

"They're probably at the Fogg Ministries."

"Oh," he says like there's a longer story to tell.

"Is it still technically following me, if I'm in the passenger seat of your truck?"

He nods and helps me limp into his SUV.

On the way, Clete coaches me. "Lily, in this kind of conflict you've got to practice what's called 'ironic detachment.' It's when you know what's happening, and at the same time, you can step outside and see it from a dispassionate perspective."

"Clete, what does this have to do with anything?"

"Lately, you're under suspicion at the label, because you've been acting like a disgruntled employee."

"Clete, everyone there is disgruntled. That's the corporate ID. Our tagline should be 'Def Kahn-5—Stay Pissed.'"

"True, but you should see the irony in this situation."

"You want me to be detached when my baby's just been kidnapped by her religious fanatic father? Would you?"

"No, the irony of why you were hired in the first place."

"Yeah, I know about Kahn's nasty plans for me."

"You do?"

"He wants me to turn the label into a real business operation, but it never will be. Now, with this Bunyan business, who knows what he wants."

Clete shakes his head. "You have no clue, do you?"

"Guess not."

"Good to hear."

We arrive at Gramercy Park, the Fogg Ministries, Hank and Ivy—I hope.

Clete flips his cell phone and calls his little brother, Gervin.

"Where are you?…Where?" He looks around. "I don't see you. Do you see the Hummer? Then why don't you walk up to it?" Putting away his phone, Clete shakes his head. "Gervin's sweet, but none too swift."

A slimmer, Scooby Doo version of Clete, strolls up. "Yo bro, who's that?"

"Lily White. She's from the label. It's her daughter we're here to get."

"Nice t' meet you." He reminds me of the country boys back in Puce with that "aw shucks" body language.

"Thank you for helping me."

Clete throws my coat in the backseat. *Hey, my knife.* He takes a deep breath. "Okay, let's bring that little girl home."

As we cross the street, Clete says, "Ironic detachment."

"My big bro's one word wizard, ain't he?"

"One can't go very far without a strong vocabulary."

Can't talk. My ankle is really hurting now. *Can't stop.* Up the stairs. I'm trying to ignore the feeling I may have to throw up again. The building itself shows no signs of being a church, except for the words under the buzzer.

Fogg Ministries
Enter Ye Whom Seek Epiphany
NO MENUS

Clete knocks on the large wooden door. Fogg answers in his shiny yellow and green striped pajamas. His slippers are green patent leather, trimmed in white fur and scream "The Pimp at Bedtime." The entire congregation stands behind him, choir-like. They outnumber us ten-to-one.

My stomach drops into my swollen ankle.

If Ivy's there, it'll take some expert negotiating. Clete and Gervin separate Fogg from the group. They quietly threaten to break Fogg's skull unless he or Hank hands over Ivy.

What happened to "ironic detachment?"

The Reverend yells upstairs at Hank to bring Ivy out. Hank refuses. Fogg hollers that if he doesn't comply, he'll slide back to a sixty percent spiritually disability. "At least come downstairs, Astronomous. Greet thy wife. After all, you avowed to th' girl."

"Not with that fornicatress!"

I limp to the bottom of the steps. "Hank, you come down here, right now, or I'm coming up there."

Silence.

Halfway up the stairs I realize I'm halfway up the stairs. My ankle burns, but I'm going to get Ivy back if I have to ironically detach Hank's head from his shoulders.

At the top landing, I see him. This is the first time I've actually been eye to eye with Hank in a year-and-a-half. I imagined what our meeting would be like. My little scenario went from grand, sweeping embraces, as the camera circled us in a field of tall grass, romantic music swelling. Later, that changed to a polite reconciliation with long, painful silences. Most recently, I've fantasized that Hank and I are in mortal combat. Each of us, trying to bludgeon the other to death with unpaid bills. Now, I look at him—his sunken, lost eyes—and I feel like crying. He seems polished. Not as in manners, but as in Turtle Wax. He has this shine to him—like you see in someone who's dying.

It breaks my heart to realize what he has and hasn't become.

His jaw tightens. He's not giving up Ivy without a fight.

Well, I'm ready for that.

"Lily, you need some help up there?" Clete yells.

Hank looks more scared than me. But that makes him more dangerous. My eyes stay on him as I yell back over my shoulder to Clete, "No, I just need a little time. Please, be patient." To Hank. "How've you been?"

He turns away and grinds his teeth. My skin crawls.

Take a deep breath. "I've thought about you a lot."

The grinding stops. "You won't get Ivory back," he squeezes out of his tight jaw.

"I know. Not until I get you back."

That throws him off.

"Hank, can we go somewhere and talk in private?"

He thinks, then walks to a door and opens it. "Words can't undo your sins."

"I know."

We enter a small living room. The furniture looks like it was old when it was built. The couch is covered with a black and red crocheted blanket. Next to it is a cracked green pleather chair. The Reverend must have sent people looking for street treasures just before the garbage trucks came to carry them to their final resting place.

"You'll repent for eternity before you'll see your daughter again, fornicatress."

It takes all my willpower not to slug him, but I've got to practice ironic distraction. I limp to the couch, sit and put my leg up. "So how do you suggest I repent?"

"It isn't that easy, Jezebel. You have sinned too much with the black devils of Ishmael."

"That's because you never contacted me or Ivy."

Just added out-and-out lying to fornication.

He can hardly breathe. "I, I, I wrote you missives and left messages on your machine."

"I never got any. And when I called here, they said you weren't in or available."

He's thinking. "You never heard from me?"

"Do you know what it's like, not hearing from my husband, our baby calling for her Daddy?" I shake my head and act like I'm about to cry.

"I didn't know... Had I, I would have..." He stops for a moment and then rages. "What difference would that have made? You fucked that nigger, and broke our marriage vows. I pity your afterlife. The Lord abhors whores."

"Mary Magdalene."

"Who?"

"Mary Magdalene," I say quietly. "Jesus forgave and respected her for changing—in her heart. If he could, couldn't you?"

Hank looks away.

I realize what I have to do. "Give me a chance, Astronomous. I, Magdalene, ask your forgiveness for my sins. Let me show you the future—the good one—the one the Lord desires."

I motion for him to sit next to me.

Hank looks confused, but I have to get him focused on my target, not his. I touch his hand, and pull him to the couch. "And she layeth next to him, and was cleansed. Her sins purged from the depths of her heart."

He's shaking. For the first time I'm grateful that my mother was a religious fanatic and a spouter of Bible BS. I lift his gray hand and kiss the palm. "He that forgiveth a sinner, and maketh a cleansing, shall liveth in the house of his countenance forever."

He stiffens.

I pull him to the sofa, next to me. "He maketh me lie down in green pastures."

I undo his pants. He's turneth into stone. "For thine is the kingdom..."

His eyes widen. I reach in. "And the glory."

His knees lock as I start to stroke. He moans. "Whatever it taketh."

I stroke harder.

His hips pump up and down.

I squeeze tighter.

"He is risen."

He's bouncing off the couch.

I ram him hard.

With each stroke, he screams in tongues. "balaBAZINGEfer nanaZINUGEfer BLAT!"

He freezes. His eyes open wide. He howls and then explodes all over everything. Hank is God's little geyser. "He is come!"

His final response: "BLAT! BLAT! BLAT!"

I milk him until he relaxes. "Thou hast epiphanied."

Hank stares at my hand that holds his shrinking thing. He mouths something—what—a prayer?

Finally, I let go. My fingers have cramped-up. I work them back and forth to get the feeling back.

"Epiphany," he whispers.

"What?"

"I've achieved Epiphany." Hank is enraptured.

"Epiphany?"

"I've seen the coming of the Lord, as foretold in 'Matthew.' Hell, I'm gonna change that. Think of it, the 'Gospels of Magdalene and Hank.'"

"Shouldn't that be 'The Book of Astronomous?'"

"Naw, that was just a loaner. Now, I am that I am—Hank 'Prophet' White."

He's out of his mind. I've got to focus mine. "Hank, we've got to get Ivy out of here."

"We shall go forth into the land."

There's a knock at the door. My hand is sticky, so I wipe it on the crocheted blanket. "Yes?"

Clete opens the door. "You okay?"

"We're fine. Aren't we, Hank?"

He does a Mona Lisa smile. "We are bles-sed."

I notice his fly is still open. So does Clete, who rolls his eyes. "You going to be here long?"

"No, we were just about to get Ivy." I look at Hank. He looks at me. There's color in his face for the first time.

Could he be coming out of it?

"We must fetcheth the Hank-Child," he says.

I didn't think so.

Clete, Hank and I walk to the third floor, where Ivy's asleep—safe. I want to cry out, "My baby's okay!" But the lump in my throat stops all sound.

I pick her up gently. If I hold her any tighter, she'll wake up screaming. I refuse to feel the pain in my ankle.

Slowly, we "step-by-step" our way down the stairs. Below, Gervin, The Reverend and his followers are talking about guns. They turn and gaze upon us, as our processional descends.

Hank is stuffed with inner peace. He stops on the final step before the ground floor. Peering down on the congregation, he smiles. "Reverend, my work here is done. I must go spread-eth the word."

The Rev raises his hand and face to the sky. "PRAISE THE LORD, HALLELUJAH AND GOOD LUCK!"

The entire congregation joins in the Hosannas.

Yelling above the "Praised Be Hee-Haws," I say, "Gervin, could you take Ivy to the truck? Clete, please stay here."

I hand Ivy to Gervin, who cradles her carefully.

Hank follows. I limp quickly to get in front of him.

"You're not going anywhere."

He must not hear me, because he keeps walking.

I put my palm on his chest. "Hank, stop!"

That gets his attention. "I, I don't understand."

"You're not going with us. In fact, if you ever show up anywhere near Ivy or me, I will have you planted under a parking lot in Jersey City, near some bootlegs." I look at Fogg. "KnowhatImean?"

He does.

"Hank, you made your hell, now live in it."

Fogg squirms. "Fuck, lady, that just ain't Christian."

"Actually, it is. He doesn't stand a chance out there, so he stays in here."

Hank nervously smiles. "But I want to spreadeth the word."

"Nope."

"But I've achieved Epiphany."

"Congratulations."

Hank's eyes fill with tears. His voice breaks, "But what about what we did up there?"

"We both got what we needed. It's a win-win."

I start to leave. Got to get back to my own life. That one, standing there, staring at me is over.

Hank cries, "Magdalene, I will be so alone without you."

"Yeah, I know. Isn't God great?"

20

The Village Vidiot

"ENTRÉZ VOUS!"

Inside the small production trailer, a round, dark ginger-tanned man with bright white Appaloosa patches on his skin sits in a lotus position—sort of. He wears orange and black tiger-striped football pants, and a torn black t-shirt with "Welcome to New York Fucking City" on it. A flip-flop dangles off one foot and an unlaced Timberland boot covers the other. No socks. His hair looks like black asparagus—tied together, ready for steaming. Tattooed on his left arm is 완전히 바보가 (Korean for "waste of space"). Around his middle is a scabbard. He waves a short sword to punctuate his words. Bagel Tigerthighs, music video director, does cutting edge work.

Kahn assigned me to oversee the video shoot of Jess-up's first single, "Tongue-Hung," a little epic about the length of his lady's tongue.

It's amazing how many words rhyme with "lick."

Outside the production trailer is a slew of women. Each one thinks she's the featured "Tongue-Hung" Girl. That's because, Jess-up promised every one of them the title role.

A few fights have already broken out.

In the trailer, Bagel Tigerthighs is killing time, because Jess-up has been "on his way" for the last four hours. So with his sword unsheathed, he lays down a line of coke the length of the blade.

Bagel asks me if I'd like to take a stab at it.

"No thanks. I need all of my senses." Kahn wants me to make sure everything goes smoothly. I'm his eyes, ears and nose. Never having done anything like this before is no drawback—that's what he said.

"DK-5 paid for it. It's good shit," Bagel burbles.

"Thanks just the same."

He runs his nose across the full length of the blade, inhaling everything but the chrome finish. "Ahhhh, that's better," he huffs. "Nothing beats an Assagi."

"Excuse me, but where did you get your unusual name?"

Still snuffling, Bagel enlightens. "It was awarded to me by my Korean Sensei." He points to his tattoo.

"Sensei?"

"My spiritual and martial arts master, Oxcart Pudbuddy."

"I beg your pardon?"

"That's his name. And I honor it, because the last person that made fun of it got their balls handed to them. He's a twelfth-degree black belt in Sun Tzu. What's your name?"

"I'm Lily White."

"Lily White? Does it have a meaning?"

"No, just something I picked up in Missouri."

He slaps his right fist into the palm of his left hand and bows as deeply as his midriff will allow. "I understand and honor it."

"Mr. Tigerthighs, could you tell me your ideas for the video?"

His Buddha brow wrinkles in contemplation. "It's about the tongue chi, the energy of a woman's, a special woman's, long tongue. A metaphor. The long tongue reaches down into the soul to touch the life force." He loses his balance and uses the sword to keep from falling. Bagel re-pretzels his legs into a lotus position, but his thick mid-section fights back. As Bagel teeters back and forth, he expounds. "Jess-up has hit upon a question that needs to be answered in today's numb-nuts world—what does it take to make us wake, see, feel and understand the life force around us? Whoops." He falls sideways. "Pretty fucking fly, ain't it?"

"Yeah, real fly." *Is this guy trying to pull my wool?*

Why did Kahn ask me to oversee this video? He said to make sure we didn't waste time and money. How to do that, I hope, will become self-evident because I don't have a clue about what things cost and how long they take.

Bagel reloads his Assagi.

"Won't that stuff interfere with your responsibilities, I mean, your artistic judgment?"

"Should have known there'd be a suit on the set." His nose travels the length of his sword again. This time he slices a thin red line across his top lip. Blood trickles, forming a red mustache.

Feeling faint. "I, I have to check some things outside."

"In a former life, I was a great warrior princess" are the last coherent words I hear from Bagel Tigerthighs.

Outside, girls of all shapes, sizes and levels of undress—bosoms, bottoms and bare-midriffs fight for attention.

"Yo, I'm da one who's da Tong Girl." She extends her tongue and does circles with it.

"I be da Hong-Kong Girl dat Jess-up pick for."

"No you ain't. He promisin' me da Gung Ho after we done the nasty. That what."

"Ladies, ladies." I raise my arms. "This will be all straightened out when Jess-up arrives. Until then, let's just be respectful with each other. Okay?"

A bit of calm—I can actually hear the traffic noise.

One tiny woman, dressed in a yellow beret, thong, and cowboy boots, buttonholes me. "Do you know what the rate is for today?"

"Rate?"

All the ladies are listening now.

"I was told four-hundred." She glances at the others with a slight smile.

"Told me a hundred."

"Me, too," says another angry Jess-up promisee.

The yellow-thonged, miniature says, "The obvious reason for the difference is I'm Sha' Dinga…"

Sha' Dinga?

"…and I'm the Thong-Gong Girl." She lashes her tongue and spins her eyes to confirm her credentials.

That ignites a tongue-war. I leave the ladies and try to see what else is, or isn't, going on?

"Has anyone heard from Jess-up or Mae?" I'm trying to get the the film crew's attention. But they're munching sticky danishes and sipping cups of their favorite on-location beverages.

The only person who responds is the producer. She's nearly six feet tall, blonde and has a big smile that makes you feel happy, until you realize she's clueless. And that's an assessment from me—someone who doesn't know what they're doing. "Little problemo, Miss White. No one can find the Mitchell or the Arri."

"Who're they?"

"The cameras. Good part is, we have plenty of film."

"I see. Now if I'm not mistaken, we may not be able to shoot this WITHOUT THE CAMERAS, RIGHT?"

"Hey, y'know, everything's under control, totally."

"Oh really? Have you seen Bagel Tigerthighs lately?"

"He's meditating in the trailer, right?"

"Meditating? More like medicating." I can see she doesn't understand the difference. "Why don't you join Bagel? Maybe, you know, to slow his coke consumption to once every ten seconds. I'll wait here for Jess-up, and when he arrives, I'll get you. Like, totally! Okay?"

"Ho-kay!" She flits though the rioting ladies and enters the production trailer.

Kahn really did it to me this time. There's no way we'll stay within the budget. We don't even have a camera.

One of the ladies approaches. "'Scuse me, but if I ain't the Tong Girl, I ain't stayin'. I gots a career to upkeep."

"Well then, we wouldn't want anything to upset the upkeep of your career. So if you need to go, just return your costume to whoever is doing the costumes."

She looks at what she's wearing, a see-through tube-top and a short orange leather miniskirt that exposes her behind. "This ain't no costume, it's m' own clothes."

"Oh really? Well, oops, my mistake."

As I walk away, looking for a bit of sanity, she hollers, "Jess-up be kickin' yo' pale ass, dissin' me like that."

Help! I'm surrounded by blind, deaf and dumb ambition.

Thirst—there's something I can accomplish. I'll go get something to drink, but all the LoCaterers have out is watery coffee and Zip Lime-Flavored drink.

I've lost my ability to swallow anyway. That's because, we're in the Meatpacking District of Manhattan. It's a location used in many videos, mainly for it's cobblestone streets and authentic warehouse facades. What you don't get on film is the smell. The only way I can describe the odor is rotting flesh in August. A century of meat products has left its USDA Grade-A stench in this area.

The effect on our crew is apparent. Two strict vegans have thrown up. The non-smokers are standing next to the smokers, inhaling deeply to mask the odor.

Me, I'm breathing through my mouth—a trick I learned at Mr. Jensen's pig farm in Puce.

I can't stand this much longer.

The producer plows into me. I lose my balance. She grabs my arm on the way down. "Sorry. You need to come, stat!"

"Is there a problemo?"

"Just a teensy one."

"What is it?"

She pulls me towards the trailer. I pull back.

"What's going on? Tell me now!"

She stops, looks to see if anyone is listening, and blurts out, "Bagel's burnt."

"He's what?"

"It'd be a lot easier to show you." Drawing circles around her eyes with her fingers. "See for yourself." She grabs my arm and pulls me to the production trailer.

Inside, Bagel's in a fetal position, singing—off-key. We try to get his attention, but he's channeling Henry Mancini.

He's on all fours, head-butting the storyboards.

"WADDA YOU GET WHEN YOU FALL IN LOVE?"

"Bagel, it's me, Lily White, remember?"

"GUY WITH...PIN TO BURST YOUR BUBBLE."

"You need to start directing the video."

"DAT'S WHAT YA GED FOR ALL YOUR TROUBLE."

I finish the song for him. "I'LL NEVER FALL IN LOVE AGAIN. Bagel...Bagel Tigerthighs, the video shoot? Hello. Remember? Jess-up? 'Tongue-Hung'?"

"Thung Gung?" gurgles from his gullet. His eyes flicker. Then, he grabs his storyboards and starts to eat them.

"Mr. Tigerthighs," cries the producer. "Bagel, please don't eat the concept."

CHOMP! CHEW! GULP!

I join in. "Bagel, I'm warning you! Give me those ideas NOW or I'll call Bigar Kahn!"

We manage to save some of the boards, but they have large chunks missing.

Bagel, full of concepts and coke, snoring, snotting, a dab of drool dribbling from his mouth, is now unconscious.

We just stare.

"Kinda bitchen. What do we do now?"

I turn to her and raise my eyebrows. "We?"

"Well I'm not going to be held responsible for his unprofessionalism, just mine."

We're five hours into production. No film has been shot. How do I explain this to Kahn? I won't. So I gather the cast and crew in front of the trailer. Standing on the top step, so I can look taller, I raise my hands. "Hey, everyone, I need your attention!"

A crowd of confused faces looks at me. *What now?* For a moment no one is rioting for a role or nauseated from the location. They just stare.

Think of something. "Bagel Tigerthighs is unable to complete his assignment. That's why I'm taking over. My name is Lily White. I'm from Def Kahn-5. So, ladies, get into your costumes and make-up. Crew, let's set up wherever the set up is set up...to be."

An older man steps up. "We don't have a camera."

"What? Oh, yeah."

I look around. The producer is gone. *Maybe she's not as dumb as I thought.*

"Shouldn't we get one?"

He says, "We could call around."

"What's your job here?"

"I'm the DP."

"And that means..."

"Director of Photography. I frame each shot and sometimes operate the camera, when we have one."

"Oh. Well then, I guess we, you should make some calls."

Of course, we can't find a camera on such short notice. But one of the ladies has a camcorder with her. We negotiate a fee.

She'll let us use it, if she can be the Tongue-Hung Girl. I tell her she's the one. *What I don't tell her is, I'm not sure if that means anything, in the big picture.*

Luckily, the tiny camcorder fits on the huge camera dolly. It looks silly, but now we're ready to roll. Reading the chewed-up storyboards that I pulled from Bagel's mouth, I try to figure out the right order of the shots.

The Director of Photography is amazing. He suggests where we point the camcorder and place the girls. He's done this many times before, and I am so grateful.

To each girl separately, I whisper, "You're the Tongue-Hung Girl, but please don't tell the others."

It's sneaky, but now they're in front of the camera, gyrating their hips and snaking their tongues. I realize that there's supposed to be a choreographer, so I invent some moves that the ladies try.

They look ridiculous. "Forget what I just showed you—just get jiggy with it," is my only direction.

We do a couple of takes with music playing from a speaker on the set. The DP says we should do some handheld close-ups.

"Okay."

Each girl is filmed shaking her booty on my instruction. Since I've seen so many of these types of videos, I know what body parts are important. And guess what? I'm being listened to like a general, like I'm the boss.

This is so cool.

Everything's going okay, until a stretch limo and two large black SUVs drive up. Their brakes squeal. Jess-up and Mae step out. The SUVs expel about twenty people—chickenheads, family members, managers and assorted hangers-on. Mae looks relieved to be outside. She smoothes her tight, red skirt and tucks in her charcoal sleeveless blouse. The black Prada calf-length boots with red piping are perfectly Mae, except that she's walking like a penguin.

Everyone on the set rushes to Jess-up, who eats up the adulation. His security retires to the caterer's table.

"Jess-up's ma man! He fuckin' be MA-MAN!" one of the hangers-on pronounces, for all the world to hear.

Mae gives me a funny look.

"What kept you?"

She tilts her head towards Jess-up.

"Sorry, it's just that everyone's been waiting. We've wasted a lot of time before we could even got started."

"What are you talking about? We're here on time. The call was for eleven a.m."

"No, it was for six a.m."

"That's for the crew."

"Kahn told me everyone was to be here at six."

"Whatever."

I can see she's uncomfortable.

"Mae, what's wrong? You look so sad."

"Sad?" She whispers, "Honey, you don't know what sad is 'til you been fucked in the ass by that pig's dick. Can't hardly walk, sit and breathe."

Maybe I should change the subject. "Bagel Tigerthighs is conked out in the trailer."

"That supposed to mean something?"

"The director...of this video. He had an interesting concept for the song, but he ate most of it and did too much coke, so now I'm directing..."

"We can talk about this after I get me some Preparation H. I'll concentrate better without this pain." Mae waddles to the limo, talks to the driver, slides very carefully into the backseat and leaves for her ointment appointment.

The producer approaches. "Jess-up's in make-up."

"Where have you been?"

"On a break."

"For an hour?"

"I saw this cop car drive by, and since we don't have a permit to shoot here, hey, I just didn't want to get hassled."

"Why is everything so messed up?"

"Nothing to do with me. Mr. Kahn refused to okay everything we suggested. You know, like a director who's not a cokehead, a choreographer, make-up and costume crew, and a shooting location permit from the city. Not our job to question The Man."

"But Kahn knows a strong video drives sales..."

"Not my departmento." She walks away.

What is Kahn doing? He said that this video is very important to get Jess-up's first release moving. Now, it's like…like he's trying to undermine this project. No preparation was done and then he sent someone who doesn't know the first thing about video shoots to oversee the whole thing—me. *Why?*

The DP walks up quickly. "Looks like rain is on the way. I'm guessing twenty to thirty minutes. So we need to get Jess-up's master performance shot soon."

"What's that?"

"It's where he sings the whole song in one take."

"Oh."

To keep things moving, we shoot a scene, where each girl compares how long her tongue is. Sha' Dinga wins.

We shoot the clouds, the cobblestones and cars driving by. I'm running out of ideas.

Finally, Jess-up walks out of the trailer. The ladies are all over him like gnats.

It's getting cloudier.

He says, "Girls, don't be messin' wid me right now. I gots to git inta a caracter." A Marlon Brando hush descends over the hootchies, as he approaches. "You like m' Armani's clothes?"

"Jess-up, you look great."

"I dunno, I'm not feelin' them. More inna Gucci frame o' mind. KnowhatImean?"

"Well, since there's no way we can get to a store right now, that may be a problem."

"An' maybe you don't git my statement. I ain't doin' no video in the wrong clothes."

"Look, Jess-up, you look so sexy. Those ladies can't keep their hands off you. They're fighting over who's going to be your Tongue-Hung Girl."

He looks at me, confused. "We ain't doing "Tongue-Hung." We be doing 'Butt Wise Girl.'"

"Jess-up, this entire shoot is about 'Tongue-Hung.'"

"Bigar tol' me we was doin' 'Butt Wise Girl.'"

"Kahn may have said that, but I'm the boss on this set, and you're going to do 'Tongue-Hung,' or you can get back in your limousine for the last time, because your career is over. That means, no more money, no more Armani's clothes, and no more Guccis or hootchies grabbing at your scrawny behind. You get my subtext here?"

He gulps. "Okay...But I'm holdin' ma jacket over ma shoulder, like this."

"That I can live with."

We start shooting. The camcorder does it's magic. The DP tells me not to worry. We can fix and edit this mess in post-production. *I hope so.*

Everything's cranking. Jess-up's not half bad.

A garbage truck drives up. We stop shooting to let the truck's steel claws pick up a large dumpster, raise it high, and empty it's contents—animal bones, gristle, guts, cartilage, and God-only-knows-what—INTO THE STREET! This causes the cast and crew to scatter like a bomb went off.

The driver gets out, sees the mess and yells, "Shit!" He starts to sling the carcasses into the back of the truck.

It starts sprinkling.

The playback on the audio keeps blasting "Tongue Hung," along with the sound of bones being crushed.

The slaughterhouse fumes overcome everybody. Some people vomit where they are. Others are doubled-over, looking for relief in trashcans.

But, come smell or high water, we're going to finish.

I grab the camcorder off the stand and yell, "Get back on the set, now!" I'm breathing through my mouth, and screaming over the music and the crunching sounds of bones being compacted in the truck.

Raining a little harder now.

"Stick out your tongue, Jess-up." I yell, "Come on, sell it!"

"D, Don't feel s' good. My Armani's drippin'."

I keep going, "Sha' Dinga, roll over on your back and show me your tongue."

Like a pro, she does, and spews a fountain of LoCaterers food into the air—special effects.

I'm a shark shooting through a swarm of fish. Everywhere my camera points, drama unfolds.

Everything and everyone is soaking wet. The flooding rain drives the garbage right at us. We're engulfed in guts and blood—an orgy of ooze.

The rain suddenly comes down in sheets.

"LILY!"

I hear my name, but nothing's going to stop me.

"Look into the camera!" I scream at one of the crew, who's spasming, "Keep doing that! More! Lose control! That's it! More! More! Great! Great!"

"LILY!"

I zoom into his mouth. His extended tongue looks like a big purple landscape. He vomits. Got it. Perfect.

"LILY, WHAT THE FUCK IS GOING ON?"

Who's bothering me now?

I turn. In the viewfinder I see Kahn staring at me. Next to him is Clete, holding a large umbrella. Both are wide-eyed and open-mouthed.

Looking up from the camcorder, I yell over the storm, "What are you doing here?"

"I want to know what you're doing here."

"We're getting a few handheld shots. Just about done."

"This is part of the video?"

"Got to keep things moving. Don't worry, everything will be fixed in post-production."

"And where is the director?"

"You're looking at her."

"I see. So now you're a director? So, Miss Director, look at these people. Shouldn't someone yell 'cut!'"

"Why?"

"Because that's how you stop a scene."

"But I don't want to stop it. I'm still shooting."

"CUT! CUT! CUT!" Kahn waves his arms. He looks at the cast and crew. "That guy by the garbage truck isn't cutting."

"Uh, uh, Caterer?"

"I send you to be overseer of the shoot, and you end up killing the cast?" He points at the animal carcasses.

"I didn't…"

"Money down the drain. A simple job, and you cost over-ruin

the entire production."

Everyone that's conscious is watching.

"Mr. Kahn, could we talk about this in the trailer? In private?"

"You are the last person I want to be private with."

"This is all about the sale to BUG, isn't it?" That gets his attention. "Okay, if you want to discuss it out here."

He thinks for a minute, then walks to the trailer. As he passes me. "You're gonna pay for this."

"Okay, everyone. Take a break." No one's around to hear my command—just a waterlogged Kahn and Clete, and a super-soaked me.

Kahn enters the trailer. I follow. Clete stays outside. Once inside, the rain drumbeats on the metal roof.

Kahn looks around and sees the unconscious Bagel.

"Who's that?"

"Bagel."

"Bagel?"

"Bagel Tigerthighs, the director. You hired him."

"I did not." Kahn looks at him. "What kind of fucked up name is Bagel whatever-ties?"

"He got it from his Korean Sensei, Oxcart Pudbuddy."

"What the fuck do I care? I'm talking about you. This was your chance to do what's good for the lego, and look what happens. You turn this whole thing into a big, stinking pile of shit sandwiches." He rips the Bruce Lee towel off Bagel's wall and dries his face and arms.

"That's not true. I've been getting things done."

Kahn stares at me, calmer now. "Okay, so you wanted to talk? So talk."

"Why did you put me in this position?"

He puts the towel under his shirt and rubs himself. "Oh, where's the Lily, that first day, on the floor at my feet, who promised to make DK-5 a professional company? She's not here, not in this trailer. She's out there, making people sick."

"Look, there were some major problems to overcome, like the director, no camera, no choreographer, Jess-up was five hours late and a producer who doesn't know what she's doing. She said that you made all this happen..." Something in Kahn's eyes stops me. "But that's it, isn't it? There was no way I was going to succeed in this, right?"

His silence tells me I'm right. The vicious smile, the narrowing eyes and the way he moves his head to crack a vertebra, these are his signals that he's playing you, like a pimp.

"Lily, your presence at Def Kahn-5 is no longer desirable. Your big mouth and sticking your nosiness into business that isn't yours has made me a disappointed label head. You have proven to be non-competant."

"So you're going to fire me? What about Bobby Bunyan?"

"Yes, he will be disappointed, but I'm sure he'll survive the lamentabilibull loss of Lily White."

"Oh, you think I'm going to disappear, just like that?"

"Lily, Lily, Lily, I need a star in this position. You aren't even a supportive player. I blame myself, but mostly I blame you. I wish things were different."

"How could they have been different?"

Kahn shoves the Bruce Lee towel into his pants and dries himself vigorously—front and back. "It's too late for that discussion. Now's the time to focus on taking care of your little girl. Think of tit this way—you'll have more time to breast-feed."

"I haven't done that in over a year."

"See? Times change."

Does he rehearse this stuff?

I'm fighting to keep my job, and he's talking like I can't see through what he's doing. I'm not going back to where I was. I can't. That Lily White is history. This one can't afford to be.

So I swallow my pride. "I've done so much for this label, and so much for you. Can't you give me another chance?"

He reveals a new smile from his a la carte menu. "Lily, you know I'm not a cold-hearted person. I care about people. Call me a sentimentalist. So I'm going to be forgiving, but only if you're for giving me some sign of your loyalty."

"A sign?"

"Yes."

He removes the towel from his pants, sniffs it and smiles.

Kahn sits down on a cushioned bench in the trailer. He uses the unconscious Bagel as a footstool. Undoing his pants, he pulls them down, then his underwear, and exposes himself. He holds up his bent penis. "You're gonna have to show me something real special, real commitment, real intensity. If you're gonna continue in this company, I need to see you'll do whatever it takes."

He waits.

I'm staring at his warped thingy.

Finally, I have a clear job description. "Okay."

"You know what I'm talking about here, my subtext?"

I get it. For the first time I get it. This is what "it" means. I nod.

He leans back, holding "it" up for me. I crouch, using Bagel to cushion my knees. My hands rest on Kahn's pasty thighs. His eyes close. His head arches back. One small movement forward, that's all that stands between him and me. My mind stops working. It's all autopilot now.

Dad said *never put anything in your mouth you don't want to see in the toilet tomorrow.* If only...

Bagel moans. That stops me for a moment. I see Bagel is barely holding his Assagi. Here I am, kneeling on Bagel Tigerthighs, once-great warrior princess, about to...

I grab the Assagi and place the sharp tip under Kahn's ballbag. His eyes open wide. The sword makes its impression. His thingy shrinks to a mini pigtail.

"Sorry, no Pecker's Chicken to save you today, Bigar."

"Wha, what are you doing?"

"I'm trying to get you to see my point—one way or another. Now, you either make sure I keep my job after the sale, or I'll lower your rating on the Big Balls/Dick Slinging Grid, permanently. You understand my subtext here?"

He nods.

Bagel shifts, knocking me over, and mumbles, I'LL NEVER FALL IN LOVE AGAIN!"

This gives Kahn just enough time to get away. I reach for the sword. He scrambles over Bagel towards the exit, and stands. I grab his leg. He trips. His head bangs into the trailer door, opening it. I let go of his leg to grab the sword with both hands. He crawls out. I follow.

Outside, he tries to run, but trips on his fallen pants,

screaming, "HELP! HELP! SHE'S TRYING TO KILL ME! HELP!"

He can't get traction, because the rain and ooze have made the cobblestones slick.

Clete bolts towards us. "Lily, drop it. I'm warning you. Just lay the sword down."

I swing wildly, slicing vents into Kahn's pants, before Clete knocks me down.

"He tried to rape me. Clete, look at him. His pants are down around his ankles."

Clete is now on top of me. "Not the way to handle it."

"No? How would you handle it? What book have you read that explains what to do?"

He stops for a moment to—what—think of a book title?

"Please, Clete, you're crushing me."

"Promise not to get violent?"

"You've got the Assagi, and the weight advantage."

He gets up and brushes himself off. "So this is an Assagi? Interesting weapon."

Kahn screams, "I want her whacked. You hear me, Clete? I want her made into a hamburger!"

Clete points to the small crowd that has gathered to watch. "Maybe you should pull up those trousers before you say anything that might be taken in the wrong way."

Kahn realizes he's exposed. He does up his tattered pants, and gives me one of his throat-cutting looks. "I'm through with you, you ungrateful cunt."

I spit back, "No, you've only begun with me, Bigar."

His mouth quivers. "Nobody talks to me like that."

"Yeah? Well, wait till I tell Bunyan what happened in that trailer. How do you think he'll see it? Going over budget on a shoot or rape? Over budget or rape? Rape, budget, rape, budget? Guess what? Rape wins!"

After a moment of shocked silence, he gathers himself. "As of this momentum, you are not what's good for the lego." Kahn struts to his limo, his legs showing through his sliced-up pants.

Clete looks at me with sadness. "Lily, your big mouth just turned you into an outsider."

"Yeah? So when was I an insider?"

Sitting on Your Laurels

"Please, don't. Please, Lily, it hurts too much. Oh, I can't believe it. Girl, you done that motherfucker up real good. Oh my, you making m' asshole scream!"

I'm on the way home with Mae in a limo.

She's laughing so hard about what I did to Kahn that she can't find a comfortable sitting position. I learn that Preparation H reduces the swelling, but not the pain—that's Tucks Pads. I've also learned that you can use Preparation H to get rid of the rotten meat smell by rubbing a little in your nose. Of course, since it contains shark-fin oil, you're substituting the aroma of rotten meat for dead fish.

It's amazing what tidbits you pick up in the music business.

"Mae, Kahn fired me."

"Hell, he's fired all of us at one time or another. Didn't he fire you a while ago, too?"

"Yeah…"

"So soon as he needs something, he'll forget about it."

"No, Kahn thinks I'll mess up this BUG business."

"What business?"

Does she really not know about the sale?

Mae shifts from one cheek to the other and moans.

"You okay?"

"Hon, I'll survive this, and so will you."

"Not so sure. Got a feeling Kahn set me up somehow. Exactly why, I don't know."

"He's pretty much an in-yo-face-muthafucka. Kahn never fired no one, permanently. Most of the time, they leave on their own, or in an ambulance."

"This is different. BUG makes it different. What I can't figure out is why Bunyan wants to buy DK-5."

Mae stares out the window. "You're worrying about something that hasn't happened."

"Well, it's happening, and no one seems to understand what that might mean for all of us."

The limo stops quickly. I put my arm out to keep her from

flying forward. Mae grits her teeth from the pain.

We're stuck in traffic.

She smiles at me. I smile back.

Neither of us talks for a few seconds.

Mae says, "Just thinking, if I was worried about this like you, I'd try to get to that guy, Bunyan. Find out what's up with that."

"I know where he lives."

"You sure about this BUG thing?" She looks at me.

"Something is going down that will affect all of us."

She leans into me and whispers, "Good place to start a conversation is at a party, or somewhere there's lots of people—a friendly atmosphere, where everyone's relaxed. Then drop some interesting info—in the direction of where you want things to go. That's how I'd start it."

Despite Mae's impressive ability to assess and manipulate a situation, I can't help thinking that she also made the choice that led to her sore rear-end. But...

"You think that'll work?"

Mae looks to see if the driver is listening. "Look, I'm only telling you what I'm not supposed to know, understand? Seems a good way for a person to get to another person, especially if that person has heavy security around him."

"Maybe I could mention to Bunyan that I just directed the video, and tell him how wonderful it will be. Then I could tell him about other things I've done at the label, then he'd..."

"How much time you think you'll have? Maybe five seconds before a bodyguard kicks you out the door. You gotta drop that interesting bit of info before 'Hello.'"

"Why is everything such a struggle? After all I've done, I thought Kahn would show a little loyalty." My stomach starts acting up.

"Loyalty? There ain't no loyalty! Get with the program, girl. It's about gettin' what's yours, takin' what you can, while you can. Nobody gives a shit about you, your daughter, your feelings, even whether you live or die. All you have, or will ever have that's real, is them Benjamins. Learned that in the Projects. Learned that in the shiny office buildings. Time you learned that too." She shifts to find a comfortable position. "Look at me. You know what I call this?" She points to her behind. "Motivation. The pain makes me get off my ass and get me something real in return. Everything else is just bullshit."

My stomach is pumping acid. Need Tums.

The driver opens his door and checks the traffic jam.

Time to contact Bunyan. I turn to Mae, who's found a comfortable position. "Got business to take care of."

"Be careful. Kahn doesn't like to lose."

Stepping out of the car in my soggy clothes. "Neither do I, and I've already done that."

Guess what. I really am fired. Tried to go to work. My cardkey was disabled, I wasn't allowed into the offices and Clete escorted me out of the building. He said they would ship my personal things to my apartment. Guess that's that.

That's DAT

Next day, I have lunch with Jiggity. I tell him that I need to meet with Bunyan to reveal what's happening at the label, and maybe, to get my job back. He discourages me. Why? I don't know. I tell him that Bunyan seemed to like me and I need to cash in on that.

He sips some water and says, "I wouldn't."

"You wouldn't, but our situations are different."

I sip some water. "One thing bothers me." My eyes narrow. "Why didn't you take your masters, when we risked our lives to get them?" He looks away. "After all you've been through and the way the label has disrespected you."

He starts to sip, but lowers his glass. J Man looks down and quietly says, "They were DATs."

"So?"

"Back when I recorded my songs, we used two-inch tape, not DATs. Those weren't the masters. They were copies in that new digital format—to make bootlegs."

"You mean Kahn is bootleging his own catalog?"

"Actually, looks more like piracy or counterfeiting."

"Why would he pirate what he already owns?"

That's when I got the call.

21

Remembering

MY DAD DIED PEACEFULLY in his sleep a few days ago. I'm standing by the coffin, trying not to laugh. Didn't mean that his passing was funny.

Holding Ivy on this blustery Missouri day, I see about half the population of Puce standing by his grave. What's funny is that I can imagine what Dad would be saying about some of the people assembled here.

The Reverend Wilton T. Forthright conducts the service, as if Dad ever went to church. He's respectful, and all, but Dad would say that he's being nice to him—finally.

The Reverend bombasts, "Willy Lamb was a man, a man who was not a believer, but who believed in those of us who are. And we are grateful for that."

> *I believe you don't believe that I don't believe in your beliefs.*
> *Believe you me, I don't.*

I can hear Dad saying that and it makes me want to giggle, but I shouldn't. Not here.

The Reverend's son, Garner, who constantly reminds us that he's the best car salesman in the county and that he's also running for County Chairman as a Republican. His waistline matches his weighty accomplishments.

> *Looks like they'll be a chicken in every potbelly, if he's elected.*

Don't laugh.
Wow, look at Gar's hairpiece.

Next to him stands his wife, Alice. How did he end up with the most popular girl in school? Went to Puce High with both of them. Now, they look like a yard sale political team. Garner has become a bulldog with a poodle haircut, and Alice—a poodle with bulldog determination. The winds may budge their beliefs, but never their coifs.

But he'll probably get elected…by a hair.
Why am I hearing Dad's voice so clearly now?
As I look around, I see people that still owe him money.

Guess paying respects is easier than paying debts.

Dad! God, I miss your sense of humor.

When I got the call from my brother that our dad had passed, I dropped everything and headed to Missouri. On the plane, I kept wondering what I'd feel like when I took my first look at Puce since moving to New York. The flight was awful. Ivy wouldn't sit still the whole time. Driving here from the airport, I opened the car window. The smell of Puce gave me memories. Couldn't fight back tears. Had to stop at the side of the road. Ivy stared at me not knowing why I was crying. She never met him. That really made me feel guilty. She had the right to know her grandpa. They would have loved each other. Dad once said, *things always work out, whether you want them to or not.* Now I know what he meant.

My dad and I are so much alike—were alike—except I wasn't as talented, and he wasn't a go-getter. But we shared an offbeat way of seeing the world.

Seems the pigs at Jensen's farm fattened up, since they voted for Reagan.
I've got this song in my head, but I don't know which one.
Never come back to Puce, unless you have to.

That last piece of advice I took to heart. But Dad needs someone to stand up for him—his real self. Otherwise, all these goody-goodies will make themselves feel self-righteous at his expense. After all, he did pay for this funeral. He thought out every detail—the blue steel casket with a treble clef on it, his musician buddies, Willy Lamb and His Swinging Flock, playing

Sinatra, even the people he invited, none of whom ever went out of their way for him, were on his list.

Dad wrote the invitations ahead of time. He seemed to know something was up. He also knew that my brother, Roy, wouldn't be able to handle it very well. That's why he asked my brother's high school football coach, Dolph Erickson, a big Swedish guy, to put his arm around him during the service. Dad somehow knew that Johnny would need help to hold up.

The only plan he didn't include was for me.

He admitted, "I never make any plans for you, Lily, because you seem to have plenty of your own."

Wish I'd planned better for the knot in my stomach and the tears, waiting to gush, when I get a few moments alone.

Thank God for Wilmer T. Forthright, the Puce version of Foggmaster-D. Thanks for Garner and Alice. Without their cartoon charisma, I'd be a blubbering fool.

And that would wake up Ivy.

My arms are getting tired holding up my sleepy girl.

The wind swirls the autumn leaves into dancing funnels. This is the time of year when school begins. Our new clothes announcing how much we'd grown over the summer. Stories, told breathlessly, reliving every crucial detail of our vacations. Later in the term, we would start recognizing the same clothes, the tired old stories and the numbing tedium.

I see a huddle of teenagers in oversized jackets, backward caps and unlaced sneakers. Must be high schoolers. They're about a hundred feet away, keeping to themselves at a "cool" distance.

What are they doing here?

The Reverend says a final prayer, then invites me to place a flower on Dad's casket. I carefully place the red rose on the treble clef. I'm guessing it's where middle C would be. I start to cry, but suddenly, the band breaks into "Night and Day." They sound worse than the Puce High Marching Band at halftime—and that's God-awful. The reason is, the Swinging Flock is crying and playing. Those guys are so pathetic and touching. They're trying so hard to make this moment special. I walk up to them and kiss each one on the head, which makes their music worse.

Hopefully, Dad hears what's in their hearts and sees how

much Willy Lamb's Swinging Flock loved him.

One player, who stands out, is John "Rainy Day" Sedler. He's on saxophone. John is the only black man I knew until I started at Def Kahn-5. In his lifetime he went from being called a "nigger" to "nigra" to "black" to "African-American." What Dad always called him was "my rainy day friend." They used to sit around our dinner table and talk music, agreeing on Bix, Pops, Dizzy and Coltrane, arguing over Ella, Dinah, Billie and Sarah. I used to roll my eyes whenever they started up.

Ba-de-ba, ba-de-ba, ba-de-ba…Boop!
Biddl-dee, bop. Ba deedly-do-wop!

They riffed a language only known to them. My brother Roy's middle name, Rainy, is named after "Rainy Day."

Now here, on this day, Dad's friend is playing some last licks, like he's still communicating with him.

The service ends. We head for home.

There's an After Party?

After a Puce funeral, people gather to meet, greet and eat. That's what we're doing—a community gathering at Dad's house.

Ivy took a breath of Missouri air and went narcoleptic. She's asleep, encircled by coats, on my old bed. As she gently snores, the activity continues in the rest of the tiny house. In the living room on a table filled with chips and onion dip, sits a studio portrait of Dad, when he was a seventeen-year-old aspiring concert pianist with expressive fingers and wavy hair. But that's the picture he requested.

It's funny when kids see their parents as young people. His chin rests lightly on his hand, eyes staring to a point beyond the photographer. So posed, so goofy, so young. My guess is that's how he always felt inside—young, with potential and hope that's just beyond the picture.

"Eeyoo!" Alice cries. She just spilled some yams on her black silk shoes. Garner, kneeling, wipes the orangy blob with a napkin.

"Bring a sow to a gatherin' and you invite a mess."

"You just get that before it stains or I'll…" Alice realizes eveyone's listening. She smiles, and changes her tone. "That Gar, he's just too precious. Look how he takes care of me."

Andy Jackalop, Garner's political opponent, yells across the living room. "That Gar's a regular footman for her royal heinie."

Alice, oblivious, beams, "That's right."

"Hey, Gar," Andy brays, "Careful you don't muss up that hair. We're all out of Elmer's Glue."

Everyone breaks up, except the Royal Family of Puce. Garner raises his head. His hairpiece moves a second after, revealing a scalp that's turning red.

Alice pulls her shoe out of his grasp. "I told you not to start wearing that thing."

Garner snaps back. "And I told you not to wear your good shoes for something like this."

That quiets the crowd. I realize that this shoe reference has something to do with my Dad's standing in the community—or lack of it.

Luckily, my cellphone rings. I give a warning look to Garner and Alice, then hinge open the phone.

"Lily White."

Alice whispers loudly enough for me to hear. "She thinks she's so above us…"

I want to say something to her, but I'm also trying to find out which of our female artists just shot up a beauty salon.

> *"Keisha, why are you calling me about this?…No, this is not a good time…I'm…Is she in jail or hiding? Look there's nothing I can do about it now. I'm in Missouri…Tell Ma'am-Ree to call Rich. Make sure she loses the gun AND the press-on fingernails…Because the police will blow her away if she looks armed in any way…How hard is that to understand? No gun, no press-ons, and nothing sharp…Yes, I'll be by the phone."*

Keisha hangs up. I close the cell. Great, I just buried my father and Kahn fired me last week, but they still call so I can solve their problems.

I turn. Everyone's staring. Alice has this sneer on her face, so I walk up close to her. "Is there something you want to say?"

She turns even whiter.

Garner steps in. "She, Alice…you know her…her big mouth. She doesn't know half of what she's saying. It's those Valii she takes. I mean, it's legal, being a doctor's prescription and all."

Alice clenches her teeth, "Shut your mouth before I put my yam-stained shoe in it."

I look at them. "What's happened to you two? You used to be so happy. Now you're like nervous puppets. Who's pulling your strings up there?"

Need to change the atmosphere in here. "Gar, you remember when we won that bet with Andy and who else was it?"

"I don't recall."

"Sure. Andy and, I think it was Ben Blaisedell, bet that you couldn't kiss me. You told me about it and we got them to raise the stakes. Then we split the money. You must remember…"

All the oxygen has left the room. The silence makes me realize that this isn't New York, and this is no longer the place I remember. In bringing up the past, I've broken some sort of ancient Puce taboo.

Change the subject. "Hey, everyone, I want you to know that as of this moment, I absolve you, all of you, of any and all debts you owe my Dad."

Oops! Half the people suddenly make excuses to leave. The other half waits for the right moment to get away. Garner works the door for votes. Alice gossips to the other women, who hastily Saran rip and wrap the bowls of potato salad, pickled beets and other assorted dishes.

The party is definitely over.

Feeling like an intruder, I look out the window, where Dad used to spend hours just staring into space. What was he looking at or for? The sunset is gray and pink. Under a large tree, sits the Puce chapter of Hip Hop wannabes. The same teen posse I saw at the funeral.

What are they doing there?

"I hope you're happy." I turn. Angry Alice glares at me. "You ruined your Daddy's funeral with your New York superior attitude." Her face twitches like she's lost control of herself. What's scary is that I remember who she used to be—head cheerleader, popular beyond belief, the girl who walked the school hallway like she was on a homecoming float, waving at the rest of us on the curb. Now she's become a bitter woman, trapped in a parade of hate.

"What's happened to you, Alice?"

My question stops her for a moment. She bites her upper lip. "You can't talk to me like that. You're not so high and mighty just because you live in God-forsaken New York City."

"Alice, I'm not…"

"At least I've stayed with my husband, not like some people. I haven't given up on my obligations."

"I'm warning you, Alice, don't go there. I'm not about to be judged by an over-the-hill prom queen."

Her face goes from pale to red.

"ALICE!" Garner jumps in. "We should be going." He takes her arm. "Time to get home. You've done enough damage." Gar turns to the few people left. "Got to get that yam-stain out of m' lady's shoe. You all be good now. But if you can't be good, be careful. Ha-ha."

On the way out, Alice fumes, "How can you let that woman talk to me like that?"

"Just keep walking."

The last thing I hear her say is "She works for that devil's Rap music. Look at those hoodlums over there. That's her fault. She did that."

I did?

The Puce food patrol leaves the kitchen clean, the leftovers gift-wrapped and the house neater than when they came. With their lined faces and deep dishes, they are life's caterers. At births, weddings and funerals, these angels appear and feed the crowds with country manna, effortlessly. Having graced this gathering place with sustenance, off they fly to prepare for the next milestone.

Earlier, for a moment, I squinted at and imagined everyone here was black. This could be BronxSkee's home—Garner could easily be Uncle Smelly. The ladies who cook and wrap must all belong to the same union—the IUFFL—The International Union of Food, Fixings and Leftovers. And Grandma. Was anyone here like her?

"Made me a plate to take home, Lily."

It's Rainy Day. In one hand, he's holding a plate of tin-foiled leftovers. In the other hand—his saxophone case. I give him a hug. He puts his forearms around my shoulders. I start to cry. So does he.

"Rainy, I miss him so much."

"He was very proud o' you, Lily. Your Daddy always said that. He said that you got the gift."

"Gift? What gift?"

"You know." He looks into my eyes.

"No I don't."

He checks to see if anyone is listening, then "Bah-da-be-bah..." and points to me. He scats again "Bah-da-be-bah..." and points again.

"Boop!"

"That's it, girl. That's the gift."

I have no idea what he's talking about. He gives me another big hug. The warmth of his leftovers plate soaks into my back.

He leaves, humming " Bah-da-be-bah...Bah-da-be-bah..."

Boop! Like that, everyone's gone.

It's just too difficult to think of spending the night here. The house seems so small and the memories so big. I miss New York City with the crazy people on the street and the misfits at the label. For a moment, I forget I was fired, and just warm myself in the insanity my life has become.

I actually love it.

Got to step outside to take a deep breath.

The last light is disappearing. It's crisp and cool. There's a faint smell of burning wood and wet moss. I need to talk to someone. Who'll listen? Funny, but I can't think of anyone off-hand. I open my cellphone, flip through the numbers stored in the memory. There's Jiggity Man's number. I press send.

"Hi. Thought I was going to get your voicemail. It's Lily. Okay, I guess...There's things to wrap up here...Like the house and my Dad's stuff...The funeral was exactly what my Dad wanted...I appreciate that...I'm doing okay. Actually,

> *I'm not. I want to go home. I mean New York. Funny, I used*
> *to think this was home, but now…"*

Jiggity says soothing things. But I'm not feeling better, because he asks me about when I was working at the warehouse. Could I describe who borrowed the masters?

Have to remind him that I just buried my father five hours ago. Business, especially our business, can wait. He pulls back and says that he's sorry he's being so insensitive. But there's something about the way he asked me—like my situation wasn't that important. That's the kind of behavior I'd expect from Kahn.

I tell J Man I've got to go.

Folding my cellphone, I glance at the giant Bur Oak that I used to climb when I was a kid. Under the tree, sit the group of kids that were watching the funeral.

"Hey," I say.

They look at each other as if they've just been caught.

I wave with both arms.

A couple of them decide to leave their perch.

"How goes it?"

I put out my hand.

One of the boys gives me a ghetto handshake.

That's a surprise.

"Y' know, s'cool." he says through the collar of his baggy jacket. "Chillin'." His head bobs and weaves.

"Yeah, I know, bro," I say without thinking.

This makes them sit up. All it took to break the ice with this crew is one well-placed "bro."

The Puce gangstas all start talking at the same time.

> *Wassup*
> *Word*
> *Wreckin'*

"Whoa," I say, "One at a time. I'm only two ears."

A little guy, whose clothes swallow him up says, "We be down wid dat. Yo, let me in on the scoop wid Axx¿. He be da bomb. Tell me the truth. He be all that?"

"Yeah, he be all that." I'm not going to pop their bubble. They wouldn't believe that he's a middle-aged pedophile. "What're all of you doing out here?"

A big ol' redheaded, freckled country boy ambles up to me. His hands are large enough to milk a cow dry in one squeeze. "We hear you be comin' back, an' we wanna get down wid ya's. Pay respects to your fam'ly."

Another kid says, "Yeah, we be sorry 'bout your Dad."

Another says, "The man was a fly dude."

They all touch fists, which touches me deeply.

Am I in the right place? These Future Farmers of America are acting like they're right out of the hood. They're sweet and respectful.

It hits me—what we do at DK-5 actually has an effect well beyond big cities. I wonder if in Fiji, I'd find Polynesian kids wearing their caps backwards and their underwear peeking above their low-slung baggy pants?

"You wants t' hang wid us at th' new mall?"

"There's a mall in Puce? Where?"

"Out yonder." One of the crew points. "By Elam's Run."

"That be da bomb diggity," says one of the girls, "For sure, when they's finish buildin' th' thang."

"It's not built yet?"

"Nearly. Needs bricks, stores, and bang-bang, it be done."

"How can you hang out at the mall that's not built yet?"

The small guy says, "We be stakin' out terr'tory...early."

Another farmboy adds, "Yeah, we wants t' keep it away from the Crips. We be Bloods, knowwhatImean?"

"Uh, yeah, I think."

My cellphone rings.

"Lily White...Oh, no. Can you get her on the phone? Never mind give me her number..."

I say to the kids. "Excuse me, I have to make this call."

They don't take the hint, so I turn my back and dial.

"Ma'am-ree, this is Lily White from Def Kahn-5. What's up?...Why did you do that?...But you can't shoot up a

beauty shop, even if Bitty Betty dissed your hairdo. She's just jealous cause you're selling more records than her...I know...Yes, but that kind of response can undermine your parole. Are you at home?...Good. Are the police outside your door? ...Oh. Remember, they will shoot you if you do something foolish...Here's my suggestion: get rid of the gun, put on something very conservative. Do you have a blue business suit?...Well, do the best you can. After you change, call the police and tell them you'll give up if they promise not to shoot...Of course, that makes sense...I'm on your side, girl...I'll always be there...Right. Look like a businesswoman, because you need to be taking care of business now...Right?...NO, NO, NO, DON'T EVEN THINK OF GOING AFTER BITTY BETTY!. YOU UNDERSTAND ME? I'll call Kahn and make sure he gets you a lawyer...Yes, the best lawyer...Just stay cool and things will work out...Of course, you're beautiful...Right...Bye."

I hang up, take a deep breath and realize the kids are staring at me. I've just become the fifty-foot woman, scoring an eleven on the BB/DS Richter Scale. Here, in small-pond Puce, they think I'm the big fish.

"Kids, I've got to go inside. One thing I'd like to tell you is playacting Hip Hop culture is fine, but living it can get you in trouble, or even killed. KnowwhatImean?"

Obviously, they don't. "Look, thank you for coming to the funeral, and thanks for your kindness."

"Word," says one of them.

The others respond, "Word."

I hope they'll outgrow this. Maybe one of them will become the best used car salesperson in the county.

Word.

I turn quickly and go.

Inside, I see all the things that I loved and hated about this place. What do I want to take back home? Looking room by room, I'd say, almost nothing—almost. My eyes keep drifting back to my father's picture. That's what I'll take. I feel badly that

I don't have anything from my mother, but she willed all her things to Reverend Forthright's church. Their tag sale brought in about a thousand dollars for their activity fund.

Dad said that she gave her life to that church. Her possessions should follow her obsessions.

Bah-da-be-bah...Boop.

In my old room, Ivy is still asleep. I take her in my arms. Tears pour out of my eyes.

She wakes up. "Mommy cry?"

"I miss my Daddy, honey."

"I you little girl."

"I know. I'm crying because I'm no one's little girl anymore."

Coiled Up

Life's not a straight line. It's a spiral.

Which direction do you see the spiral moving—from inside out or outside in? Imagine your life as a dot traveling along that curve. Is it traveling inward or out? Now, imagine my life up to this point. Which direction would you guess I'm headed? Inward, outward, spiraling out of control or what? Before you answer, take a look:

The Three Laws of Hip Hop Motion
1) A body at rest tends to go nowhere
2) A body in motion stops when it hits a brick wall
3) For every action there's an opposite, but not necessarily equal, reaction

So how does this pertain to my life? Simply this, even though I increased my motion at DK-5, I've gone nowhere. I hit a wall. I am invisible. Kahn bricked me in. Left me out.

At first, I thought that he felt threatened. That somehow I made his plans go off-target.

What those plans were—I can only guess..

BUG is going to buy DK-5—something I thought Kahn would never allow.

But he seems to be doing nothing to stop it.

I know that he hired me to be his "cuntingency plan." If things got bad, it was me who would hit the fan. That's why he gave me assignments that were sure to fail. Of course, he didn't count on me actually accomplishing anything—but I did.

My Dad used to say that *Life's a pasture. The only choice is which cow paddy you're gonna sit on.*

So here I sit in my paddy, wondering how I got here—jobless, husbandless, and aimless. Since I let the babysitter go, I've spent more time with Ivy. But soon as she's napping, I run into the bathroom and cry. I try to watch "I Love Lucy," but it's hard for me to laugh, even when Lucy's crushing grapes and fighting that Italian woman.

And I really miss my Dad.

I called Roberta to see if she could help me find a job. She's gone out of business. Even her home phone's disconnected. So I called the "Martha Stewart" of that women's group. She said, "Roberta found a lovely Arabic man, married him and moved to Beruit or Hauppauge."

Bobby Bunyan can't be reached. Jiggity Man hasn't returned my calls. Tried talking to Mae, but she's too busy to chat. Seems like everyone's avoiding me.

I miss having a challenge. I even miss my ugly office.

And my refrigerator is nearly empty. *In the beginning is the end, and vice versa.* That was my Mom's quote.

When I hold Ivy, I find that my leg starts pumping up and down—not like a "playing horsey" way, but like a racehorse pawing the ground, waiting for the gate to open.

But it never does.

At least Ivy gets some enjoyment out of it.

Now, I don't know where to take my next step.

So if you haven't guessed by now, I'm not spiraling.

I'm in limbo.

22

A Regular Riot

YOU'RE INVITED to the dopest, loudest, illest
movie of the year—Fantazy Strip. Be down with it at
8:00 p.m., and get down with it at the Madison
Square Garden Fantazy Premier Party.

I keep reading and rereading the invitation. Luckily, no one ever implemented my idea to scrub and centralize the contact sheet. So nothing's changed, and I'm still on the company's mailing list.

Call Mae and ask her about the screening and premier party. She says that it's going to be a big event. Even a "friend" I haven't seen in a while is going to be there. She is all but saying Bobby Bunyan.

THIS IS MY CHANCE! I hop around the room, screaming. Ivy joins in. We're both jumping around and singing the Barney song. "I LOVE YOU. YOU LOVE ME. WE'RE A HAPPY FAMILY..."

Gangstas scream about how life is a nightmare. Players scream about how great life will be when their dreams come true. That's how I'd sum up Rap—screaming and dreaming. Kind of like what I'm feeling now.

I was about to go out of my mind. Being banned from the office isn't the worst part. What's hardest is the loss of routine, not being around adults, and the twenty-four/seven at home with Ivy. "...WITH A GREAT BIG HUG AND A KISS FROM ME TO YOU..."

A confession: Ivy is wonderful, but I feel like a constant slave. Being a mom is much harder than babysitting artists. At least with Rappers there's a good chance that they've been completely potty-trained.

Been so involved with Ivy's needs, that I haven't thought too much of my own. And eventually, the rent will come due, and it's nice to eat—you know, stuff like that.

So I have to get to Bunyan because, through him, I have a chance to get my job back and prevent my refrigerator from being empty.

Screaming and dreaming.

I'm not going away quietly. If I've learned anything from this business it's that noise, bluster and threats are legitimate negotiating tactics. While not very clever in execution, these techniques come in handy when the job needs to get done. Thanks to Kahn's assignments, I've learned to employ and deploy them in the field.

My plan is simple: Get to Bunyan. Tell him that Kahn tried to rape me and then fired me when I fought back. Then talk about the bootlegs.

Just get past security, make stimulating conversation, and secure my job in ten seconds.

"...WON'T YOU SAY YOU LOVE ME, TOO."

Suiting Up

A black, backless Versace dress, which I intend to return tomorrow, and my knock-off Manolo Blahniks. A simple "almost" gold rope and my DK-5 pendant. My small green sequined purse holds lipstick, a make-up mirror, cab-fare, my work ID, and a company beeper.

And Ola agreed to babysit tonight.

Before leaving for the premiere of "Fantazy Strip" and the party afterward, I hold Ivy. When's she's tired, she sucks her thumb and curls her hair with her finger. She yawns, "Don't go, Mommy." I hold her until she falls asleep.

One last insult from Ola about my parenting, and I'm gone—to make it happen—to collect what's due me.

The Plot Sickens

The Fantazy Strip Plot: The Fantazy Four, America's dopest Rappers, decide to bust a move on Las Vegas. They arrive to find the concert they've booked has been mysteriously canceled. In fact, they're kicked out of every hotel lobby and casino in town. What de dilly yo? While trying to "make it happen," they discover that their new Vegas girlfriends are informants for Sly Eagle, sinister publisher of "Black Eagle Magazine," whose goal is to destroy the group. The Fantazy Four take it to the street and start rapping in front of a casino. A crowd gathers and grooves to their beat. The police arrive to arrest them, but get caught up in the rhymes. Eventually, their girlfriends are so smitten by the Four that they repent their wrongdoing and start to sing back-up. All is forgiven and the Fantazy Four join Las Vegas in a giant Rapfest, as Sly Eagle literally explodes with rage. They be da bomb—but Sly go ka-boom!

What a horrible movie.

But our soundtrack is da bomb-diggity.

The director thanks us for being supportive of his dreams, and I want to thank him for the movie being only eighty-eight minutes long. Even at that length, thought I was going to crawl out of my skin.

Bunyan wasn't there. Maybe he'll be at the premiere party.

Now, I'm moving with and hiding among the same people who shouted and howled throughout the screening. Our herd rushes out of the theater towards Madison Square Garden and the premiere party for "Fantazy Strip."

We're guided to The Garden, past a snaking line of blue barricades and helmeted police holding back thousands of screaming fans. Light bulbs flash. People crane their necks to see if they can spot anyone famous. We wind our way to where security checks invitations and frisks partygoers.

A tuxedoed guy at check-in looks at me. "Invitation?" I hand it to him. "Name?"

Before I can answer, a woman security guard grabs my purse, empties it, looks in my mouth and says to spread my arms and legs while metal-detecting me. Then she sticks her hand up my dress and feels around.

"I said, name."

Should I use my real name? My work ID is on the table.

"I worked on the soundtrack."

"That's great, but you can't enter without a name."

I pick up my work ID and show it to him.

"Lily White." he reads, then looks at his list.

"You're not on the list."

"But I have my work ID and an invitation."

"Can't let you in without..."

"But I worked on the soundtrack. My name is on the album."

"Congratulations, but you can't come in unless..."

I bum rush my way to the entrance, but a female security guard grabs my arm. "Don't cause me no problems."

I've seen her before. "Isn't your name Er-Mine?"

"I know you from somethin'?"

"You should, we both worked for Jiggity Man."

"You be workin' fo' that pimp?"

"No more. He dumped me for, well, you know how the game's played."

"Don't I, really. What for you tryin' t' come in here?"

"I helped produce the movie soundtrack, but I think Jiggity's trying to keep me out. All that work, and he's disrespecting my contribution. KnowhatImean?"

"Don't I, though." She looks around, then whispers, "Folla me. Act like I's kickin' yo' ass out. Then when we gets 'round the corner, just turn left and keep goin'."

We walk, just as she suggested. She gives me a push. I stop and look at her.

Er-mine says, "Go on. Can't let that muthafucka run us no more." I smile. "We gots t' look out fo' each otha. This be a rough life."

"Don't I know it, girl," I say. "Thank you, Er-mine."

She smiles and winks.

I turn and strut into the party.

BOOM! The crowd noise and our soundtrack explode around me. It takes a moment to get oriented.

Wow. This enormous arena has become "Fantazy Strip," a Las Vegas environment with chorus girls, dancers, singing groups and gambling. Between the croupiers and slot machines, are sports fantasy areas where beautiful people play basketball, hit baseballs and toss footballs at a target. And a boxing ring. Kind of silly to be all dressed up in designer clothes, while pretending you're a jock. But I can live with it.

Circus aerialists and tightrope walkers balance above us. At the outer edges of the floor are trampolines, an elephant ride and a small ice rink, where nearly naked people skate. An enormous banner in the rafters, among the retired jerseys and numbers of sports legends, reads "All proceeds tonight will be donated to the DK-5 Foundation for Mental and Social Well-Being." That's Kahn's fake charity. He unfurls it when money needs to be disinfected.

So Kahn has turned this promotional tax write-off into a charity write-off, which makes everyone think Bigar's a humanitarian. Then he double-dips the deductions.

But he does know how to throw a party. Vegas-type circus performers and waiters, walk around balancing trays. Some have large pheasants, surrounded by rows of tiny glazed drumsticks. Looks like colorful birds with centipede legs flying above and through the crowd.

BOOM!

DUCK! Hundreds of plastic-wrapped candies shoot from mini-cannons onto everyone. Guess Rich didn't see the potential lawsuits blowing up with each volley. Over there is a Cleopatra server with—wow—never heard of Egyptian corn-on-the-cob before. To the left, a woman stands on a man's shoulders. She balances flaming shish-kabob and a fire extinguisher. He offers me some with a napkin and dip.

Tasty and totally tasteless at the same time. Love it.

Focus. Find Bunyan. There's got to be a VIP area somewhere, and I bet he's there. Have to find it, get inside and close enough to recite my speech:

Mr. Bunyan, before you consider buying Def Kahn-5, please consider this: Do you know the reality of the financials? Be very skeptical about the figures you hear tossed around. Conduct an independent audit before you sign anything. Also, did you hear about Kahn trying to rape me? When I refused, he fired me. I didn't press charges because it would hurt the label. And then there's the bootlegging…

Blah, blah, blah. Don't know which stinks worse—my plan or the elephant ride next to me. Got to get upwind of both.

Oh my God! I'm standing next to Harry Belafonte—one of Dad's favorites. There's Aretha Franklin! And Kiwi Smith, the Executive Producer of "Fantazy Strip," talking with two former mayors of New York City—the very short one and the very bald one. No doubt about it, I'm watching the rich and famous be, well, rich and famous.

A guy walks up to me, lays down on his chest and pulls both of his legs back behind his neck, lifts his tray over his head and asks, "Pretzel?"

"No, thanks. But I could use a drink."

He points a toe. "By the Fantazy Tent."

"Thanks." I start to leave, but look down at him. "I have to say, 'that's amazing.'"

"It's a living."

Walking to the tent, I realize that my work on the soundtrack helped make this party happen. I feel like taking a victory lap. Finally, I was starting to get some recognition. There are people who would only do business with me, in spite of their feelings about Kahn or DK-5.

But now, I need to not be recognized—until I'm inside the Fantazy VIP Tent and…

From behind me, "CUNTRUBBING, DICKSHITTER!"

What was that? My neck tightens. I turn slowly.

There…is this very short gorgeous black guy smiling at me. "Hey, little lady." His head is shaved shiny bald, and he's wearing a camel-colored suit and a cream-colored shirt. His skin is the color of Godiva nougat. His light green eyes twinkle at me. Wow, just gorgeous. *Where did that sound come from?*

"Noticed you walkin' by and had to..." His head twitches and he screams, "FUCKINGSLUT CLITHOLE!"

"Excuse me?"

"Could I take a moment of your time?" He smiles.

"You already have."

He offers me his business card. "My Name's Kamal. BITCHTASTING BUTTFUCKING PENIS. You must be from Def Kahn-5."

His business card exactly matches his outfit.

"What makes you think I'm with the label?"

"DK-5 necklace. COOZSUCKING ANALFINGER."

"What are you doing?"

Kamal's head does that double-twitch again. He makes a loud growling noise, then bares his teeth.

People are looking at us. Just what I didn't need—attention.

"Look, I have some business to..."

"I'd like to discuss something with you. PUSSYFART SODOMIZER." He purrs like a cat.

"I, I've got to go."

"Oh." He touches my hand, tenderly. Kamal leans over. *Is he going to kiss it?* "Maybe another COCKREAMER STUFFERPISS BLOWJOBBBER time."

I yank my hand away and realize that I'm holding a small package. "For your consideration." He disappears into the crowd. *What was that all about?* Walking away, I tear open the small brown paper package.

A DEMO! Perfect, just perfect. A guy, speaking in tongues, just handed me a demo.

At the Fantazy Tent, I see the unmistakable continent called Clete blocking the doorway. He's motionless. Only his eyes move as he scans the arena.

If he sees me, I'm toast.

A group of partiers gives me enough cover to walk to the side of the tent, where the nearly nude ice-skaters are making figure eights. *How do I get past Clete?* Maybe there's another way in. Can't find it. If I had something sharp, I could cut my own entrance.

All I've got to work with is my make-up mirror, red lipstick, the useless cellphone and the demo. So I frisbee the only thing that won't ID me—the demo—at Clete. It grazes his head.

Oh, no. I didn't mean to hit him.

He starts investigating. I run the other way around the tent.

He moves to where I was. I move to where he was.

I jump into the Fantazy Tent. It's filled with movie stars, studio executives and, as usual, a flock of chickenheads—each one screaming for attention. Our soundtrack blasts in the background. It's Marquee da Shade screaming his rhymes. That works in my favor. No one will notice me in this ambitious crowd. I motion to the bartender for a drink. Looking around, I see Simon Luftig, the film's Music Supervisor. He acknowledges me with a raised glass. I lift my drink in response. Don't worry, he's not going to invite me over. He's too busy campaigning to get his next job.

No Bunyan here.

Where's the very, very (VSOP) VIP area?

There, by an inner tent-flap, stand four very large, muscular, tuxedoed men and, thank the Lord, Clete's brother, Gervin.

Maybe he doesn't know I've been exiled from DK-5. *Can I fake it?* Have to. I march up to Gervin, put my arms around him. The other guards watch me closely. I plant a big kiss on the bottom of his chin—that's all I can reach.

"Gervin, how are you? It's so nice to see you again." While he's trying to recover from my hug, "I would love to have you and Clete come over for dinner some evening. It's the least I can do for you after helping me find Ivy."

"Aw, you don't have to go to no trouble. We just wanted t' make things right."

"Well, I owe you—big—and I'm not forgetting that."

I enter the inner VIP area quickly. *He bought it.*

As I walk through a narrow corridor, I notice the music changes. It's quieter—less Marquee Da Shade—more Sadé.

Turning left, I enter a large room. It's like a sheik's magnificent tent—Persian carpets, artwork, silver vases with large ferns and plush chairs. Gloved attendants stand ready to pour and serve. This is the inner, inner circle. And there, sinking into big cushions, sit Kahn, #2Girl, Rich, Bobby Bunyan, and ...JIGGITY MAN!"

What is he doing here? Their backs are turned to me. I hear Kahn's voice. "We hope to have collected enough money to help the DK-5 Foundation become handsome."

Bunyan nods his approval. "Quite handsome indeed, Mr. Kahn. The board will be ever so impressed."

I step towards them, then...

...a pair of enormous arms wraps around me. I'm pulled away and back through the tunnel, back through the flap, past Gervin, the other guards, and past the crowd in front of the tent. It's like traveling back in time. One moment you're where you are and the next you're where you were.

I'm standing in front of the Fantazy Tent. My expensive dress is sticking to my clammy skin. I finally take a breath and turn around to see Clete. He's got his "scary" face on. But I don't feel scared, just amazed at how quickly he got me out of there.

"You trying to get me fired? Lily, why'd you do that?"

"Do what?"

"Make me leave my post? Hit me in the head?"

"I didn't mean to hit you, just get your attention. I really need to talk with Kahn. Important business."

"You picked a strange time to do that."

He bought it—Just don't mention Bunyan.

"Clete, I need face-time with Kahn. It's very..."

"LIPLAP PISSFART SHITEATER."

Oh, no. I turn. Kamal grins and takes my hand. "Was hopin' we'd run into each other again. Must be fate."

"Yeah, I was just passing your demo by Clete."

"Great. KISSDICK GASHMASH PUSSYJUICE."

"STOP TALKING TO ME LIKE THAT."

His head does a double-pump to the left.

"Calm down, Lily." Clete lowers his voice. "The man can't help it."

Kamal looks down. "Sorry," trying to stifle a "FINGERFUCK CUNILIGUS BUTTPLUG. Didn't realize it had started up again. Must be nervous about your reaction to my SODOMY BASHNUTS DILDOBREATH demo."

Clete says, "The DK-5 Foundation helps people like him learn to control..."

"I thought it was to teach music to inner city kids."

"That was last year."

I give up.

Walking away, I hear, "Please, ma'am, please give me another COCKSUCKER TURDPACK SNOTSPERMER."

The cannon booms, showering me with candies—some down the front of my dress. I try to fish them out.

Great, just great. No way I'll get to Bunyan now.

I head for the lady's room.

Wait a minute. Why was Jiggity Man there, chumming it up with both Kahn and Bunyan? Has he been pimp-jiving me all this time? Have I just been played, like some girl he just primed at the P-A-B-T?

I turn back to the Fantazy Tent, to talk with Bunyan—and that's what I'm going to do. I march a straight line up to Clete. He doesn't see me coming. In one movement, I reach inside his overcoat, pull out his Street-Sweeper, and take a step back.

Okay, now what am I supposed to do with this overloaded shotgun?

Clete extends his hand. "Lily, give me that weapon."

I take another step back. I've learned to keep my distance from Clete's disarming ways.

"Clete, Don't come any closer. I don't want to hurt you. I have to talk to Bunyan."

"Bunyan? Lily, don't do this. Kahn's got too much riding on this deal. We're talking real danger here. The best thing you can do is lay low until the deal's done. Soon as he sees the money, he'll forget all about you. Go home. Go anywhere, but here. Because the next time I see you, I might not be so nice about it. You hearing me straight?"

"You finished? Good. Now, get away from the entrance. I mean it, Clete. NOW!"

"Okay, just be careful with that gun. The trigger is very sensitive." He moves to my right, towards the entrance.

I thought he was supposed to move the other way.

Just then, Clete's right hand makes a quick upward motion to grab the shotgun, but he misses. Then he swings his left arm upward, forcing the barrel point to the ceiling, which makes the gun roar.

Madison Square Garden is silent—for a second.

The DK-5 Foundation banner, full of holes, flutters down from the rafters and covers the crowd near the gambling tables.

I drop the shotgun. It goes off again.

People start running and screaming.

Is Clete all right? He and the gun are gone.

The Fantazy Tent is leaning to the left, because people are pouring out of a newly torn exit.

Was anyone shot?

It seems like I'm the only one not in motion.

A pained groan catches my ear. I turn to look. The elephant is going berserk. The entire floor of Madison Square Garden rumbles with footsteps and fists. "Fantazy Strip" is being broken apart and flung from one end of the arena to the other. Chairs, ice skates, acrobats, food, cellphones, beepers, canapes, champagne bottles, and anything else not tied down, fly through the air. Individual curses and screams join to form the sound of a blender—set to liquify.

Behind me, the Fantazy Tent creaks, snaps and finally falls flat.

The poor elephant is now sliding across the ice rink, body-checking skaters. Every time it tries to stand, its legs go in different directions, making the terrified beast relieve itself wherever it splats.

Something hard and shiny hits me in the face. For a moment I'm stunned. I touch my right cheek—blood.

Another gunshot.

Ladies and gentlemen, the riot is now officially underway.

I dive under a serving table, causing caviar and toast points to rain down on me.

And another gunshot. Screaming, the crowd moves like a huge school of fish being chased by sharks. Two more shots. I've got to get out of here. Crawling from one table to another, I manage to get close to the door as the police in riot gear "hut-hut-hut" into the Garden.

The contortionist is on his back. His legs are still stuck behind his head. He's whimpering. I try to help un-pretzel him, but a cloud of tear-gas turns me into a bad Samaritan.

Nose running, eyes flowing, I'm running, doubled over, sweat pours out of every pore, my coughs rattle my spine. I use the bottom of my dress to cover my face. "Fantazy Strip" music is still pounding. The place is filled with fear and tear-gas. *Got to get out.* To shield myself from flying objects, I crouch behind an overturned roulette table, and then roll it towards the exit. I slide on poker chips, playing cards and party dip, straining for traction and breath.

Finally, the exit ramp. I hit the outer doors, as the crowd inside starts to sound like one of my mother's revival meetings— wailing, stomping, "help me lords" and music blaring.

Wonder if Bunyan still wants to buy the label now?

Outside, on Seventh Avenue, the crowd noise is replaced by traffic sounds. I take a full breath and exhale. That's when my knees buckle and my stomach starts to churn.

Shaking and scared, the taste of tear-gas still in my mouth— OH, NO. WHAT DID I JUST DO?

My stockings are torn. *Where are my fake Blahniks?*

Police cars pass, their lights flashing. But I can't hear the sirens. After a moment I don't even see them.

I did it. I'm deaf, dumb and blind—to everything.

23

Nothing Business—Just Personal

When you're caught in a tidal wave, it's too late for swimming lessons.

DAD SAID THINGS like that as he stared out the window, letting his thoughts float.

Now, I'm floating, numb, lost, tired, scared, thinking, walking —for who knows how long?

Central Park West: A doorman, wearing a long maroon coat and hat, hails a cab for a woman and a teenage girl. They look like the older and newer versions of each other. The older one keeps an eye on me. The doorman sees her seeing me.

Wonder what Ivy will look like as a teenager.

The doorman blows his whistle. A taxi pulls up. He opens the back door, shuts it behind the passengers and salutes. The cab pulls away.

He walks to me. "Can I help you, ma'am?"

"I want your job."

He laughs. "Let me tell you, you don't. Gets crazy around here sometimes. Still, made enough to send two kids through college. Not too bad, if you ask me."

"Not too bad."

"Excuse me for being personal, but seems like you might need some help."

"Yeah, need to get my job back."

"What do you do?"

"Whatever it takes."

The doorman runs his hand down his mouth and chin like he has a beard. He's studying me. "Look, I ain't got a judgmental bone in my body, but if you're looking for extra work, leave me your number. Not promising anything, but sometimes the residents ask for, you know, 'personal services.' I'd only ask for fifteen percent."

"Fifteen percent?"

"Hope you don't mind, but clean you up and you'd make out like a bandit."

"Bandit?" I touch my cheek and cringe.

"That's quite a shiner."

"Shiner?"

"You hooked up with a pimp?"

"Not anymore."

"You want to leave me your number?"

"Number?"

"Look, don't mean to be a bug about it, but I'm..."

"BUG? The number. From the dumpster. On Fifth Avenue. BUG's address."

"...just trying to help."

"You did. You did."

I try to hug him, but he pulls back. "I'm happily married."

"I'm not—but thanks."

With a little more energy, I cross the street, enter the park and follow the roadway. Cars pass. Honk. One, with its headlights off, stops. "You looking for a ride?" I look at the guy. "Jesus, what tha fuck?" He steps on the gas.

My feet are completely out of my ripped pantyhose. With each flap, flap, flap across Central Park, they creep a little higher. Up the East Side—Fifth Avenue. Blocks of barefooting, and I'm at the large ornate building. Inside, two doormen stand guard.

This is where Bunyan lives.

Should I put my left foot in or my right foot out? Before I can shake it all about, should I do the Hokey-Pokey, and turn myself around? After all, that's what it's all about.

I enter the lobby. What's that between my legs? It swings back and forth. It puts a swagger in my stride. It makes the doormen look at me like I'm trying to smuggle a bowling ball between my knees. I raise a finger—One moment. Turn my back, lift my dress and look. It's the DK-5 pendant. Must have fallen down in the riot and snagged on my pantyhose. Snagged. Maybe later. I smooth out my ruined Versace and turn. "Here to see Bobby Bunyan."

"That so?" One of the uniformed doormen stares at me like I just dropped off the back of a garbage truck.

The other one lifts the receiver, as if it doesn't matter where I dropped from. He asks me to sign in. Lost my ID.

"I have a visitor to see Mr. Bunyan...I will." He hangs up the phone. "Ma'am, Mr. Bunyan's security says that no one is expected. Can't let you up without authorization. Sorry."

"I'm from Def Kahn-5." The two doormen look at each other. "Look, I have proof."

I lift my skirt and expose the DK-5 pendant stuck to my pantyhose, one of the men inspects it carefully. He takes a moment to think, then whispers, "Excuse me, but I have this demo I've been working on…"

"Sure." I lower my dress. "Always looking for hot joints. Twenty Mott Street. My office." He grins. "Need to see Bobby Bunyan…"

The "demo" doorman turns to his companion. "Maybe we should call up and say she's from the Def Kahn-5."

"Tell them I'm Lily White."

The other doorman looks at my dirty feet and shakes his head. "Okay, but you'll take the blame for this one. I'm on my break." He leaves.

"Don't mind him. He doesn't understand the record business." Guy's grinning at me like I'm his ticket to glory.

He calls again and adds Def Kahn-5 to my description, and says that I might need some assistance. He hangs up.

"Take that elevator to the penthouse. I'll drop the demo at your office in the morning."

"Yeah, do that."

A young guy with white gloves holds the elevator door.

The doorman says, "Ms. Lily White to Mr. Bunyan's suite."

The elevator operator salutes. "Please, watch your step."

Wish someone had told me that at the beginning of the evening.

The doors close and I slump against the back wall railing.

Too bad though, because the dark, wood-paneled car has large copper mirrored doors. Oh my God, who is that? Her black dress is torn under her chest and the skirt is ripped up to her thigh. It's stained and sticky with extra dry champagne, and smells of old caviar. The face looking back is pale, except where mascara has run down to meet the blue and purple bruise on her swollen cheek. Hair matted down. So, like a stranger in an elevator, I ignore myself.

The elevator operator looks in the mirror. "You in the music business?"

"Do I look it?"

He turns, looks, shrugs and faces forward.

What am I doing? Something. I'm doing something. Try to remember. What?

The elevator glides to a stop. A quiet ding and the doors silently open. Bunyan's security force bristles in front of me. Some have holstered guns. Others have all the firepower they need in their arms.

The operator says, "We're here, ma'am."

"Thank you." My legs and back ache. Rising from my slump, I step into the vestibule, trying to squeeze out some dignity. The elevator door closes. I turn to look back. Suddenly, from between my legs, the DK-5 pendant plops to the marble floor.

There's a hush, as the bodyguards stare at my dropping. They look at each other in silence. Then two muscular women in matching spandex tank-tops and pants advance towards me, pulling on rubber gloves.

It's my move. Either I can step forward or faint.

I do both.

"I'm Lily White, of Arts and Repertor, Reper..., Repet..." I take a deep breath. "...Re-pet-twar and artists from Def Kahn-5. Important...I need...talk...to Bobby. Important."

Did they hear that, or am I only talking in my head?

The two women grab my arms and lift.

"You're hurting me." They let go.

I'm barely standing, then I'm not.

"Please follow us, ma'am." I look up at the dark-haired one. Her tree trunk arms point the way. I want to follow, but, right now, I'm enjoying the floor. The male guards talk into their cufflinks. Tiny earpieces with clear wires corkscrew into the collars of their dark blue sport coats. One of them says my name.

He listens, nods and then says, "Proceed."

The two bulging babes make a move. Each one takes an arm and Beany Babies me away.

"Excuse me, ladies, where are we going? Hello, where are …Taking me to the weight room?"

The blonde twists the upper half of her physique and head in one sharp motion. Her blue eyes pop through her third-degree tan, but she says nothing.

"I mean, waiting room." Better shut up. This is a no-win tag-team situation. They continue carrying me down a hall. "Could I take a bath?" That stops them. "Can't meet Bobby like this. Come on…fish goop on my dress. I smell like a bait-shop in summer."

The blonde looks at the brunette. "She does, you know." The brunette wrinkles her nose in response.

"Need ice for my shiner. Rough night at the Garden. How's Bobby? He alright?"

The brunette nods to the blonde. They lug me down another hall. The blonde opens the door to a living room. It looks like a living room, except for the large sunken tub and the marble throne of a toilet.

The blonde starts the water running, then leaves. The brunette gets me two large towels, a white terrycloth bathrobe with BB on the chest pocket and matching slippers.

She helps me peel off my dress, then the rest of the mess. I get in the hot water and just soak. The blonde returns with an icepack. I put it on my left cheek. The shock wakes me up a bit.

The three of us sit there and say nothing. I decide to call them Wham and Bam—in my head. After a few seconds of trying to make small talk, I realize they aren't here to enjoy my company.

Lean back, close my eyes and let the hot water do its work. What am I doing here? I had a plan. I'm inside. Now what? Too tired to give Bunyan my speech. Too sleepy...

I'm standing at the bottom of an escalator at the bus station. Hank is a pimp, selling Herbalux. Mae comes down and licks his face. Behind her is #2Girl. She opens up her shirt, revealing her chest, one breast is the head of Kahn and the other is Rich. Ivy descends. Hank approaches with a syringe full of Herbalux...

"No!" I scream. That wakes me up.

Standing beside the tub, is the pumped-up blonde holding up a towel. She clears her throat.

Bath time is over.

Drying, I say, "You could swim laps in here."

They look at each other.

Did I confuse them?

Wham wraps me in a fluffy bathrobe. She helps me with some slippers, which make me feel better. Bam cleans and butterflies the cuts on my cheek.

Wham holds up my dress with a mop handle. It's ruined.

I sigh. "It's Versace. I was going to return it tomorrow."

They lead me down a hallway. The walls are covered with art. The floors are green stone inlaid with white marble. Persian carpets run the full length of the hall. Every ten feet or so, there are statues of people from some ancient nude civilization.

"The rent on this place must be something."

No response.

We stop at carved mahogany doors. Got to be twelve feet high, at least.

The brunette opens one and motions me in.

Entering the room, I turn to Wham and Bam. "Thanks. You've been very nice."

The door slams in my face. I turn around and...oh, my, this isn't a room. It's a convention center. To make it look more intimate, furniture has been arranged in groupings. There are areas for playing cards, chess and boardgames, areas for conversation, another for reading and one for jigsaw puzzles. Other furniture-groupings seem to be for no other reason than to just fill up space.

A piano plays from the other end of this blimp hangar. My

slippers flap, flap, flap towards the distant music. It gets louder as I approach. I can't make out the tune, but it's sad. There, on a small stage is a large piano, a Bosendorfer. Dad said that's about as good as it gets—as far as pianos go.

So how far will Lily go to get what she wants? Whatever "it" takes, even if doing "it" is part of the bargain. This girl may not be the sexiest woman around, but she is the most freshly-bathed.

Under the piano I see two legs in pajamas with a musical notes pattern and slippers with pennies in them. It's Bunyan. His feet move on the pedals. I come around the shiny black monster and step onto the small stage.

Without looking up, "I wrote it on a lonely day." His face is covered in small band-aids. I wince. "I must look dreadful."

"Oh, Bobby, did that happen at the Garden?"

He continues playing. "Actually later. The car overturned. I thought we had escaped the mob, but the police decided we were armed and dangerous. So a chase ensued. Mr. Clete sped ahead at a frightful pace. As improvidence would have it, we bashed into the island that contains the lovely landscaping along the center of Park Avenue. So I guess you could say, we escaped one garden only to be upended by another. No real harm done, except poor Mr. Kahn—whiplash." Bunyan finally looks at me. "Lily, poor dear, you look like you've been battered by a brute."

"I was lucky. There were gunshots."

"Yes, I suppose in the Rap music business that's considered tolerable behavior. What?"

"Bobby, could I ask you something? Are you still interested in buying DK-5?"

He pauses and then speaks quietly. "I'm advised by my board, it is a lucrative endeavor."

"What if it's not the moneymaker you thought it was? There's so much about it that you may not understand."

"I agree."

"Then why do you want to buy Def Kahn-5?"

"Let me assure you, Lily, Bunyan Under Garments has always been a forward-thinking company. It all started when we introduced the first trap doors into long johns. That made us our first fortune. Then we put the front slits in boxer shorts—our second fortune. We've grown from two to forty styles of gentlemen's and ladies' undergarments. To tell you the truth, there's not much more we can do to improve undies. That's why we expanded to shopping carts, oil refining, canned vegetables and auto parts. We have been future-faced for over one hundred and thirty-eight years. So when Daddy asked me to think about what's next for BUG, I did consumer research, and learned that entertainment is what the world wants. It's why people use our core products in the first place—to go out to be entertained. And have you ever noticed all those street urchins who expose their underwear in public? Our focus groups have determined that it is all for show. It's a perfect fit. Ergo, the logical extrapolation of undergarments is show business. "

"Logical?"

"Lily, the underwear business and the music industry work the same way—create, manufacture, market and distribute."

What he's saying makes no sense, so I put my hand on his shoulder. "Would you play a song for me?"

"Really?"

"Yes. You know, my father was a piano player."

Bobby's grin widens. "Certainly." He plays and sings.

Mediocre would be a compliment to what I'm hearing.

When he's done, I applaud politely.

"That was nice."

"I love music so."

"Is that why you're buying the label?"

"Actually, I would love to buy every recording label, but my financial people would put up such a row. So I've decided to exercise prudence and own only one of each musical genre."

Did I just hear him right? He wants to collect recording companies like some people collect albums? Could this wimpy little guy have the biggest ego of all? Even Kahn has to manipulate to get what he wants. But little ol' Bobby here, wields power with a wave of his checkbook.

"DK-5 seems to be the most desirable Rap recording company. So, naturally, I wanted it."

"Naturally." *Naturally?* "Encore."

His voice is a whiny, off-key will-o-th'-whisper. He has no

breath-control, but his diction is flawless. Bunyan sings of love, so unrequited that you'd barely know it exists. But, in his own way, he's passionate about what he's doing. And I'm not going to say anything to make him feel otherwise.

He sings a ditty about "Love, where is it now that I can love?" and another about "I would stalk you, and love to walk with you and talk to you."

I applaud. "That's lovely." Here I am, sitting next to this underwear billionaire, trying to figure out how to beg him for my job. That makes me laugh.

"What's funny?"

"I was just thinking about how perfect this situation is."

"This situation?"

"Yes. Here you are, about to buy a record label, and by coincidence, you're also a musician."

"Its no coincidence." He smiles, looks around as if someone might be listening, then whispers, "Would you like to know the real reason I want a music label?"

"Yes, I would."

"You see, Lily, I want to share my music with others, and this is the best way to…" He must see the shocked expression on my face because he gets defensive. "I've studied composition, practiced daily, ever since I was a boy."

OH-MY-GOD! He doesn't want to go into the music business. He wants to record his own music! He's building a vanity conglomerate. Who's crazier—Kahn or Bunyan?

This boy has just taken the lead in that race.

Did Kahn know that this was happening? He had to. Kahn's not that stupid. In fact, he reads people pretty well. He had to see this guy was about pure ego. But why would Kahn go to all this trouble to woo Bunyan, when BUG could crush him?

Who's the pimp here and who's being played? "So your advisors think DK-5 is a good investment?"

"Yes, but they usually tell me what I want to hear, then convince Daddy to say no. So this time I stepped in with my Acquisition Commandos."

"Acquisition Commandos?"

"They never fail. Mr. Kahn was actually one of our easiest

conquests. You see a privately held company like DK-5 is very hard to acquire without some leverage on the owner. Can you keep a secret?"

"Yes."

"I'm going to tell you something you may not want to hear. Bigar Kahn has done some things that many would find questionable. Even illegal."

"I've heard rumors."

He leans in. "What did you hear?"

Where do I start? "Have you ever heard of bootlegging?"

He interrupts, "Oh, poo, I've had full knowledge of that little side-venture for months."

"You did?"

"Yes. Peanuts. And I know about his skimming, money laundering, drug selling, prostitution and what a list it is. More peanuts." *Kahn has been a busy boy.* "That was our leverage. He did not want to sell until he saw his choice—prison or a capitulation."

"We were even going to keep Kahn as COO, but he had this silly idea that as a side venture, he could take a salary and sell his little pirated bootlegs through some charity fronts. I was very disappointed in his petty dishonesty."

"But honesty has nothing to do with a Rap label."

"It will—as of the first of the month."

HE'S SERIOUS. This is it—as high on the BB/DS Grid as a person can score. Now, here I am, face-to-face with moneyed-mediocrity. His very presence tells me that all my grinding work, all my knowledge and all my struggling means nothing.

But that's the trick. Hank and Kahn kept me in line—by promising better times if I stuck it out. Promising that my hard work would pay off. Always promising. Well, I'm tired of promises. "Bobby, I have to be honest with you. Running a Rap label is not the same as running other record companies. I suggest you let me introduce you to this strange business. First of all, it's based on years of hard life circumstances. Circumstances you know nothing of. I'm sorry to be blunt, but unless you have some sort of major dysfunction in your life, you wouldn't understand. You can't relate to the artists and the audience. There are forty employees and twenty-two artists who make up the label. We understand what the public wants. Why? Because we're just as dysfunctional as our audience." *Trying to get Bunyan to understand that it takes one to know one.* "And that riot tonight? It was planned. (Okay, so I'm lying). An industry party gets mentioned on Page Six of the Post, if you're lucky. A riot makes page one— more publicity."

"But not the right kind of publicity, is it?"

"It's perfect for the Hip Hop demographic. They all want to be insiders and at the same time they want to be rebellious. They want their artists to color outside the lines and be dangerous. If they could riot, they would. So it's the artists that riot for them. Think of it as commercialized chaos. And that spills into the business side."

"This is more complicated than I thought."

"It's important for you to know what you're getting into."

"Yes, well..." Bobby stops to think. "Do you think this would affect me recording my songs?"

"I don't know. Not many label heads do anything outside of their comfort zones." Bobby looks disappointed. "But I would."

"Oh?" he perks up, but then looks sad again. "Oh."

"What's wrong?"

"I had become disillusioned with Mr. Kahn as a visionary. His criminal behavior was one factor. The other was that he never seemed to have time to enjoy my songs."

"So now you need someone to run DK-5?"

"Well, you see, I had asked Mr. Man, as an expert, to be a BUG intelligence source. He's been very helpful with gathering information. Quite a knowledgeable fellow, that Mr. Man."

"Mr. Man? Who's Mr. Man?"

"Mr. Man, you know, Mr. Jiggity Man."

"Jiggity...?"

"Yes, I've asked him to become the new label head."

"You what?"

"He's been ever so helpful."

THAT SON OF A...

"And I'm sure he'll lead us all onto victory, or whatever they call it in Hip Hop lingo."

"How, how did this all happen?"

Bunyan tells me that Jiggity contacted him after he heard about BUG's interest in DK-5 and offered his time and services as an 'expert' consultant."

So J Man was using me to get information to Bunyan. And now, he's going to be rewarded with DK-5 on a platter, and even if I keep my job, I'm going to be serving someone who used me worse than Kahn ever did.

"Mr. Man says that he wants to bring Rap back to its roots. Old School, I believe he calls it."

Great, just great, a bunch of dentured Rappers, sitting around the label, taking hits off stool softeners—VSOP, reminiscing about when eight-track was king.

> *Yo, Bro, gimme a beat*
> *Blood pressure's fuckin' me up*
> *Gots m' choppers in a bedside cup*
> *Baby says she wants me to try-ee*
> *That hotdog helper they call viagr-ee*
> *Boyeez...*

DJ-Geritol and MC-Polident. The label will smell of mothballs and we'll be out of business in a year. *Do something. Say something.* "Has Mr. Man ever taken the time to enjoy your songs?"

"Once, but he had another appointment, and well, he seemed to be in a hurry."

I smile. "Could you play me another one? There's nothing I like better than music from the heart."

What some people won't do to get ahead—including me.

Enthralled, I sit there, applauding when each song is finished, and sometimes when it's not. Even manage a few tears. Finally, after I've heard all the words that could possibly rhyme with love, I look at him. "Bobby, your songs speak so beautifully to so many people. It's a shame no one will ever hear them."

"Why, what exactly do you mean?"

"Well, according to Mr. Man. He says he's taking the label back to the Old School. As far as I know, that doesn't include songs like yours."

"Oh, really?" He thinks for a moment. "You know, I had the

feeling he wasn't impressed with my compositions. But being me, I'm apt to give someone the benefit of the doubt. Well then, I'll just have to keep Mr. Kahn in place and find another area for Mr. Man to occupy."

"But Mr. Kahn has never allowed any ballads to be recorded. I've studied the entire DK-5 catalog. Not one to be found. Knowing him, as I do, he would be hesitant to start now. Old dog—new tricks, you know."

"Oh, I, oh my."

"Of course, the best solution would be to start a sub-label, dedicated to your 'special' style. You see, I come from a family that understands the appeal of your music. It's my heritage. Plus, I have a great deal of industry experience. A perfect combination, if you ask me. What's really important is, I'd always make sure that the world could have a chance to share your music, while BUG makes a fortune on Rap."

His eyes are in the stars.

"LoveBUG Records. How does that sound? Love-BUG."

"LoooveBUG." He takes a moment to dream. "I don't know. It might be rationalized as a brand extension. The corporate ID people would object. We had a real disaster with BUGbites Chocolate Drops. Undies and chocolate drops do not make for a pleasing taste experience. Took a year to clean up that mess. LoveBUG is just too close to BUG Industries."

"Then, how about Love Bobby Records?"

"Love Bobby Records." He wraps his imagination around that, and beams.

"What do you think?"

"We could use an English Bobby for the logo." He's excited now. "You know, a Copper."

I nod. "It's simply perfect." I keep smiling. "So anyway, Bobby, that's what I'd do, if I were the boss."

"Okay."

"Okay what?"

"It's yours."

"It's mine?"

"Silly Lily, you can be the head of Love Bobby Records."

Oh no!

"Uh, wow." I try to sound enthusiastic.

"Congratulations, Lily White, CEO of…"

I can't let him say it. "What about Def Kahn-5?"

"Oh well, if you want that responsibility too," he adds, as if it's no big deal. "Of course, it's yours. Truth be told, I've found Rap a little too O-T-T for my taste."

"O-T-T?"

"Over The Top. What?"

"What. Over The Top—Ex-actly."

Am I dreaming this? Am I really head of the label? I'm not being rewarded for the work I did, but for working a rich boy.

Like that, he's handed me my own set of Big Balls and unlimited Dick Slinging (+20 points, + 20 points, Bro).

Notes to myself:

A) Get rid of Kahn's crew ASAP

B) Get the masters under tight control

C) Ask Clete to explain Machiavelli's "The Prince"

AND MOST IMPORTANT OF ALL

D) Figure out how to keep Bunyan busy

I'm scared, but it's a good scared.

My most favorite billionaire continues his recital. We sit on the piano bench next to each other, bath-robed, at the Bosendorfer—Bobby Bunyan and Lily White, flapping our slippers to the beat.

To find gold, some things have to pan out.

24

Make It Until You Fake It
(November 1992)

I'M PACKING UP. The contents of my office are neatly divided into boxes—each labeled—one for desktop items, one for CDs, assorted by artist. Another box contains framed drawings and photos of Ivy, marked "Fragile Handle with Care." Large cartons contain pictures of artists and me, acting like we're buddies. Leaning on the floor against one wall, are my gold and platinum records. Not mine artistically, but mine in a "got my hands really dirty with these" sense. I'm very proud of these dust-collectors.

To tie up some loose ends, here's where things are today.

An Executive Summary

Jess-up and Bagel Tigerthighs are riding high after their video, "Tongue Hung," won just about every major video award. Bagel's unique blend (sic) of handheld camerawork and post-production magic has revived his directorial career. He's slated to direct Jess-up's next single, "Put Your Na-Na There." Can you imagine that shoot?

Hank wanted another chance to make the marriage work. He wouldn't accept my "no." I guess the divorce papers clarified the situation, because he moved back to Puce to start a chapter of the Fogg Church. With his sales ability, he'll put God out of business in a month.

Sik and **Topp Dogg** left to start their own label—"SikDogg Records." Wish them luck. They'll soon find out blunts don't constitute a business plan and you can't "prop-up" a start-up without some effort. They'll be back. Then what?

Clete is now Head of Security. He writes memos about, "Looking After Your Stuff" and corporate policy on "How To Handle A Shoot-Out." Told him, "Not on my watch!" We've installed metal detectors and guards (Er-Mine, being one of them) in the reception area. But what gives Clete Clydesdale the most pleasure is the "Need to Read Book Club" that he started. We've covered Kafka, Rimbaud, Balzac and Baldwin. I Iave to—pop quizzes.

Beany Baby is now VP of Police Relations. Why not? He knows most of the cops in our precinct. Each one has carried Beany out at one time or another. Now, he's carrying out my orders to keep the SWAT Team assaults on our offices to a minimum. The number of "official" visits has dropped to nearly zero. Even so, there's always a cop or two in here. They make unofficial visits, especially during lunch. Works for us. Now, we have double the security, for the price of a few orders of ribs.

Mae is VP of Artists Relations. That means she's no longer treated like a piece of meat. Now artists look to her more as a big sister to help them with their problems. And "closing the deal," means signing a contract—with a pen. We've found, rather than appealing to an artist's sexual appetite, we appeal to his greed with a signing bonus. It costs more up-front, but we make it back. That's because it's taken out of their royalties as a legitimate expense. You could say, Mae's in charge of doing to the artists what they used to do to her.

Rich and **#2Girl** jumped to another label. He heads their legal department—until they discover he's not a licensed attorney. Rich will move from record company to record company. He'll stay one step ahead of the truth and two steps behind the bar exam. #2Girl found another Kahn. It's what she does.

The Right Reverend Sky Fogg, PC has started "Foggarhythms," a religious Rap and Gospel label that records and distributes the "Lord God Almighty" albums and videos. The Reverend records in his church basement, and then distributes the DVDs by mail order and door-to-door, using salespeople-parishoners to spread the word and the debt. It's a faith-based pyramid scheme. Isn't God Great!

Bobby Bunyan lost interest in recording his own love songs. He soon discovered how much work actually went into writing and recording music professionally. We've had to purchase back most of his CDs from the stores. No one buys his songs and no one buys into LoveBobby Records. Now, Bunyan's latest flirtation is the film business, which leads to…

Bigar Kahn. Oh boy, where do I start? First of all, he's now the Chief Consulting Officer of BUG. He oversees the entire underwear process—from manufacturing to marketing to recycling. He seems to have a nose for it. Kahn came by one day, to visit, and spent most of his time trying to convince everyone that what he's doing touches the lives of more people than Rap ever could. I doubt it. It's hard to skim or scam in the skivvies biz. That is what I call a karmic wedgie.

The Label. And then there's the new DK-V. We've remodeled. The decor now looks like the inside of a computer motherboard. Each office is a portal into the future. I like that analogy. Light shoots between the circuits on the walls. Pictures of our artists fade in and out all over the place. And my favorite part is that you leave electronic footprints on the floor. So now you can look back and see where you've come from. In the last two years, we've evolved from an urban environment, to a death star, to virtual reality. With all the changes, we had to do something about the name. The label is now called DK-V. We kept the DK for branding purposes, but changed 5 for the Roman numeral V. It now stands for Def Karma-Vibes. Don't want to throw our cachet away.

My Official Bio
Lily White, CEO of Def Karma-Vibes Recording Company, started as an A&R Coordinator at Def Kahn-5. In a short time she has grown into one of the most respected executives in the music business, having helped many marquee artists, such as XYZee, Jess-up, Filthy Lukre, Clo-Rocks, Axxe and BronxSkee go platinum. Her goal, as head of DK-V, is to "Make It Real—Keep It Real."

You should see the picture that goes with this bio. I still wear the blue "I'm in business" suit. In this game you have to develop an image, and stick with it. Anyway, I'd look foolish in Hip Hop fashions. So I dance with who brung me, clothing-wise.

One big change—the way I deal with people at work. But rather than talk about it, join our A&R meeting in progress.

> *Ditch*
> *Hitch*
> *Itch*
> *Kitsch*
> *Mitch*
> *Niche*
> *Pitch*
> *Rich*
> *Stitch*
> *Twitch*
> *Witch*

Zilch. We're trying to find a word that rhymes with "a female dog" so that Scabbee's first single can be played on the radio. His song, "Da Bling-Thing," is about how he's going to get even with all the women who've used him. His constant reference to them as a—starts with "B"—is the reason radio won't play it. Bleeping out a word just draws attention to the fact that you bleeped it out. It's more creative to substitute a word that has the same feeling.

And then there are all the "motha-f…s" too. "We will have to bleep them unless you come up with an alternative." Scabbee threatens me and I say, "I'm frustrated too, but that Glock isn't going to convince radio programmers, and the FCC, to change their rules. Scabbee, relax, you simply can't say MF on FM."

We're holding our weekly A&R meeting in our new high-tech conference room. The chairs are silver metal mesh, and comfortable for about five minutes. The oval table is eight feet wide and about twenty feet long. The top is clear blue plexiglas, embedded with visible wires and computer chips. Lightwaves constantly flash from one end of the table and back.

What was I thinking when I agreed to this design? Everyone said it was "da bomb" on blueprint. Now, I'm getting an exploding headache from the décor.

"We're spending too much time on this."

Mae is sitting there in a black skirt and gray blouse, opened just enough to show that she's still got it.

"Anyone?" Silence. "I'd hate to bump this release, because we can't find a plan B-word. Don't mean to put a gun to your heads, but if I don't, Scabbee's mom will."

Janine Scott, efficient with an MBA from Wharton, has become my #2—She's black and speaks with a valley girl singsong. "Maybe we should tackle this later. Okay?" She's the "Mistress of the Meeting Agenda." First, old business; then, new business; next, old problems; after that, new problems; and finally, action items. Yet, somehow, chaos always finds a toehold.

Still have a notepad and two pens in front of me, but I hardly ever use them. Need to see and listen more. And I don't have an executive or management style. Just make some top-level goals, and spend the rest of the time using those as benchmarks to measure results. So far, it seems to be working. DK-V is making bigger profits than it did under Kahn. I attribute it to the fact that I'm not stealing any money from the company, and can still increase our "honorariums" to radio and TV programmers.

Sorry, but Play Money is a reality in this business.

"Okay, Janine, what's next?"

She checks her notes. "Next up is Killer Pepe."

Everybody groans.

K-Marx, our new head of A&R, jumps in. "That boy be wack. Wack, wack, wack. Wack juice all over that sherm stick."

K's got the new DK-V logo shaved into one side of his hair. There's one spot on the back of his scalp, where a dreadlock ponytail sprouts. The rest of his head is shaved. Add to that, the matching chin beard that's tied with a piece of plaid ribbon, and you get the picture. He's half-black, half-Puerto Rican—pure street. K-Marx is also our chief tastemaker. That's a person who tells the others in his crowd what's dope or wack—an influencer.

"What's the problem?" I ask. "I haven't heard his demo."

Mae says, "He doesn't speak English. He doesn't speak Spanish. Killer Pepe is un-languaged."

"But I thought you liked his music."

"Did, but now we aren't sure he sung it." Mae tries to explain. "His Uncle Titi says that he raps phonetically. You know, like that 'Hooked on Phonics.'"

"So we don't know if this guy is for real or Milli Vanilli?" Everyone looks at me like I just said Guy Lombardo. "They were the guys who lip-synced their songs. That was just two years ago.

Am I the only one who remembers them? Everyone nods like they remember, but I see they don't. "The point is, folks, that someone has to go into the studio and watch him."

Mae says, "But his uncle won't let anyone in. He says it has a negative effect on Killer Pepe's creativity."

"I guess he doesn't realize that cancelling his contract might have the same effect. Look, I have a barnstorm. Clete..." He looks up from "Sense and Sensibility." "Could you go to the studio and just listen politely. If anybody tries to stop you, ANYBODY, kick them out. That includes Uncle Titi."

Clete places his DK-V Book Club bookmark inside his Jane Austen and takes a moment to travel from 1810 back to today. He says, "What if the real Rapper is the uncle? What if Pepe is fronting for Titi?"

Mae says, "Then what about signing the uncle instead?"

"I'M NOT HAVING AN UNCLE TITI REPRESENTING US, YOU HEAR ME? It's bad enough with that label-killer, Pepe. Uncle Titi? Are you kidding? Can you imagine a four-foot tall guy with half-a-tooth in his head representing DK-V? And that moth-eaten beard. I will not let that sleaze-ball turn us into a 'they're-so-over' label. Great, just great! Didn't anyone do due diligence on them?" No answer. "What kind of label are we running here? Janine, no more Killer Pepe and no more Uncle Titi. Pass on them. Executive Decision."

Remember, "What's good for the lego?" Well, "Executive Decision" is my version of it. Some concepts endure. You could say that I'm sampling from Kahn's management repetoire.

"What's next?"

Janine reads off her tablet. "Axx¿'s parole hearing."

"Oh, yeah. Everybody, I need to get some brains together and decide what we're going to do about Axx¿. He's up for parole, but his "Records From Stir," are blazing, which worries me. I have a feeling that if he's freed, the uniqueness of his sound will disappear, along with his sales. Any thoughts?"

Mae says, "We could record him somewhere else with the same acoustics."

"That's not what I mean. He won't be in jail anymore. He'll just be another ex-con Rapper. He'll lose his marketing hook."

K-Marx says, "He be bouncin' outta, thinkin' he be ballin' young cat, but he be endin' up bama in th' hood. That be bunk for his crew. He be out, that bro be over like a creakin' ghost."

Have to fill you in on K-Marx. For this or any label he is the find of a lifetime. A former street soldier, starting at eleven-years-old, he put up posters for albums and shows all over the city. Then, as a tagger, he built a reputation for placing graffiti in the hardest places for the Sanitation Department to reach. He was a legend before he was drafted into the obligatory street gang. Lucky for him, he spent years twelve to fifteen in juvenile detention homes. Lucky, because when he was finally released his entire gang was either dead or serving time. So he came back to street soldiering. But it wasn't enough. One day, he decided to put together a concert of political Rappers. He spreads the word on the street and then makes the artists feel like they're going to be left out if they don't perform. The one thing he doesn't have is a venue, or a permit.

That doesn't stop him.

K-Marx, with all the confidence of a sixteen-year-old, convinces the police that the Mayor's Office has approved the concert on the grounds of Gracie Mansion—THE MAYOR'S HOUSE. CAN YOU BELIEVE IT? THE NERVE, THE SHEER GALL OF IT!

I guess everyone in the government was too busy, doing their jobs to…do their jobs. No one checks up on him.

The night of the concert, a fleet of blacked-out SUVs, filled with Rappers, and about forty thousand restless youth, all under police protection, enter the gate of the Mayor's residence. The artists set up on the veranda of this quaint Victorian mansion.

The Mayor must have been in a soundproof bunker, because, not until the third act was blasting away, did he and his bodyguards look out the window. The Mayor opens the front door of Gracie Mansion, which is behind the performing artists. The crowd goes crazy with appreciation. He joins in the fun, and takes a bow. By now his anger has become political instinct. Cameras flash, reporters shout questions, and the crowd cheers. This Republican gets credit for bringing a night of joy and song to people who have never even thought of voting for him. But the Mayor eventually remembers he can't run again—term limits.

K-Marx goes into hiding, until the next administration is sworn in.

He came looking for a job and I hired him on the spot. You've got to have a guy with big "you-know-whats" like that in your company.

Now, I'm going to tell you a secret. K-Marx should run this label. He knows the streets, the music, and what's the next hot thing. One little problem though, he speaks his own version of Hip Hop that even people in the ghetto find hard to understand. But as time goes by, I'm getting the hang of what he means, which makes me even more impressed with his capabilities. He reads people better at eighteen than I do now. He's what people mean when they say "keepin' it real."

But it's Janine who will eventually run things. The industry is changing from a Hip Hop to a corporate culture. With all her efficiency, organization and systems, she will be successful. But she will never get to the heart, the understanding of Rap. With her it will be all business—nothing personal. The problem is: What makes Rap great is that it is "personal." You can't crank it out efficiently like some fast food meat patty.

Where were we? Oh yeah... "I agree that the Axx¿ situation is a problem. If he gets out, how will it affect sales?" I look around the room to make sure everyone hears.

At that moment, a flash of light criss-crosses the table. In turn, each person's hair stands straight up. This wasn't in the original decorating plans. We've gotten used to it, and try to ignore that we look like banshees.

I continue. "What if we make sure he doesn't get out? What if that girl he raped and her family are at the parole hearing?"

Janine says, "Cannot do. We paid the girl's family to keep quiet. What kind of message does it send if we turn around and ask them to testify? Anyway, it goes against your policy about not glamorizing violence."

"My policy? When did I make that policy?"

Janine smiles. "When you first took over this label."

"I did?" *What was I thinking?* "Look, the policy's changed, slightly. We still don't glamorize violence. We, we, uh, only hold up a mirror to it. Violence exists in the world and our artists recreate the world as it is. There's nothing to be proud of in violence. But we take pride in our role to reflect the truth, or something like that. Janine, make sure someone wordsmiths that. It's a great answer to the press, when they get on our case. Next? Oh yeah, Axxȩ stays where he is. He's more valuable to us behind bars, than hanging out in them. Jail sells—Executive Decision. And tell the family of that girl to go to the Parole Hearing and testify." I'm not going to have that animal released to harm someone else's daughter. Okay, Janine, next."

"The Christmas compilation. Need to decide on the title."

Totally forgot about this. "What do we have so far?"

Janine reads, "'Ho Ho Hos,' 'Nuclear Mistletoe,' and my pick 'Gift Rappings.'"

"What's that last one about?"

"That's the one with rapping about presents."

"That's kind of nice. What do the rest of you think?" Silence. "Is it that bad of an idea?"

K-Marx says, "Ballers ain't getting' their jammies jumpin' 'bout wrappin' rappin'. They gonna gas face ghost."

"I take that as a 'no.'"

"Word is bond, Lily. Chuck that Gift Rappings.' That 'Nuclear Mistletoe' be da holiday bomb, no diggity."

"Anyone else?" No one can disagree with K-Marx when he comes to a conclusion. "Okay, we call it, 'Nuclear Mistletoe.' What's next?"

Janine whispers a little too loudly, "What about Jiggity Man's masters?" She knows I want to keep this quiet. I guess this is how she gets even for not choosing her Christmas album title. I'll remember this at her next performance review. I might even tell her that she's the only one who does get a performance review.

Mae laughs. "Lily, haven't you already given Jiggity what he desires most in the world?"

Before I blush anymore. "I'm glad you brought this up. I've decided to hold onto his masters for a little while longer. I want to add it to this box set concept I have. It's called "The Four Fathers of Rap." It will be four CDs—one for each of the giants on whose shoulders we stand today—ScratchMaster P, Cool

Funkspinkter, Foggmaster-D (Yes, the Reverend) and, of course, Jiggity Man."

There is a reverential hush in the room. Only K-Marx can talk, but barely, "Droppin' science, girl. Dime!"

Now that's a compliment.

My only problem is to keep Janine's mouth shut while I figure out a way to tell J Man he won't be getting his masters back. But, hey, the box set will let him relive some of his fame. He's owed some respect, even if he did work me. Nostalgia is sweeter than revenge, especially when it's wrapped in cash.

Janine says, "One more item on the agenda."

"Okay."

"The Shit-Doggy CD will have to carry a Parental Advisory sticker on it," she says as if she's revealing the secret of the ages.

"So?"

"So? You asked me to make sure all the seven bad words were edited out. I did that. Why do we still need to have that sticker?"

"Janine, what's the title of the CD?"

"Shit-Doggy."

"And what word in the title looks, smells and reads like one of the seven bad words?"

She thinks for a minute. It dawns on her. She shakes her head. "I'll guess we'll have to change the title."

"A little late for that, isn't it? The artwork's done, sales have been solicited, Vishnu's started the promotion campaign, the CDs are manufactured, and the artist's management is breathing down our necks. Now why on earth would we want to change the album title?"

"Uh, to prevent having the PA sticker slapped on it?"

"Wrong! We want it on that CD. PA stickers sell more records that any marketing budget could. Janine, you should know that. K-Marx, can you tell her why?"

He clears his throat. "Stickers be mad business and original gangsta at one time, no legs pull."

"Just make sure the parental stickers cover the first word and we're good to go."

"But that covers the title."

"Janine, THE TITLE IS THE PROBLEM. WHAT IS

WRONG WITH YOU?" I know I'm treating her badly, but this #2 has to see the obvious before she'll be able to understand the obscure. Maybe I'm too harsh. Sometimes I feel like I'm acting like that word we're trying to find that rhymes with itch—no legs pull, bro.

"Lily, we still have to find a word that rhymes with bitch." She read my mind.

"Janine, keep working on it. I'm sure you'll find one. Okay, folks, meeting's over."

Then Clete's bear growl: "Don't forget about the pop-quiz on 'Sense and Sensibility' tonight." We all groan. He tucks the Uzi deeper into his overcoat and starts to leave. Clete turns. "And it's gonna be wicked."

I stand. My hair is standing up too. "Okay, you all know what to do. Need help? You know where I am."

Everyone does his or her exit routine. The door opens and Beany Baby rushes in. "Didn't want to interrupt, but we has a bit of a problem."

Before I can ask "what?" two cops walk in, holding large white paper sacks. The thin one is relaxed. The other, with a donut-belly, yells like an angry six-year-old at Beany. "I ordered the extra-hot sauce, and you gave me the mild. Is it too fuckin' hard for you to get it right?"

"I said I's sorry." Beany turns to me. "Even offered to go out and get him some hot sauce."

The angry officer says, "Yeah, and by the time you get back, my ribs'll be cold."

Got to diffuse the situation. "Microwave them."

The cop can hardly speak. "Micro…wave? Ribs?" Bits of barbecue spew out of his mouth at me. "Are youse crazy? You ever tasted ribs after they've been nuked?"

"No, I've never…"

"They get soggy, and I like my barbecue dry. All I want is hot sauce. That too much to ask for something simple? How do youse guys run a business around heya?"

Unbelievable. I'm listening to this overfed beef jerky, complaining through grease-stained lips, about his free lunch.

"Who's in charge of this shithole?"

I get in his face.

"I AM."

Acknowledgments

Claudia Menza, Moshe Lazarus and Andy Cialone have graciously given us their expertise and encouragement. In return, we offer our gratitude.

About the Authors

Marcella Andre's career spans the stage, music and film businesses. At Columbia Records, she created the book, "Columbia: Portraits of a Label." She is currently a marketing executive in the film industry.

Joseph Bergmann has been a writer for over 30 years and loves *almost* every minute of it.

www.ingramcontent.com/pod-product-compliance
Lightning Source LLC
Chambersburg PA
CBHW071250170626
46809CB00001B/156